TWO COMPLETE WESTERN NOVELS IN ONE LOW-COST VOLUME!

HANGMAN'S RANGE

Alder City, Montana, was a town gone wild with gold, girls and gambling. Every lawless bastard West of the Rockies had flocked there after the War. But Dean Bowden and his men had had enough—they swore to clean up Alder City no matter how many bullets it took.

SADDLE PALS

Jess Roberts and War Dog Smith were hardened by life on the range, where bullets were more precious than gold. When they heard an old friend needed help, they rode fast to back him up. But Mack Orcon had accidently started a range war, and it would take more than two men and a couple of six-guns to stop the massacre that was about to shake the frontier.

HANGMAN'S RANGE AND SADDLE PALS

LEE FLOREN

LEISURE BOOKS   NEW YORK CITY

A LEISURE BOOK®
February 1990

Published by

Dorchester Publishing Co., Inc.
276 Fifth Avenue
New York, NY 10001

HANGMAN'S RANGE Copyright©MCMXLVII by Phoenix Press
SADDLE PALS Copyright©MCMXLVII by Phoenix Press

All rights reserved. No part of this book may be reproduced or transmitted in any form or by any electronic or mechanical means, including photocopying, recording, or by any information storage and retrieval system, without the written permission of the Publisher, except where permitted by law.

The name "Leisure Books" and the stylized "L" with design are trademarks of Dorchester Publishing Co., Inc.

Printed in the United States of America.

HANGMAN'S RANGE

Chapter 1

RIDE ON, TEXAN!

Dean Bowden left his Cross U trail-herd at Sulphur Springs, telling his Texas punchers to keep the herd pointed north; then he rode toward Alder City. The afternoon of the second day found him on the rimrock above that gold-mad town. Hidden there, he squatted and watched them lynch two miners, watched with the casual indifference of a man who already had seen too much death.

An hour later the lynchers had ridden off and he rode down the trail that twisted into Alder City, heart of the gold-diggings there in the Montana Rockies. When he passed the hanged men, Bowden did not stop, but rode on into Alder City. A sudden dust storm ran down Montana Avenue ahead of him, then died between the raw buildings. A wagon train was leaving, going east toward the new diggings in Last Chance, a hundred miles away over the Continental Divide.

He sent the gray ahead, moving around the wagons, and stopped in front of the low long building, just beyond the Lady of Chance Saloon. He sat his saddle and looked up momentarily at the warped sign that read, *Henry Potter, Sheriff*. The door to the office was closed.

He asked a passing miner, "Is the sheriff in, fellow?"

"Try the door."

Dean Bowden leaned back against his cantle and thought: *Hospitable gent . . . like hell*. He stepped down then, tall, lean, and clean-shaven. He wore battered, brush-scarred Texan chaps and run-over Justin boots. Although just over twenty-four, his face was too gaunt, his eyes too quiet; the war had done that to him.

He entered without knocking. Two men were inside. One sat behind the desk; he was big and bluff and a star was pinned to his open vest. The other was thin—too thin, and too restless. He was taking a drink from the pail in the corner, but when Bowden entered he laid the dipper down quickly and came forward slightly, limping badly.

Bowden spoke to the big man. "I take it you're the sheriff?"

The big man's eyes were dark and heavy as they went slowly over him. "Yes, I'm Sheriff Henry Potter. And you?"

"I'm Dean Bowden. A Texas man."

Potter said, "Glad to know you, Bowden," but he did not rise and shake hands. He leaned back hard against his chair. "You a cowman?"

"I'm trailing a herd in," said Bowden. He added, "A small herd."

"Where from?"

"Texas. They're at Sulphur Springs now; my men are moving them north. I rode ahead to look things over. I bought the Jackie Bell place."

Potter nodded and said, "Only two other cow outfits around here, Bowden. Marcella Gray runs some over on Bitter Crick. Her dad died two years ago and left her the outfit. Len Carberry runs a big spread though, back in the north hills."

"Lots of room here," said Dean Bowden.

"Maybe," murmured Potter.

Bowden looked at him and felt a small irritation. He had not come there to discuss cattle. He glanced at the lame man. "Your deputy, Potter?"

"No. Why?"

"I'd like to talk to you alone."

"Limpy Gault's my friend; he can hear what you say. What's on your mind, Bowden?"

Dean Bowden was tired. "Two men were lynched about two hours ago south of the town. They were miners. I saw it from the rimrock."

Potter said heavily, "Another lynching, huh?" He glanced at Limpy Gault suddenly. Gault stood there quietly and looked at Dean Bowden. He had moved his right hand down and now his thumb was hooked in his gunbelt.

"Just thought I'd tell you," murmured Bowden, and turned to leave; Henry Potter's voice turned him back again.

"Tell me some more," said Potter.

"They had been working at their sluice boxes there in the creek. They put up a fight, but the odds were too big. I was about a mile away. I didn't want to ride into trouble, so I waited."

"A mile away, huh? Then you weren't close enough to recognize anybody, huh?"

Bowden said, "A mile is quite a ways."

Limpy Gault went to the window and looked out at Bowden's gray and turned to Henry Potter. "He's got field glasses tied to his saddle, Henry."

"You saw it clear, then?" asked Potter.

Dean Bowden realized that the pair were too quiet, too serious. He leaned back against the door seemingly loose on the surface, and watched them.

Potter got to his feet and stood beside his desk. He had a Winchester rifle lying across the spur-scarred top.

Limpy Gault had moved forward a little, his hand all the way back now. His small eyes were sharp, quick. He said evenly, "Texas man, huh? And a cowman? This range ain't got no room for Texas men or Texas cattle, Bowden, Ride back and turn your cattle back south into Idaho and Utah."

"You forcing my hand?" asked Bowden.

"You could call it that," said Gault, almost savagely.

Bowden knew then there was something behind the man's attitude, something that was forcing them into trouble with him. He deliberately raised his elbow, and Limpy Gault fell for the trick. Gault was reaching, then. He had settled down; his gun was coming up. Dean Bowden's two bullets hit him; then Bowden held his gun on Potter and he was cold inside.

Gault fired once, his bullet wild, then his knees buckled and let him fall. He rolled over very slowly and lay there, dead and dark against the worn floor. Henry Potter hurriedly pulled his hands back from the rifle.

He looked at Limpy Gault and said, "He's dead, Bowden."

Bowden said, "He should be. . . ."

Potter's eyes lifted, steadied. He had himself under control now, and he scratched his head. "Now why did Limpy pull against you, Bowden? You two have never crossed trails before somewhere, have you?"

"No."

There was a silence. Bowden let it build up until it had weight and thickness. Then, and only then, did he put his gun back. He wondered what was behind all this, why they had forced him. But then, he knew he would find the answer later. The war had taught him great patience.

Boots were coming up the gravel walk outside. And Bowden, who had been raised in high-heeled boots, knew from the sound they were riding boots, not the heavy broad-heeled boots of the miner. He moved to one side, and the door opened. The man was tall, almost as tall as Bowden, and he was thin, too. He wore a neat gray suit with the legs crammed into hand-stitched boots. He was, Bowden saw, a cowman.

Dean Bowden noticed another thing, too. A heavy gold watch chain hung from across the man's vest, and from the chain were suspended two dried human ears. Time had withered them and pulled them into small accurate miniatures. A sharp knife had cut them from owner's skull and punched holes in them to fit them to the chain. Bowden found himself wondering idly if the man who had lost them had been dead or alive at the time.

The man looked down at Limpy Gault. "What happened, Potter?"

"Limpy went for his gun. Dean Bowden here—this stranger—drew and killed him."

The man looked at Bowden. "Why?"

"He went for his iron," said Bowden. "I had to protect myself. Now who are you?" He made his voice deliberate.

The man's lean fingers played with the dried ears, sliding them back and forth. "Limpy Gault worked for me. I'm Len Carberry; I own the Lady of Chance Saloon next door and some of the mines and the Rocking Chair cow outfit north of here. Now who are you?"

"Texas man," said Bowden, almost too quietly. "I'm trailing some cattle in—just bought the Jackie

Bell ranch."

"Oh," said Carberry. "Now, well, that means we're neighbors. Not that I really need any neighbors, Bowden. This range is overstocked as it is."

"There's room for more cattle," said Bowden. "There's room for Texas men, and Texas cattle."

His voice was low but still it held a rough grain. He watched Len Carberry, and he saw this roughness rub against the man. He watched the lean fingers move the ears slowly to the left of the chain.

"You pack a hideout gun, I see," said Bowden.

Carberry's hand halted. The fingers played with the ear; then he drew it back across the chain. He said, "You're up, Bowden, you're up. I could use you, man. How many head you trailing in?"

"Three thousand. Cows and bulls."

"Aim to start raising calves, huh? I'll buy the bunch and hire your punchers. I need a man like you. How about it?"

"I could have sold them in Denver for a better price," said Bowden.

Carberry spread his hands flatly. "No offense," he murmured. "But I don't think we're going to get along, Mr. Bowden. Now to get back to Limpy Gault. He—"

Potter said quickly, "Bowden was telling me about a lynching out in the south hills. For some reason, Gault didn't like a Texan interfering with this country. I guess I better ride out that way, Carberry."

Carberry said, "Another lynching, huh? Those hijackers must have jumped another claim, Potter." He turned to Dean Bowden. "There's a local gang preying on miners; robbing stages, stealing gold, jumping claims. So far, Potter has had little success in catching them. Of course, he's got a few—we hung those."

"They follow gold," said Bowden.

Len Carberry bowed slightly. "We shall meet again, Bowden," he said. "You are welcome at the Lady of Chance. We run all kinds of games—monte, stud, draw, roulette, faro—and our drinks are the best."

Bowden said, "Thanks."

He turned, left, and went to his gray. The shooting had attracted a few men, and one miner asked, "What happened?" but Bowden did not answer. He found his stirrup and went up and rode ahead, riding through and around rigs and packtrains, heading toward the livery barn there at the head of the narrow street.

The Montana gold rush had run for over a year. The story had moved rapidly across the world and brought adventurers and miners and cutthroats from the far edges of civilization. And with these had come traders, gamblers, saloonmen, and women. The names of Alder Gulch and Alder City were known all over the world.

Six months before the town had been wild—too wild—but the leveling file of time had dulled its edge. On the long trip up from Texas, Dean Bowden had heard stories about the town and its wildness, but he had not listened very carefully nor had he retained much of them.

The war had taught him to take things as they came. It had taught him never to worry or fear. The lesson had been bitter but thorough. It had been repeated at Vicksburg, at Shiloh, at Richmond.

But now the war was over and Appomattox was history. A sniper's bullet had gone through his high ribs; even now that spot of pain burned against his right lung. Sometimes the ache was dull in his thigh, sometimes it felt as though a sharp blade were being drawn across it. He had left something back there, something vital. He knew now it had been his youth.

He had seen too much at the lynching; therefore, Limpy Gault had pulled against him. That meant that Len Carberry was involved, too—for Gault worked for Carberry. And where did Henry Potter, the sheriff, fit in—if anywhere? He was thinking these thoughts when he rode into the livery and dismounted.

An old man, bent with age, came from the office, wiping his mouth with a hairy hand, and Bowden caught the fleeting odor of whiskey.

"You want oats for the hoss, I reckon?"

Bowden said, "He's come a long ways."

The oldster peered at the gray's brand. "Cross U on the right hip. Texas iron. Panhandle country, aroun' Lubbock. Old Ike Bowden's brand. You any relation to Ike?"

"My dad."

"Ike still alive?"

"Dead," said Bowden.

"He was a good man," said the oldster. "I rode a herd once when he was trail boss. What brings you into Montana?"

"Cattle," said Bowden. "We're trailing in a herd."

"What's wrong with Texas?"

Bowden smiled quietly. "All shot to hell, fellow. Carpet-baggers moved in after the war. Fences came in and cotton started on the panhandle. Cattle had to go."

"How many head you trailing in?"

"About three thousand."

The man spat. "'Tain't many compared with what the old Cross U used to run. About a hundred thousand, wasn't it?"

"Around that."

"I'm worse than an old woman," said the old man, "but curiosity has got the best of me. How come you want to buy a spread in this section? You have to cut hay for winter feed here, you know. The N Bar N drove in from Oregon on the Sun River. They tried to get by without feeding the first winter and they almost lost their whole shebang."

"Bought a place through a Denver outfit. The Bell place, I guess they call it. The way I hear it we got some big hay meadows with it down along the creeks."

"Heard Jackie Bell was selling it," said the oldster. "Len Carberry runs in that section. So does Marcie Gray. Her and Carberry might not like it, Bowden."

Bowden said, "They might not." There was a black gelding munching hay in the next stall. He had two white stockings on his front feet. Bowden looked at him, remembered him, and then asked: "That black is a nice-looking animal. He belong to somebody around here?"

"He's Sheriff Potter's horse."

The old man went into a side room, carrying a grain scoop. Bowden moved over and looked at the black more closely. But when the old man came back with the scoop full of oats, Bowden was stripping the gear from his own gray.

The sight of that black had told him many things. He knew now why Limpy Gault had tried to kill him. And he knew too that Sheriff Henry Potter was definitely his enemy.

He had seen the black before that day. Seen him back there when riders had lynched two miners to a cottonwood tree under the rimrock.

Chapter 2

TROUBLE TOWN

Bowden went down the plank walk, his boots rapping against the timber, and entered the Antlers Cafe. It was in the middle of the afternoon, the idle period, and back in the kitchen the cook was scraping a pan. The waitress was a small girl with bright, quick ways and hair as dark as ebony. Bowden ordered steak and coffee, and he ate with slow enjoyment.

"Fine food, Miss," he said.

She said warmly, "I'm glad you liked it. I haven't been in business long but I have managed to get a good cook. Anyway, he's a good cook as long as I can keep him sober!"

Bowden smiled. "You're like me, then—new to Alder City."

"Not that new," she corrected him. "I've been here for over two years. My uncle died, and he left me his cattle and ranch—but I'm no hand with cattle, so I sold the outfit a month ago and moved into town and started this restaurant."

"This is a rough town," said Bowden.

"It's quieted down some, but there's still a gang

that go around robbing sluice boxes, hanging miners, and killing innocent men. The sheriff doesn't seem to make much headway against them."

Bowden nodded.

She asked, "Didn't you kill Limpy Gault?"

"I did."

She said, "Good riddance, Mister—"

"Bowden. Dean Bowden."

"Why," she said, "you are the one who brought my ranch!"

For the first time, Dean Bowden really paid some attention to her. Her face was small, well-formed; her nose short, her lips full. She wore a plain housedress and a small apron that accentuated her full breasts. She was pretty—not beautiful; but she was wholesome.

"I bought my ranch from a man," he said. "His name was Jackie Bell."

"The Jackie," the girl said, "is short for Jacqueline."

Bowden leaned back and smiled. "Well, I'll be damned," he said. "Miss Jackie, just what was wrong with your iron to make you sell out that-away?"

Her smooth forehead showed a frown. "Well, it was just too much for a girl to run alone, and I don't know anything about cattle. Then Len Carberry's outfit edged mine on the east, and Marcie Gray ran cattle on the west. And it seemed to me my cattle began disappearing—I feel sure the miners, Carberry's miners, were eating my beef."

Bowden nodded. "Could be so," he said quietly. "But when I bought your ranch the Denver outfit said you still had some cattle on the spread and they would go with it. Where are they?"

"They're back of the meadows, back in the high mountains. I sold out all the rest, but these were too much trouble to round up—they're really wild, Mister Bowden. Yes, they went with the ranch."

"How many head would you say?"

She thought; then: "Oh, about two thousand, maybe more. But they'll be hard to run out of those cliffs, Mister Bowden."

"Dean," he said, "not mister. Or just call me Bowden; that's what all my friends do."

"One of my former cowboys told me the other day that both Marcie Gray and Len Carberry were running cattle on the old Lazy Z range, my old range."

"They'll have to get those cattle off," said Bowden.

"How many head are you driving in?"

"About three thousand." He paid for his meal, a thin smile on his lips. "The last of a proud Texas outfit, ma'am. An outfit that once ran thousands and thousands of head."

"The war?"

He said bitterly, "Yes, the war."

"Texas men are tough men," she said. "My father was a Texan."

"They make their way," said Bowden quietly. "Who's out to the ranch now, Jackie?"

"An old *mozo* of mine. Kirk Myers."

Bowden said, "I'm riding out that way today—about twenty miles out, ain't it?" She nodded and he went on. "How are the buildings?"

"The house and barn and corrals are down on Rock Creek. Rock Creek flows all the year around. The house is in good shape but you might have to do some work on the corrals and the barn and bunkhouse. Kirk Myers knows you should arrive in a few days."

She told him more. The patented land covered twenty sections down on Rock Creek. This was all hay land, raising wild bluejoint grass. Her uncle had

16

dammed Rock Creek up high and turned the water down into irrigation ditches. This irrigated the lands so there was never a bad crop of hay.

Bowden had checked the description of the land thoroughly, and it all dovetailed with Jackie's statements. The rest, the girl said, was government range, land to be grazed on by the cattle of the outfit that was the toughest. And from what she said, the Carberry riders were tough and, for that matter, so were the riders of Marcie Gray.

Bowden murmured, "Thanks," and went to the door, where he halted, turned and asked: "This man Carberry has two human ears tied to his watch chain. Where did he get them, Miss?"

"He cut them off a Frenchman named Henri Laval. It seems the Frenchman and Len Carberry had had some trouble before, down in Colorado, and Laval had escaped meeting Carberry. Well, they met in this town one day—Carberry killed him, a gunfight, and while Henri Laval was dying, Carberry cut his ears off. That was about two years ago, I guess."

"You say Carberry owns mines, too?"

"Yes, he owns most of the diggings. He has some tough miners working for him, too."

Bowden went outside. Sheriff Henry Potter came riding down the street, sitting the big black, and drew rein beside Bowden. He said, "Those dead men were miners, Bowden; you were right. I buried them out there."

Bowden said, "I see."

Potter rode on, going toward the livery barn. There was a girl standing across the street, talking to a cowpuncher, and Bowden gave her a slow steady glance. She was, he saw, a pretty girl; her hair, peeping from under her small Stetson, was clear and spun fine. She was taller than Jackie Bell, and there was greater hardness in her full, tan face. She wore a split buckskin riding skirt and a beaded buckskin jacket and a full silk blouse.

Bowden was walking past the Lady of Chance and he saw Len Carberry through the open door. The thin man was drinking at the bar alone. Bowden went in and stopped beside him.

Carberry asked, "Drink, Bowden?"

"Beer," said Bowden, and added, "A small one, barkeeper."

"You drink them mild," said Carberry.

Bowden said, "Blame it on the war."

Carberry looked at him. "You fight for the North?"

"A Texas man," said Bowden, "fighting for the Yankees?"

"My error," said Carberry.

Potter came in. He walked hard, his spurs jangling. He said, "Whiskey," to the barkeeper, and then, to Bowden and Carberry: "How do, men."

"What'd you find out?" asked Carberry.

"I buried two men," said Potter slowly. "That was all I could find. The same old thing, Carberry. No evidence, no proof, a cold trail."

Bowden did not look at Potter's face when he spoke. He watched the man's fingers curled around his whiskey glass. "You ride a fine black horse, Potter. A good horse, I'd say."

The fingers stopped turning the glass. They tightened around it and the knuckles stood out.

"He's a good horse," said Potter.

"I'd like to buy him," said Bowden.

The fingers suddenly lost their tightness. The knuckles slid in and color came across the big hand.

"He ain't for sale," said Potter.

Bowden drained his glass. "You men want one on me?" He did not wait for their answers; he ordered, but did not drink again. He was tired, the past was catching up again; his lung ached.

Potter said, "If somebody presses you, come to me, Bowden. Marcie Gray has a tough bunch of riders. They know how to use their guns."

"I tromp my own snakes."

Potter looked at him. "I'm the law," he said quietly.

Bowden was quiet for a time. He let this grow, and let it take effect. The man, he knew, was not tough; he was big but he was not dangerous. Just the same he would bear watching.

Bowden repeated, "I kill my own snakes."

Something moved through Potter and held him; then Potter's thick face fell back into its heavy complacency, and the eyes were thin and flat.

"I'll be in town," murmured the starman.

Carberry had suddenly glanced into the backbar mirror. Bowden had caught the edge of the glance, and he followed it. A man, seemingly a loafer, sat behind him, his chair tilted idly back against the wall.

He was tall, his face thin, his lips loose.

Bowden asked quietly, "Another one of your bodyguards, Carberry?"

Carberry asked, "Who?"

"The man sitting behind us."

Carberry glanced into the mirror. His right hand came up and played with the dried ears on the gold watchchain.

"Oh, him. Yes, he works for me. He's Dunc Cross."

Bowden said, "So long." He went to the door. He ran his boot out, hooked it around Dunc Cross' chair and dumped the gunman on the floor.

Cross landed sitting down. He was pulling his gun from the hand-tooled holster when he saw Bowden's gun; then he slowly shoved his weapon back. He got to his feet.

"What the hell's wrong with you, Bowden?"

Bowden said, "So Len Carberry's already told you my name. You weren't sitting there by accident, Cross." Bowden looked at Potter and Carberry.

Potter's heavy jowls were gray, his lips twisted, but Carberry's thin lips and eyes were without emotion.

Bowden said *"Adios"* and stepped outside.

Chapter 3

MOUNTAIN RANGE

Bowden walked down the main street. The territorial courthouse, a raw plank building, stood on the corner of Montana Avenue and Bozeman Street, and he entered its open door. A balding man of about fifty came to the rough counter. Dean Bowden introduced himself.

"I was supposed to have some important papers here," said Bowden. "They should have arrived from Denver by this time."

"They came in yesterday," said the old man. "They had to go to Helena, the capital, for registration there, too." He spread out the legal-looking document. "This is a deed to the Lazy Z, the former Bell ranch."

"Record it for me?"

The bald man nodded. "All right; the fee is one dollar."

Bowden turned to leave, stopped. "Another thing. I want to register a brand. I'm putting the Lazy Z on the shelf for good. I'm registering my Texas brand in Montana—the Cross U."

"Here's a form to fill."

Bowden dipped the pen and wrote slowly. The point was jagged and made the work harder. He drew a picture of the Cross U iron. The brand would have to go into Helena for recording in the book of brands there and, if there were no other Cross U brand in the territory of Montana, then he would get the brand. Otherwise, if some other cowman were running his cattle under a Cross U iron, he, Dean Bowden, would have to rebrand all his Texas stock with another brand.

But Bowden had made a search through the use of the mails and he had found no other Cross U brand in Montana records. This, then, was a mere legal formality. He shoved the completed form across the desk. The clerk was still studying the deed.

"Jim Bell didn't sign this," he said.

Bowden asked, "Who's Jim Bell?"

"He's Jackie's younger brother—only brother she has, for that matter. Guess the kid must be eighteen or a little over."

Bowden remembered suddenly. "Oh yes, they told me that when I bought the place in Denver. The lawyers said Jackie was his legal guardian and could sign for the boy. I figured all the time that Jackie was a man."

"Well, *she* ain't," said the clerk. He added, "Splendid young girl. She sure has gained the respect of this community—that is, among those having any respect left—for the way she told Len Carberry to go to hell."

"How's that?"

"Carberry wanted to double up the two outfits. Run one wagon and brand one iron, cutting the cattle on shares. Jackie told him to go to hell."

Bowden asked, "Where's the young fellow, young Jim?"

The older man hesitated momentarily. Then he

said, "He's riding for Len Carberry, Bowden. Didn't Jackie tell you?"

Bowden shook his head.

"Almost busted the girl's heart, it did, to see her brother turn in with Carberry. They had some harsh words, too, but Jim's a wild young one and he'll have his fling. It might lead him to some serious trouble."

"I see."

"Maybe that's why she never told you."

Bowden said, "How do Len Carberry and this other girl—the one that owns the Turtleback outfit—get along?"

"You mean Marcie Gray, huh?" The man pointed out the door. Bowden turned, and from where he stood he could see the blonde girl he had admired as he had gone into the Lady of Chance. "That's Marcie Gray."

Bowden said, "She's pretty."

"And a fighter, too. She's fought Len Carberry tooth and nail. She won't like you moving cattle in on Alder City range, Bowden."

"Maybe not," admitted Bowden. He paid for the brand registration and went outside.

The afternoon sun pounded down on the dust and on the unpainted buildings. Marcie Gray was going into a store when Bowden came up and said, "Miss Gray—a moment, please."

She stopped, looked at him, and waited.

He said, "I'm Dean Bowden, a Texas man, Miss Gray. I bought the Lazy Z and am changing it into the Cross U outfit."

She said, "I'd heard the place had been sold," She added, "What are you going to do for cattle, Mr. Bowden?"

"I'm trailing a herd north," said Bowden.

She was, he noticed, a trifle nervous. Her white

teeth played with her bottom lip, and she hit the flare of her split buckskin skirt idly with the lash of the quirt she carried. There was color, there was fire, behind that impassive, calm face; he thought of this, and he found that thought good. She would be warm and kind to the man she loved, and to no other. He got this glimpse back into her inner person; then her gray-blue eyes hid her feelings. It was like shutting a door upon something fine.

She was hard again. She said, "Well, I hope you like it here in Montana." She turned to go. "I'll see you again, of course."

Bowden said quietly, "Just a minute, Miss Gray. I understand you have your Turtleback cows running on my range."

She stopped and looked at him. "Both the Turtleback and Len Carberry's Rocking Chair run cattle on what was Lazy Z range. The land is government land, you know, and it is unfenced."

Bowden said, "Yes, it's government land, that's true. But the Lazy Z cattle used to run on it and I claim squatters' rights. That has, I understand, been upheld in a Montana territorial court."

"I thought you were a Texan?"

He said, "I'm no lawyer, Miss, but the Denver firm that I bought this ranch through looked that up for me. I'll have to ask you to take your cattle off of Cross U range, Miss Gray."

She said almost angrily, "And if I don't?"

"Then we move them off!" He felt a brief, quick anger; but he held this in and kept his feelings back. He saw anger turn across her face, and again he glimpsed that strength, that hardness. But he had the feeling suddenly that it was not real; it was forced.

"I have riders, Mr. Bowden."

He said simply, "I came to Montana to find

peace, Miss Gray. There's room here for all of us if we cooperate, but if we don't, there isn't anything ahead but war. I bought this ground and I bought grazing rights with it. I bought the patented lands along the creeks and intend to cut hay on them. I am, to put it frankly, here to stay and run cattle."

She said, "I'll think it over."

"I'll give you two days," he said, "to start moving your cattle."

She asked suddenly, "Do we have to be enemies?"

"No," he said, and added; "That's up to you."

She said, "Good day, Mr. Bowden," and went into the store. He turned and walked to the livery stable. Jackie Bell was saddling a young sorrel mare. He nodded to her, and spoke to the old hostler.

"I'd like to rent a good horse; my gray is sort of tuckered out. I'm riding out to the Lazy Z to look the spread over; then I'm going back to my herd. I'll leave the horse here in the evening and pick up my gray then."

"That roan's a good horse."

Bowden untied the blue roan and bridled him. He was a long-legged, thin horse but he had stamina built into him. Bowden put the Navajo blanket across his back, smoothing out the wrinkles, and then lowered the Houston hull on him and cinched it tight.

When he rode out the back door, Jackie Bell waited on the sorrel.

He asked, "You riding somewhere, Miss Bell?"

"I thought I'd go out to the ranch with you and show you around. You might like to see where the boundaries are and learn some things about the place you don't know."

He lifted his hat. "That would be nice of you, ma'am." Then he added, "But your place of business—can it get along without you?"

"The cook is sober now, and I have two girls working for me during the rush hours. There won't be many miners in tonight because it is the middle of the week."

They rode for a few miles in silence. Dean Bowden rode heavy in his saddle, and his thoughts were many. Somewhere, ahead, a meadowlark sang, and Bowden remembered other meadowlarks and their songs on the long trek north. A curlew piped along the deep grass of a wild mountain stream and somewhere a mother cow bawled for her errant offspring.

The trail lifted over a hill, then ran down into a small bottom. The spring thaws had left waterholes there; they stopped and watered their mounts. Young frogs, recently escaped from their polliwog prisons, leaped into the water, swimming toward the center of the pool, where they came to the surface and floated with their eyes wide behind their veiled eyelids. Bowden's horse drank deeply, filling the hollow spots in his flanks.

"He was thirsty," said the man from Texas.

"Old Matt is usually drunk," said Jackie Bell. "Sometimes he forgets which horse he has watered that day and sometimes he forgets to water any of them."

"Bad habit."

She said suddenly, "I saw you talking with Marcie. How did you two get along, Mr. Bowden?"

"I don't know," said Bowden frankly. "We didn't get off to much of a start, Miss Jackie. I asked her to move her Turtleback cows from my range; whether she will or not is something else."

"She's stubborn."

"She's a beautiful woman," he said.

She glanced at him. "You've noticed that already?"

"It only took one glance," said Dean Bowden. He

leaned back in his saddle and thought: *They always hate each other. . . . Or maybe it isn't hate; maybe it's envy or whatever a woman suffers from the most. . . .* "If she doesn't have her riders move them, me and my men will put them on Turtleback range."

"And what about Len Carberry's cattle?"

Bowden said, almost too quietly. "We'll move them, too." He turned in his saddle and looked at her. "You never told me you had a brother. The clerk down at the courthouse mentioned him to me. Jim is his name, isn't it?"

"He's eighteen," said the girl.

Bowden speared into the dark, feeling his ground. He said, "If he wants a job, Miss, there's one for him at the Cross U."

"He's working," she said. He noticed she did not tell him where, or for whom he worked.

They gained the rimrock and the land rolled away beneath them to the north. Dean Bowden ran his eyes slowly across the range and filled his lungs with clean air. It was, he suddenly decided, nice to breathe clean air again. The dust of the trail herd had irritated his wound. But there in that high and dry Montana mountain air, the spot would heal more quickly.

"There's Rock Creek," said Jackie. She lifted her hand and pointed, and Bowden followed her finger. The creek ran out of the snow-capped Rockies, running down a deep gorge to the west, winding in a canyon cut for centuries by water and the elements, then turning abruptly to the south and leveling out on the bottomlands, building meadows between the lower hills. The grass was green on these and lay like a green blanket under the shimmering air in the distance.

"And back there—right where the canyon

ends—is the dam," said the girl. "The main ditch takes off to the right there, and runs along the foot of the valley, heading along the edge of the cliffs and hills."

"Nice-looking outfit," said Bowden.

It was just that. There in a land of hard, cold winters with blizzards and heavy snowfall, hay was worth much to a cowman—without it, his stock would starve and die. And the Rock Creek irrigation system was well planned and well executed.

They rode down to the ditch that ran along the edge of the hills. The water was clear and sparkling, swirling against the gravel bottom and sides. Bowden opened the barbwire gate without dismounting; they rode through and he closed it behind them. A trail skirted the edges of the meadow and they rode along this until they came to the buildings.

They came upon them suddenly, the hill falling on a long reach below them, and revealing the ranch. The barn, made of pine logs, was not high but it was long, and could hold quite a few horses. One corral was behind it, fastened on to the ends of the building, and three other corrals were sprawled along the creek bottom. They were huge corrals, made of native pine rails and pine posts; they could hold thousands of head of cattle during branding and weaning time.

Bowden noticed that they would, as Jackie had said, need some repairs. A few of the rails were down, a number of posts would have to be replaced, and one gate sagged on its hinges.

The house stood higher on the hill, where the gravel was plainly apparent. There, during the rainy season, the higher ground would have better drainage. The house was typical of the cow country, with the long porch on the side that faced the corrals and the creek, and paint that had chipped and peeled with the passage of time. But it was a good house and strong—it had withstood the Montana elements, and it would stand many more winters and summers. There was plenty of room in it.

The bunkhouse, a log building, ran along the hill beyond the house. It was a long, low building with a shingled roof and many windows. Below it, farther down on the slope, were other smaller buildings—a harness and saddle storeroom, a blacksmith shop, and a granary.

Kirk Myers, a stooped old man, came out of the house. "Well, bless my buttons," he said, smiling, "if it ain't my girl, Jackie!"

"Hello, Kirk." Jackie introduced Dean Bowden. The old man's hand was a scraggly claw, but it had strength. He peered at Bowden through weather-aged eyes. "You look all right, Mister Bowden. And take it from me, you really bought an outerfit."

"Looks all right," said Bowden.

They went into the house. The place was neat, the furniture old but dependable, and Bowden liked what he saw. He went out and inspected the rest of the buildings. They needed a few minor repairs, true; but everything was in pretty good shape. Even the harness, freshly oiled and cleaned, hung on pegs in the harness room, and a few saddles hung by stirrup-leathers beside the harnesses. Bowden made a slow, thorough inspection that took almost an hour, then returned to the house.

Jackie had a meal on the table.

Bowden said, "Now I didn't expect this, Miss Jackie."

She spoke slowly, almost too quietly. "You needed a welcome to your new home, Bowden; you didn't get a very good one down in Alder City. You'll find this a good ranch—a ranch that I'd never have parted with had my brother—" She checked herself in time. "We'll call this your welcome to the Lazy Z. You'll probably make this ranch your home for a long, long time."

"For a long time," repeated Dean Bowden.

Kirk Myers said, "I got a bottle hid. We'll drink on that." He hobbled into the kitchen. . . .

Chapter 4

BACK-ROOM MEETING

Len Carberry stood and looked at Dunc Cross. He had the sudden thought that what he was planning would be tough: this Bowden waited for no man; he went out and took what he wanted. Dunc Cross got to his feet, wiping the sawdust from his pants; he righted his chair.

Carberry let the silence grow and gain form and contour. Cross slammed the chair against the wall.

Carberry said, "Don't take your temper out on a chair, Cross. The man you want to take it out on is walking down the street."

Cross said suddenly, "He's seen enough, Carberry. He's tough, and damned tough."

Potter turned and looked at Len Carberry. "He knows a lot, Len," he said. "He saw us lynch them miners—he saw it through field glasses. He knows I was in on it; that's why he asked about my horse—that black. He used that question just to tell me he knew. He'd walk out of his way to get into danger."

Carberry said, "Don't talk here," and turned and they went into his office, there behind the Lady of Chance. Carberry swung his lanky body in the swiv-

31

el chair; he looked out the window at the tin-can-littered alley. Potter settled heavily in a chair, but Dunc Cross squatted beside the door, a cold cigarette on his underlip. Carberry knew these two men and he waited; finally he spoke.

"He'll be tough," he admitted. "You can't buy him—I tried; you can't scare him, he showed that. And when you can't buy a man or scare him, there is only one thing to do to get rid of him."

"Kill him," finished Dunc Cross.

Len Carberry leaned back and smiled thinly. "He sure ran the Injun sign on you, Dunc. . . ."

Cross said, "He'll pay for that." After a while he added, "And pay through the throat."

Potter said angrily, "You talk big, Cross, but you do little." The big man walked the floor savagely. His boots were strong and heavy, and his tread ponderous.

"Sit down, you big ox," said Carberry.

Potter turned and looked at him. The arrogance in Carberry's sharp order rasped against the lawman's thick hide. But underneath there was a touch of cowardice; the struggle was short and sharp, and that cowardice won. The sheriff sat down again.

Carberry said, "It comes down to this, men. We got outfoxed on two points. The first was when I tried to buy the Lazy Z and Jackie Bell wouldn't sell it to me. The second was when I tried to buy it indirectly but that Denver firm got wise and refused to sell to my agents."

"That's old stuff," said Potter.

Carberry went on speaking, picking his words carefully. Potter leaned back and watched him, and Dunc Cross shifted his weight slightly, letting it rest on the other leg.

"You made a mistake, Potter, when you rode that black horse. I thought you would have better sense than that. Maybe you don't know it, but the local citizens have organized a secret bunch, the vigilantes, they call themselves. One misstep on your part, Potter, and they hang you."

"I'll be a hard man to kill," said Potter.

Carberry studied him. "You're big and when you hit the end of a rope, you'll hit it hard. But I don't think this Bowden man will talk to anybody and tell about that black, Potter. He'll play his cards close and keep what he knows to himself."

Potter said, "You've got miners on his range."

Carberry nodded. "And Bowden owns the mineral rights to the Lazy Z, too; his deed reads that way. There'll be trouble there, but we'll let the miners take care of that. Somebody'll have to kill Dean Bowden, it looks like. Let's hope it's one of my miners."

"Or me," said Dunc Cross.

"But you've got Rocking Chair cattle running on his range," said Henry Potter. "Len, why in the hell don't you sell that outfit? There's gold in this country and one day on a good stream brings in more than those cattle would bring in in a year. Instead, you keep building the spread up."

"Your big nose," said Carberry, "gets in way of your eyes, Potter. These gold pockets are playing out, man. A year from now and they'll all be done. Then what's next?"

"Last Chance gulch over by Helena."

"And Last Chance won't last long—maybe six more months. Then what is there? There's sign of gold in the Black Hills. No, this is the end of it, Potter. I followed it from California north into Idaho and now Montana. Cattle's the thing here; it'll pay, and pay big."

"What if Bowden and his men shove Rocking Chair cattle off their range?"

Carberry said simply, "It'd mean war."

"He'll do it," said Cross.

"We got men," said Carberry. "We got shotguns and rifles."

Potter said, "This range'll tear open from end to end and turn into a red ball of hell, Len. And where will Marcie Gray stand, I ask you? Against him and against us; she'll fight him and she'll fight us. There'll be two against us. This country is getting too damned hot for me."

"Don't try to ride out," said Carberry.

Potter settled down suddenly. He said, "I didn't mean it that way, Len," and then he added: "Why not join up with Marcie Gray? If you can't whip them, Len, join up with them. Why not try that?"

Carberry smiled with his lips only.

"It might be possible," he said. "We'll ask Jeff Walton when he rides in tonight. The way I understand it, Bowden gave Marcie Gray two days to start moving her cattle off'n his range. That means, I reckon, that he gives us the same length of time."

Potter asked, "We wait then . . . for a while?"

Carberry dug into his desk and came out with a quart of whiskey. He pulled some glasses out of the drawer too, and he filled each with the amber liquid. "Yes, we wait for a while. We got something big on our hands for the next few days with that shipment of gold going through from the Idaho mines to the smelter at Denver."

"I don't know about this kid," said Henry Potter suddenly. "Damn it, Len. I can't forget that he's Jackie Bell's brother. He knows too damned much, I tell you. What if he took a notion to holler on us and tell?"

"He won't."

"How do you know he won't?"

Carberry said, "He's too ignorant, Potter. He's in

deep himself, and I never let him forget that. He thinks he's a big gent, now—and he does dirty work that either you or Cross would have to do if it wasn't for him. He's getting paid enough and he has a big ego to feed with braggadocio."

"Talk American," growled Potter.

Carberry said angrily, "You big ignorant—" He checked himself and smiled almost gently. "All right, fellow. The kid thinks he's playing a tight, fast game—he craves excitement and money, and we're giving him both. We'll use him and then drop him. How does that strike you?"

"Better drop him soon," said Potter.

Dunc Cross got to his feet. He crossed the room. He poured another drink. His eyes were tight over the glass as he raised it. "Henry's got shifty feet, Len," he said evenly and slowly. "This Bowden gent seems to have pinned the deadwood on him, recognizing that black horse, and Potter's pulling on the bit. Hell, Potter, there's other black horses in this country with stockinged legs."

"Okay," said Potter, "forget the whole thing."

Dunc Cross drank quickly and set his glass on the table. He went to the window, moving fluidly, and he looked out. He said, "There goes Marcie Gray now, heading north into the hills. She's a lovely woman, Carberry." He turned and his eyes showed something and Carberry noted it. "A man who leaves a crooked trail sure raises hell with his thoughts, Len."

"Don't think then," snapped Carberry.

Dunc Cross stood there and watched Marcie Gray ride into the hills. The girl did not ride fast; she held her pinto to a running-walk. She was riding north, heading for her Turtleback ranch.

Dusk was moving across the ridges, settling in the low draws, when she reached the high point on Signal Hill, and from there she saw the two riders leaving the Lazy Z and pushing toward Alder City. They rode hard and a thin line of dust turned in the air behind them. She recognized the riders as Dean Bowden and Jackie Bell, and she thought again of Bowden and their talk on Alder City's main street.

When she rode into the Turtleback, dusk had settled into twilight, shadows were gathering and building and taking form. She was tired, and she shouldn't have been; she left her horse to the old *mozo* to unsaddle, stable and grain. She went to the house, beating the lash of her quirt slightly against her buckskin thigh, and she felt the lift of impatience inside of her. But when she entered the house, she hid this behind her eyes.

She said gaily, "Hello, Janie!"

The woman came to the kitchen door. She was heavy, with thickness and width, and she wore old house slippers. Her housedress was shapeless and without form.

"Supper's ready, girl."

Marcie laid her quirt on the davenport and washed her hands and face on the outside porch. The water had just been pumped from the well and it was cool and brittle. The heat left her face, then, and she wiped roughly with the towel and brought the color back. She glanced in the mirror and liked what she saw, and her smile showed it.

"Have a good day, Janie?"

"It was hot," said the heavy woman.

Marcie kissed her on the forehead. "You work too hard for me, dear," she said. The hardness left her face then, and showed the girl's true nature; but she drew it back, and sat down.

They ate in silence. Marcie ate slowly, enjoying her food, yet finding her thoughts insecure, without strength. Janie had raised her when her mother had died at childbirth, and the heavy woman knew every mood, every whim, of the blonde girl. She had watched her grow and had seen the hardness come in.

She said, "What happened today in Alder City?"

Marcie looked at her. "Why do you ask that?"

"You're too quiet," said Janie.

Marcie said, "Jackie Bell has sold the Lazy Z to a Texas man, Dean Bowden. That means there is trouble coming, Janie."

"You can take your cattle back," said the housekeeper. "That way there'll be no trouble."

"But I won't," said Marcie.

"Why not?"

"He wants trouble," she said slowly.

She toyed with her food, wondering at her thoughts. "He's tall and he's strong; already, he killed Limpy Gault. They had words in Sheriff Potter's office and Limpy reached for his gun and Bowden killed him. He crossed Len Carberry and ran over Dunc Cross. They're out to get him, I understand."

"That doesn't mean you have to trail with them," said Janie. "Limpy Gault got only what he needed. He's walked in the shadow of the gallows and the gun too long. You could pull your cattle back—"

"And have people point me out," finished Marcie Gray. "No, Janie, not that. My dad was proud, and I guess I'm proud, too. I'm his daughter."

"And he was stubborn," finished the woman. "Stubborn beyond the point of his own good."

"He was my father."

"You sure it isn't because of Jackie Bell?"

"What do you mean?"

Janie said, "You know what I mean. . . ." She was a woman and because of that, she saw beneath the surface. "You don't like Jackie Bell, do you. . . ."

"I don't dislike her. Maybe it's because we both made a fatal mistake: we both turned out to be women."

"Is that all?"

"Jackie Bell has made her boasts—she says I never ran her off the Lazy Z, but Len Carberry and his men did." There was a great arrogance in the girl, and the elder woman, who knew it well, understood and saw it now. And she knew, then, that Marcie's pride, for it was such, would get her into trouble. "I guess I'll show Jackie Bell that nobody else can run on Lazy Z range."

"You talk like a woman in love," said the housekeeper.

Marcie got to her feet and walked to the window. She turned and said, "Look, Janie, it's this way. I fought Jackie Bell and I fought Len Carberry and the thing got too hot, and Jackie Bell gave up."

"That isn't true," said the woman. "Jim Bell went to hell, and it broke his sister's heart. You can't fight with a broken heart, Marcie."

Marcie Gray shrugged. "Well, she fell out . . . That left only Len Carberry. Our cows and Carberry's Rocking Chair stuff are running over Lazy Z range. Sooner or later, Carberry and I will have trouble. Maybe we won't, but I think we will. This range isn't big enough for anybody but Carberry . . . and you know he thinks that way, Janie. It's still the same vicious circle. Only now, instead of fighting a woman and a man—I fight two men; maybe it will be easier."

Janie said nothing.

Marcie looked at her suddenly, and asked, "Why don't you say something?"

"Your mind," said the woman, "is made up."

Chapter 5

TRAILHERD

Bowden rode into Alder City with Jackie Bell, left his borrowed horse at the livery, and rode out on his gray, heading toward the trail herd that was in the south.

A strange contentment rode with the tall cowman. For the first time in months, he felt some resemblance of happiness. The causes prompting it were elemental and essential. He had found the land and the range he wanted and, though an undertone of discord and danger ran across this rough land, the land was good.

The ride in from the Lazy Z had been eventful. Jackie Bell had shown him the boundaries of the range, and he had seen Rocking Chair and Turtleback cattle grazing on his grass. He had seen miners, too, working on Rock Creek with sluice boxes and with pans. He had ridden down on one group.

They had been a suspicious, tough lot. Most of them were big, bearded men who had followed the lure of the yellow metal around and across the world. He noticed that they stayed as close to their rifles as they possibly could while they worked and that each, despite inconvenience and discomfort, packed a short gun in a holster. Their eyes never left him as he spoke.

"I'm Dean Bowden," he said. "I bought this Lazy Z range. I own the mineral rights on this creek."

"T'hell you do, Bowden. We took up claims."

"Don't get reckless," said Bowden quietly. He had made Jackie Bell stay back on the ridge and had ridden down alone, anticipating trouble. He deliberately kept his hand away from his gun. He knew that, if the occasion arose, he could still draw and shoot before any of the slow men before him. "How much gold is there left in this creek?"

"About another week's shakin', I reckon. We got it purty well worked, Bowden; but ain't our claims no good?"

Bowden shook his head. "There's been some mistake made, men. You figured the mineral rights on this place were open. Well, they ain't; I got the word of my Denver lawyers to back me up."

"Then you'll claim our gold?" demanded one. "By hell, I don't aim to let you walk off with my hard-earned—"

"Hang onto yourself," warned Dean Bowden. His hand had moved back and was settled on his gun now. "I ain't asking for your gold. You worked for it, panned it, and it's yours. Are there any Carberry hands here?"

"I'm one," said a thick man.

"Me, too," added another.

"You'll have to move on, pronto," said Bowden. "The rest of you can stay a week. By that time, if your diggings are worked out, you got to move anyway. That's fair enough, ain't it?"

"Fair to me," said a man.

Another added, "Okay, Bowden. And thanks for

the chance, fellow. We figured the mineral rights were open."

The thick man—the Carberry hand—said, "What if we don't move, Bowden?"

Bowden put his spurs to his horse. He rode forward, his gun rising; the thick man, too, had reached. Bowden's gun came down sharply. Sunlight glistened on its steel barrel. The gun rose, but this time the sun did not glisten on it. The barrel showed blood and hair.

Bowden put the gun on the other Carberry miner. He said, "Don't pull that, fellow, or I'll kill you." The man did not hesitate. He drew his hand back, and raised both hands up. His tongue snaked out and wet his lips.

"I'll move," he said. "Don't shoot."

Bowden studied him, then slid his .45 back. He said, gesturing toward the thick man, prone on the ground: "Take your pard down to the creek and pour some water on him. Then get him outa here, fellow. Tell him to be careful who he pulls a gun against after this."

"We'll leave."

Bowden hollered to the ridge, "Jackie, keep your gun handy as I ride out," and turned his horse. He came to the top of the slope, his bronc breathing against the stirrups, and found that Jackie Bell had her rifle on the men below.

He said, *"Gracias, senorita."*

She said, "I had my rifle out all the time."

He glanced at her. "I told the two Carberry men to pull out right away. I gave the rest a week. The creek, they said, would be panned out by that time."

They had ridden on into the dusk, and there had been little conversation on the road into Alder City. The calmness of evening was settling and girding the land with freshness and coolness. Bowden felt this, and liked the feeling. They rode into the livery and dismounted.

"I'll see you again," murmured Bowden.

He unstripped the hired horse and put the rig on the gray. The brief spell of rest had put new strength into the animal. When he rode past the Lady of Chance, Carberry, Dunc Cross, and a thin young fellow stood on the sidewalk and watched him. He swung his horse in close and pulled up.

"Carberry," he said, "I had a run-in with two of your miners. They're on Rock Creek and they're getting off my land *muy pronto*."

Carberry was silent.

Bowden said, "You've got some cattle on my range; they'll have to be moved. I gave Marcie Gray two days to move in. I give you the same."

Carberry said slowly, "I see."

Bowden sat there and looked at him. Carberry was angry, his face thin and tight. Dunc Cross was silent, but his eyes were too small. The kid stood there, and Bowden looked at him the longest.

He was light, and his whiskers still limber. He wore a beaded buckskin shirt and California pants. His boots were of calfskin, his spurs of Mexican silver. Across his slender face was stamped a mingled egotism and arrogance, coupled with immaturity. He was not brave, but he was dangerous because he was reckless.

Bowden turned the gray. Time was pressing on him, and he lifted the beast to a long lope. When he rode past the cottonwood, he saw the two graves of the lynched men. They were fresh and gray against the green ground. He put the gray over the rimrock, retracing the path he had used to ride into Alder City.

Bowden's men had moved the herd rapidly and

far. He met them about ten miles to the south, and old Panhandle Smith was riding point. He signaled to Ken Shaden to come up and ride point, and then he and Dean Bowden swung off to the side and drew in as the herd went by.

"How'd you fare?" asked the trail boss. He had been born to the saddle—he was wiry, muscular; he had seen cattle across the Indian territory, had lined his rifle sights against Apaches and Navajos. He rubbed his long angular nose and looked at Bowden sharply.

"Nice range we bought," said Bowden. "But there's liable to be a little trouble, Panhandle."

"A man could expect that," drawled Panhandle Smith, rubbing his nose vigorously. "There's a gold rush on. With gold, comes crime. The war has just been over a short time. Montana's northern ground, even if it didn't get into the war. We're Texas men; rebs, beaten men. Which will be the worst—the crime element that moved in, or will we have to fight the Civil War over again?"

Bowden smiled. "Ain't heard a thing yet about us being rebs. I guess the war didn't touch this country much, everybody being too busy digging for gold. The crime element, as you say, will be the worst. But then, too, there's a lady involved."

"Lady?" Panhandle Smith stopped rubbing his nose. "You mean you've met a good-looking heifer and can feel yourself slipping?"

Bowden laughed, leaning back. "Two good-looking ones, Panhandle," he said. He told him the entire story: about Marcie Gray and her outfit, of Jackie Bell and the Lazy Z, and of Len Carberry and what he had seen there under the rimrock when Sheriff Henry Potter and the Carberry men had lynched the two miners.

"Maybe you're wrong about the sheriff," said

Panhandle slowly. "Maybe it was another black horse, some other bronc than his?"

"His horse," said Bowden. He settled in his saddle, watching the cattle go by. They were tough to the trail; they had moved all day—yet they were hard. Cows, some of them heavy with calf already; and a mingling of well-bred bulls.

Bowden said, "Keep this under your stetson, Panhandle."

The lanky trail boss nodded. "You're a marked man, Dean," he said. "They know you saw that, and that marks you—they'll have to kill you to silence you. Looks to me like you made a mistake when you rode in and told the sheriff about the lynchings."

"Sure I did, but how was I to know?"

Panhandle Smith bit off a chew and rolled it slowly. "Well, this might prove interesting at that, Bowden."

The drags were moving by now, and the dust was thick. They put spurs to their mounts, and rode to the point. Bowden said to Ken Shaden: "We'll guide the herd in, Ken; you ride back and help Harry and Wyatt with the drags. Spread the word around that we have to run these cattle right through Alder City's main street."

The cowboy said, "They might stir up a ruckus, Bowden. Ain't there no other way to get them through?"

"We have to go through Alder Gulch. Can we help it if they built a town right in our way?"

"I'll spread the word," said Shaden.

Shaden loped back, circling the herd, and then went back to the drags. The dusk was heavy when they reached the rimrock and the cattle smelled the tumbling mountain water below; they crowded the steep rimrock path. Two riders moved up, closing in and pinching the herd, building a bottleneck and letting the cows move through this, and thus stringing them out along the thin trail.

Below the high point, Bowden and Panhandle Smith pulled their horses off to each side, sitting there to keep the cattle on the trail. They came over the edge hard, running and bawling, sliding in the shale. They ran down on the lower reaches, bawling and hurrying, and the leaders plunged into the creek, grabbing water and pushing ahead as the others rammed them down the stream in their haste.

Bowden saw them run over the new graves.

"Push them," he hollered. "Don't let them drink too much; they'll log on us."

Punchers rode into the water, their broncs' hoofs shooting spray. Bullwhips popped and cattle moved. They hurried them along, cropping the green grass along the banks, grabbing a mouthful of water as they traveled. They hurried them along to where the creek took a sudden turn and roared down a small waterfall. There the leaders left the stream and the banks and turned on the trail that led into Alder City.

Night found them a few miles out of Alder City. Bowden, too, had not liked the idea of trailing the herd through Alder City, but he had no other choice —to get to the Lazy Z ranch, they had to move the herd through the mining town. The moon was coming lazily over the mountains when they reached the outskirts.

The cattle, tired from their long trek, nevertheless became spooky when they lumbered down the main street. Bowden and Panhandle Smith were riding point; they pushed the leaders hard, running them straight ahead. Word had gone around and townsmen stood on the plank walks and in doorways watching the cattle run by them.

The Texas cattle ran down the dirty street, swinging the dust in the moonlight behind them. Kerosene lamps in saloons and stores cast huge rectangles of light on the sidewalk and dust and the cattle shied at these, spooky and frightened. There was only one thing to do and that was to drive them harder.

Bowden swung his gray sharply, and rode back. Already the leaders were leaving the main street, taking the north trail that led to the range under the mountains. Bowden breathed heavily; the thing was working well—more than one half the cows were already through town.

Back there, a dog started a sudden barking, and other dogs took up the clatter. Cattle were bawling and a cow was kicking. Bowden cursed and started back, riding his stirrups, but he was too late.

A pack of curs were harassing the edges of the cattle, snapping at the cows, who were breaking into a terrified run despite their weariness. Bowden rode in, his bullwhip popping. The lash hit a dog, sent him ki-yipping, and knocked him flat. But the damage was done.

The cows were running, and running hard. They swelled up, driving the side riders, on the sidewalks, penning them and their horses against the buildings. Hoofs beat on the walks, and a cow hooked a horn in a store window. Bowden heard the smash of glass, and rode that way.

They were moving fast now, moving under the moonlight. They spread out and hit the sidewalks. Men and women were running for protection into saloons and stores. A bull, blinded by dust, ran into the outside rail that held the pine awning over the doorway of the Lady of Chance.

The rail broke. The canopy sagged. Another rail popped, and the canopy fell. Hoofs ground over it and broke the pine lumber. The incident did not last long, though, because most of the herd had already passed the saloon. The last of the cattle brushed by it and reached the outer edges of town.

Bowden said to Panhandle Smith, "We better ride back."

Men were moving on the streets, and some were cursing. A girl, standing in the doorway of the Congress Bar, was laughing hysterically. The street was pocked with hoofs and in a few places the sidewalk had been torn up. The merchant was out looking at his broken window when Bowden rode up.

"Those dogs did it," said Bowden. "We'd've got the whole herd through all right if those curs hadn't started in. I'll make good your window, mister, and whatever other losses you've had. That goes for everybody in town that has suffered some damage due to my men and cattle."

"That glass came in by wagon from Butte," said the merchant.

"You order it," said Bowden, "and I'll pay for it."

Panhandle asked a man: "Anybody get hurt?"

"Nobody that I know."

They swung around and rode to the Lady of Chance. Len Carberry and some of his men were picking up the broken canopy. Bowden drew in and said, "Send me the bill, Carberry."

Carberry said, "T'hell with you, Bowden!"

Bowden was quiet for a little while; then he said: "All right, if you want it that way," and turned and rode off. Sheriff Potter stood on the corner, dark and heavy and bulky in the night.

He said, "Bowden, I could arrest you for this."

Bowden rode close and said deliberately, "Now you really don't mean that, do you, Potter?"

Potter read the undertone in Bowden's voice. He said finally, "If somebody swears out a complaint, I'm serving it on you."

"Come ahead," said Bowden.

Panhandle Smith was stirring in his saddle, and Bowden glanced and saw that the trail boss had his hand on his gun. Potter saw this, too, and he saw his way out—there were two of them and only himself, and he could tell that to Len Carberry as an excuse.

Bowden said, "There's nothing here, Panhandle."

They put in their spurs and caught the herd. They grazed the hungry cattle over the hills, and they were dark dots moving under the moonlight. They were hungry and they ate as they walked, and the progress was slow. When false dawn came they had the herd on the rim of the hills that overlooked the Lazy Z ranch house.

Panhandle Smith looked at the indistinct buildings below. "Nice-looking ranch," he said.

"I think so," murmured Bowden.

Chapter 6

NIGHT RIDERS

Jeff Walton left the Turtleback outfit at dusk of the next day, reaching Alder City long after dark. He tied his horse back in the alley and went to the Lady of Chance. There was a lamp lighted in Carberry's office, and Walton leaned against the wall beneath the window and listened. Finally he went to the door and knocked and said quietly: "Len, it's Jeff."

The door opened and Jeff Walton entered, pulling it shut behind him. He stood against the wall and said, "Hello, men," to Sheriff Potter and Dunc Cross and Len Carberry.

Potter, seated across the room, nodded quickly, and Dunc Cross, squatting on the floor, looked up from his cigarette. "Howdy, Jeff."

"We been waiting for you," said Carberry.

"This Gray woman is a witch, Len," said Jeff Walton. "Tonight she wanted me to go over the payroll for this month with her. I begged off, saying I was coming in to see the doc."

Carberry asked, "Maybe she's suspicious that her foreman's friendly with me, huh?"

Walton shook his heavy head. He was a thick man, not too short, but heavy. His pale gray eyes were set under heavy brows, and he was about thirty. "She don't suspicion a thing, Len."

Dunc Cross asked, "Where's the kid? Where's Jim Bell?"

"He'll be around soon," said Carberry. "He's got our horses down along the creek. We drift out separately and meet down by the rapids. Jim took the broncs down there and tied them up for us."

Jeff Walton spoke slowly. "I've heard quite a bit of talk about these vigilantes, Len. Some of the Turtleback hands been talking about them. Seems as if nobody knows who they are, but they're growing in strength, they claim. Some of these stage robberies and these miners being robbed and killed ain't setting so purty with them, they tell me."

"Who's in that bunch?" asked Potter.

Carberry looked at the star-man and smiled a little too tightly. "You sound like you're a-scared, Potter," he said.

Potter said, "They find out about me and—" He drew his forefinger across his throat.

Walton asked, "Yeah, who is in the gang?"

Carberry dropped his thin shoulders. "Probably local merchants and townsmen," he said. "Hell, that's nothing new. They were secretly organized in California and in Idaho—"

"And look what they did," finished Potter. "Hung anybody they suspected—and hung 'em high. Nobody's even asked me to join—you don't suppose they figure I'm—"

Carberry said angrily, "Drop that talk, Henry." He settled back in his chair and looked at them. "We'll take care of these vigilantes when we know more about them. And we'll know that later on. You see, I'm one of the charter members."

Potter stared. "You're what?"

"You can hear," said Carberry distinctly. "One of them came to me and sounded me out. I led him on and went in on the scheme. I wouldn't worry about that, men."

Potter looked at Dunc Cross. "Well, I'll be damned," he said. "The biggest crook in Alder City leading a bunch of vigilantes!" The tenseness left and he leaned his head back and laughed. The sound started low, rumbled up, and was too loud. Carberry's face showed a touch of disgust.

The back door opened and Jim Bell said, "Everything is ready, men." He was the flashily dressed youth that Dean Bowden had seen with Dunc Cross and Len Carberry the evening before when Dean had ridden back through Alder City. "Horses are set to travel." He pulled his head back and closed the door. They heard his boots go down the alley; then the sounds died.

"Got your masks?" asked Carberry.

Potter dug into his jacket pocket. "Got mine," he said. The others nodded and they went out. They split up and went to the street between buildings. The night was still dark, but soon there would be a moon. A few minutes later, they regrouped in the brush along the creek.

Len Carberry looked them over, marking them well in his mind, knowing each man for his capacities; then he stepped up. They were riding dark horses and they had the brands smeared over with pitch. They were tough horses that could carry a man a long way before daybreak, but Carberry knew they would not be ridden far.

They did not follow the wagon road to the west; they rode across the swelling undulant hills. Carberry took the lead, and a pace behind him rode Henry Potter. Jeff Walton and Dunc Cross rode together, with Jim Bell a little bit behind and riding alone.

The moon was up, and they wanted that. They did not ride fast, but hit a long trot; they had plenty of time, and there was no hurry. Each packed a rifle in his saddle scabbard and each had a short gun around his hips. And tied to each man's saddle strings were some gunny sacks. On top of these were tied dark slickers.

They rode a high ridge, and Carberry saw the Turtleback outfit below them, still miles away but discernible under the uncertain light. Accordingly, he swung his horse around, and held him in until Jeff Walton moved up.

He said, "How does Marcie Gray take this Cross U outfit, Jeff?"

"She's goin' to fight the Texan," he said.

Carberry said, "That's good—feed her lot of that talk. Maybe we can get her to fight him for us—and maybe she and her men can run them off. Anyway, they can whittle them down and we can move in for the kill."

Jeff Walton was slightly hesitant. "I laid on a butte and looked over them gents through my glasses this afternoon," he said quietly. "They ride in pairs, Len, and they carry rifles, too. There's seven of them; they've seen the cattle trails, and they know cattle and shooting irons."

"So Marcie says she won't move her cattle, huh?"

"Claims she won't, Len."

"That's good," said Carberry. "That's the way we want it." He added matter-of-factly, "Neither will I haze off my cows, either."

"There'll be a range war," said Walton. "I've read these signs before."

"They point that way," said Len Carberry. They rode on in silence for some distance. "If you wanta win something, Jeff, you've got to fight. When this is over, you'll ramrod the biggest cow outfit in Montana."

"Or else be fertilizer for wild sweet peas," said Walton.

Carberry looked at him and smiled twistedly, but the smile was not friendly. "Your Justins got ice in them, Jeff?"

"I'm in," said Walton, "and in deep. I go all the way, Len; whole hog or none, that's it."

"That's the talk," said Carberry.

They crossed a small creek. Their horses wanted to drink but they held them up, and their steel-shod hoofs plumed the silvery spray around the riders. They climbed the far bank, their horses slipping in the sand, and gained the ridge. Dunc Cross glanced at Jeff Walton.

"Len's miners ain't got no guts, Jeff," he said. "This Texan son run off two of them, after bumping his short gun off'n one's skull. They came into town tonight, their bellies full, told Len, and then drifted out on the evening stage for Drummond. Claim the diggings around Helena are better than these anyway."

"Why in the hell do you fool with those dirt movers, anyway?" asked Jeff Walton. "Here they make good money digging—keeping all they dig—and you pay them wages besides. I don't get it."

"What do you use for brains?" asked Carberry. "How do you suppose I get this gold shipped out of the country without arousing suspicion? What if I didn't hire any miners and then, all of a sudden, I make a big gold shipment? You don't figure local people would get suspicious of me, do you—as to where I got the gold? Especially with these miners being robbed and these stages being stuck up?" His voice was cynical.

"But one of your own miners was robbed," said Walton.

"That's what he said. How would it look to people if every miner but one of mine was held up, and mine never got touched?"

Jeff Walton had to smile. "You play them close, Len," he said, "and you don't miss no bets."

"Not if I can help it, Jeff."

The moon rose and arced and started to fall. Then it was that they reached the high summit there in the Rockies. The wind was raw—it was blowing off snow and glaciers—and they pulled on the slickers. The oilskin cloth, used to shed rain, turned the wind, too, and also hid their identities, covering even their saddle cantles and forks.

Jim Bell's fingers were cold. He was glad when they reached the fringe of scrub pine that topped a rocky ledge. They dismounted there, tied their broncs to the trees, and took their rifles out. The hour, Jim Bell knew, was past midnight.

"They oughta be rollin' that stage along soon, Len," he told Carberry. "Lord, it's cold up here in this high air!"

"Not too cold for straight shooting," said Carberry dryly.

The stage road was to their south, twisting through the cuts and fills, dipping along like a tired ribbon under the waning moon. They moved ahead with their rifles up, and nobody spoke, and they came to the timber along the rim of the road. There was the exact summit of the pass. And there, at this point, the stage would be slowed to a walk—the horses would be tired from the climb, and ready to stop.

They settled in the brush, and each man had his thoughts. But whether these were disturbing or reassuring, nobody knew except their owner, and he did not disclose their nature. They had done this before on other points along the trail, and they had carefully rehearsed their plans in Len Carberry's office— the thing was clear to them, and they knew just where each man was to be stationed, and what each man should do when the time came.

They sat there for some time, smoking cigarettes. Then finally Len Carberry said, "Here it comes, men."

They saw the stage then. Four horses were pulling it up the hill, toiling in their tight traces. The sweet jingle of the tug chains came across the stillness. They could hear the rattle of rims on the gravel.

"All right," said Carberry quietly. "You each know your job; don't muff anything."

Jeff Walton and Henry Potter went down the road a piece, then pulled back into the brush. They were shapeless forms under their slickers and now both wore their bandannas over their noses and lower part of their faces. The brush settled behind them, and they were hidden.

Dunc Cross moved up the road a bit, and settled back. That left Jim Bell and Len Carberry in the center. Carberry glanced at Jim Bell and murmured, "Kill anybody that gets in our way, Jim."

Jim Bell said, "It'll be my neck if I don't Len."

They settled back then, rifles ready. Carberry squatted on his rowels, and said no more. Jim Bell felt that gnawing feeling in his belly, that feeling he always had before action. And, as usual, he wished he were somewhere else.

But, he thought, *you're in too deep, Jim Bell*. . . .

Fifteen minutes later, each carrying a part of the gold, they rode back over the hills, drifting before the high shrill wind. Behind them the stage burned with the flame lifting against the dull gray sky. The horses, after the double tree's pin had been pulled, had stampeded down the trail, running around a bend and getting out of sight, the doubletree beating them on the hind legs and rump as they ran.

Jim Bell, feeling a little sick inside, glanced at his fellow riders. Carberry's thin face was without emotion, without heat. Henry Potter's heavy jowls were just a little too white, and his lips too loose. Walton was light in his saddle, his face bleak. Dunc Cross was the same: he showed nothing.

"I hated to have to kill that driver," said Jim Bell quietly. "I've known old Hans for a long time, Len, ever since I was a kid."

"Either you or him, Jim," said Len Carberry quickly. "The fool should've known better than to jerk your mask off. If he'd been allowed to live, and got to talk, his words would have hung you, Jim."

"I reckon so," said Jim Bell. But he still didn't feel right.

They drifted across Dean Bowden's outfit, cutting across the edge of the hills, and day was breaking as they rode into Alder City. They drifted in, one at a time, and finally met in Carberry's office. There the sacks and their yellow metal were put in the saloonman's safe.

"We'll cut it later," said Carberry.

Chapter 7

OPEN RANGE

There was much to do at the Lazy Z. Alex Tooping took a team and drove into Alder City for grub, horseshoes, and other necessities. Bowden had bought some horses with the ranch, and most of these were workhorses used to put up hay during the haying season.

The whole outfit was tired—men, cattle, and horses. But with the green grass shooting up as the sun increased in intensity, the cattle and horses would soon regain the tallow lost on the long trail between Texas and Montana. Bowden rode through his stock, strung there along the length of the hills, lying above the fences that held them out of the hayfields.

The cattle, he knew, would not drift far for a few days. They would stay close to water and feed and shade, building up from the trip. It had been a slow, difficult job trailing the stock north. Had they been steers instead of bred cows, the trip would have been easier and faster. And to add to the slowness, the herd had been started early in the spring, even when there was snow on the ground. Some of the old trail drivers had warned Bowden it could not be done at that time of the year, but the Texan had had to take the chance.

They had lost some cows, of course. Some had become too weak to travel and had been abandoned at various ranches. Numerous accidents had taken others. But all in all the loss had been only about ten percent. Bowden knew that luck had ridden with him.

He was almost broke, except for a thousand odd dollars. But his men had consented to wait for their wages until he had built the spread into a paying ranch. The trip had cost him more than he had figured; in Utah he had had to buy hay for a week to feed the stock up before moving on. That had cut his roll drastically.

The next forenoon he and Panhandle Smith rode over the new Cross U range. And what the wizened trail boss saw made his eyes pucker in satisfaction. They rode down on the creek where the miners were located. Bowden sent a glance over them, and saw that the Carberry men had left.

"Getting much gold?"

One man said, "Not too much. The pocket's out, Bowden."

Bowden nodded, looked at them, then rode away. Panhandle Smith said, "Damn, we could use that gold, Bowden."

"We'll make it all right," the Texan assured him.

They rode silently, each with his thoughts. Neither man, for that matter, ever talked much, and when they rode together they rode mostly in silence. Panhandle Smith had put Bowden on his first horse, back there more than twenty years ago, and he had been a pallbearer at Ike Bowden's funeral. They had, after all, nothing much to talk about. Each knew the other too well.

They stopped and looked at some cattle bedded down under a grove of cottonwoods on a slope.

"Rocking Chair and Turtleback brands," murmured Panhandle Smith. "Don't look like they aim to pull their stock off'n our range, Dean."

"They've got another day," said Bowden.

Panhandle Smith shrugged his shoulders. "Let's hope they run out riders tomorrow," he said.

The Rocking Chair and Turtleback cattle were farther back from the creek, grazing on grass higher on the hills. Bowden did not look for them to mix with his Cross U stock because his cattle would stay close to the creek for a few days.

They came in to the ranch at noon, ate, and then rode out. They were in the foothills, looking over the wild cattle, when they saw the two riders in the distance. Bowden put his field glasses on them.

"Sheriff Henry Potter," he told Panhandle Smith, "and a young fellow with him. Saw the young fellow down in the town the other day."

"Wonder what Potter's doing on our range?"

Bowden said, "Let's find out."

They rode down the hills and met the pair. Bowden said crisply, "You're off your range, Potter."

Potter said, "I'm the law. I can ride any place."

Bowden nodded and murmured. "Oh, that's the way you think," and looked at the young fellow, marking again that recklessness that was dangerous. "And who are you?"

"The name's Jim Bell."

"Your sister was telling me about you."

Jim Bell smiled crookedly. "I guess she'd tell you all she knew, too," he said. He licked a cigarette into shape, lighted it. "But I guess that's a woman's privilege, huh, Bowden?"

"I guess so," said Bowden. He suddenly said to Sheriff Henry Potter: "Where you two riding for?"

"The stage was held up sometime last night," said Potter. "Luckily, there was only the driver on it—besides the gold, of course. Whoever did it killed the driver, and set fire to the wrecked stage. They got the gold, of course."

"Seems funny that they'd send out gold without a guard," said Bowden.

"The Placer Company up in Ribbon Gulch were shipping it out. They'd lost so much with a guard on that they decided to run it through without a guard, figuring that the guard just told everybody there was gold on the stage."

"Somebody's got wind of it," said Bowden.

"Looks that way." Potter scratched his head. "Well, we figured we'd mosey out this way an' look for tracks. But we sure ain't found much, Bowden."

Bowden said, "Is Carberry going to move his Rocking Chair stock off my Cross U range?"

Potter shrugged. "You'd have to ask him."

"You don't know?"

Potter looked at him. "How would I know?"

Bowden let that ride. He said, "Tomorrow morning's the deadline, Potter. If Rocking Chair and Turtleback cattle still run on Cross U range, I'm rounding them up and holding them in pound. According to the law, I can hold them fifteen days and, if nobody has come to redeem them at that time, I can rebrand them with my iron and claim them."

Potter said, "That'd mean war, Bowden."

Bowden said, "I know that. If they want war—war they'll get. *If* I have to round up their stock I can charge them two dollars a head for expenses due me when they do come to collect, if they do."

"Carberry'll come with guns," said Potter.

"That'll have to be it . . . if he wants it that way."

Jim Bell said, "Bowden, you're reaching too far.

Somebody'll chop your arm off . . . with a bullet."

Bowden rode close. He said, speaking low: "Listen Bell. You're on the wrong track; you're riding the wrong color horse. I've seen kids like you start out. The trail you're hitting will lead you two places: to the pen or to the gallows. Or maybe a third: you can die under bullets."

Jim Bell had his hand on his gun. He looked at Bowden, but his eyes were none too steady. He said, "You aren't talking to me that way, Texan."

"Don't pull on me," said Bowden.

Jim Bell was silent for a long time. Potter sat in the saddle, his breathing heavy. Panhandle Smith was watching Potter very closely. Then Jim Bell drew his hand back.

"This ain't Texas, Bowden," he said. "This is Montana."

"Maybe not," said Bowden.

Potter said, "Let's drift, Jim," and lifted a hand, and they rode off. Bowden sat his horse and watched them go and he found himself smiling slightly. When he looked at Panhandle Smith, his eyes were twinkling.

"I hope I scared him."

Panhandle shook his head gloomily. "I doubt it. Dean. Why did you do it?"

Bowden thought of Jackie Bell. "For his sister's sake," he said. He looked at the two men, now in the distance. "Potter ain't out here to look for tracks. He's out here spying on us for Carberry."

"Well," said Panhandle Smith, "he ought to know where we stand. . . ." He looked at Dean Bowden sharply. "This man Potter may look big and tough, but I got a hunch he's got a wide yeller streak under his thick hide. He knows you saw him help lynch them miners, and he's the sort to take to the brush with a rifle and do a little bushwhacking."

Bowden said, "I've got an ace there, Panhandle."

Panhandle frowned. "In what way, fellow?"

"From what I hear, the vigilantes are getting pretty strong down in Alder City. If they knew that I saw their sheriff out there they'd hang him tomorrow. When the time is ripe, I'm letting them know—and we're watching big Henry Potter hang."

Panhandle Smith nodded.

An hour later, high on a ridge, they sat their horses in the sandstones and looked down on Len Carberry's Rocking Chair ranch. The spread lay at the base of a sprawled out hill. Bowden handed the glasses to Panhandle Smith, who looked long.

"Nothing much going on down there," he said.

Bowden said, "That means, then, they don't intend to start hazing stock off our range, 'cause if they were they'd have horses up and there'd be riders."

They swung across to the west, and rode into the Turtleback ranch at dusk. Punchers were coming out of the mess house after supper. They rode past them and drew rein in front of the long porch that ran the length of the two-story frame building. Marcie Gray and an elderly woman were sitting on the porch. Dean Bowden lifted his hat and Panhandle Smith moved his horse back a little, and then sat quietly.

"Hello, Miss Marcie," said Bowden.

Marcie Gray got to her feet. She came forward and said, "Miss Gray to you, Mr. Bowden."

Dean Bowden smiled. She wore a gingham housedress that held to her closely and built up her girlishness. He liked what he saw.

"What brings you to the Turtleback, Mr. Bowden?"

Bowden said quietly, "Cattle, ma'am, cattle. Are you moving your Turtleback stock from my Cross U range, or do me and my riders have to impound them and hold them until you either pay for the gathering or lose your herd to me according to territorial law?"

"We won't move them," she said, "and you won't gather them."

Bowden said, "Miss Gray, I'd hate to fight a woman."

A few of the riders had moved up. One of them said, "You aren't fightin' a woman, Bowden. I'm the ramrod of this outerfit." He was a short man with long, powerful arms, and a bestial face.

"What's your name?" asked Bowden.

"Jeff Walton. And I'm asking you to head off'n Turtleback range, and stay off. Do you hear that, Bowden?"

"I'm not deaf," said Bowden. "I've heard a little about you since I come into this section, Walton. And damn little of it was good."

Walton came forward. He said: "I'll beat your face in, Bowden. Step down off'n that horse, and I'll work you over."

Marcie Gray said, "Jeff, quit that talk."

Bowden was very quiet. He glanced back at Panhandle Smith and saw that the oldster had his gun out, covering the Turtleback men.

Panhandle Smith said, "Remember those bullet holes, Dean. That army doc told you to take it easy for two years."

"Step down, you reb," said Jeff Walton.

The reb did it. Bowden came down, and Jeff Walton came in. He moved in fast, almost blindly, because his head was too low. His fists were out in front of him, and he staked everything on his strength, for he had plenty of that as could be easily seen.

Bowden moved back, moving quickly. He caught

the sight of the spectators on the rim of his vision, and he saw the horror scrawled across Marcie Gray's face. He noticed, in that instant that the hardness had left the blonde girl, and then he lost consciousness of all that, being only aware of Panhandle Smith's rasping orders.

"Stand back and let them fight, you Turtleback men. First one that interferes, or reaches for his sidearm, gets a slug from me!"

A fist dug into Bowden's ribs, almost on his wounded lung, and he felt fire run through him. He was going back, and going back fast. He saw the right coming, and went under it; the left caught him beside the head, and stung him. He moved in then, feeling the edge go from Jeff Walton's strength.

They fought in, close; Bowden heard Walton's whistling, straining breath. He hit the man twice, both fists ramming in, and Walton gave ground. Bowden came in, fighting harder now, fighting with calmness. Walton was going—he had paced himself too fast, but he was still strong.

They went down once, falling in the gravel, but Bowden was up too fast. Walton blew the blood from his nose and came in, more deliberately now. Bowden swung him around, and got his back against the porch. Walton felt the rough lumber behind him, and it pressed against his shoulders and back—he tried to fight his way clear. But Bowden braced his feet, and was hitting hard.

Jeff Walton moved to the right, and Bowden blocked his way. Walton started caving, his knees turning in, and Bowden hit harder. Then Walton went down and fell on his side in a flower bed of pansies.

Bowden stepped back. He said, "You better get him out of there, he's ruining those flowers, Miss Gray."

Marcie Gray asked, "Are you hurt?"

Bowden looked at her. "I've been treated worse," he said. She let the hardness come back into her again and he did not like her so well that way.

Two men were helping Jeff Walton to his feet. He said indistinctly, "I'll kill you for this, you reb," and then he went into the bunkhouse. Bowden looked up at Panhandle Smith.

"Hurt much, Dean?"

"He wasn't so tough," said Bowden.

Marcie Gray said, "You men better ride on." And then to her riders, "Go back to the bunkhouse."

The heavy, elderly woman had come off the porch. Her tone was bitter when she said, "All right, you hired hands—get back where you belong." She looked at Marcie Gray and said, "Marcie, you're a fool. Pull your cattle back or there'll be death, I tell you."

"They're my cattle," said the girl. She spoke now to Bowden. "I fought Jackie Bell and whipped her. I ran her off this range. I'll run you off, too, Texan. You corral my cattle and me and my riders are coming after them—with guns!"

Bowden said, "I'm sorry, ma'am," and went to his horse. They rode out slowly, with Bowden thinking of Marcie Gray, and that hardness she didn't own. Finally Panhandle Smith spoke and said, "We better stop at a stream and let you wash up, Dean."

Bowden smiled. "Guess I'm not a pretty sight," he agreed.

Chapter 8

A CHANGE IN PLANS

Sheriff Henry Potter and Jim Bell broke company five miles out of Alder City. Potter played his hand close: he did not want to be seen with any of Len Carberry's men. The fact that Panhandle Smith and Dean Bowden had happened on them together, back there in the hills, still bothered the heavy-set sheriff.

Potter rode straight in, while Jim Bell circled and came in from the other direction, riding into the livery. Old Matt was drunk, as usual, and Jim Bell tossed him a gold piece.

"Buy a few on me, Matt."

"You're in the money, Jim."

"There's more where that came from."

Jim Bell saw that Henry Potter had already reached town. Potter's horse stood in a nearby stall.

"Sheriff been out for a ride?" asked Jim Bell. "See his horse looks like he's covered some ground."

"He just came in," said old Matt. He put the gold piece deep into his watch pocket. "He come in from the east. Guess he's been out there lookin' over that stagecoach murder."

Jim Bell shook his head. "I'd like to get my hands

on the fellow that killed old Hans," he said. He kicked off his chaps and hung them up beside his hand-tooled saddle. He went to the washbasin, pumped it full of cold water from the cistern, and washed his face. He squinted into the cracked mirror and carefully combed his dark hair. One strand was unruly and he had to work with it for some time before it lay correctly.

When he went toward the Lady of Chance, shadows were grouping across Alder City's main street and hiding the ugliness of the raw buildings. But he had no eyes for the beauty of the encroaching night; he went to the bar.

"Old Crow, Jack."

The bartender shoved out a bottle and a glass. The night trade had not drifted in yet.

"Where's Len, Jack?"

"Ain't seen him for an hour or two. He ain't back in his office."

Jim Bell poured a drink. He felt a little angry because Len Carberry wasn't in the saloon. The whiskey was hot and strong, and he had not eaten since early noon. The stuff hit him rather hard.

"I'm getting something to eat, Jack," he said. "Tell Len I'll be down at Jackie's place getting supper."

"All right."

Sheriff Potter was eating in a booth with Martin Johnson, the owner of the Mercantile, and George Carson, owner of the hardware store. Jim Bell glanced at them and took a chair at the counter. Jackie was waiting on a table there.

"Where have you been, Jim?"

"Don't start getting that way," he said quickly. "I'm old enough to take care of myself, kid."

"What do you want to eat?"

He studied the menu with deliberate carefulness.

67

"Wish you could write so a man could read it," he said. "What's this?" He held his finger on the writing.

"Lamb chops."

"Lamb chops for a cowman," he said. "Hey, what is this, Jackie? Where did you get hold of lamb chops?"

"I butchered Mary's little lamb."

"I'll try them," he said. "I've never eaten them before. Yes sir, I'll take a plate of them."

"You don't need to tell the whole restaurant," she said.

He shrugged and watched her go into the kitchen. He had to wait for some time, and impatience tugged at him. He was eating when Henry Potter and Johnson and Carson had finished and were going to the front to pay. He saw that Potter paid for the three meals and then the trio went outside. He was drinking his second cup of coffee when Jackie stopped in front of him, her slim arm holding up a pile of dirty dishes.

"I want to see you, Jim," she said, "back in my office."

"Some more preaching?"

Her lips tightened, but she went on. He followed her, going through the kitchen, and entered the door to the side room. There were a small desk and a safe that had been hauled in by wagon from Spokane. He took a chair and leaned it against the wall. After a while she entered.

He said cynically, "Shoot, kid."

She looked at him. He wondered: *What is she thinking about?* and then he felt a surge of anger. He said again, more roughly this time: "All right, shoot. Pull the trigger. I'm ready."

She asked, "Where were you last night?"

"In my room, of course, up at the hotel."

"You weren't," she accused him. "I was up there. You were gone."

He felt his breath catch; he hid it. He asked, "What time was that?"

"About eleven."

"I wasn't there, then; I was in a poker game in Carberry's office." He added, "The game broke up about one and I went home then."

She said, making her voice level: "You're also a liar, Jim. I was up to your room at least five times. The last time was at three-thirty and you weren't in then. You came in sometime this morning."

"Why all this?" he asked.

"I've got eyes. Carberry wasn't in town last night; neither was Henry Potter. Dunc Cross was gone; you were gone. And last night the stage got robbed and Hans got killed."

"What are you talking about?"

"Where were you?"

He shrugged. "In my room, I suppose. You didn't knock hard enough to make me hear you, I'd say. I sleep sound; you know that."

She let her shoulders drop. She was whipped, and her dark face showed that, but her eyes were quick. She said, almost too softly: "Jim, you're my brother. There's trouble here, Jim. Dean Bowden is a hard man. You and Carberry's men will go against those Texans. They went through the war, they've killed men. They'll kill you, Jim."

"I can handle a gun."

"I rode with Bowden yesterday. He's quiet and thoughtful but he's steel underneath. He's seen the worst of it, back there in the war—"

Jim Bell studied her. "You in love with him?"

"You can leave that out, Jim," she said.

He got to his feet and rolled a cigarette. "Well, we know where we stand," he said. "You string along

69

with Bowden and I play my cards with Len Carberry. We're in opposite camps, Jackie, but we've been that way for some time now. So I won't feel too bad, you know."

She said, "Jim!"

"You're my big sister," he said. "I've heard that, too. Listen, girl, I'm free. I'm making good money—Carberry's paying me, and he's paying me plenty. Maybe you're right—maybe a bullet will tag me. But what the hell's the difference? You got to die once and twenty or thirty years too soon won't make any difference to you or to anybody else."

"Is that all?" she asked.

He looked at her small, dark face. Her hair was back, drawn into a severe knot. The lamplight glistened from its ebon surface. He had a moment of weakness then—but he'd gone too far; he'd killed. And he hoped his face had hidden his sudden relenting, short though it had been.

"That's all," he said, and left.

He went out the back way. The night had settled, and the air was sharp and cold and he realized for the first time his cheeks were hot. He looked at the stars and thought: *She's right: I'll die that way,* and then he went to Len Carberry's office.

There was a light inside. A crack of lamplight played between the bottom of the drawn blind and the sill. He said, "Len it's me—Jim." The bolt came back, and the door opened.

Dunc Cross was there, squatting beside the door. Jim Bell had a sudden distaste for the thin, silent man. He said, "Don't you ever sit on a chair, Cross?"

Cross' eyes were dull. "What the hell difference does it make to you, Jim?"

Carberry cut in. "No rough talk here," he ordered.

Cross looked at Carberry. "Nobody's crossin' my

trail," he said evenly, "let alone a whiskerless kid."

"I told you to can that," said Carberry.

Cross leaned back. "All right," he said. But the thing wasn't over with and all three knew it.

Carberry said to Jim Bell: "What do you know, fellow?"

"We rode out there on Bowden's range, like you wanted. You got about a couple of hundred head of stock on his grazin' land. Marcie Gray has more than you have—she must have aroun' half a thousand running on his grass, I'd say."

Carberry settled back in his chair. He built a slow pyramid of his fingers and looked at Jim Bell over its apex. He was silent for some time. Then he asked, "Did you see any sign of Dean Bowden or his riders?"

Jim Bell smiled, "We met him and his trail boss—run right into them. They was ridin' the rough country and they seen us before we seen them and they rode down on us. We never had no words, though."

Carberry scowled deeply. "Damn it, I didn't want anybody to see you and Henry Potter together. How would it look to this town if they saw one of Len Carberry's gunmen and the local law hobnobbing together?"

Jim Bell shrugged his shoulders. "They just happened to su'prise us, Len. We split up, though, right out of town and came in from different directions. Maybe Dean Bowden won't think anything of it, him being a stranger here."

"Maybe he won't," said Carberry, "and maybe he will."

"He told Potter there'd be trouble unless you move your cattle right *pronto*."

"Dunc Cross's starting a wagon out come morning," said Carberry.

Cross' back stiffened. "What're you talkin' about?" He studied Len Carberry carefully. "Is this a joke? I thought you aimed to fight these Texans."

Carberry smiled. "There's an old Chinese proverb, Dunc, that I learned when I was dealing faro down in 'Frisco. *'A fool uses only the one style of attack, a smart man changes his in battle.'* We can sit by and watch Marcie Gray's Turtleback riders fight this fight for us, and when the time is ready we can step in and take the winnings. No, we move a wagon out tomorrow."

"We won't need a wagon," said Cross. "We can do it in a day or two from the home ranch." He considered. "One day is enough, I guess."

Jim Bell said, "Dean Bowden says he's going to hold Turtleback cattle and make Marcie Gray pay so much a head for gathering them. Then, if Marcie doesn't come through in fifteen days, he claims he can legally brand these cattle with his iron. Is that right?"

"That's right," said Len Carberry.

Jim Bell threw his cigarette away. "Then where do I fit in?" he asked.

"You can ride out and punch cows for a few days or just stick around town close. I may need you, Jim."

"No cow prodding for me," said Jim Bell. "Those days are over, Len." He yawned. "Guess I'll climb the stairs and hit the hay. Wonder if my sister'll check up on me tonight, too?"

"She's been checking up on you, huh?" asked Carberry.

"So she tells me."

Jim Bell left by the front door. Miners were coming in and the opening of the door brought in their boisterous talk and made the bang of the piano sound louder. The door closed and the office settled to its former state.

Finally Dunc Cross said, "That kid's getting too cocky, Len. That sister of his might get wise to us and what we're doing, seeing she's following him so close."

"I've thought of that."

"He can't talk to me that way."

Carberry said, "Maybe we better get rid of him."

"I think so."

Carberry thought. He said, "After a while, Dunc." He opened a drawer. "Want to play a little stud?"

"With you?" asked Cross. "You think I'm crazy?"

"Penny ante," said Carberry.

"For that," said Cross, "I'll stay around. But no big stakes; I want to get out of here with a roll—a big roll."

"You'll do it."

They played for three hours. The night pulled out and became darker, and finally somebody knocked at the back door. And a husky voice said, "It's Jeff, Len."

Carberry unbolted the door. Jeff Walton came in. He had a black eye, and his lips were swollen. Carberry stared at him.

"What happened? A horse kick you, Jeff?"

Jeff Walton's voice was cynical. "Yeah, a horse. His name was Dean Bowden."

Chapter 9

ROUNDUP

Dunc Cross slept for a couple of hours there on the bench in Len Carberry's office. A miner had come in from the back country and the stakes were running high in the poker game Carberry and a gambler had started. Cross pulled his hat over his face to cut out the lamplight.

Len Carberry shook him awake. "It's time, Dunc."

Cross sat up, blinking a little. He yawned and then sat there, holding his head and looking at the floor. "That last drink I had didn't sit very well," he told the world in general. "Who's winning the blue chips, gents?"

"Not me," growled the miner.

Tim O'Murphy, owner of the Congress Bar, had heard about the game and come to sit in. The fourth player was a sallow-faced gambler, one of Carberry's housemen. Cross knew just what chance the miner had with those three in the game.

"Look you up later, Len," he said.

Carberry nodded.

Dunc Cross went outside. Dawn was rimming the

east and the night air was chilly. The Chinaman's was open and he got a cup of coffee there. That settled his head and he went to the livery barn. Old Matt was snoring drunkenly in a manger. Cross glanced in on him and noticed the old man was in his shirt sleeves. He got a fork full of hay and dumped on the oldster. Matt kept on snoring.

Cross thought: *That'll help keep the old stiff warm.*

A few minutes later he rode out on a lineback buckskin. The horse was big and tough, and Dunc Cross let him have his way and set his own pace. The buckskin was a hill horse that had been raised on the Rocking Chair and he headed over the ridges for his old home range.

Cross said, "Damn, it's cold."

The dawn was growing clear and brush was taking form and significance. When they reached Rimson Ridge the sky was turning a brilliant mixture of gold and fire. The buckskin was losing his edge, and Cross rode him with his rowels. An hour later, he loped into the Rocking Chair ranch.

Smoke was coming from the cook shack but there was none from the bunkhouse stovepipe. Dunc Cross put the buckskin to the cookhouse door and called, "Hey, Luggy, I wanta talk to you!"

The cook was a homely, long-faced individual with sad-looking, limpid eyes. "Figured you'd stay in town until about noon," he said. "What brings you out here at such an ungodly hour, Dunc?"

"Roundup ahead," said Cross.

"Only thing this outfit has rounded up for months has been drunks when they wanted to get outa town and come home," said the cook. "Try another one, Dunc."

Dunc Cross smiled. "No fooling, Luggy, that's straight from the shoulder. We're runnin' Rocking

Chair stuff off'n Bowden range an' back on our grass."

Luggy stared. "Come again?" he invited Cross.

"You heard me the first time. Kick out some grub and get it on the boards fast. I'm waking up the crew." Dunc Cross pushed the buckskin on and rode up to the bunkhouse. He pulled one foot out of the stirrup and kicked hard against the door, driving it open. He leaned and stuck his head in the door. "Come on out, you scissorbills, and start punchin' cattle."

"You gone crazy, Dunc?"

"He's drunk," said a man. "As drunk as a bartender's bar towel."

Dunc Cross felt a touch of anger for some reason. "Get out and bust daylight open! We're filling our bellies and then heading for Bowden range. Come on, you cow pushers; step lively."

"You mean—we're raidin' Bowden?"

Cross had to smile. "No, the boss has had a change of heart. Today's the last day to get Rocking Chair cattle off Cross U range, and Len orders that we work Cross U range and get every head of our stock off before tonight."

"Has Len gone crazy?"

"You'll have to ask him, Soderbern."

Thirty minutes later, washed, fed, and still grumbling, the crew was on horses, heading across the hills. Dunc Cross rode in the lead, and when they reached the lower foothills he drew rein and gave his orders.

"Four of you fellows swing out and work the south hills. Drive your cattle toward this direction. Two of you others—you two there—go across the hills and work back, holding the middle of the range. You won't find many cattle there because they're all up on the higher spots. Then you other three can work the north ridges with me."

"Just head them in this direction, that it?"

"That's it. We change broncs at noon. The horse jingler and old Stovey will have a change out here for us. You got cold grub in your saddlebags. Eat it at noon and wash it down with alkali water if you ain't got sense enough to get fresh water. All right, let's go."

"What if we run into Cross U men, Dunc?"

Dunc Cross frowned. Then he said, "I don't expect you'll have no trouble. They'll be cutting Marcie Gray's Turtleback stuff today, themselves."

"We'll meet them, then, huh?"

"Remember, no trouble though. Those are Len Carberry's orders." Dunc Cross shrugged his shoulders. "Don't ask me why Carberry don't want to fight, I just work for wages too. Everything clear?"

They rode off into the morning sunlight, and Dunc Cross looked at the Cross U ranch through field glasses. Men were stirring there and smoke was rising lazily from chimneys and horses were being saddled. He saw a man he identified as Dean Bowden, and Dunc Cross focused the glasses sharply, watching Bowden walk to the corral where he roped a horse. Panhandle Smith came up, his lasso trailing behind him.

"Riders moving on the high country, Bowden," said the trail boss.

"Been noticing that," said Bowden. "I was watching them through my glasses; they came from the Rocking Chair outfit. Looks to me like they aim to work our range for their stock."

"Thought Carberry was going to let us round them up and then take them away from us," said Panhandle Smith.

"Must've changed his mind."

Chunky Wyatt Jones came up. "They're shoving cattle around, Dean," he said. He put his field-glasses on them. "They're cutting stuff and pushing some stock back toward the Rocking Chair. I can't read no brands, though—too far off."

"Give me the glasses," said Bowden.

He studied one rider for sometime, then lowered the lenses. "That's the Rocking Chair sure enough, men. Dunc Cross is out there."

"See anything of Len Carberry?" asked Panhandle.

Bowden looked again. "Carberry ain't there," he said.

Panhandle Smith shoved back his hat and scratched his scraggly hair. He rubbed a hand over his ironlike whiskers. "Guess I oughta shave," he said absently. Then, "Who's crazy here, Dean? Me or you?"

Bowden shrugged.

They went into the cook shack where Harry Westcond, who had been elected cook, had hotcakes and coffee and bacon. They ate slowly and when they came out the sun was rather high. They squatted in the shade on the north side of the house, watching the riders in the northern hills.

Nobody had much to say. To a man they watched the hills that lay between them and the Turtleback outfit. And Dean Bowden, chewing thoughtfully on a cold cigarette, found himself wishing that Marcie Gray and her riders would come for Turtleback cattle, and there would be no trouble.

He shifted slightly. The ache was across his pelvis, and when he put his weight on the other hip, the pain left slightly.

"What time is it?" he asked.

Somebody said, "Almost nine, Dean."

He got to his feet. "They ain't coming, men; the

deadline is past." They started for their horses at the corral, and they were a sober lot of men. They roped horses and saddled and each man carried a rifle in his boot and some checked their short guns for loads.

Bowden broke the crew up and assigned each rider to his job. Panhandle Smith took two and worked the south hills; two of them rode the center; and Bowden took Chuck Baggett with him. Dunc Cross saw him and Baggett and turned and rode toward them, one hand high in the sign of peace.

"We're taking our stock off, Bowden," he said.

Bowden nodded and said, "Why the sudden change of heart, Cross?"

Cross lifted his shoulders. His dark face was without feeling. "The boss's orders," he murmured. "Guess he figures this ain't no time to start a fight. I don't know much about it, fellow. I just got my orders to push Rocking Chair stock on its home grass and to keep it there."

"Don't thank me," said Cross. He was quiet and thin in his saddle, and Bowden felt again that the lanky man was deadly, and he felt the hate that Cross had for him. "But it don't look as though Marcie Gray and Jeff Walton are sending men out to cut the Turtleback cows home."

"Don't look that way," murmured Bowden.

Dunc Cross studied him. He had not had enough sleep lately, had drunk too much, and his eyes were slightly bloodshot. "None of my business," he said quietly and in a dead tone of voice, "but what do you aim to do?"

"Gather her stock," said Bowden. "Shove it over on Turtleback grass. A man can't hardly fight a woman, Cross."

Cross smiled a little. "I fought one for two years,"

he said. "They call it matrimony. . . ." He sobered and said, "Seems to me you're changing your tune a little, Bowden. . . . Could it be because Marcie Gray is a damn fine-looking woman?"

Bowden said, "You talk too much, Cross."

Cross braced both hands against the fork of his saddle. He shoved against it, and Bowden saw his knuckles were tight and bloodless. Finally Cross said, "That Texan tongue of yours'll invite a bullet through your heart," and he looked at Chuck Baggett, who had his hand on his gun. He said *"Adios"* and rode off.

The gathering was comparatively easy. The Cross U cattle had not drifted far back; they were along the creek in the shade and close to water, and all that the Rocking Chair men turned back were Turtleback brandings. Bowden and his men took these, and headed them toward the west, driving them lower down onto the flatlands, where the cattle came trotting in and made a herd.

The day stretched out; they saw no sign of Turtleback riders.

Bowden rode with wild abandon, letting his horse run the cattle. He was loose and fast in the saddle, for the taste of the land was wild in him, and he liked it, with the high mountains, the singing pines, and the mad young creeks that roared from the glaciers and ice high on the peaks. But always, rimming the edge of his thoughts, was the presence of danger and death; this kept him alert and yet it brought him no pleasure.

He had thought it all over that night, lying between the blankets and feeling the chill come from the timbered slopes. Marcie Gray was young and she was a woman, and he felt toward her as every man feels toward a woman who is young and who is beautiful. He had changed his plans then; he would take it easy for a while, and try to reason with her.

He had thought: *She's stubborn and proud.*

And, also, there was something else there; and he could not understand it, at first—why was Len Carberry moving his cattle from Cross U range? Carberry wanted a fight, and he would get it sooner or later, and yet suddenly and for no apparent reason, he had ordered Dunc Cross and his crew to swing out and haze Rocking Chair stock from this range.

He said to Panhandle Smith, "I can't understand it, Panhandle."

The trail boss rubbed his chin thoughtfully. "There's something behind it, huh? There has to be, ain't that so?"

Bowden nodded soberly.

"Never rush against time," said Panhandle suddenly. He was thoughtful again, and then he said, "We got most of the stock in this herd, ain't we?"

"Might be a few back in the hills," said Bowden. "But if there are any it ain't many head."

They had gathered the Turtleback stock and had the cows grouped along a waterhole, and now they started them toward the Gray ranch. They ran them hard with bullwhips popping, and the herd gathered momentum as it started, breaking into a wild run. Calves bawled and the dust rose. They whopped them across the borderline, running them harder than ever, and they spilled down into the coulees and draws, running toward the ranch house that lay below them.

The Cross U riders pulled up. Their horses were breathing heavily. Young Chuck Baggett wiped the dust from his long face with the back of his sleeve. Wyatt Jones reached and got his plug and bit off a chew. Ken Shaden was thoughtful, as was his wont.

"Maybe they'll drift back," said Panhandle.

"They might," agreed Dean Bowden. The dust

had settled in his lungs and caused an irritation there. "But we'll have to chance that. Turtleback riders might keep them back."

"But if they don't?"

"We could build a drift fence."

"Barbwire," murmured Panhandle. "I hate the sight of it. I guess I saw too much in Texas. But what if they do drift back, Bowden?"

"We'll corral them and hold them."

Chapter 10

LADY OF CHANCE

Marcie Gray had slept poorly that night, for the thought of the morrow was with her, driving sleep away. She was up early and thought she would be the first awake in the house, but when she came into the kitchen Janie was stirring about, wearing her faded, shapeless robe and worn slippers.

"You're up early, child."

"Insomnia," said Marcie. She made herself gay. "What is it for breakfast, Janie?"

"Wheatcakes."

"And coffee," said Marcie. "Lots of coffee, Janie."

The heavy woman stirred the batter while Marcie fed dried cottonwood twigs to the thick iron range. The twigs crackled and sparkled and burned quickly and made her feed the stove often. She wriggled inside her blouse and split riding skirt and said, "It's cold, Janie."

"Late spring."

Marcie looked at her friend. Janie had been her mother's friend, and she had never married; when her mother had died Janie had taken over, and raised her and sent her through grammar school.

She had cried on Janie's wide shoulder, and laughed on her lap; Janie had helped her with her first party dress, and she had waited up that night until she had come home.

"You're quiet, Janie."

The obese woman's eyes were level. "Who would have much to say, when red hell is going to break loose across this range and men are going to die? Marcie, you're going to bring those cattle of yours back—tell me you will?"

Marcie shook her blonde head slowly.

"Why not? You've got plenty of range. You ran cattle on Turtleback range only before Jackie Bell came to take the outfit. You don't need to run cattle there; you have plenty of feed."

"But I'm running them there," said Marcie.

"Your pride, then?"

Marcie shrugged her thin shoulders. She shoved a handful of twigs into the stove. They crackled as the fire caught them and twisted them.

"Maybe you could call it pride," she said. "Maybe it isn't. I'm not taking orders, Janie, from anybody. And down in Alder City a man stopped me and ordered me to take my stock off his range."

"Dean Bowden's a Texas man, girl. Maybe he spoke a bit too quickly. He's come out of the war and he's been wounded. His nerves are a little too jumpy, and he may have spoke too fast."

"The cows," said Marcie, "are staying there."

"Bowden will gather them and hold them. And then what?"

"He can't hold my cattle. I'll take Jeff Walton and my riders and go over there and take my cattle out of his pasture and turn them loose. They're my cattle, aren't they? He can't hold something that doesn't belong to him, can he?"

"He can make you pay for gathering them," said

the older woman. "Or he can hold them for fifteen days and then claim them and brand them. The laws of the territory read that way."

"We'll change that law. We'll make our own. He's making his laws; we'll make ours. We'll take the cattle away from him."

"That means gunplay."

Marcie was silent. "Yes, I guess it does."

They let the conversation die. Marcie was sick inside; she tried not to show it. She was wrong, and she knew it, and that hurt her; but she was proud, too, and she was too young—she wanted her way. She had, she told herself, gone too far; she could not turn back now. She had made her boasts, and she would stay with them.

They ate in silence, and the sun was rising when she went outside. Punchers were washing at the bunkhouse pump and they nodded at her, but few of them spoke. Jeff Walton was wiping his face on the roller towel, and she noticed he did not rub hard, and that he was careful.

"Today's the day, Marcie."

"I can read a calendar."

"What're you going to do?"

"My stock stays on Cross U range."

"There'll be trouble," said Jeff Walton. "Lots of trouble." He added, "But maybe it's for the best."

Marcie went to the horse corral where she roped a cream-colored buckskin gelding. He was a rough horse with rough ways, but he was strong underneath. He snorted and fought the rope, rearing and striking, but she jerked him down to the ground, and he landed hard on his hoofs. She reached out and pulled him in and stroked his velvet nose.

"Tuffy, you old fool."

A few minutes later, she rode out toward the south hills that rose between the Turtleback and Alder

City. When she reached the rimrock Tuffy was breathing heavily from the climb; the rim of his leather headstall and the cheeks of the bit were flecked with foam. She dismounted beside the sandstones and settled there and watched the Cross U ranch through her glasses.

Time dragged on, and she saw the Rocking Chair men ride on Cross U range, and she identified one as Dunc Cross. The question grew in her: What were Rocking Chair men doing on that range? And it found its answer when she saw Cross and his riders turn the Rocking Chair stock back and push it off the Cross U ground.

She thought: *Len Carberry's giving ground to Bowden,* and that thought was unpleasant. That left her against the Texans, and already the Texans were riding out, gathering her cattle. She watched, the question going unanswered, and then she saw Bowden and his men turn her stock to the west, and she knew they were not holding them; she saw they would only put them on her range.

She mounted and rode toward Alder City. Dusk was falling across the wide land and the wind was moving it in; shadows grouped and separated and gathered again, the dusk pressed down and became night. In yonder cottonwood motte an owl gave his thick hoot, and above her she heard the booming wings of a nighthawk as the bird slipped down through space, hunting flies and insects in the bottom air.

The town was boisterous. Miners were moving on the street and the stage from Butte had just arrived. Tugs were jangling as they changed horses and a woman was entering the Concord, lifting her hoop dress high above her ankle as she stepped inside. She swung Tuffy around this, riding at the fringe of the crowd, and she stepped down and tied him to the rack in front of the Lady of Chance. There was a dun horse tied to the rack, and she looked at him as she tied Tuffy; he was one of her horses, and he was in Jeff Walton's string.

She thought: *Walton's ridden into town sometime today. Now what is he doing in here? He seems to come in plenty often.* She saw a man coming toward her, and she waited and said, "How do you do, Mr. Johnson."

He lifted his hat. He was a big man, and his face was square; he was Nordic, and his face showed stubbornness. He said, "Miss Gray, this is a pleasure. What are you doing in town this fine evening?"

She said lightly, "Business."

"If you want some supplies from the Mercantile, I'll open the door for you and serve you myself."

She smiled, "Thanks."

He turned; he looked at the Lady of Chance. From inside came the rap-rap of a piano, the sigh of an accordion. He said, "You're not going in there, I trust?" He was joking, of course.

"If Len Carberry's in there, I'm going in. I want to see him."

His smile left, and his character showed through. "Marcie," he said slowly, "I don't know how to say this, but you know me well, I think. There's nothing that either Mrs. Johnson or I wouldn't do for you. But if you don't mind my saying it, I think you're acting wrong."

"We ran on Cross U range before, and we have claims to it. Even if I have to hook up with Len Carberry, I'm using Cross U grass."

"Not according to law—"

"Dean Bowden boasted that he made his laws. I'll make mine."

Martin Johnson was a patient man; he spread his thick, heavy hands. He said, "Be careful, Marcie girl," and then watched her go into the Lady of Chance. One of the batwing doors went too far open and it stuck, and he watched her go up to the bartender and then he saw her go toward the door of Len Carberry's office, there at the far end of the wide building.

He stood there and watched, and he felt a stirring of something inside; he tried to reach this and analyze it, but there was little to his thoughts. He had been in the town before the gold rush, and he had seen it grow. He had his finger on its pulse, and he had felt that pulse sicken; he and others of the same peaceful cut had gathered, and soon they would act.

Sheriff Henry Potter came up and said, "Hello, Martin."

Johnson said, "Hello, Sheriff."

Potter moved on down the street, big and wide in the crowd. Jim Bell came out of the Antler Cafe, a toothpick between his teeth; he leaned against the building and looked at Martin Johnson, and when Johnson looked his way Jim Bell let his gaze switch idly away, but still he kept the merchant at the edge of his sight.

Marcie Gray had reached the door to the office, and Johnson turned to go into the night. Marcie knocked and Len Carberry said, "Come in," and she entered. She had never been in the Lady of Chance before, and therefore she had never been in his office, and she sent her glance around it before focusing her eyes on Len Carberry, who sat behind the desk.

"So this is the center of the web," she murmured.

He did not get to his feet. He said smoothly, "Miss Gray, I swear . . . Now what brings you through the den of iniquity that the Ladies' Aid calls the Lady of Chance, and what brings you to my office?"

She said, "I thought you were going to fight Dean Bowden."

"Am I not?"

"Your riders pulled your cattle back!"

His eyes fell and became lidded; his fingers went to the dried human ears and he pushed them along the chain. Finally he said, "My men had my orders, Miss Gray. I did not choose to fight in that manner." His eyes lifted, and they were sharp beneath their laziness. "Did you drive your Turtleback cattle back on your range?"

"No."

"Then, I understand, Bowden corralled them?"

"No."

The eyes were sharper now. The thin fingers ran across the dried surfaces of the ears, finally rested.

"Then what did he do with them?"

"He drove them back on my range."

There was a pause. She watched his fingers, there on the ear; she saw them tighten perceptibly, then relax. They lifted, letting the ears dangle, and they rested on the table.

"That was considerate of Bowden," he said quietly. He looked down at his fingers, and studied them. She had the feeling, then, of something that was dangerous; the man was too quiet, too silent, and she wished momentarily she had not come, and she wondered just why she had come at all.

"Are you going to fight him?"

He smiled, with his lips only, and said: "You seem impatient, Miss Gray. Yes, I'll fight him, I guess. Is that why you came here—to find that out?"

"Yes. Then we go together, is that it?"

He shook his head. "The Rocking Chair fights alone, and in the way it deems fit." He got to his feet and moved over beside her. "Women aren't tough, Miss Gray. They talk, but they seldom act."

"Don't judge me by your dance-hall harpies!"

He lost his smile, then he found it again. He bowed low and said, "You will excuse me, of course, but I have work to do. No, not that way—you may go out the back. Nobody will see you leave and confuse you with one of my harpies, as you put it."

She slapped him then, and she slapped hard. He lifted his hand to his jaw, and then his anger died, and he was himself again.

"A thousand pardons," he murmured quietly. He opened the back door and said, losing his polite veneer for a long moment, "Get out!"

She stepped into the night.

Chapter 11

THE VIGILANTES

After driving the Turtleback cattle off Cross U range, Dean Bowden and Panhandle Smith rode on and into the Turtleback ranch, while the rest of the Cross U punchers returned home. They pulled up in front of the porch and Bowden dismounted and knocked on the door. Janie answered.

Bowden asked, "Is Miss Gray at home?"

"She left this morning," said the heavy woman, "and I don't know where she went; maybe she went to town."

Bowden said, "Thanks," and walked back to his horse and mounted. They rode down to the corral where Jeff Walton and his men were branding some colts. They were good-looking stock, Bowden noticed; long-legged, hill-bred colts with a hint of hot blood in them to give them their long legs and height.

Jeff Walton was handling a branding iron. He put it in the fire, pushing it in deep, and when he got to his feet from where he crouched beside the embers, he pulled his gun forward a little on his hip.

Bowden said, "We didn't come for trouble, Walton."

"You aren't wanted on Turtleback ranch," said Walton huskily.

Bowden settled in his saddle, his eyes watchful. The Turtleback men had become very quiet, and he gave them a long glance. They were, he saw, just run-of-the-mill hands; they were cowboys, not gunslingers. They differed in that respect from the Rocking Chair hired hands.

"We'll ride off soon," said Bowden quietly. "We just came to tell Miss Gray we shoved her cattle off Cross U grass. She isn't home, I guess, so I'm telling you, Walton. If those cattle come back, I'll corral them and hold them."

"They'll drift back," said Jeff Walton.

"You better watch them," said Bowden. He addressed Panhandle, "Let's go, fellow," and they rode away.

Panhandle murmured, "I don't like this, us putting our backs to them. . . . More than one man's been knocked from saddle with a slug through his spine."

"Those men aren't gunmen," said Bowden.

They gained the low crest of the long slope, and Panhandle Smith said, "What if they drift back, Dean?"

Bowden shrugged. "Guess we'll have to hold them in the lower pasture, or else string that drift fence."

Panhandle Smith rubbed his jaw and scowled. "We're new to this country, and maybe we ought to ride light of trouble, Dean," he said. "What say we run that drift fence, huh? Won't be many miles of wire to set and the boys need the exercise after the long ride they went through."

Bowden nodded. "All right, Panhandle. We got some wire on the ranch; about eight spools of it, I guess. That'll do most of the stretching. I'll head into town and order some more—about two more spools—and take them out on a pack horse. I can get one at the livery barn. You swing back to the ranch and get things ready for the crew to go out in the morning. I'll come back sometime tonight."

"Take care of yourself," said Panhandle Smith.

The night was dark, pressing hard against the spring earth, when Bowden rode into the livery, Old Matt, reeking of liquor, sat on the bench dozing, and Bowden shook him awake.

"I want a pack horse and a pack saddle. You got either?"

"There's a sorrel down in the back stall," said the old timer. "He's broke to pack. There's a saddle down there with him. Say, were you the gent that dumped the hay on me t'other night when I was sleeping in the manger?"

Bowden smiled. "Not me."

"Damned fool," mumbled old Matt, "had me pickin' foxtails outa my whiskers and clothes for a whole day. You got a drink?"

"Seldom touch it," said Bowden.

The old man studied him from under craggy brows. "What t'hell do you do for excitement?" he wanted to know.

Bowden had to smile. "I get plenty of excitement," he assured the oldster.

He went to the Antlers Cafe. The restaurant had its evening trade, but he found a stool at Jackie Bell's end of the counter.

She said, "I haven't time to talk now, but I would like to see you later on. We close around nine. Could you meet me here about that time?"

"I'll be here."

He ate slowly, enjoying his food; he liked the conviviality around him. He had been too long in the war and too long on the trail. He paid for his meal and went outside, going up the street toward the hardware store. When he went past the Lady of Chance he saw two Turtleback saddle horses tied to the rack; he recognized one as belonging to Marcie Gray and the other he had seen under Jeff Walton's saddle. That meant Walton had cut in ahead of him, and ridden into town—or else he had just ridden in, coming in after Bowden had and while he had been eating at the Antlers.

The hardware store was dark but he tried the door, seeing a dim light back in the office. But evidently it was only a night light, and he turned away. Somebody behind him said, "Just a minute, Mr. Bowden," and George Carson came out of the night. "Is there something you want out of the store?"

Bowden asked, "You know me?"

Carson introduced himself and said, "I've had you pointed out to me, Mr. Bowden. Martin Johnson and I were talking about you today. Johnson, as you know, is our biggest storeman—he owns the Merc."

"Say anything good?" asked Bowden.

George Carson said, "A little," and laughed. Bowden liked the way he laughed; the sound was real and unforced. He followed the short, heavy man through the door, and Carson turned the wick up on a lamp and lighted it. The yellow rays went out and showed the store's interior.

"Hate to disturb you," said Bowden, "but I got into town late. I want about three—no, make it four —spools of barbwire."

Carson looked at him. "What's the fencing job?"

Bowden told him about the Rocking Chair and Turtleback cattle, and how Carberry had pulled his cows back, and that Marcie Gray had not moved hers. "Now we aim to run out a drift fence to keep Turtleback stock out."

Carson said, "Don't seem natural that Carberry would back out on you. . . ."

Bowden shrugged. "Can't tell anything about a human," he said.

They went to the back storeroom, with George Carson carrying the light. He had a few spools of wire. "These came around the Horn," he said. "I did get some overland through Fort Benson from the Missouri River boats, but these made the long trip. That makes them rather steep, Bowden."

"I'll have to have them," said Bowden.

Carson thought for a while. "Your credit's good. You can pay for them later on, if you'd rather."

They carried four spools out and put them on the back porch that faced the alley. Bowden told him he'd come along later with the pack horse and pick them up, and they went inside. Carson locked the door behind them.

His heavy face was serious. "Bowden, there's trouble here. I said that Johnson and me were mentioning you—well, we were. Somebody's got to stop these killings and this robbery. Some of these men have become drunk and boasted about their robbings and killings. Us honest folks have to do something."

"Organize the vigilantes."

Carson nodded, eyes lidded. "We have a pretty tight organization. Day by day we're building it up. We want you in with us."

Bowden said, "I'm new here, Carson."

"We trust you. The day you saw them hang those miners you came right in and reported it to Henry Potter. A dishonest man would never have done that."

Bowden smiled. "That ain't much to judge a man on, Carson."

"It's enough," said Carson. "We have our suspicions, of course. They point to Len Carberry and his gunmen."

Bowden thought of the men who had lynched the miners when he had first ridden into Alder City, and he thought of Sheriff Henry Potter's black horse. "Where does Potter stand?"

"We don't know," said Carson.

Bowden leaned against the wall and said, "All right, I'll be with you. When you need me, send for me. My trail boss, Panhandle Smith, will be with me."

Carson said, "We swear each other to secrecy. Lift your right hand, please." Bowden did, and the man swore him in. He spoke in a soft, low tone of voice, and the quietness of the ceremony impressed Bowden greatly.

"Your plans?" asked Bowden.

"We have to spy, of course. I own the warehouse behind the Lady of Chance Saloon. We are digging tonight—even now some of the members are working —and we are sending a tunnel under the alley and coming out under the floor of Len Carberry's office."

Bowden murmured, "Good idea."

They went out the front and George Carson locked the door. They stood for a long moment under the board canopy, neither man speaking but each playing with his thoughts as he looked over Alder City. People were moving up and down the boardwalk, and pleasing, and it moved across the night and its depot, waiting for the stage in from Drummond. A dog barked and a piano rapped out a tune and a woman sang in some dive. The sound was smooth and pleasing, and it moved across the night and it sounds, and Bowden felt the edge of it and found it strong and good. He said, "Good night, Carson," and moved forward.

Carson said, "I'll see you again," and stepped on

the street and went the other direction. Dean Bowden walked slowly, feeling the tides and the moods of the night and of the wild mining town. The stars were bright and clear overhead; they lay across the dark sky—and under all this men moved and fought and loved, and death was high in the mountain wind.

When he came to the Lady of Chance, he saw that the horses of Marcie Gray and Jeff Walton were still at the tie-pole. He had seen Walton in the Congress Bar, but he wondered idly where Marcie Gray was and what she was doing in town that night. He stepped into the saloon.

He took the widest space at the bar, and stepped into it and ordered beer. He was setting the glass down, his curiosity and appetite satisfied, when Len Carberry came from the side room. Carberry saw him and came up.

"Drink, Bowden?"

"Just finished one," said Bowden. "A beer." He added, "Thanks, though."

Len Carberry poured a drink. Bowden saw he was a little nervous, and he wondered what caused that. "My men move my cattle off your range?" he asked.

Bowden nodded.

"I told them to," said Carberry.

Bowden said, "That's good," and then he waited. Carberry lifted the glass and tossed the drink down and filled it again. Bowden let the silence grow up until it had weight, and then he said, "You aren't going to stop fighting me, are you, Carberry?"

Carberry was raising the glass. He set it down very slowly, and then he turned and faced Bowden. His right hand had dropped to the ear on his watch chain and he shoved it gently back and forth.

"Bowden," he said, "are you here for trouble?"

Bowden lifted his shoulders and looked at him.

"We got it ahead of us, Carberry. You know and I know that grass isn't free and that blood will buy it. You're not walking off and leaving that range to me."

Carberry said, "Don't jump to conclusions, friend," and then drank. He set the glass down; he was calm now. "Sure you don't want a drink?"

Bowden said, "No."

"Too bad," said Carberry. There was some trouble at a far table and Bowden heard a miner's raised voice. Carberry said, "Excuse me, please," and went that way. Bowden turned, looked the place over with studied indifference, and went out. Marcie Gray was stepping up on her horse and he went to her.

"Miss Gray, a moment, please."

She looked at him, her face flushed with emotion, and she recognized him, and he saw the fleeting expression die, leaving her face without thoughts. He marked this in his mind; stored it there for future consideration.

She said, "Yes."

He came to her horse; he put his hand on the beast's shoulder. "I was over to see you, but you had already left. We shoved your cattle on your range today."

"I saw that." She added, "They won't stay there —they'll drift back. Unless, of course, I send riders out to run the line. And I might not do that."

He said, "I'm putting up a drift fence." He saw something in her face then, and he knew it was relief. This, he thought, was her out. He would put up the fence, then her cattle could not cross; he had protected himself against her. This was no retreat, no giving away, for her. . . .

She said, "That's a good idea," and turned her horse and rode off. She moved in and out of a freight wagon slowly coming into town, and he lost sight of her. He remembered that Jackie Bell wanted to see him, and he looked at a clock in a jewelry shop, and saw it was almost nine-thirty.

The front door was locked, but she opened it to his knock. She was counting the day's receipts, and back in the kitchen the cook was washing his pans. She said, "Come in," and added, "I can talk when I work."

"Most women," he said, "can talk any time."

She glanced at him. "You made me miss my count," she said. She started over again. She was smart, bright; she was quick. He reached out and took her hand and she looked up at him.

"You can count that later," he said.

She pulled her hand back slowly. "It's Jim," she said. "He—I don't know what to do. He'll do something desperate and then—"

He said, "He's old enough to take care of himself."

"I don't look at it that way," she said quietly. "Maybe I'm a little bit—wrong, you could call it. You see, he's my only relative; that is, outside of an uncle and aunt back in Indiana." She looked at him. "Would you talk to him?"

"I did," said Bowden. He told her about meeting Jim and Sheriff Henry Potter, out there in the rough country—he told her how he had talked roughly to Jim, doing it on purpose.

"What do you suppose he and Henry Potter were doing out there?"

He shrugged. "I don't know." Then he added, "I was wondering that myself. Are Potter and Carberry —or Carberry's men—very friendly?"

"Not in town."

He spoke in a low tone. "You see, Jackie, you can't do anything for Jim, and neither can I. Your folks gave him a good home, you tell me, and despite that he has gone astray. I saw the same happen to my kid brother. Dad and mother brought him up right, but he had just so much wildness in him, and that broke out and ran over their teachings, and the wildness won out. The same thing is happening to Jim. . . . Nobody can do anything for him except Jim."

She said, "What happened to your brother?"

"He's dead," he said. "The war: Lookout Mountain." He wanted to help her; and he knew he couldn't—he had seen such cases before. The pattern was old; it always ran the same, and brought the same results.

She said, "You are at odds with Len Carberry. Jim rides for Carberry. I want you to promise me one thing. Don't hurt Jim—for my sake."

He said, "All right. But if it's his life or mine, that is a different thing. I can't promise that."

"That would be different," she said, "and I wouldn't ask you to promise that. Let's hope it works out for the best for all of us."

"Let's hope so," he said.

She smiled and said, "I'll start counting again, then." The cook stuck his head in and said, "Goodnight, Miss Jackie."

"Good night," she said.

"You'll have to say good-night to me, too," said Bowden. "There's a long ride ahead, Jackie."

She let him out the door and he went to the livery barn. Old Matt was drinking out of a quart; he lowered it and said, "I saddled that pack horse for you. He's back there in the stall."

Bowden saw that Marcie Gray was seated on the bench beside the old man. He said, "Hello, Miss Gray," and she answered. He led the pack horse out and returned in fifteen minutes with the laden animal. Marcie Gray sat her horse in front of the barn, and old Matt had saddled his horse and she held the reins. She said, "This way, Bowden; here's your horse."

He said, *"Gracias,"* and went up, dallying the pack horse's rope around the horn. She swung in behind him and said, "I'll ride with you to the fork," and they rode off at a running walk, the pack horse pulling back a little.

Bowden asked, "Why the honor, Miss Gray?"

"A long night ride," she said quietly, "and maybe I wanted company." Her voice was throaty and he tried to see her eyes, but the night was too heavy. He found himself comparing her with Jackie Bell, and he wondered at the difference of his feelings. She was sharp and sultry, and more mature. Jackie was too young yet; not in body, but in talk, in feelings. She was the kid sister he had dreamed of and never had . . . or was he wrong?

They talked of many things. She mentioned Texas —she had lived for some time in Houston—and they skimmed over the talk of the war; she had felt it little because it was so far away. . . . And as she talked, Dean Bowden found himself probing into her character, trying to read her and decipher her, but he was only a man and she was a woman, and the riddle was deep and endless.

Midnight found them at the fork; here the high trail ran over the ridges, heading for the Cross U and the low trail took the creek, leading into the Turtleback. She swung her horse around and said, "Well, good-night, and thanks for the company."

He reached out. He took her reins. He asked, "Is that all?"

She looked at him. The mask had come back; her face was hard. "What do you mean, Mr. Bowden?"

He had moved his horse to her horse's shoulder. He put his arm around her and kissed her, and then he wished he hadn't. She was rigid and unyielding against him, and her lips were cold. He felt the push of her firm breasts, and then he let her go; and he felt a minute of regret that he had given in to his longings.

She said softly, "I'm sorry that you did that," and then she rode away. She did not ride fast; she rode at a running walk, and he sat saddle and watched her for some time, before he turned his horse and rode away.

The hour was late when he reached the Cross U.

Chapter 12

DRIFT FENCE

Calf roundup was some weeks away, and Jeff Walton felt the slow dry tick of time, and measured it methodically. There were chores to be done; machinery to be overhauled, fences to be fixed, and odds and ends of other work—repairing saddles and harnesses, putting new corral bars into place. But Jeff Walton found that time ran slowly, and he waited for it to build up and break and run over into action—for the suspense was too tight.

He said, "You had company yesterday afternoon, Marcie. Too bad you went to town and missed him."

"Oh," said Marcie. "Who was it?"

"Bowden was over. His foreman was with him. They are running a drift fence and keeping our stock off the range."

"I talked with him in town," she said. "By the way, I saw that you were in town, too, last night."

He looked at her sharply. "Had to buy some tobacco for me and some of the boys. If I'd a-known you was riding in I'da had you buy it and save me the trip."

"Guess I should have told you," said Marcie. She

had asked about the tobacco stock from some of her riders; they had assured her every man had plenty of smoking and chewing. Why, then, this statement from Jeff Walton?

Walton went to the corral where he roped a stocky black gelding. He saddled the beast and rode out, heavy in his Miles City saddle. This was buildup, adding up—and there would be hell and gunsmoke. He wanted to get out, but then he thought of Len Carberry and the high wages he was drawing, and he decided to stay for some time. He wished nevertheless he hadn't made that decision.

Bowden had called him; he had faced him, whipped him. He had a gun and he knew how to use it; and deep inside Jeff Walton, burning with a small flame, was a touch of fear. He put the black ahead, hitting him now and then with his star-roweled spurs; he reached the apex of a ridge and he pulled up there for the black to get his wind, and he looked back on the Turtleback outfit in the valley below and to the north.

He sat there, deep in his thoughts; then he turned the black and swung to the east, riding the pine-clad ridges. The endless wind sang through the pines and spruce, and there were splotches of unmelted snow yet among the rocks where the shadows were thickest. An hour later, he gained the spot he wanted and he dismounted. The wind was sharper there and it was cold; he untied his mackinaw and took the field glasses from their case.

He left the black there and went ahead, lying prone on the lip of the rimrock. From there he watched the Cross U men below. They were cutting diamond willow poles from along Rock Creek and hauling them by wagon out of the creek bottom. Others along the hills, were driving in postholes with bars, and others were stringing wires along the poles.

He swung the glasses to the west, running his vision over the hills and draws. Cattle were moving down out of the rough country, and they were Turtleback cattle. A cow, he thought, is like a man in one respect: she likes to roam close to one spot, she hates to move and change her range habits. . . . All day he lay there—the sun rose and had heat and then lost it—and by that time the Cross U men had two wires up.

Still he lay there, watching. The shadows pulled down and became dusk. The Cross U left one man behind to ride line while the others returned to the house. Turtleback cattle stood on the other side of the fence and already some of them were bedded down.

Jeff Walton rode into the Turtleback. He left his horse with the *mozo*, and went toward the house. The sound of the piano ran across the thin air, and he stood in the doorway for a while watching Marcie Gray play. He thought: *She's a beautiful woman*, yet he had no desire for possession.

She saw him and turned on the stool and asked, "What is it, Jeff?"

"They're stringing that drift fence, Marcie. I saw them today. Our cattle are grouping up against it."

"They don't need that range," said Marcie. "They have plenty of water and grass on our side of the fence. I guess those cattle just want to get back on their old range."

He said, "We could cut that fence."

"But we won't."

His eyes were sharp. "Then you're kowtowing to the Texans?"

She said, "Walton, you're not hired to think."

He felt his anger come up, but he held it. He said very distinctly, "All right, Miss Gray," and then he went out again. He stood there and looked at the night and wondered if he should ride into Alder City, but the distance was too far and this rubbed against him; he decided against it.

Payday had been the day before, and a few of the punchers had some money left. He went to the bunkhouse and leaned against the wall, his eyes pulled shut against the lamplight, and looked them over silently. A few, probably broke already, lay on their bunks and were reading; another sat and sewed on a boot with a Martin sewing awl; another slept, fully dressed and breathing heavily. One of the men from the table looked up.

"Want a hand, Jeff?"

Walton came forward and took a chair. "A stack of blues," he said. "Some whites and reds, too."

"Thought we hit you pretty hard last night," said the dealer.

"Jeff always has money," a man said.

Walton let that ride. "Two cards," he said.

Next afternoon he rode out again, this time riding another black, and this time too he had a pair of wirecutters tied to his saddle. He reached a high spot at dusk, and saw that the fence was complete—the wires stretched taut and stiff. More cattle had moved down from the hills and stood grouped against the wires. One man, he noticed, rode the line fence.

The man made a mistake as he rode; he was singing, and this told where he was all the time. Walton waited for darkness and then he rode down. The Cross U rider came to that end of the fence, and Walton waited patiently, squatting there in the dark some yards away. The Cross U rider turned his horse and rode away, singing in a low tone, and when he was gone Walton moved in.

He cut the wires quickly. His nippers clicked; the strands parted. He went to his horse then and circled some cattle, shoving them into the break. Other cows saw them moving through the fence; they hurried and ran in on Cross U grass.

They were dark spots moving in the night. Jeff Walton rode ahead, and when he had gone half a mile, there were more Turtleback cattle against the fence; he stopped there and, without leaving saddle, bent down and cut the wires. Then, riding at a walk, he headed west.

Some distance away, he halted in a dark motte of pine and listened. Below him, cattle were moving—he could see them running through the breaks. They came out of the hills, heading toward the cut—in a matter of time, they were all on one side of Cross U grass.

Jeff Walton saw the rider coming back. The man stopped and looked at the break, and he sat there for some time, silent and without movement. Walton knew the man could never see him with the night and the trees against him, and he let a smile form on his lips.

He saw the rider turn and head for the Cross U ranch. Jeff Walton turned and rode hard, and when he rode into the Turtleback he turned his horse loose himself. Sometimes he slept in the small shack back of the granary, and he went there now. He lay alone in the room, his hands under his head on the pillow, and sleep was slow in coming. . . .

A puncher came in that morning when Walton was at the corral. He said, "Somehow our cows got through that drift fence, Jeff. When I was riding bog down on lower Rock Creek I saw Cross U men hazing Turtleback cattle on their side of the fence. They're corralling them down on Wheeler Springs in a wire pasture they've built there. Now what t'hell do you suppose happened to get them cows on their side of the fence?"

Walton shrugged. "Talk to any Cross U men?"

"I don't wanta get shot."

Walton went to the house. He told Marcie what had happened. The girl frowned, and said, "Now how'd my cattle get through that fence? Maybe I ought to ride over and tell the Cross U men—"

He said, "I don't think that will be a good plan," and then he added, "I'll go into town and talk with Judge Morgan. I don't think that they can legally string that fence and keep our cattle. Why not leave it to me for a while, Marcie?"

She thought. "All right."

He reached town by noon, riding slowly on the way. The thing had run out right, and it had reached its goal. He tied his horse to a hitchrack down the street, and then he went into the Antlers Cafe, where he ate a slow and full meal. He went out, the weight and heat of the food pleasant inside of him, and he ducked between two buildings, coming out into the alley.

A man with a rifle said, "What're you doing here, Walton?"

"I could ask you the same," said Walton. "Or has Len Carberry got out some guards now?"

"I never knew you to work with Carberry."

"You know now," said Walton drily. He went to the door and knocked, and Carberry opened it. The day was raw and the wind cold, and inside the air was warm and laden with tobacco smoke. Dunc Cross squatted across the room beside the door, and he nodded and did not speak, but Jim Bell said, "Howdy, Jeff."

Walton murmured, "Hello, Jim," and then he looked at Carberry, who sat behind the desk. He said, "I cut that drift fence last night, Len, and Turtleback cattle went through. Bowden put them in the pasture on Wheeler Springs."

Carberry said, "I know that."

Walton felt a tinge of anger; he had wanted to break the news. But he hid it and said, "You get around, Len."

"I don't," corrected Carberry, "but my men do . . . Henry Potter was out that way this morning."

Walton said, "We could bust the hell out of that herd tonight." He looked at Carberry levelly. "That's your plan, ain't it? And then Cross U men will blame it on Turtleback riders?"

Carberry nodded.

Dunc Cross shifted. "Potter said to leave Dean Bowden for him, that Bowden is his meat. I guess he's remembering what Bowden saw. . . ."

"Kill Bowden," said Carberry.

Walton said, "That Panhandle Smith is a tough gent, Carberry. The sooner he's got out of our way the better I'll like it . . . for one."

Carberry said, "We'll get him. Get that: set your sights on this Panhandle gent, and kill him when you shoot."

Dunc said, "I hit what I aim at, Len."

Jim Bell rolled a cigarette. He asked, "When do we hit the herd, Len?" and Cross looked up, his eyes thoughtful.

"Around midnight."

Chapter 13

NIGHT RIDERS
MEAN GUNSMOKE

Dean Bowden and Panhandle Smith rode through the broken fence at dawn, and hit Jeff Walton's tracks. They swung around and rode the high country and followed them; Bowden was quietly dangerous and Panhandle Smith was with few words. They cut the trail, following it across the ridges and rocks, and then they saw that it led into the Turtleback Ranch, and both pulled up and looked at the outfit that lay miles away to the west.

"I didn't think she'd do it," said Bowden.

"You can't tell about women," said Panhandle. "Or maybe you ain't like me, Dean, 'cause I never could."

Dean Bowden thought of the ride out from Alder City the night before. "I still can't quite think so."

Panhandle shrugged and looked at Bowden levelly. "The track is there for eyes to read, Bowden. She's pretty, but them is the kind to watch. Or so they tell me." He smiled quickly. "But I don't know, of course."

Bowden was thoughtfully quiet. "Yeah, you wouldn't know. According to my reckoning, you only been married three times, and then you used to run cattle through Indian territory."

"None of them weddings caught," said Panhandle. "And that's odd, ain't it though? Three times, they say, is the charm; well, it sure ain't in my case. What say we ride down and meet this haughty lady, huh?"

Bowden shook his head. "No use in doing that, Panhandle. The sign points her way; she asked for war, we didn't. She'll have to either fight for them cows to get them back or buy them back. That's the funny side to the thing; she stands to lose her cattle."

"Maybe she figures on forcing the issue and running this into one big fight, and getting it over with for once and all."

"That must be it."

They turned and rode back through the cut fence. Cross U punchers were bunching the Turtleback cattle and pushing them toward the pasture down around the springs. Bowden had a wire stretcher and some rolled up wire on his saddle, and he dismounted and took the stretcher and clamped it to a loose strand.

"We better tie the other hole together," said Panhandle, " 'cause if we don't we pull on this end and just pick up the slack."

"We'll tie them here," said Bowden.

They made a loose set of connections on the wires, using the lengths Bowden had on his saddle. Then they rode to the second cut and fastened the stretcher there. Bowden pulled the slack up, making the barbwire taut, and Panhandle wired them together, using a pair of fence pliers.

The wires settled back after the stretcher was removed, and Bowden saw they were still tight. They reached their stirrups and went up and rode across the creek bottom to where the rest of the Cross U men were pushing the Turtleback cattle toward the springs.

Wyatt Jones rode up. "This means trouble, Dean," he said. "They'll come after these cows, sure as hell. They ain't giving them to us."

"The sign points that way."

Jones' blocky, husky face showed worry. "That's the hell of it," he said. "A man has to fight for everything. He fights for his living, his woman, his horseflesh. The whole thing is designed wrong; things come to a man too hard. Or maybe if it wasn't for a fight this would be a lonesome world."

"We'll keep a guard out," said Bowden.

"The crew is tired," said Jones. "The trail was damned long and they got saddle boils. Otherwise, we'da had more than one line rider out last night, wouldn't we? Then maybe this wouldn'ta happened, huh?"

Bowden said, "If there was to be trouble, there had to be trouble. So maybe it's best we got it over with soon. We did our best to ride around it, but I guess our pony shied somewhere."

They ran the cattle into the fenced square, and then shut the gate and rode to the house for breakfast. There was a plume of smoke coming from the cook shack's stovepipe, and it curled in the air like a question mark against the morning light. From the slope of the house they could see the cattle in the fence, and there was no use stringing out riders around the barbwire.

Harry Westcond came from the cook shack and hit the triangle with a mixing spoon. After washing in the basins by the well, they stepped down and tied their horses to the corral and went in to eat. The water was cold and sharp, and Bowden liked the sting of it against his skin.

No man rode away from the ranch that day. They stayed close to the buildings: Some worked in the blacksmith shop putting sharp caulks in horseshoes, grinding mower sickles for the coming hay season, getting mowers in shape for the cutting ahead. Others worked over harnesses and riding gear in the barn: lacing on new latigos and working over riggings, and two men spent their time at the corrals, digging postholes and putting in new rails cut the day before along the creek.

The day was overcast, with a raw wind, and the chill was bitter. Clouds rolled across the moving sky and the sun shone little. Bowden and Panhandle Smith played checkers in the living room, and the oldster was morose and sharp, beating Bowden each time.

Panhandle Smith glanced at the alarm clock. "Getting around five," he said. "I wonder if they hit tonight?"

"All of us better ride tonight, Dean."

Bowden said, "I don't know." He jumped two of Panhandle Smith's men. "Better keep your mind on the game."

"What're you worrying about?" said Bowden. "You've lived a long time; too long, I've heard certain people say. And then I don't think there's a bullet made that can dent that hide of yours."

"One made for every man," said Panhandle.

Most of the men had already knocked off work, and were in the bunkhouse. Bowden knew they were tired, and they did not know what the night would bring, and they wanted to get a little rest. Therefore, they ate late; the meal was a taciturn one, with little bantering, and the current of thoughts was deep and strong. When the meal was almost finished, Bowden pushed his chair back.

"We all ride out tonight, as you probably know.

Be sure you have plenty of shells for your short guns and rifles. There's some boxes in the bunkhouse. I put them there right before coming to eat. Ride in pairs, and when and if trouble starts, shoot straight and shoot to kill."

Chuck Baggett said, "That's hard to do in the dark, Bowden. There'll be no moon tonight with these thunderclouds."

Bowden said, "Chuck, you can stick home, if you want to."

The youth looked at Bowden hotly. "I hired out in Texas as a hand," he said. "I rode my share of the point and drag on the way up, Bowden."

Bowden said, "Let's get horses."

They had their broncs selected: dark horses, all of them—they would not be seen easily against the night. They selected a password, too; it was the old one the vigilantes had used in California: *Innocent*. They rode to the pasture at about nine, and already the night was dark.

Bowden said, "Two men stay at the fence; the rest go back on the hill and hide. Then, if something does break, you can come riding down, and you can come in faster. Panhandle and I stay at the fence."

They moved into the brush higher on the slopes, and Dean Bowden and Panhandle Smith pulled into a motte of wild rose bushes and sat there. The night darkened and moved out against the hills, and the cattle found beds beneath the boxelders and cottonwoods around the springs. There were the usual night sounds—the slipstream of a nighthawk flying above them, and the bawling of a cow in the distance across the hills. The wind stirred the trees, making a murmur run through them, and when you got closer to the trees, you could hear the creak and rub of branches, and this sound had no menace or hint of harm.

Finally Panhandle Smith asked, "I wonder what time it is, Dean."

"Hard to tell," murmured Bowden. "I don't want to light a match and it's too dark to see my watch."

"These trees make a lot of noise," said Panhandle. "Those branches rub together and the wind makes some noise, too. I wonder if a man could har some riders if they—" His voice fell down. "Dean, cattle are getting up out there . . . I hear them."

The gun spoke its red piece into the night. Bowden was already riding ahead, his short gun out, and Panhandle Smith was behind him. Cattle were moving and riders were coming down; and already guns were telling their positions. Bowden rode ahead, and the essence of their plan lay clear and without obstruction.

The raiders had hit from the east. The cattle, terrified by the guns, the flares, would run west toward Turtleback range. Even now they were snarled in barbwire and posts were creaking. They were on the run west, and they were running hard, and nothing but tiredness would stop them.

Bowden hollered, "Swing wide, Panhandle," and rode to the right, pulling his bronc hard to skirt the foremost of the stampeding cattle. He saw Panhandle swing left, and then the herd roiled the dust between them, running with clashing horns. He felt a tinge of anger, and with it was a touch of remorse. He had played the girl wrong, she had let him get the wrong impression—and then she had run her men against his.

A rider came by, drifting in the dust and night, and the cry came. "Innocent," and Bowden held his fire. The raiders were turning and running, their work done; they had started the cattle—and they were pulling out, riding fast in the dark with their guns talking red.

Bowden felt the tug of impatience, and then he saw a rider come out of the night. He hollered, "Innocent," and a gun spat across the darkness. There was no whine of the bullet, for the roar of the herd hid that. Bowden lifted his piece, swung his horse, the weapon kicked and kicked. He saw the horse run on, and he thought the saddle was empty, but he was not sure.

The dust was thicker now; he was at the drag of the herd. The herd moved past him and left him, and there was no more; just the dull receding of the sound, and the darkness. The impression was quick and clean; the thing was over with and somewhere, out there, riders were drifting fast on tough horses, and they were hidden by the night. He rose in stirrups, and called loudly:

"Innocent."

The cries came: "Innocent."

A man called, "Bowden! Oh, Bowden!"

He recognized the voice. "This way, Chuck," he said. Then another called, "Keep yelling, Bowden, so we can tell where you are," and he lifted his voice. They came in, then, and he looked at them.

He asked, "Who isn't here?"

Alex Tooping said, "Where's Panhandle?"

Something prodded Bowden. He said, "Lord, men, no," and he called, "Panhandle, where in the hell are you?"

They listened. Somewhere they heard the snarl of taut barbwire cracking; the sounds of the cattle were more distant now, and had lost their meaning. "They've run through the drift fence," said Ken Shaden.

"Who were they?" asked Chuck Baggett. "Did you recognize any?"

Nobody had. Bowden said, "I saw one clearly." He added, "He was Jeff Walton, I think. I shot at him but I missed."

"Then it was Turtleback men," said Westcond.

Wyatt Jones demanded, "Who else would it be?" He had a rasp in his voice. "Where is Panhandle? If they've got him."

"Get lanterns," said Bowden. "We'll have to look." He felt sick; he asked, "Did anybody get any of them?"

"I got one," said Chuck Baggett: "A big fellow. He fell back yonder. Come with me, Wyatt, and we'll look for him."

They rode off; the night took them. Bowden got down and leaned against his horse. The night had settled down; the run of the cattle had died; somewhere men were riding off, and those men had knocked Smith from his horse. Bowden thought of that and he thought of Texas, and he remembered then that Panhandle Smith had showed him how to handle a rope, those years ago. The scene was clear, cameo clear; he wondered why, and he felt sick.

"Hey, Bowden," called Chuck Baggett, "here's the man I got. He's dead."

Bowden walked over there and Chuck lighted a match for some time, and then it burned his fingers. He swore.

"Who is he?" asked Wyatt Jones.

Bowden said, "Henry Potter. He was the sheriff."

Jones cursed rapidly. "The law, huh, riding with killers! Well, that's the end of him, huh? How come he rode with Turtleback men, though?"

"I don't know," said Bowden.

Lanterns were moving, their yellow rays like small darting eyes. They stood there, the three of them, and they watched; they had the same thoughts. Finally one lantern stopped, and Bowden saw men bend over.

Alex Tooping called, "Here he is, Dean." There

was a silence. "He's dead."
Bowden just stood there.

Chapter 14

GUNSMOKE!

They carried Panhandle Smith to the house and put him on a bed. Chuck Baggett came riding up, leading their horses. They had found Henry Potter's black, running through the night, and they had tied the dead sheriff across the saddle. Bowden came out and looked at the black and thought. *Well, Henry Potter'll never kill another man.* . . . He said, "Everybody got rifles and pistols?"

"We have," said Wyatt Jones. He asked, "What's next, Bowden?"

Bowden tied the reins up on Potter's black and went up. He said, "Those raiders went east; that means they'll have to swing around and head in to the west to get home. When they get there, we'll be waiting for them."

Jones said, "That's it, Bowden."

They put Potter's horse ahead of them, and they drove him hard. Although they had tied the dead man securely, his great weight still caused him to bounce up and down. They headed due west, and they rode fast; time was against them, and urgency was a mean spur.

They took the path of the cattle, splitting the stragglers, but they had no eye for the stock. Streaks of gray marred the sky to the east, and Bowden knew that dawn was ahead. When they reached the high ridge, he reached low and grabbed the reins on Potter's horse, and he tied the panting black to a tree. The dawn was gray now, and the Turtleback ranch lay before them.

Wyatt Jones said, "I can't see anything of Turtleback men behind us, Dean. It wouldn't be possible that they could have beaten us here?"

Bowden shook his head.

"They might have a guard out," said Chuck Baggett.

Bowden said, "We'll ride him down."

They moved down the slope, the shale running and jumping ahead of them, and they hit the flat hard, their broncs' shoulders jarring under the sudden fall. They split up then, fanning out across the plain, and they took the ranch from all directions. They came in fast, dropping from running horses over rifles, and although it looked scattered and confused, the plan was clear and strong.

A man moved out of the shadows. He said, "What goes on—" Ken Shaden swung his rifle and the man went down, his own piece falling to the ground and being trampled by Shaden's bronc.

Bowden hollered, "Come out, you who are here!"

Somebody hollered from the bunkhouse, "Lay off that noise," and Bowden pounded on the door, pushing it open. The light was dim but he saw men sitting upright in bed; one wore a red nightgown and he had a white nightcap. Bowden saw that almost all the beds were occupied.

"What is this?"

Somebody said, "That's Bowden. I saw him in Alder."

Bowden moved back. Something was wrong. These men shouldn't have been in bed; they should have been out riding. He said, "Where's Jeff Walton?"

"His bunk is empty," said a man. "Maybe he slept out in the shack last night. It's out behind. What t'hell is this anyway?"

Bowden said to Ken Shaden, "Keep your guns on these men," and he went outside. There was an error there, and he had made it: that was the thought that kept prodding him. He came to the shack and kicked the door open. The bed had not been slept in.

Jeff Walton, he thought, *wasn't here last night*.

Marcie Gray came running from the house toward him. She had on a dressing robe, and it clung to her closely. The heavy-set woman stood on the porch, and she had a rifle.

Marcie said, "What is this, Bowden? What's wrong?"

Bowden drew back. He looked at her sharply. "Raiders stampeded your herd last night," he said.

She frowned. "What herd?"

"Don't tell me you didn't cut my drift fence." He made his voice cynical.

She said, "I didn't. Nor did any of my riders."

Bowden leaned back. He was cold. He said, "Your riders cut my fence. Your cattle came on Cross U pasture. I corralled them yesterday. Raiders struck them tonight and stampeded them in this direction."

"What makes you think they were my men?"

"Jeff Walton rode with them. I saw him."

She started toward the shack, and he caught her shoulder. She said, "Get your hands off me." He pulled his hand back. "Walton's in there, asleep."

"No, he isn't."

"Then he's in the bunkhouse."

121

"I was just there."

She looked at him. He saw her eyes clearly, and she was thoughtful. "Bowden," she said, "I won't fight you. Yesterday—last night—not a man of mine has ridden off this ranch. If you saw Jeff Walton among the raiders, he was not with my men."

He said, "Thanks, Marcie." The weight left him; he felt light. "I was in your bunkhouse. Your men never left this ranch. Jeff Walton is riding with somebody else. They killed Panhandle Smith; he raised me . . . in Texas."

"I—or my men—never had anything to do—"

"Hush," he said. "Your word is good." He saw her shoulders move. "You'd better get back into the house. The air is cold."

"And you—"

He said, "Walton rode with those killers."

She understood. "I have wondered about him before," she said slowly. "He was the only man who ever looked at me as though he didn't want me. Maybe that is why I felt that way about him—I sort of disliked him, and I wondered how honest he was." Her eyes were on him. "You'll be careful?"

He said, "We'll leave that drift fence down, I guess. Your cattle will come on my grass and mine will go in on yours."

"Leave it down," she said. She turned and went to the house. Alex Tooping came up and said, "Those weren't Turtleback raiders, Dean."

Bowden nodded.

"But Walton rode with them," said Tooping.

Bowden said, "He's sold out to somebody. It must be Len Carberry. He wanted the Turtleback to fight his battle for him; then when we were both weak he'd step in and win. Walton is his man on the Turtleback crew."

"Wonder where they went?"

"Back to town, I guess. Where else could they go?"

"Ken Shaden said that when Potter got knocked down, another rider tried to pick him up and take him out, but Ken scared the fellow off. That means then, that Carberry's given orders to pick his wounded or dead up, and thereby hide the fact that himself, and not Turtleback men, did the dirty job."

"That would be it, Alex."

Ken Shaden and Chuck Baggett came up. Ken said, "We're on a cold trail here; all that's paying is our noses. What do the next cards say, Dean?"

"You and me ride into town, Ken. The rest of you drift back to the Cross U. We'll take Potter's body in."

"I'd like to go with you," said Chuck Baggett.

Bowden shook his head. "No, just the two of us, kid. We've been out-tricked once; they might swing back and burn the ranch down. The rest of you ride back and keep your eyes open."

"What about Panhandle's body?"

Bowden thought. "We'll have a coffin sent out. We'll bury him on the ranch." He added, "I think he'd like that."

They went to their horses and rode out, going fast on a lope. The guard had come to and he was washing his head carefully. He looked at them as they rode past and then he looked at Bowden and Ken Shaden, who were going to their horses.

"You play for keeps," he said.

Bowden said, "Sometimes, yes."

They rode to where they had left Potter's horse. They pointed the animal toward Alder City, and he started for home. The day was brighter now and the shadows had gone; the day would be clear, for the wind had chased the clouds into the mountains. Bowden looked at the snow-tipped peaks and the clouds around them, and then he let his gaze run to the west until sight and distance merged and became blue air.

Ken Shaden was tough; the saddle had worn him, but had only polished him. He said, "You'll move against Len Carberry now?"

Bowden said, "If he was the one that killed Panhandle, yes."

Shaden's eyes were somber. "We don't know who killed him," he said. "That dust and the night. . . . Wish we could have seen who else rode there. . . . Carberry's the enemy; why not fight him?"

"We don't know that, for sure."

Shaden shrugged. "Who else would it be?"

Bowden said, "Look at it this way, Ken. Maybe Jeff Walton was playing a lone hand; maybe he ain't in with Carberry. Maybe him and Henry Potter had some deal cooked up to run this range."

Shaden said, "Sounds fair, but no man knows. There are drifters here, and miners, and the whole recipe is mixed up."

"Busted up," said Bowden.

"We'll get Carberry later?"

Bowden felt irritated. "If the sign runs that way."

They rode into the barn, and old Matt rubbed watery eyes. "Is the big son dead, Bowden?"

Bowden said, "Dead." Matt took their horses. Bowden asked, "When did he ride out?"

"He left here last night sometime. I was asleep."

Bowden glanced around the horses in the stalls. "Does Carberry keep his horse here?"

"That's him there."

Bowden went over; he looked at the horse. There was no sweat on him and he had been curried but he was tired; Bowden saw that by his legs and thin shoulders. "Did Carberry ride out last night?"

"I don't know. I—well, I got drunk."

They went to the Antlers Cafe. They took a stool in Jackie Bell's section. She said a cheery good morning.

"Your brother," said Bowden, "Was he in his room last night?"

"I never checked." The dark eyes rested on him and he saw alarm. "Why do you ask, Bowden?"

"Just a question."

Ken Shaden said, very quietly, "There's Jeff Walton, Dean. He's across the street—see him?"

Bowden slid from the stool and said, "Hold that order, Miss Jackie, will you?" and he went into the street. He moved forward, almost running, and he hollered, "Hey, you, Jeff Walton!"

Walton turned sharply. He saw Dean and he stepped ahead; then he halted. He said, "What is it, Bowden?"

Bowden was a few feet away. Ken Shaden came up. Carberry and Jim Bell saw it from the Lady of Chance; they came to the door. Dunc Cross moved out of the doorway and stood apart, his eyes heavy.

Dean Bowden said, "Pull your gun, Walton!"

Walton was calm. He asked, "Why?"

Bowden said clearly, "Here's why!" and he hit Walton hard. Walton went back, and as he went he drew—and he drew fast. The move was unexpected and quick, and Bowden was reaching. He moved in, twisting, and Walton shot, but Walton was falling, and he slipped his bullet wild.

Bowden shot three times. The roar tossed against the buildings, built up waves and came in, and then died. Ken Shaden said, "Don't waste another bullet, Dean," and his voice was too quiet, too low.

Bowden looked at him, saw Shaden's drawn gun; he followed the course of the barrel, and then he saw Carberry and Bell and Cross. He said, "Come with me, Shaden, and keep your gun on Cross and the kid."

Ken Shaden said, "At your side, Dean."

They moved across the street, with Bowden holstering his gun. Jim Bell had pulled back, fanning out a little from Carberry, and Bowden knew him as dangerous because of his recklessness. Dunc Cross had slid against the building slightly; he was smaller, and he had his hand down.

Shaden said, "I got them, Dean."

Bowden came up to Carberry. He said, "Where were you last night, Carberry?"

Carberry studied him for a long time. His hand came down; long fingers played with the dried ears. Finally he said, "At home, of course. In bed. Why?"

Bowden said, "I think you lie!"

Carberry pulled his eyes down. His fingers were still now. He said quietly, "Don't call me a liar, Bowden! Don't call me that unless you want to pull—"

Bowden hit him then. He hit him once, and his knuckles fitted into Carberry's jaw, landing smartly under the bone. Carberry went back; he sat down. He held his head in his hands, and finally he looked up.

"Some day, Bowden, I'll kill you."

Bowden said, "Just talk, that's all," and looked at Jim Bell. Bell was a trifle pale against his darkness and Bowden caught again his close resemblance to Jackie. He was immature—but he had courage. He lifted his eyes to Dunc Cross, who was dangerously silent.

Townspeople were coming in and crowding close. Bowden thought: The time wasn't ready . . . I rushed in too fast. He said to Ken Shaden, "I guess we'll move on."

Shaden nodded gravely. "I guess so," he said.

Chapter 15

DEATH ON SWAN CREEK

They went back to the Antlers Cafe where Bowden washed his skinned knuckles. When he came back into the dining room Jackie had his breakfast on the counter. The girl was watching him, and he felt the silent scouting of her eyes. He was on his cup of coffee when the thin elderly man came in.

"Bowden," he said, "I'm the coroner. I've got Jeff Walton's body down at my shop. Who's going to pay the bill?"

"The old money angle," said Bowden. "The Cross U'll have to bury its own dogs, I guess. Send me the bill but don't make it too high—he wasn't worth much."

"How about Potter?" asked the man. "Old Matt got his body down to me, too. Who'll pay for him?"

A man down the counter said, "Potter's got money in the bank, Taylor."

Taylor said, "I'll bury him on that," and turned to go. Bowden's voice halted him. Bowden said, "I suppose you have coffins, too. I want one for a man— not a big man—about the size of the fellow there. Send it out to the Cross U as soon as you can, and send the minister with it. Can you get it out there tonight and get the minister out by morning?"

"I'll do that."

Jackie asked, "Who's dead at your ranch?"

Bowden told her about the raiders and the running fight over the stampeding cattle. Her face was dark and thoughtful, and some of the quickness left her. She said, "I should leave, I guess, and take Jim with me. We could go back east to Indiana, and I could keep him out of trouble."

"He probably wouldn't go," said Bowden.

He and Ken Shaden finished their meal and went outside. The sun was bright and warm and lay smoothly on the rutted street. Freight wagons moving out for the Continental Divide were stirring the yellow dust lazily with their iron rims. On their way to the livery barn they passed in front of George Carson's hardware store and the man called them inside.

Bowden said, "This is one of my men, Ken Shaden. You can talk in front of him, Carson."

"You beat us to the sheriff," said Carson. "We aimed to hang him pretty soon, Bowden. We got five of them last night on Strawberry Creek robbing an honest miner. They were the fringes of the gang that hangs around the Lady of Chance."

Bowden said, "What did you do?"

"Hung them."

Bowden was quietly sincere. "Rough medicine," he finally said, "but the only treatment, I guess. I suppose you were masked, weren't you?"

"To protect ourselves, we had to be. Later, when we get stronger and we whittle down the opposition, we can go about it openly. Of course, we held a court —but what could they offer as evidence. We came there when they were looting the miner's sluice boxes."

"And the miner?" asked Ken Shaden.

Carson said, "He was dead; they'd murdered him." He looked at Bowden. "Now what happened last night at the Cross U?"

Bowden told him.

Carson asked, "You don't know who killed Panhandle Smith?"

Bowden said, "No. How's the tunnel coming?"

"We have men sitting right under Carberry's office right now. We finished it this morning; dug right under the guard's feet, you might say."

Bowden said, "I'm killing the man who got Panhandle Smith. I want to ask one thing of you, Carson. If you—or anybody else—finds evidence that points to Carberry or Cross as Panhandle Smith's killer—or Jim Bell, either, for that matter— I want you to tell me. I want you to give me two hours to kill that man in. Then, if I'm dead, you and your vigilantes can take over."

Carson said, "I promise, Bowden."

Ken Shaden asked, "Did any of those men you hung last night get around to talk or confess?"

"Couldn't get a word out of them."

"A tight organization," said Dean Bowden. "But it's bound to break soon." He was thinking of Jackie Bell, and her love for her brother. "It'll be tough on the girl, Carson."

Carson understood. "Lord help her," he said.

They went to the livery barn and got their horses. Bowden had bought a quart of rye for old Matt, and the oldster's watery eyes showed doglike gratitude. They swung around the corner across from the Lady of Chance, and Bowden saw Carberry standing in the doorway watching them. Carberry stood there and watched them go, and his rage was a fine, spun anger. He thought: *If the town and people couldn't see me, I'd drop Bowden from saddle with a bullet through his back* . . . He watched them until the edge of a building screened them, and then he walked back into the Lady of Chance.

He said, "Bourbon," and he poured with quick fingers. Dunc Cross came up, his eyes deceptive, and he asked, "Are we sicking the kid on that miner tonight, Len?"

"Tonight's the night."

"He rides alone, huh?"

"One miner—one gunman. You thinking about last night, huh?"

Cross said evenly, "They hung five men, Len. They hung them all together on the ridgepole of the old Peabody ranch corral. They're hanging there yet, they say. Nobody dares cut them down."

"Dead men are dead," said Len Carberry. "What difference does it make whether they blow with the wind or are weighted down with tons of sod? They're still dead in either case, Dunc."

Cross said, "The vigilantes hung them, Len. Somehow they've got wind that they were going to raid that miner, and the vigilantes came in and hung them. That puts you in a bad spot, doesn't it? These vigilantes, whoever they are, aren't fools; they know that these men were rather close to you. How do you suppose they got wise?

"Ike Press got drunk down in the Bucket of Gold, and I've heard he talked too much. That looks to me what has happened; whiskey loosened his tongue and he hung himself. They can't connect us up with that very well. He never talked in the Lady of Chance."

Cross nodded. "But what about Henry Potter? We used to have the law on our side, but with Potter dead. . . ."

Carberry asked, "Have a drink?" but Cross shook his head. Carberry poured and toyed with his glass.

"Henry Potter was no 'count," he finally said. "He talked too much, too; I'm kind of glad he got killed. But we made one bad move, and Bowden will never forget it; that was when we couldn't get Potter's body last night. That looked bad for us, but when you get down to it, Bowden found out that the Turtleback hadn't stampeded his cattle, so there was nobody else but us Rocking Chair men."

"He's dangerous," said Dunc Cross.

Carberry studied him sharply. "You getting snow in your boots, Cross?"

Cross said quickly, "No, not that, Len. But a man has to consider the odds. Me, I think this thing, is getting too big, too powerful. I've seen these vigilantes before. I've run into them. When they get stronger, they'll pull out of those masks, and they'll come out openly. I thought you were a member of them?"

"I was talking with Ike Press. He claimed he was a vigilante. He wouldn't tell me who else was in the gang. I joined up with them to see what was going on, but I don't think Press was really in with them; somebody had just approached him and maybe so they offered him membership—just to gain his confidence before they hung him. I'm as much on the outside as you are, Dunc."

"They work that way," said Cross. They worm inside and eat out."

"Play your cards close," said Carberry. "Keep your liquor supply low, your gun handy, and your mouth shut, Cross."

Cross said, "I'm no idiot, Len."

Carberry drank his whiskey neat. The alcohol burned against his bruised lower lip, and he thought savagely of Dean Bowden. He looked into the backbar mirror and saw Jim Bell come in.

He said, "You tell the kid, Dunc, in the office."

Cross said, "All right, Len," and went back, walking through the saloon, and Jim Bell caught the cue. He moved over idly and watched a dull morning poker game; he stood there for some time, then he went to the office. Cross was hunkered against the wall, and his cigarette was cold.

Jim Bell asked, "What'd you want, Cross?"

Cross settled back. He lighted his cigarette and blew through his nostrils; he watched the blue smoke lazily. He said, "There's a job for tonight . . . for you alone." He made his voice very low.

Bell said angrily, "Why doesn't the boss tell me about it—I'm hired out to him, not you."

Cross shrugged. He had seen Jim's kind before: they had the sharpness, but they lacked the steel behind it, and their edges soon became dulled. He said patiently, "There's a miner out on Swan Creek. He's running a set of sluice boxes and he's doing some pan work in pockets. He's located where Bend Creek comes into Swan. You mind where that is, Jim?"

"Where Bend comes into Swan? Yes, I know. How much dust has he got, do you reckon?"

"About ten thousand, we judge. The cut is half of it, Jim, for a few hours work, and where else can a man pick up five thousand that easy?"

Jim Bell got to his feet. "I'll take it," he said. "I'll do it tonight." He went out.

Dunc Cross squatted there for some time, and then he got to his feet. He was lean and somber; things were closing in, he could already feel the stranglehold of events, and inside he felt cold. He crossed the room and shut the door behind him.

He went up to the bar beside Len Carberry. Carberry glanced at him knowingly, and Cross nodded slightly. He turned and walked into the street and then stood with his back to the Lady of Chance. The sun was warm and sometime a man would be out of it for a long time, he thought.

Ross Matthews came out between two buildings, and Dunc Cross thought: *Now what is he doing out there in the alley—and him one of the town's leading lights?* He watched Ross go into the hardware store and dismissed him.

Ross Matthews said to George Carson, "I want to talk to you, George," and he and Carson went back into the hardware man's office, where Ross Matthews shut the door carefully behind them.

Carson asked, "What is it, Ross?"

Ross Matthews said, "I just came out of the tunnel. Ronald McIntyre is there now; he stayed there. Two men were talking in Len Carberry's office. One of them was the kid, Jim Bell. I don't know who the other was. I heard him call the kid by name, but Bell never mentioned his name. He talked awful low, too."

"Was it Carberry?"

"I don't know, George. I couldn't say for sure. We can't hang a man until we have some evidence against him. We don't want to be as ruthless as the killers we've set out to exterminate. We're bringing in law and order, not gangsterism."

Carson said, "Quit throwing those big words at me. What did you hear?"

"Jim Bell's riding out on Swan Creek tonight. You know where Ned Churchill is working gold—where Swan and Bend join—that's who he aims to rob, George."

Carson said, "He won't rob Churchill. We'll see to that. I'll tell the others, Ross. You go back to that tunnel and listen."

Ross Matthews said, "I hate to think of his poor sister . . . Jackie's a fine girl; there are none better. It'll break her, Carson."

Carson was thoughtful. "There's no other way out," he said slowly. "If Jim Bell does this, we'll have to hang him. For we know this now: he's in with these killers, and if he is in with them, he's killed before." He shook his head. "The rope," he said, "the rope."

"You notifying Dean Bowden?"

"Yes."

Ross Matthews was silent; then he said: "Bowden won't want to move against the kid; Bowden likes that girl. If it weren't for Marcie Gray, they would get along better. But that Marcie's gone over the deck like a shipwrecked sailor leaving a mud scow."

"Time somebody tamed her."

"I'd like to be him," said Ross Matthews.

Carson smiled. He said, "Get out of here, you old Romeo."

Ross Matthews left. Carson hung up his apron and went out the back door. Martin Johnson was in his office in the Mercantile working on his books. Carson told him what had happened, and Martin Johnson's bluff face was solemn and tired.

Carson said, "You get the men together, Martin. Be damned sure you sprinkle out of town a few at a time, and I'll ride for Bowden. Then I'll swing in and we'll meet at Bend and Swan, and we'll set the trap."

"The girl," said Martin Johnson; "damn, it'll be tough on her. I hope, for her sake, the kid falls through and doesn't ride out there."

"Let's hope so," said Carson.

Carson reached the Cross U when the sun was swinging down. He hailed the guard and rode in, and Dean Bowden met him in front of the house. He told Bowden, and he saw the man's face change.

Bowden said, "I can't ride with you, Carson."

"Why?"

"I promised the girl—his sister."

Carson leaned back; he understood. He said, "There will be enough of us, and thanks. Could a man get a bit to eat, Bowden?"

"I'd have ridden with you, otherwise," said Bowden. They walked to the cook shack. Harry Westcond dug out some stew and plenty of bread and accessories. Carson ate slowly; he had time.

"Maybe he killed Panhandle," said Carson.

Bowden looked at his fingers. He said, "I promised the girl; my word is good." He looked up. "Try to get the boy to confess, get him to talk. He might tell a lot, Carson. Then if he tells who killed Panhandle, come to me. Is that right with you?"

Carson nodded.

Chapter 16

WHILE THE
HANGNOOSE WAITS

They laid their trap that bright spring night, and young Jim Bell rode into it. He had swung wide and he came in from the north, riding the ridges and the brush; he pulled up once and looked down at the winding silver tongue that lay between the rough hills, and recognized it as Swan Creek. He sent his gaze to the south, and another streak of molten silver lay under the moonlight; this was Bend Creek. He brought his eyes down it and came to the junction with Swan; they saw the light in Ned Churchill's log cabin.

He thought: *He's home . . . that's good.*

He sent his horse down the slope, riding hard against the fork of his saddle, and gained the bottom. He sat there for some time in the high wild rosebushes, and looked at the house with the light. The Creek ran and jumped beyond him, dashing over rocks and around boulders, hurrying and running toward the bottomlands. The wind moved through the ash and spruce; the wind was lazy.

He thought he heard a movement to his right. He looked toward the sound, but it was gone, and he thought: *Might have been just a squirrel or an owl and then it might have been a cougar or bear* . . . He felt tight inside; the band was around his belly, and it was cold.

Jim left his horse there, tying a cloth around the beast's jaws, took his rifle and went forward, still holding to the protective brush. He got opposite the house and stood there, then he went ahead. He had put on his mask and his breath stirred the black cloth. He came up to the door, his rifle up and ready; he kicked the door, and it went in.

He stepped inside. The lamp stood on a log table, but there was nobody there. A warming trickle hit his belly; he turned quickly. One thought stood out suddenly clear; maybe Ned Churchill was down by the creek tending his sluice boxes. But no, there had been no man along the creek.

He stepped outside and the barrel of a rifle tore into his belly. The blow almost doubled him, and he tried to bring his rifle up. Something came down and hit his wrist and drove the rifle from his hand. He dropped it, then fell and reached for it, but a boot kicked him and rolled him over.

A voice said, "Get up, Jim Bell!"

He was surrounded by men. They were all dressed alike in mackinaws and their faces were masked with red handkerchiefs. He wondered how they knew who he was: he, too, was masked. He got to his feet, cold inside.

"Who are you men?"

"Vigilantes."

He was quiet. Something was running inside of him; he felt it move. He finally said, "What do you want with me? Can't a man come and visit another man in this country?"

"Not when he's wearing a mask and carrying a gun."

Ned Churchill came up. He alone was unmasked. He said, "Take that off, Bell," and he reached out and pulled off his coverings. He was a heavy man, and his voice had depth. "You'd murder me in cold blood for my gold, is that it, Bell?"

Jim Bell felt all alone. He thought of Len Carberry, of Dunc Cross, and of Jackie. He was very quiet now. Something had flowed into him; it had settled in his veins; the end was there and he'd never see the sun.

"How did you know?" he asked.

One man said, "We have ways of knowing, Bell."

"Did Cross or—" Bell halted suddenly. He said, "To hell with you, you damn fools."

A man grabbed him and tied his hands behind his back. The rope came up; the noose had already been built. He looked at it and counted the coils in the rope and saw there were thirteen. He felt it fit around his neck. One of the men went to the cabin and came out with a chair.

"Here," said a man. "Under this cottonwood."

Jim Bell walked to the tree. The branches were heavy and made a cover and he could hardly see the moon because of the thick leaves. The rope sang out and settled over a strong limb and rough hands put him on the chair. He felt the slack take up and the rope tightened; the knot rubbed against his left ear.

Somebody said, "It's anchored tight, men."

Ned Churchill was pale. He bent over suddenly and lost his supper. Jim Bell looked at the man and said, "You'd think you was hanging him."

Churchill turned and walked to the cabin. He went in and shut the door. This sound banged out and then the rattle of the rapid stream hid it. Jim Bell listened to the roar of the stream and thought of Jackie.

Somebody said, "Carberry squealed, Jim. He told

on you. Talk up, fellow."

Jim Bell said, "Carberry squealed, huh? Now what would you mean by that? And what have I got to talk about?"

"Did you kill Panhandle Smith?"

Jim Bell thought. "No," he said. He added, "I know who did, though."

"Who did?"

"To hell with you," said Jim Bell. A touch of braggadocio hit him and warmed him. "I killed old Hans, the driver, though. What is this: a hanging or a jury trial?"

"Any last words?"

Jim Bell looked at the rim of the moon. He said, "Tell Jackie good-bye. Tell her I was thinking of her." The silence built up and the stream broke it. "That's all. Go to hell, all of you!"

A man reached out and jerked the chair. Jim Bell fell, stumbling as the chair went out—and the rope took the slack sharply. The noise of the stream seemed to rise, and then it fell back. Somewhere an owl hooted, and the sound was low and filled with eeriness.

A man said, "Had he gone right he'd made a valuable man." He added, "Damn, it'll be hard on that girl."

"She couldn't help it; she did her best."

Somebody called, "Churchill, it's all over with," and Churchill called from inside the cabin, "I can't stay here tonight; I just can't. I'm going up the stream and see old Jake Hawkins."

The miner came out without looking that way and turned into the brush. One of the vigilantes had a heavy cardboard hanging around his neck from a piece of rope. He took this off and hung it around Jim Bell's neck. The wind turned Jim Bell a little and the moonlight showed the words printed on the cardboard.

> MONTANA VIGILANTES HUNG
> THIS MAN
> HE WAS A MURDERER AND
> THIEF
> SEE THAT YOU ESCAPE A SIMILAR
> FATE, GOLD THIEF!

They heard Churchill riding through the brush. They took off their masks. The man who had worn the cardboard counted the others he had around his neck. The swinging body of Jim Bell came between the man and the moon. The shadow flitted across the seamed face and the man moved from under it.

He counted the cardboards. "We have three more to distribute tonight," he said. "We better be moving."

"Got a long ride ahead," another said.

George Carson looked up at Jim Bell. He asked, "Could you boys get along without me the rest of the night? No, I ain't got ice in my boots, but I got a little riding to do. Dean Bowden's waiting for word from me as to whether I found out who had killed Panhandle Smith." He sighed, "I'm tired, too, men."

Martin Johnson said, "Sure George, we'll get along." He was big and bluff and his face was carved by what he had just witnessed. "This way ain't nice, George, for any of us, but it's what we have to do if we want peace—if we want your son and mine, and Bill's son, to walk down a good street in a good town."

"We better ride," a man said in a low voice.

George Carson went to his horse and found saddle. They had their broncs scattered all over and they were hidden well and they met and rode on, turning to the south. Carson watched them for a long moment, his face without color or emotion, and then he turned toward the north and rode up the stiff mountain, heading for the Cross U ranch.

He rode fast after he reached the summit; he wanted to get away from the spot along Swan Creek. The brush was high and he put his sorrel hard, swinging across trails and riding his spurs; he came to the foothills and the brush thinned down, and the sorrel had easier going. He met Bowden five miles beyond the Cross U riding toward him, and Bowden pulled in with his rifle up.

Carson called, "It's me—Carson. That you, Bowden?"

"This way," said Bowden.

Bowden swung his horse around and pointed him toward the ranch. Carson reined in and pulled down, and they rode stirrup to stirrup. There was a warm night wind and it moved in silence across the green growing grass.

Carson said, "This late spring is good for hay, Bowden. The grass has more of a chance to grow before the sun gets too hot. And it gets hot here in Montana in July and August—and sometimes even into September."

Bowden nodded.

Carson lighted a cigarette and the flare showed his seamed face clearly. The light died down; he pulled on the tobacco. The ember glowed and receded and came back again. Finally Carson spoke. "He didn't talk," he said. "I asked him, too. He said he knew, but he wouldn't tell."

"He's dead, then."

"He was a man," said Carson. "Maybe he talked a lot, but he had sand. When the time came, he looked at the moon and waited."

Bowden hid his feelings. He lifted his shoulders,

let them fall. "A man builds his life," he said.

Carson said, "If it had been Henry Potter who killed him, I think Jim Bell would have said so. Jim said he'd killed old Hans, the stage driver, but he said he hadn't killed Panhandle."

Bowden said, "I'll get the man."

Carson was studiously thoughtful. "This is pulling in, Bowden," he finally said. "The thing is breaking, and the end is near. Of course, we got to get to the kingpin, and we think it's Len Carberry. Somebody'll talk and then we can move—but, of course, you get first chance at Panhandle's killer, if we finally find him."

"The rest of your men?" asked Bowden.

"They had another chore or two to tend to yet." Carson felt tired and without feeling. He swung his horse off the trail and drew up. He said, "I'm drifting now, Bowden, but I'll see you in town tomorrow."

Bowden looked at him inquiringly. "Tomorrow?"

"Yes, in the afternoon." Carson stretched in the saddle and settled back. His horse stirred, then rested. "Gold is going out of the Runback mine tomorrow on the stage for Drummond."

"You think they'll hit it?"

Carson studied his saddlehorn. "They might," he said. "If they don't hit that, they'll hit some other time. We'd appreciate your help."

"I'll be there," said Bowden. "Ken Shaden will ride with me."

"I like him," said Carson. "Quiet, but a good man. He sits a good saddle." He turned his horse. "So long."

Bowden heard the chop-chop of his receding hoofs. This sound died finally, and only the soft murmur of the wind came. He thought again of Jackie Bell—even now she slept, and her brother hung at the end of the rope. The wind was pushing quietly through her window and across her bed and the same wind turned the body of her brother in slow circles.

He came into the Cross U, and the guard hailed him. He said, "It's me, Wyatt," and rode on into the barn. There was hay in the stall and he ran his fingers through it; it was bluejoint and fresh. He unsaddled and led the horse to the trough and the beast stuck his nose into the cold water and drank. Bowden leaned against the trough and thought; the horse lifted his nose, the water dripping from it, and nuzzled at Bowden's sleeve.

Wyatt Jones came in with a rifle. "They hang him, Dean?"

Bowden said, "They hung him."

Wyatt Jones set the rifle down, and he leaned against it. He said, "A man's fate is a funny thing. Maybe he just speaks lines somebody else thinks up for him. Maybe he's just a puppet and somebody else—I read something like that once, I remember."

Bowden said, "Damn it," and walked to the house.

Chapter 17

GET OUT—OR DIE!

Somebody was knocking on her door. The sound was vague at first—a long way off and without meaning. It rose and fell back, and then it came again; it was strong and potent with harshness. She sat up in bed.

"Who is it?"

"It's me, Jackie. Old Matt—the livery man."

A hand reached out and held her breath. She thought: *Oh, Lord, no; not that, Lord,* as she pulled on her slippers. They were cold against her bare feet —she remembered that afterwards—but she was not conscious of it then. She pulled her robe around her and held it tight.

"Matt," she asked, "what is it?"

She smelled his breath and there was whiskey on it. But his voice was sincere. "Jackie," he said, "you have to be brave, girl."

"Jim?" She waited for him to say no but she knew he wouldn't. She was lighting the lamp and the match would not catch—she scratched the head from it, and took another from the table. This caught and the flame touched the wick of the lamp and she turned the wick up.

"Yes," he said, "Jim."

She found herself studying the burned match. She thought of that afterwards, too, but she was not aware of it at the time.

"A bullet, Matt?" She added, "Or a rope?"

He said, "A rope, Jackie."

She forced herself to be calm. "Where did it happen and what was it over and who did it, Matt?"

"The vigilantes hung him. He was going to steal from Ned Churchill. The vigilantes heard about it and warned Ned, and Jim walked into the trap. They hung him and rode off; Ned Churchill went to Jake Hawkins and he told Jake. Jake got somebody to take the body to town. They're taking him to Taylor's now."

She said, "There's nothing I can do." She felt tired. The past came rushing up and it ran across her, and she thought of a hundred visions and memories, and still they were without meaning, without form. "I guess I knew it would come all the time. Now that it has come I guess there's nothing left to fear. It seems funny, Matt, now—there's nothing left to fear."

She came to him and he put his arm around her. She had her head against his old coat, and she smelled hay and whiskey there, and with this was the male scent of raw tobacco. She thought she would weep, but she didn't. *Maybe*, she thought, *I've wept inside for months and years, and there are no more tears.* . . . She felt his gnarled hands against her hair, there at the base of her neck; the feeling was strong and she found comfort in it. She drew back.

She said, "Thanks, Matt."

"If there's anything I can do—"

She said, "There's nothing anybody can do. What

has been done, has been done. He built it that way and it didn't have a foundation."

"I guess so," he said. He added, "But if there is anything—"

"There's nothing, Matt. Thanks."

He shut the door behind him, and he shut it softly. She heard him mumble. "I'm going to get a drink, damn it," and she went to her dresser. She took out the pint; it had never been opened, and she broke the seal, thinking that it had been there for months. She poured some into a glass, and drank hurriedly.

The whiskey stung; she grimaced. But it was warm and she felt it. Dawn was tiptoeing into the window and the wind ruffled the curtains uncertainly. She dressed and went to the Antlers Cafe.

The cook was starting the fire. He looked at her in surprise. "What brings you down so early this morning, Jackie?"

"Jim's dead," she said. She saw the question on his thin face. "The vigilantes hung him."

"Oh," he said. He tried to think of something else to say but he couldn't. He stirred the fire and shivered against the cold. Finally he said, "I'm sorry, Miss; I am, you can bet on that."

She said, "Well, it's over with." She felt, in a way, a touch of relief; the load had been heavy and the road long. She looked at him. "I guess a person shouldn't say such things, though?"

There was an awkward silence.

She asked, "You got any money, Pat?"

"Why, a little, yes. I bought a quart last night, but I got some left." He glanced at her. "Why ask?"

"I'm leaving," she said. "I'm taking Jim East. I'll never be back; do you want to buy the Antlers?"

"I haven't much."

"You can mail me payments," she said. "Your

word is good." She got to her feet. "There's Taylor at the door."

She went into the dining room and opened the front door. Taylor had a team outside, with a coffin in the spring wagon; Reverend Rassmussen was with him. When the minister saw her come to the door he climbed off the seat and came in with Taylor. He was a tall, gaunt man, and he had seen many men die.

He said, "May the Lord keep you, Jackie."

She said, "Thank you, Reverend." She looked at Taylor. "You're hungry, I suppose, and you're taking that coffin to the Cross U?"

"We would like some warm coffee, Jackie."

She called back into the kitchen, "Pat, how's the java?" and the cook called back, "In a little while, Jackie."

She said, "In a short while, men." The silence gathered and grew tight. "I want to take Jim back home," she said to Taylor. "You'll have a strong coffin, I suppose, and I want you to embalm him."

Taylor said, "I'll take care of that."

She glanced at him and said, "Thank you, sir," and then she rested her head on the counter. Taylor put his hand across her ebony hair, thinking of something that had happened long ago and he had thought dead, and he was silent. Reverend Rassmussen lowered his head, and Taylor saw his lips move but he could not hear what the man of God had said. Time ran out and built its length and then she looked up.

She said, "You'll forgive me—your coffee should be ready." She went through the swinging door to the kitchen and when she came back she had the coffee and her eyes were clear. "A woman's strength is weak, sir."

"No," said the reverend, "it is strong."

They ate slowly; then they went to the spring wagon and drove out of town, turning to the north. Dunc Cross came out of the Lady of Chance, stood there in the morning's strong sunlight and watched them go. He stood there for some time, adding everything up, and wondering what the answer would be. He did not know, but he was conscious of one thing: Time was rushing by and building death behind it, and he wondered what his relationship to that death was.

He turned, and went to the Montana House. He said to the clerk, "Good morning, Casey," and then he climbed the stairs, listening to the creak of the planks beneath him. The sound was sharp and without meaning, and he thought of it with indifference, for already his mind was running ahead, building up and running on into the future and to what it held.

He knocked at the door sharply and waited. He got no answer, and he knocked again, and this time a voice said, "Who's there?"

"Cross."

"What'd you want, Cross?"

"Open up," said Cross, "or I'll kick the door in."

He heard Len Carberry come to the door. The knob turned as the chair propped on the inside was removed. Cross entered. Carberry wore silk pajamas. Cross said, "What next?"

Carberry sat on the bed. "What'd you want?"

Cross said, "Jim Bell's dead; the vigilantes hung him last night. They caught him at Ned Churchill's. Jake Watson came into town at dawn toting his body over a mule, but that ain't all, Len."

Carberry ran his hand down; then remembered he wasn't dressed and didn't have his watch chain and the ears. He felt at a loss for something to do with his hands. "Now how did they find out? Or did they just blunder on it?" He didn't wait for Dunc Cross' answer. "But what ain't all, Len?"

Cross said, "They hung three other of your men too—the fellows on Clear Creek. The way it seems, they hung them after they stretched Jim Bell."

Carberry asked in a low tone, "I wonder if any of them squawked about me? Did any of them tell—?"

Cross found a chair and settled back. He said, "Use your brains, Len; nobody's been here to hang you yet, have they?"

Carberry put his head between his hands. "It's cold in here." He went to the window and closed it, then stood looking down on Alder City. Cross watched the man's face; he saw the elements there—doubt and indecision and uncertainty. But there was no fear, and Cross wondered at that. He thought: *There's fear in me—I can feel it. It's inside me, and it's cold.*

Cross asked, "What's next, Len?"

Carberry was dressing slowly. He said, "The thing has run its length, Dunc. I saw it in California—and I moved out ahead of it; it happened in Virginia City in Nevada, and I got out ahead of the noose there. We've made our stake and it's time to move; we pull out soon."

Dunc Cross felt relief run across him. "But what about the Rocking Chair outfit, Len? You've got fine range and good stock there."

Carberry was pulling on his boots. He paused, holding his right boot in his hand; he turned it over and looked at the heel. Then he said, "I know, Len. I'll sell it. I can list it with some outfit, like Dean Bowden bought the Lazy Z."

"I wonder how they found out about Jim Bell?"

Carberry pulled on the boot. He shrugged. "Lord knows," he said. "How did they find out in Stockton? Or in Virginia City?" He looked thoughtfully at Dunc Cross. "But there is something funny about it, huh? Nobody sneaked up to the office and listened, you don't suppose?"

"You had a guard out."

"Nobody listened through the front door," said Carberry. "I was watching that when you and Jim were talking."

"When do we pull out?"

"Tonight."

Cross frowned. "Why wait until tonight? They hang a man awful fast nowadays."

"Don't forget," said Len Carberry, "the Runback Mine ships tonight."

Cross leaned his chair back against the wall. "Oh," he said. "I forgot. That ought to run about sixty thousand, huh, Len? That's what it ran the last time, wasn't it?" He did not wait for an answer. "We hit it, tonight?"

Carberry nodded.

Cross asked, "Who goes with me?"

Carberry ran suddenly to the door; he jerked it open. The hallways were empty. He tiptoed down the hall and placed his ear against the panel of the closest door. Cross stood in the doorway and watched him. Carberry listened for some time and then came back. He said, "Nobody's listening—that fellow is snoring. But we better talk low."

Cross asked softly, "Who goes?"

"You and four of the boys." Carberry named them. "Hit the stage at Runner's Ridge. Last time we hit it on top of Tanner Heights. We'll hit a new place, now, and throw off anybody who wants to set a trap."

Cross thought, then said, "What about the Lady of Chance?"

"I'll sell it," said Carberry. "We'll pull over to Helena and work Last Chance Gulch. I'll peddle it to somebody there."

Cross asked, "You got some gold around somewhere, ain't you? How do you figure to move that, Len?"

"I ain't got an ounce of gold in Alder City," said Carberry. "All of it is shipped out. It's in a Denver bank. You and the boys hit the stage, then, and I'll swing across country, and I'll meet you at Tucker's Creek, right below the big rocks, when you get done with that holdup."

Cross asked, "Why not ride with us?"

"I need to tie up a few odds and ends around town," said Carberry. "Now get out of here while I finish dressing."

Chapter 18

PRAIRIE GRAVE

The Cross U men took turns with the shovel when they dug Panhandle Smith's grave. Bowden had selected the spot: the grave would be on the crest of the high hill that overlooked the sweeping range to the west. The ground was gravel and made for hard digging, and the quick runoff of the snow water had left the ground dry.

Chuck Baggett said, "Here comes a buckboard, Dean. Looks like it might be the sky pilot and the undertaker."

"That's them," said Bowden.

He walked down to the house while the rest stayed on the hill. The coroner introduced him to Reverend Rassmussen and the three went inside to where Panhandle Smith lay on the bed. Then they went back to the coffin and carried it into the living room and set it on the table. Taylor had a moment of brief apology.

"Since this hell broke open—pardon me, Reverend—but since this trouble started, my coffin builder has been too busy, and this is the best job he could do, Bowden."

Bowden nodded.

"Me and the Reverend can tend to this," said the undertaker. Bowden walked outside; the sun was bright and clean. Riders were coming over the hills to the west and he looked at them, and finally he saw that Marcie Gray was in the party. His men had seen it, too; they came down from the hill.

"Turtleback men," said Ken Shaden.

Bowden said, "Yes, it looks like it."

Shaden studied him quietly. "What are they doing on this range?"

Bowden said, "We'll soon find out, Shaden. Anyway, they come in peace, or else they wouldn't come openly."

They moved out and waited. Marcie Gray raised her right hand high, and they rode in. She was sharp against the sun, and Bowden felt something stir in him. He held this under control and waited.

She said simply, "We thought we'd come, Bowden; we thought maybe we could do something."

The Cross U men loosened. Bowden said, "Step down, Miss Gray. And you too, you Turtleback men. I can't invite you into the house, Marcie. They're working in there."

She came up. She said, "Bowden, I'm sorry. I can't tell you how much. There was trouble, and a woman's heart is another thing—and it's over with now. You know that, don't you?"

Bowden said, "We'll rip up that drift fence." He added, "They hung Jim Bell last night, Marcie."

He told her what had happened. He saw the hardness leave her: he saw pity and sympathy there. He thought: *I had her judged wrong—she's clean and fine and strong underneath.* He said, "Len Carberry's behind it, Marcie."

"And you?" she asked.

"I'm here to stay," he said. "I fit in." He spoke

slowly. The pain was sharp in his lung—the war had done that, and he wanted no more of strife. He lifted his eyes to the snow on the Rockies. "This is good range."

Taylor came from the house. He said, "Hello, Miss Gray," and then, to Bowden, "We're ready if you are, Dean."

Bowden said, "The grave is dug."

They carried the coffin up the hill. The strong sun reflected from the metal handles. Reverend Rassmussen walked behind it, and the punchers trailed him. Bowden walked with Marcie Gray and she did not hold on to his arm, even though the hill was rough. He was, in a measure, thankful for that; he was wrapped in himself.

Soon they came down.

The minister and the coroner ate, then swung their rig and went back to Alder City. Bowden and the Cross U men and Marcie Gray and her Turtleback riders sat longer at the table, lingering over their food.

Marcie said finally, "We'll have to go," and pushed back her chair. They went with them to their horses and Alex Tooping said to a Turtleback man, "This meant a lot to us, fellow. And I speak for the whole bunch of us."

They found their saddles. Marcie Gray leaned and asked, "What's next for you, Bowden?" and waited.

He said, "I'm a part of this, Marcie. The end isn't here yet."

She straightened. He watched her closely. She was silent for a long moment. Then she said, "Good luck," and rode away to catch her men.

Wyatt Jones said, "Thank the Lord, that's settled."

The Cross U men went to the bunkhouse. Ken Shaden started with them and Bowden said, "Wait a minute, Ken," and Shaden stopped. He asked, "What is it, Dean?"

"You ride with me," said Bowden.

Shaden nodded. They went to the corral and roped horses. They rode out on a long lope, swinging over the hill and out of sight. The prairie ran on and on and the foothills finally reached into the land, tearing it up into mounds. Bowden felt of the land, and the feel was strong.

Neither man had much to say. They reached town late that afternoon, but they did not ride into old Matt's livery. They left their horses in the willows along the creek, and they came into George Carson's hardware store by the rear door. Carson came to their poundings.

"We were waiting for you men," he said.

They went into Carson's office. The small room was jammed with men and tobacco smoke hung across the dead air. Bowden knew most of the men, and he nodded and settled down against the wall, and Ken Shaden squatted beside him.

Martin Johnson was talking. He said, "As you all know, the Runback ships tonight. The stake runs high. The gold goes out on the evening stage and there's a guard with it. I've talked to him and if there's trouble he doesn't go into it. Neither, for that matter, does the driver."

"How about the passengers?"

"We have checked the local ticket office and they have sold two tickets. Of course, there'll be some others on it, those that come in with the stage. But that's a small item; we get them out of the way before the fireworks start."

Bowden asked, "Maybe they won't hit?"

A man said, "Dunc Cross has already left town. So has Hank Rayburg and Jess Sergeant and Jedrow. Julius Breeding—" he jammed his thumb toward a heavy man "—owns the Silver Dollar Saloon. He approached Len Carberry a while ago and asked if he wanted to sell the Lady of Chance."

Bowden looked at Breeding. "What did Carberry say?"

Breeding shrugged massive shoulders. "I didn't want the outfit, Bowden. I just did it as an experiment. We figured that if Carberry wanted to sell, he was getting ready to leave. He wants to sell, all right; he'll sell right this minute—and the price is reasonable."

Bowden nodded. "He wants to get out, then, I take it?"

"Looks like it."

Bowden frowned. "We can't let him go. We have to string men around town, and if he starts out, we have to head him off. Once he gets out in the open he'll drift."

George Carson had all their names on a card. He named the men who would circle Alder City and he named the spots where they would be located. Ken Shaden was selected to stay behind; he would watch the west road that ran over the hills and crossed Priest's Pass and came down on Last Chance Gulch.

Somebody said, "Maybe he doesn't aim to have his men stick up the gold, men. What have our lookouts under his office floor got to say—what have they heard?"

George Carson said, "Nobody's been to see him in his office. According to our information, Dunc Cross was up in his hotel room to see him, and Tony Garnett, who has the room next to Len Carberry, heard them talking but he didn't get much—they talked too low. But he did hear them mention Runback and Jim Bell."

Bowden leaned back against the wall and closed his eyes. He was tired—the days had moved along, and sleep had become a scarce commodity. He rested, hearing the outline of the action.

The men who were to guard the town moved out of the Office and Ken Shaden said, "Best to you, Dean," and Bowden murmured, "Keep your powder dry, fellow." They went out the back and spilled down the alley and then broke up and went to each man's station. The room had thinned out some; but the air was still lifeless and smoky.

"There are four of them," said George Carson. "Four of us will get the stage when it reaches the foothills. We make the passengers get out and we get in; after it's over, we can send the stage back for the passengers and it can go on into Drummond."

"Who rides the stage?" asked a man.

George Carson looked them over. "Bowden, you go." Bowden said, "Thanks," and nodded. George Carson's eyes were deep and reflective. He named the other three men, and Bowden looked at each one; they were good men and strong men—they would know their way.

The others would sneak out of town, one by one, and get their horses which were hidden along the creek. Then, when dusk came, they would ride in two bodies. One would take Tanners Heights, leaving their broncs behind and creeping through the brush to the top of the hill. The other would take Runners Ridge and do the same.

"Any other place they could strike?" asked Bowden.

Carson rubbed his jaw. "I don't think so." He added, "I guess that's all. Good luck to all of you."

The townsmen who had homes to go to filed out, but the others stayed behind. They had deemed it unwise to be seen around town, for Carberry might get suspicious. Carson had an upstairs on his store and they went there. They had hot coffee and sandwiches. Bowden squatted beside the shaded window and looked down on Alder City's main street. Hidden, he watched the ebb and flow of life through the pionner town.

The day dragged by and the stage came in. Somebody said, "There's the five o'clock stage. That's a signal we have to pull out, because the other comes in an hour."

"Maybe the gold's on this one?"

Bowden looked out. "No guard," he said. While the others left, he watched. Jackie Bell was getting on the coach. He saw them boost up the coffin and tie it across the top of the stage. They would take the body to Cheyenne and then put it on a train. He saw Jackie get into the stage. He waited until they had hooked up the new team, and then he watched the stage leave.

He was alone in the room. The bootheels of the others, moving down the stairs, ran their course and then died. He watched the stage and felt a keen sense of loss, and he remembered a few days before when Jackie Bell and he had ridden to the Cross U, and he remembered their small talk and her laughter.

He turned and left. He went down an alley, and already the shadows were building up; the wind came in from the peaks and held a sudden chill. He came out in the willows along the creek and found his horse. He went into saddle and rode slowly to the east, and gradually the three others built up around him. They did not ride far out of town—only about three or four miles.

"This is far enough," said Bowden.

The brush was high there; they hid their horses. They took their rifles and hunkered on the edge of the road. One man consulted his watch.

"Be about fifty minutes yet, I'd say."

"Sooner than that," said another.
One man said, "I wish it was over with."
Bowden said quietly, "So do all of us."

Chapter 19

BRIGHT LAND

The stage driver was in on the scheme. He tooled his four-horse team around the curve, and nodded to the guard who sat on the box with him. The guard said, "This is the spot, John," and while the driver pulled in his fresh team, the guard dropped the brake forward, pushing it hard against the steel rims.

A passenger stuck his head out. "What're we stoppin' here for?" he demanded. He stared at Bowden and the three men as they came out of the brush. "What is this—a holdup?"

Bowden gestured with his rifle. "Get out, fellow." The man was slow and Bowden pulled him; he threw him back and the man fell. He said, "What the hell do you think you're doing?"

Bowden stuck his head into the coach. Two women and a fat man were there and he said, "There's nothing to get worried about, people; this is no holdup. You'll get out and we'll get in and in a little while, not much more than an hour, the stage will come back, pick you up, and you can go on your way."

"What if we don't get out?" demanded a woman testily.

Dean smiled. "That'll be all right," he allowed. "Fact is, though, you might be mighty dead when the stage comes back—bullets have a way of killing 'most everybody they hit. 'Course, now, you can stay in."

The woman got out.

Bowden looked up at the driver while the others entered the stage. "You can drop off if you want to, friend. I'll take over the lines. That goes for you, too, guard; if you want to, you can step down."

"I'll stick it out," said the driver. "I've tooled these ribbons quite a number of miles over these roads."

Bowden nodded. He looked inquiringly at the guard. He was a big man and Bowden knew he'd be a rough one in a tussle.

"George Carson told me I could hightail," said the guard, "but I kinda figure like Leather here—this road has got some bumps ahead, but I don't figure they're big enough to throw a man off'n this high seat."

"Where do you figure they'll hit?" asked the driver.

"George Carson says either Tanners Heights or Runners Ridge," said Bowden. "Fact is, I don't know where any of them places are. I'd be much obliged if we could fix some signal between us to tell me when we're nearing either spot."

"I'll whistle," said the guard. "Slow, like this."

Bowden said, "Thanks." He said to the men inside, "I'll ride back in the boot. They won't expect a man to be back there. You know all the plans and you know what to do, and ride a close saddle."

"Same to you, Bowden."

Bowden climbed into the boot behind the stage

and let the leather apron fall. He settled back in the narrow spot and listened to the churn of the wheels on the road. It was dark in the boot, and he liked that for some reason: possibly because it gave him freedom of thought.

The noose was drawing in now and the rope was getting tight. He thought of that and wondered what the next hour would bring. Scenes kept shifting across his mind; Jackie Bell had been dark and small, and things had gone wrong and she was on the stage ahead, and Jim Bell rode above her in his coffin, his neck broken by a hangman's knot.

They were coming to the foothills now; he could tell that by the drag on the stage. He heard the quick murmur of the men inside the coach, the sound coming low and indistinct through the thin wall behind him. They, too, were thinking of the future; they were talking in low tones, and no man was saying what was inside of him. They were talking, as men do in stress, of irrelevant items, hiding what was inside, what was stored up and heavy.

Dust was seeping slowly under the cowhide flap. He put his head back, resting it against the wall, and the thoughts came again. The trail had been long and it had wound its tortuous way across mountain and plain, and Panhandle Smith had followed cattle across it, as he had sent cattle across the dim trails that now grew in weeds and thistles. He had known the raw frontier towns, and he had tasted of them—the savor had been strong on his tongue. . . .

The stage was rocking hard, slipping the earth as it ran down a steep incline, and he heard the rattle of tug chains and the quick barks of the driver. He felt the team lengthen out, the stage found a steady pace, then it lifted again and gradually, little by little, the pace ran out and slowed to a walk as the coach neared the summit. He heard something else, too.

A low whistle.

He shifted and brought his rifle around. He was crouched, ready to leap into the road, and still the stage ran slower. The steepness of the climb almost halted the horses. He felt the tenseness in his thigh and he shifted, still holding his rifle ready.

Then he settled back. For quickly the stage started running ahead, and he knew they were going down into the next dip. The dust rose again and he got some in his lung; he pulled his head low and breathed through the collar of his shirt. Wheels clanged on rock and steel-shod hoofs rang against the gravelly roadbed and the tug chains jingled with sharpness in the dusk.

Somebody in the stage said, "Well, they never hit there; it must be the other ridge, then."

"Hope we reach there before it gets too dark."

The stage hit the bottom of the slope, traveling fast and swaying. Bowden braced his feet and steadied himself, and the stage gradually settled down and lost speed as it climbed another hill. He was tight again, expecting the guard's low whistle, and he waited patiently, his rifle ready. But the whistle did not come and then the stage was gathering momentum again, rolling down the slant.

He settled back. He thought of Marcie Gray, and he wondered where she was at that moment, and what she was doing. Her eyes were blue, and he remembered the depths in them, and he thought of this. The stage lurched and rolled and he had to steady himself again. Then it lost its speed, and the toil of the hill cut the team down, gradually slowing them.

He heard another whistle.

He thought: *This should be it*, and he settled back

and waited, feeling the tick of time run out. Gradually the stage slowed down to a trot, and time dragged on. Evidently that slant was not as steep as the others because the team was still traveling at a trot when they reached the top. He felt the stage level out and pick up momentum. He thought: *Well, we're going downhill, and they never hit. They weren't out after the gold then.*

Then he heard, "That's it, stop that team! Get your hands up! This is a—"

He was aware of many things, then. He was jumping out, battering his way through the cowhide flap, and he was hitting the ground, his rifle in his hand. He landed on his feet behind the stage; the dusk was thick and the sunset was golden in the west, and they were in a cut with brush on either side. As he came around the corner, he glimpsed men leaving the stage on the off side.

Four men were there on the trail. They were masked and they wore long coats. Two had rifles, the others had short guns. One saw him and swung his rifle around, and Bowden planted his legs wide and shot.

The man grunted, dropped his rifle, and fell over it. The smash of gunfire was sharp in the narrow defile. The other three swung, their weapons out— then a gun took up a lethal chant from under the stage. Two of the townsmen lay there shooting from under the stage, and they knocked two of the men down.

The driver was fighting his rearing, terrified team. The pitching of the stage threw the guard to the ground and he landed in the brush. Men came running from the brush, and other guns took up the noise. A fist hit the man who stood up, and a rifle barrel came in, and he went down.

The guns stopped them.

The driver said, "Whoa, boys, whoa," and he kept repeating that. Finally the team became quiet. The guard got out of the brush and said, "Hell of a hand I made," and stood looking at the men who lay on the road.

Somebody said, "Rip off their masks. Let's see who we got."

Bowden went to one of the townsmen. He knelt beside him and turned him over; the man had a bullet hole above his heart. Bowden took his hand and thumbed it, but he felt no movement; he let the hand drop.

"This one is Mike Jedrow," said a man. "He's dead. He's the one you dropped, Bowden."

Bowden nodded.

Somebody said, "We won't have to hang him, then. This one is Jess Sergeant, and he's got some life in him. We'll hang you, Jess, sure as hell."

Sergeant tried to sit up, but he couldn't. "I got a wife and two kids," he said. "They're down in Californy."

"Sure you ain't got six kids?"

Hank Rayburg was dead, too. But Dunc Cross was very much alive. He sat on the ground, disarmed, with blood on his cheek. He rubbed it on his hand and looked at it, then he looked at Bowden.

"So you won, huh?"

"I helped," said Bowden.

Cross asked, "How did you get wise?"

Bowden said, "Carberry talked."

Cross studied him carefully. "When did this happen?" he asked. "Did you get Len, too?"

Bowden shook his head slowly. "No, Carberry got away," he said. "But he left word in town that you four aimed to rob his gold."

Cross spat blood. The rifle barrel had split his forehead and blood kept coming down. He wiped it back and looked at his numb hand. He said, "You lie, Bowden. Why would Carberry steer us into hell?"

The townsmen were quiet. A few of them were taking down ropes and building nooses. Cross watched them and felt his fear. Bowden looked at them, too, and bided his time; this man, he knew, would break.

Cross said, "They're going to hang us."

"Just two of you," said Bowden. "There'd be no count in hanging some dead men." A horse stomped his foot and tug chains rattled.

Cross repeated, "Why would Carberry do that to me?"

Bowden shrugged. "I don't know," he said. "But I guess he wanted to get rid of you. He wanted the whole pie instead of getting it cut up into small pieces. Maybe that was it."

Cross said, "To hell with you, Bowden."

"Your business," murmured Bowden.

They got Jess Sergeant to his feet. He was a thick man with small eyes, and his intelligence was limited. They tied his hands behind him and fitted the noose, and his eyes were bright with fear. They jerked Cross up and put the noose around his neck, placing the knot under his ear. Then they tied his hands behind him.

Somebody said, "That cottonwood tree, there— that one with the big limb that hangs across the road."

Four of the vigilantes got on top of the coach. With the help of the others, they got the two men up with them. They held them while the driver moved the stage ahead. He stopped under the cottonwood tree. They raised the two condemned men to their feet and tossed the ropes over a thick bough. The vigilantes on the ground tied the free ends hard to the bole of the heavy tree.

Sergeant said suddenly, "Lord help me—" He slumped forward and took up the slack. His heavy body hung against the rope; trying to fall but not being able to.

Carson said, "He went on. He'll choke to death."

"He'll break his neck when the stage pulls out from under him," said Martin Johnson.

Courage ran out of Dunc Cross. He sagged down and tried to get to his knees. But the rope choked him and he came up. "So Carberry sold me out?" he asked dully. "Why, damn him, I hope he roasts—"

"Maybe he will," said Bowden. "But you'll beat him there, it looks."

Cross studied him, his eyes going wild. "You can't hang me—you can't! I gotta live and kill him—hear that, I gotta live—!"

"We'll hang you," said Martin Johnson, "and what's more, you'll like it!" A vigilante down on the ground laughed in a high voice.

Cross looked down at the man. "Laugh, you idiot," he gritted. "Go ahead and laugh. The noose ain't around your neck!" His voice was losing its sanity. He felt weak, impotent; blood rushed through him. He doubted Bowden's words—and yet believed them. "If I talk, can I go free? You want to know who killed Panhandle Smith, don't you?"

Bowden said, "I do. But no matter how much you tell, you'll never go free."

Cross cursed. "Carberry's always bragged about how tough we've been. Why don't he get some of the men and ride over here and save our necks?"

"He's pulled stakes," said Bowden.

Cross thought that over. Bowden saw that old wildness run across the condemned man's eyes. "Carberry sold me out," he said, "and I'll put the skids under him. I know the whole gang." He rattled the names off quickly. One man took them down with a pencil and paper. Cross finished with, "I hope you hang the whole bunch!"

Bowden asked, "And who killed Panhandle Smith?"

Cross said, "Len Carberry. I was riding alongside of him, and I saw it. Is that what you want to know, Bowden?"

Bowden studied him. The man was telling the truth. He said, "That's all, Cross."

Jess Sergeant was choking against the rope, and he managed to stand up. Cross looked at him and said, "Stand up, you fool, and get hung like a man. Anybody got a drink?"

One man had a bottle. He held it while Cross drank. He offered it to Jess Sergeant. The man shook his head; he was dazed. The townsmen climbed off the coach, leaving only the two condemned men standing there, and with the driver on the box. George Carson lifted his hand.

The driver cracked his whip, the team leaped ahead. Jess Sergeant was silent but Dunc Cross said, "Every man for his principles! Hurrah for Jeff Davis! Pull this damn' coach—"

The driver drove down the road, then slowly turned the coach. He came back and said, "Give me a drink, Hank," and he raised the bottle. Somebody asked, "What'll we do with the bodies?"

"We'll bury them . . . later on," said George Carson. The moon was coming up and it lighted the two men who hung there so silently in the evening. "Bowden will want to ride into town first, I guess."

They looked at Bowden. They all knew of his agreement with George Carson.

"I asked for two hours," Bowden said quietly. "That'll be time enough . . . maybe too much time." He thought for a while. "I hated to lie to a man about to die. . . ."

Chapter 20

MOONLIGHT GUNS

Bowden and the men climbed back into the coach and the driver headed back toward Alder City. The rest of the vigilantes rode behind, leaving the two bodies alone in the dazzling moonlight.

They swept along the mountain road with the dust rising under the coach and the hoofs of the horses. Bowden leaned back against the leather seat and took his Colt from its holster. He opened the loading gate and looked at the cartridges. All of the cylinders were filled. He reshut the gate and holstered the gun.

"Nice evening," said a man, just by way of conversation.

Bowden looked out into the calmness of the early night. The peaks stood out clear and bright and their sides were marred by the dark growths of pine and fir. The wind was running slowly through these thickets and bringing their sound across the distance, and he found this satisfying.

He said, "It sure is."

Nothing more was said then until they reached the spot where they had left the passengers.

Leathers turned his team and Bowden and the men got out. The fat passenger looked up at the guard.

"What happened?"

"Nothin' much."

One of the women said, "We heard shooting."

"Your imagination," said the guard.

The passengers crawled in and Leathers lifted his whip. Bowden came out of the brush, leading his horse.

"Good luck, Bowden," said Leathers.

Bowden looked up at him. He said, "Thanks," and went into his saddle. George Carson pushed his horse in close and said, "We'll come in town later, Bowden; we got lots of work there tonight. We still keep the guards out. We'll wait for you."

Bowden remembered the list of names Dunc Cross had tolled off. "I guess you have quite a chore," he said.

He rode off, lifting his horse with his rowels. When he was on the outskirts of Alder City, Ken Shaden rode from the brush.

"Bowden," he said, "what happened?"

Bowden told him.

Shaden leaned back against his cantle and looked at him steadily. "So Len Carberry killed old Panhandle, huh? I'm riding in with you, Dean."

Bowden said, "Thanks."

They rode on, letting their horses walk. Shaden rubbed a match to life against his chaps. The flame showed his thoughtful eyes and then died. "Marcie Gray's in town. No, I didn't see her. But the word came along the line back yonder. She got her men with her, and our boys rode in with Turtleback riders, too."

"Where are they now?"

"In town . . . around the Lady of Chance."

She had heard about him, and she had heard

about the gold—and she had added it together, and come out with the right answer. And now she and her riders and his hands were in Alder City.

He asked, "Len Carberry?"

Ken Shaden drew deep on the fag. The coal died, came back, glowed. "Word came along the line regarding him, too. He's still in town. He tried to ride out twice, heading out a different direction each time, but we turned him back." He looked long at the moon. "I guess the old man up there will see a lot tonight, huh, Dean?"

"I reckon so."

They were on the outskirts of the mining town, moving through the shadowy street. The night wagon train, coming in from Spokane and the Idaho mines, was moving out, the burros plodding with their heavy loads. A dog barked at the moon and a cat ran along a building, hurrying and scurrying to get out of sight.

Bowden rode deep in his saddle. His thoughts ran out ahead and grouped, and he was building for the next few minutes. Carberry would have his back to the wall, but there would be no fear in the man. Carberry had seen too many mining camps, had run too many bars, and seen too much of death. He would play his cards, letting them fall to the best of his advantage; he would know no fear. . . .

Bowden thought: *He'll be tough . . . and ready.*

Shaden, too, was silent. The weight was heavy on him, and he showed it in his carved face. They rode into the rear of the livery and stepped down. The place was dark and smelled of manure and horses and hay. A kerosene lantern, hung on a hook in the middle of the pathway, did its best to light the stalls.

Bowden called, "Matt."

"Here," said the old man. He had been dozing on

the bench by the front door, and he got to his feet, his knees uncertain. "My danged pins are playing out."

"Too much whiskey," said Bowden.

"Not enough," said Matt.

Bowden said, "Take care of our broncs, Matt. Strip the saddles off them and feed them. We aim to stay for a spell; till morning, anyway."

"Maybe longer than that," said old Matt. His eyes were sharp despite the liquor. "What happened out along the road?" Bowden retold the story in short sentences. The old man's eyes drew down thoughtfully. "Carberry's in the Lady of Chance. They ain't much of a crowd there, Bowden; somehow word has got out that the place is dangerous, and most of the little crowd there is scattered around. I just came from there. Had a drink. He's probably waiting."

Bowden murmured, "Thanks."

They went out the front, heading for the brighter part of the main street. When they were passing the Mercantile Marcie Gray came from the shadows. She said, "What happened out there, Dean?"

"Dunc Cross talked, Marcie. Len Carberry killed Panhandle."

She was thoughtfully quiet. The lamplight reflected from the beads of her buckskin jacket. The white collar of her blouse was smooth around her neck. She said, very low: "Dean—then you're going against him? Is that it?"

"Yes," he said.

"Why not let the vigilantes get to him, Dean? That way—"

He cut in. "Panhandle Smith was my friend," he said. His voice was rather rough, and he hadn't meant it to sound that way.

She said then, speaking low again, "I thought

something like that would happen. Your men came in with me. My riders are here, too. They're placed around the street, and around the Lady of Chance, and they have their rifles and short guns. You'll get a square deal out of this, Dean."

He asked, "Where is Carberry?"

"In front of the Lady of Chance, I think."

Bowden took her arm. He said, "I don't know what to say, Marcie. . . ." He did not look at her, then; he said to Ken Shaden, "You stay with Marcie and cover the street."

Ken Shaden said, "Good luck, Dean."

He went toward the Lady of Chance, walking in the shadows of the awnings. Lamplight glowed from saloons and stores, but the streets were almost deserted. Word had got out about the vigilantes, and honest men stayed home and waited until the vigilantes rode in. The night was quiet and the yellow moon rode high. The dog had stopped barking, and Bowden wondered at the unbroken night.

A voice said, from between two buildings, "Walk light, Dean, he's in the shadow," and he recognized the man by his voice. He said, "Watch things, Wyatt," and then he walked ahead, and stopped when he was opposite the Lady of Chance. He drew back into the shadows, and waited there. Time ran out and he still waited. Finally he said, "Carberry. Len Carberry."

Carberry said, from across the street, "Move out, Bowden, and let me see you. Now what's on your mind?" The man's voice was level, Bowden noticed.

Bowden saw him then, settled there against the Lady of Chance. He had squatted, and he was a small, dark ball on the sidewalk—he would be hard to hit. Bowden knew, too, that Carberry did not see him, or else he would have already been shooting.

Bowden said, "Dunc Cross is dead. He told me

about you killing Panhandle Smith."

Silence grew and held, and only the wind sighed. Bowden knew then that Carberry was looking for him, trying to locate him, but that he could not see him in the darkness. He settled back against the wall and put his hand on his gun. Then, with his free hand, he took off his hat and threw it to his right, letting it fall inside the light that shone from a store. And Carberry glimpsed it and thought Bowden was moving there.

Carberry was shooting then, shooting rapidly. The roar of his gun was loud, and glass fell. Too late, he saw he had been tricked. For Bowden ran forward, and he hollered, "Here, Carberry, here!"

Carberry swung the gun, shooting toward Bowden. He was cold with fury, yet he was collected. Bowden had halted suddenly, and he had fallen to one knee. The flame of his piece was sharp and steady against the moonlight, and he shot until his gun was empty.

The high whine of a bullet was sharp overhead. The night had been too dark, and Bowden knew he had missed some shots. His fourth bullet brought a grunt from Carberry, and the fifth made him drop his gun. He rose then, grunting and trying to stand up, and Bowden's last bullet knocked back against the wall.

Carberry stood there against the wall, and then he turned and tried to brace himself against it, pushing it hard with his hands. He wanted to go into the Lady of Chance, and he took one step toward the door. Bowden knelt there, with nothing inside of him, and waited. Carberry took another step, but his knees would not hold him. His hands slid along the wall, grabbing for a hold, but they failed him, too. He sat down on the sidewalk and then rolled over slowly until he lay dark against the planks.

Men were moving on the streets now, coming from

doorways and from between buildings. Ken Shaden passed, his gun up, and said: "Did he get you, Dean?" and Bowden shook his head. Shaden went on then, and dropped to one knee beside Len Carberry. He knelt like that for a long moment; then he came back to Bowden, who had gotten to his feet.

"He's dead, Dean," he told him. He was silent then, looking at Bowden. Then he said, "I guess I'll go out and get the vigilantes and tell them and they'll ride in. This is only starting, I guess."

Bowden said, "I guess so, Ken."

Ken Shaden moved off, and Bowden heard his boots on the sidewalk. He turned and went to the livery barn. Old Matt said, "You want a drink?" and Bowden shook his head. He sat down on the bench. Only then did he see that Marcie Gray sat there, too.

He said, "You didn't watch, Marcie?"

"No," she said.

He said wearily, "It's hell to have to kill a man. There'll be blood in this town tonight, and men will die. But maybe we have to have death, and wars, to keep strong and walk the paths we want."

"Dean," she said. She stopped awkwardly. Then she said, "Think of it this way, Dean. There's wild cattle back in the hills and we'll run them out, there's a drift fence to pull out—" He saw then she was sobbing.

He said, "Marcie, girl."

She was close to him then, and this time her lips were not cold. And suddenly to Dean Bowden the shifting pattern became real and compact. The war was a thing long past; the strife was gone—it was as though a fire blazed up in terrible glory and freedom, a blaze that was bright and sharp and showed the land in all its primeval beauty and promise.

SADDLE PALS

1

Jess Roberts awoke with a hand pulling at his elbow. He mumbled, "Go 'way an' let me sleep," and rolled over on the hard cot and started to snore again. Again the hand shook him, this time harder and with a greater impatience, and Jess opened his eyes slowly.

"Go 'way, fella!"

The hand gripped him harder, its stubby fingers strong. And while the man gripped him he shook him impatiently. "Jess—Jess!"

Jess didn't answer right away. His head ached, for one thing; some devil was inside his cranium, pounding an anvil with a big sledge. He blinked his eyes and tried to steady his wavering vision. He opened his eyes once more and saw that they had been right: he was in jail again.

"Now what happened?" he asked aloud.

The hand had quit shaking him. Now a husky voice said, "You're in the clink, Jess, an' I'm with you!"

There was something familiar about that husky voice. Jess closed his eyes anew and tried to think and then gave up. The hand was shaking him again and he sat up on the hard cot and glared at the man in the next cell. The shadows were growing thick but he recognized the squat man.

"War Dog Smith!"

The toad-like, heavy-set man was standing close to the bars, one thick arm squeezed between the upright rails. Jess Roberts grabbed the hand and shook it, a wide grin showing on his dark, homely face.

"Long time no see, War Dog. How come you're in the clink?" The lanky cowpuncher grinned. "An' how come I'm behin' bars?"

War Dog told him he'd got into jail to see him, Jess. That didn't make sense to the cowboy, who reminded the heavy man that he hadn't seen him for five, six months—the last time being when they'd got oiled up in Moosetown, down in

Nevada, and wrecked a saloon by putting a dynamite charge under it.

War Dog Smith smiled. He was part Sioux and part French, his mother being a Sioux Mandan squaw and his father a renegade French trapper. He rubbed his big bottom lip thoughtfully.

"The saloon, he got up—pufff. . . . Me, I ride out with you, lose you in the night. I go West and work in the mines in California. A miner comes in an' he tells me about ol' Mack Orcon. . . ."

Jess studied him, His head still ached hard. "What about ol' Mack Orcon? Ol' Mack's all right, ain't he?"

War Dog shook his head slowly. "Ol' Mack, he in trouble. He not in Montana any more, he in Wyomin'. Somewhere aroun' Lander, town named Wishing Springs. Him dig for water there."

"Water?"

"Yeah, water."

Jess considered the man with a great amusement. "Look, War Dog. I got on a spree—downtown in a bar. The Mangy Cur, I think they called it. I got in a fight. I remember the marshal comin' in with a club. He's a pint-sized gent—saw him when I rode in this mornin'. Didn't like him right off. Well, he must've connected with that club, or I'd never be here."

"You feel your head?"

"Sure, I feel my head. I got it onto me, haven't I; I gotta feel it. There's a he-goat in there an' he's kickin' an' blattin'."

"I mean, feel the head on the outside."

Jess ran exploratory fingers across his aching scalp. There was some matted blood and he didn't feel too hard or too long. Anger against the runty marshal ran through him and made him see a pinkish color.

"Danged little runt! Ain't man enough to fight with his fists! Has to slug a man with an elm club when a fella's just havin' a little fun."

"A little fun, huh? I saw that bar right after they'd took you to the jail. What did you use—dynamite?"

Jess' grin widened despite his aching head. " 'Member once I had a gambler by the ankles, swingin' him aroun' in a circle. He hit the backbar when I let go of the scissor-bill. Busted all the bottles, an' about that time Runty comes in an' my lamps go out." Jess peered at the half-breed. "But how did you get in the clink, War Dog?"

"Me, I tripped the marshal."

"Humph!"

"Yes, I did that. I gets into town—lookin' for you—an' they take you to the jail, stiff like the planks. The marshal comes out an' I trip him an' he lands hard and he jails me next to you. I let you sleep for two, three hours—now you are awake?"

"I think so," Jess said. "But why did you want to see me? And why did you get in jail to see me? Why didn't you just come in an' talk to me without goin' to all the trouble of makin' the hoosegow?"

"This little runt—the marshal—he would not let me in to see you. So I stuck out my boot, an' I pushed him. He went down on his face, and when he came up, he was mad."

Jess considered that information. Finally one question stood out clearly against a foggy background. "But what do you wanta see me about? Why such a hurry to tell me?" He added, "You're kiddin' me about Ol' Mack, ain't you?"

"We gotta help Ol' Mack." War Dog shook his head stubbornly.

Jess let his mind dwell on old Mack. The old man was around seventy-five, anyway. Once he'd run a big cow outfit down in Texas and he'd taken Jess off the streets of Dogtown, a hungry, homeless kid of twelve. War Dog Smith had been old Mack's range boss.

For six years Jess had lived on Orcon's Circle in a Box spread. He'd learned to ride and rope and handle a gun. He'd learned how to take a balky steer out of a herd on a night so black it would booger a mountain goat. Then old Mack had peddled his spread; he was tired of cattle, he'd said.

Jess and War Dog Smith had hit out together. They'd seen a lot of territory traveling together in the dozen or so years since old Mack had sold the outfit. They'd seen lots of trouble, too. For Ward Dog Smith, although in his fifties, had a strange flair for getting into trouble—a habit that, by rights, should have belonged to a youth, not a middle-aged man.

A few months before they had been broke, so they had split up. War Dog Smith had gone to placer-mining in California and Jess had done some cowpunching back in the Wasatch Mountains. War Dog had made a little stake and Jess had also accumulated a few dollars with his rope and saddle. They had made no agreement to meet at any particular spot or at any particular time.

Yet here they were—both in a creaky old jail.

7

"What's botherin' Ol' Mack, War Dog?"

"Like I say, he up around Lander; town called Wishing Springs. I think that was the burg's handle, Jess. He drills wells up there—water wells!"

Jess Roberts leaned back on the hard cot and put his hands behind his head, and studied the half-breed with a great indifference. So old Mack was drilling wells now—water wells? Well, what about it? Mack Orcon was full of loco schemes. He'd spent two years up in Alberta raising angora goats with the hopes they'd make good sled animals for the trappers up in Yukon Territory and the Great Slave Lake region. Jess remembered a letter he'd got from Mack.

Dear Jess:
Me, I'm raisin' goats, angora goats. Goin' make sled dogs outa them, fella. You know how a goat kin climb over rocks and handle hisself in the snow? Well, I'm goin' to make a stabe at it.

Mack.

A year later, the old man was in Montana, starting a fish hatchery. Jess never knew what did become of the hatchery. Maybe Mack had got mad and canned the whole works as sardines. Jess found himself grinning at that thought. Only thing old Mack hadn't started was a distillery, and he was probably leery about that, knowing that when he ran off his first batch, Jess and War Dog would undoubtedly smell it and come to camp with him.

Now he was drilling wells. And what did he know about drilling a well? Jess dimly remembered his father. He'd been an oil-field worker, a driller. He remembered his father's talk, remembered the oil-field jargon; he had learned a little bit himself, although only a kid of ten when his father had been killed. A gusher had thrown up a bit and crushed his dad. He knew a little about wells but he figured old Mack didn't know anything about them.

"He get his whiskers caught up in the bit an' is he turnin' aroun' an' aroun' with the stem?" Jess was joking.

But War Dog's broken words took the smile from Jess' lips. War Dog had heard about it from a drifting oil worker who had worked for old Mack.

"They's a fellow aroun' Wishin' Springs named Hank Carter. He runs a lotta cattle there, Jess; heap big cowman, I understand. Him, he don't cotton to ol' Mack puttin' down these wells."

"Why?"

"Well, from what this fella tol' me, they's a bunch of farmers comin' in Wishin' Springs an' they aim to irrigate from these wells, usin' deep well pumps to lift the water."

Jess Roberts brushed some of the cobwebs off his brain and considered this angle and its merits. He'd heard about those deep wells being used for irrigation.

"So Hank Carter don't cotton to Mack drillin', huh?"

"Ol' Mack, he ees in bed."

"You mean he's got hurt in a fight?"

War Dog let his heavy shoulders rise and fall in a negligent gesture. "That I do not know. Yes, I guess the ol' man has had some fight, maybe gunplay. We get out of here an' we go to side him, huh?"

Jess sat up on the cot and looked at his boots. Finally he decided that he was hungry. His head was getting back to normal and he could stand a strong slug of red-eye. He wondered how far it was to Wishing Springs, Wyoming, and War Dog allowed that it was about a hundred miles; a guess, of course. They called it Wishing Springs in irony, the halfbreed said—the Springs were dry part of the year, and everybody wished they had more water. Hence the name of Wishing Springs.

Jess forgot his hunger and thirst and felt sorry for old Mack. He owed the oldster a big debt—a debt so big he could never hope to pay it in his lifetime. The only home he'd had when a button had been at Mack Orcon's ranch house. And old Mack thought a heap of him, too.

"We gotta get outa here," War Dog declared.

Jess got to his boots. He wobbled a little on his pins but soon strength returned to his legs. He rattled the bars in the cell door so hard they almost shook the entire calaboose.

He waited, but nobody came.

"Rattle them again," War Dog advised. He got to his feet and together he and Jess rattled the doors. War Dog sang a Sioux medicine chant as he shook, and the din of the doors and the heavy man's chant made Jess' head start aching again. Five minutes of this, and a big man broke through the door that led to the marshal's office, his face flushed with anger.

He was a human moose, standing over six feet and almost

as wide as the cell corridor. "What's goin' on in here?" he demanded.

Jess asked, "Who are you?"

"Me, I'm the jailer."

Jess grinned. "All of you? Seems to me like a big boy like you could get a job shovelin' hay an' not shovelin' food to prisoners. Don't your arms get tired carryin' them *heavy* trays of grub?"

The jailer glared at him. "What's the matter with you, cowpoke? You go hog-wild an' wreck our only saloon, sendin' four local hands to the doctor—Now you're lookin' for trouble with me, huh?"

"You can't hit me," Jess said. "Your fists are so big they can't go between the bars. An' you're afraid to turn me loose 'cause I'll beat the livin' hell outa you an' get away."

The jailer's lips trembled with anger. "Oh, you will, huh? Well, we'll see about that—" He got his ring of keys and put one in the lock. "I'll come in there an' work you over, fella." He halted, leaving the door half unlocked, and stood for a second looking at Jess. Then he relocked the cell again. "Nope, can't let my temper sway my judgment, men. The marshal tol' me under no circumstances to unlock a cell without his permission."

Jess scoffed, "Afraid of me, huh?"

Again anger colored the jailer's eyes. Jess' plan was to get him in the cell, fight with him and perhaps to whip him, to get his keys and turn War Dog loose. But he had his doubts as to his ability to whip the giant. He'd expected the runty marshal to come in instead of this moose of a jailer.

"I'll meet you any time, when you get out. That is, if you get out. That gambler you flung around by his pins has got a fractured skull, the doc says, an' he might kick the bucket on you. Then you'll face a murder charge."

"I'm hungry," Jess declared.

"Not supper time yet." The jailer consulted a cheap watch. "Over an hour yet until chuck time. I won't be aroun', but the marshal'll feed you. Now no more of this howlin' an' rattlin' or there'll really be trouble."

Jess acted suddenly humble. He'd decided to skip trouble with this fellow and to pick a fight, if possible, with the marshal. "There'll be no more trouble," he stated.

"Better not be."

The giant ambled down the cell aisle, almost filling it. The door closed behind him and they heard his boots boom down the outside steps. Then, for a while, there was silence.

"Wonder what size Justins he wears," Jess marveled. "Must be about seventeens, I'll bet. Prob'ly gets them bench-made."

War Dog sat on his bunk and looked at a string of ants that filed across the floor. "Why worry about his boots, Jess? Me, I figure you are lucky— He come in that cell an' I figure he'd almost kill you. His fists are like hams."

"Don't mention ham, please. Forget mentionin' grub; I'm hungry. Well, reckon we'll work over the marshal, huh?"

"How?"

Jess sat on his bunk and took off his right boot. He searched his pockets and found them empty—the marshal had rolled him before ducking him into the tank. He wondered where his gun and belt and pocket-knife and personal belongings were. War Dog told him he'd seen the outfit in the office when they'd taken his gun and had emptied his pockets.

Jess grinned. His hat lay on the floor and he dusted it off, remembering that it had cost him thirty bucks down in Denver two months before. He had a razor blade between the band and the crown, and he took this out and slit open the top stitching of the boot. He brought out a small flat roll of thin, steel-like wire.

"What's that, Jess?"

"Piano wire. Saved for such a time as this." Jess shoved his hat on the back of his head and his grin grew as he built a loop in the wire. The shadows were thick in the cells now and War Dog had to peer hard to see the wire.

"What we do, Jess?"

Jess explained to him, and War Dog's smile spread to his ears. They waited for almost an hour—an impatient hour—and then the runty marshal came from the office, carrying a tray of grub.

"Let's eat first," muttered Jess, "an' when he comes back for the trays, we'll pull our trick on him."

The tray belonged to War Dog. The marshal opened the small trap at the base of the cell door and slid the tray in with, "Here you are, Injun." He looked at Jess with hard eyes. "Whatcha got your hat on for, scissor-bill? You sure ain't goin' no place, not for some time at least."

"I want a lawyer."

"You ain't gettin' one. Want all you want to."

"That's not legal," Jess declared. "Every man is entitled to legal help under the Constitution."

"What Constitution?"

Jess figured the fellow was playing ignorant. "When do we get a trial?" he asked.

"The Injun gets his tomorrow mornin' in the j. p.'s court. We'll hol' you until the gambler either gets well or kicks the nosebag over. If he gets well, you go up for trial, but if he dies— Well, they like him aroun' here, fella."

Jess knew what the marshal meant. If the gambler died, there'd be a necktie party, with the bowtie fitting around his own prominent Adam's apple. He kept smiling, but under that smile was a troubled feeling. He was in a bad way, no two ways about that. He didn't like gamblers, and if the card sharp died he wouldn't feel too much regret. He remembered the card player hitting him over the head with a chair and breaking it. The gambler'd had a fair chance in a fair fight.

The marshal bowlegged down the aisle, whistling in an off key, and came back with Jess' tray. "Eat hearty, sons," he advised. "I'll be back after a while for them platters."

"Don't hurry," growled Jess.

The lawman glared at Jess again and Jess grinned back. Still whistling off key, the runt swaggered toward the office. Jess settled back to chewing his grub. It wouldn't win a prize for culinary efficiency, but he was hungry and it tasted good. The coffee was only lukewarm but it did much to clear his head.

Jess lay on his bunk. "Notice them spur leathers on that runt, War Dog? They was awful thick and strong."

"They was strong, Jess." War Dog rubbed his flat jaw. "What if the plan does not work?"

"It's gotta work." Jess got to his feet. "Look, we gotta get out to side ol' Mack. We gotta get outa this burg."

"Here comes his nibs now."

"Me, I need the luck," War Dog declared. He went to his knees and leaned against the cell bars in the corner. He started groaning and holding his belly, keeping his head down.

The marshal stood and looked at him. "What's the matter with the Injun?"

"That poisoned grub you fed him," growled Jess Roberts. "Maybe you tried to poison him on purpose. Maybe you meant that platter for me an' you had poison in it to kill me 'count of that gambler bein' a good friend of your'n."

"Shut your trap, fella!"

"My belly," War Dog groaned. "My belly, she ees burnin' up, man. Quick, water."

The marshal was leery. He looked at Jess and then knelt beside the half-breed. He reached through the bars, got War Dog by the chin, and lifted his head. Jess was down on his knees, too. But he wasn't looking at War Dog. He had taken the length of piano wire from his boot top. The marshal hadn't noticed his movements, either.

Jess worked quickly. The wire loop settled over both of the marshal's spur shanks that stuck up in the air as the man knelt. Luck was with Jess Roberts. The runt had huge spur rowels, and when Jess jerked on the wire, the noose tightened and jerked the marshal's boots back, dropping him on his face.

War Dog had wasted no time, either. He had both of the marshal's arms, and he braced himself against the bars, pulling on the arms. Together they had the marshal spread out along the outside of the cells with the half-breed stretching him one way and Jess the other. Jess took quick dallies with his wire and got to his feet. The marshal tried to holler, but Jess had his arms now and War Dog had a greasy palm tight on the small man's lips.

Jess panted, "Get his keys, fella!"

War Dog had a piggin' string in his shirt pocket. He handed this to Jess, who tied the marshal's wrists to the bars.

The marshal was wriggling like a hogtied steer in front of a branding fire. The strong weight of War Dog's hand was pushing his head back and hurting his neck, but the half-breed just grinned and pushed harder. "You get keys, Jess?"

Jess got his paw through the bars and unsnapped the ring of keys from the lawman's belt. In a moment or two he and War Dog were out in the cell aisle.

"Wonder if anybody outside hear him?" asked War Dog. "He hollered once, Jess."

Jess listened. No boots sounded outside and the only thing audible inside was the hard panting of the marshal as he tried to breathe around War Dog's hand. Jess had the man's gun and he pointed it at the marshal's head, squatting with the gun barrel just a few inches away from the man's nose.

"Okay, War Dog."

War Dog released his hand and straightened. The marshal looked at the gun, his lips quivering. "Don't—don't kill me, fella. I got a wife and eight kids— I gotta wife—"

Jess grinned. "You damn' liar, you're a bachelor. Fella told me you was a woman-hater." He was fabricating.

The lips shook more. "He—he was lyin' to you. He—he—" War Dog was taking off his boots. He took off his dirty woollen socks and put his boots back on, his not too clean feet in the worn Justins. "What're you goin' do, Injun?"

"You see soon."

War Dog sat on the marshal. He pried his mouth open and crammed a sock in it despite the muffled protests. Then he took the other sock and tied it around the man's head, knotting it hard in the back. When he got up, the marshal was gagged, and gagged completely.

"We go now, Jess."

Jess was walking down the corridor. The office was empty and they got their guns and belongings and went out the back door to the lean-to barn. Their horses were there munching hay from the stalls.

They saddled up hurriedly. "Our broncs, they get cheap feed and have a rest an' we rest, too," War Dog said, grinning.

"Maybe you call it a rest. I don't."

Two other broncs were in the barn. Evidently they belonged to the marshal and the jailer. Jess got a pair of nippers from the hook on the wall. He pulled a shoe off the left front hoof of each bronc and tossed the shoes out the windows. Two saddles hung from pegs on the wall.

He raised the stirrups on each and cut the latigos almost in two up where the stirrup leathers hid them. If a horse started to buck or prance those latigos would pop, throwing rider and saddle. Then he and War Dog were riding down the alley.

"We ride fast, Jess."

Jess Roberts shook his head. "Dark an' nobody'll see us. We ride fast, an' somebody might get suspicious of us, fella."

Once out of town, though, they put their broncs to a long lope. The horses were fresh and the night was getting cool. Come daylight they'd be miles away, heading for Wishing Springs.

Suddenly War Dog grinned. "That marshal, he will have bad taste in his mouth, Jess. He have bad taste for a day, anyway, huh?"

Jess remembered the dirty woollen sock. "For a day, humph! You mean for a month, War Dog!"

2

The big bartender said, "You gents got any money? Drinks are cash in this joint, men!"

War Dog Smith smiled widely. "Sure, we got money." He dug into his pocket and came out with a handful of change and laid it on the bar. "They do not take a man's word here, huh, Jess?"

Jess Roberts nodded dully. He was tired of the trail. From what he'd heard, Wishing Springs was about thirty miles north. From this town here on the railroad they ran a daily stage to the Wishing Springs post office. "There trouble around here, bartender?"

"There's always trouble on this range, drifter." The bartender counted out the coins he wanted, slid out a bottle and two glasses, and placed his hairy arms on the bar. "Sorry I had to act so rough, but you looked like drifters to me an' I been stuck for too many drinks lately."

"Just lately?"

"Yeah, they's no-goods driftin' north to Wishin' Springs. They come in here an' can't pay for drinks. Some goin' up to side ol' Mack Orcon an' some to side Hank Carter, I reckon. Not many to side ol' Mack, though; most of them want Carter's money. He's spendin' it too, I understand."

"Ol' Mack still in bed?" asked Jess.

"Heard tell he was up now, crippling aroun' good-for-nothin'. Me, I keep out of the trouble— There goes Hank Carter now, men."

They could see the depot through the open door. A frame building, raw and new, with unpainted surfaces, it had been built but a few weeks before when the railroad had finally reached this town of Watsonville. From there on into Wishing Springs passengers went by the stagecoach.

Now the stage had pulled up to the platform, for the local mixed passenger and freight train was discharging its passengers. Two of them were climbing into the stage. One was a fat man who carried a suitcase. Jess figured he was a drummer. The other passenger was a lanky woman of about fifty odd, evidently a spinster. Jess could see her face and form and he based his calculations on those two unattractive features.

"Which one is Carter?"

"He's drivin' the stage today."

Jess and War Dog watched Carter climb up into the boot and take the ribbons on the four-horse team. Carter was not tall or wide but still he was big enough. He packed one gun, tied down, and he wore California pants and a buckskin jacket and shirt. His gray Stetson, creased and clean, was well back on his big, heavy head, accentuating his stubborn features and showing coal-black hair.

"So that's the mighty mogul," mused Jess.

"He owns a piece of that stage line, I think. He owns so much a man can't tell just what he ain't got a finger in. Anyway, he tooled the stage into town today. He was in here for a drink. Said the regular driver got sick an' he needed a little work hisself, anyway."

Jess Roberts and War Dog Smith both nodded. Both took another drink and both went outside. They talked for a little while, standing on the edge of the plank walk, and then Jess went to his horse, got up and rode out of town on a lope, leaving War Dog sitting his horse.

Jess drew in behind some buildings, slid to the ground and walked into an alley. From there he could see the stage and War Dog but he doubted if either could see him. Pretty soon the stage came down the street with Hank Carter handling the lines, his boots braced against the dashboard, his whip in its socket.

War Dog held in his horse and hollered, "Hey there, you Hank Carter? If you are, I look for you."

The stage stopped, dust rose, horses pulled up. "What do you want, Injun?" Hank Carter glared at the half-breed. "Talk fast, fella!"

Jess could hear every word War Dog said. "Me, I got a gun, Carter. Me, I wanta use that gun."

"Go ahead," growled Hank Carter. "Use your gun. Only don't pull it against me or I'll—"

"You do not misunderstand, Carter. I want to use the gun with you—I want you to hire me—"

Carter jerked on his wheelers and set the big grays back against the singletrees. "Oh, I getcha. You wanta hire out to me. All right, Injun; tie your bronc behin' an' climb up on the boot. I wanta talk to you." Carter hauled in on the ribbons again and again the grays went back a pace. "What's your name?"

"War Dog."

"Good name," hollered Carter. "You'll see plenty of war, too."

The spinster stuck her skinny neck out the window. "My good man, isn't it time we get moving? Isn't it—"

The stage lurched ahead, chopping off her words. Jess watched it roll out of town. War Dog was on the seat beside Carter and the half-breed's bronc trailed behind, pulling a little against its hackamore rope.

Jess went to his horse and he too rode out of town. He headed across the hills, hit the stage road ahead of the stage, and loped along it, making his pony stretch. Once from a hill he saw the stage toiling up the slope, the grade slowing the horses to a long trot.

The stage changed horses once at Turner's Stage Depot. From that point to the Wishing Springs post office was about twelve miles, the agent told Jess, who kept out of sight of the stage, loping on ahead of it. About five miles out of Wishing Springs he came to a series of high, rough hills covered with clumps of buckbrush. He found a gully along the top of a grade and pulled into it. He sat his sweaty horse, hidden by buckbrush, with his gun in his hand.

He waited almost half an hour.

Somewhere tug chains rattled. Hoofs sounded, and the stage came around the bend. The grade had slowed the horses to a walk. Jess waited until the lead-horses were past him and then he rode out, gun up.

"Stop that stage, Carter!" he ordered.

He shot once, the bullet whistling high. Inside the stage, the old maid screamed, and the drummer hollered, "Hey, she fainted! She's got her arms aroun' my neck—"

The horses were tired and the shot didn't scare them much. Carter had hauled in and was staring at Jess. His voice was hoarse.

"You must be drunk, cowboy! This stage ain't got no valuables besides our belongin's—them things that belong to me an' my two passengers. 'Sides, you ain't even masked! You can't get away with this!"

War Dog growled, "Yes, he can." He put his boots against Carter and kicked his powerful legs. Carter grunted and then slid through the air, falling in the road beside the front wheel.

Jess holstered his gun and stepped down. Carter got to his feet, wild with rage. "So you're workin' with him, huh, Injun? So that was your deal, huh?" He glared at Jess. "Who are you two gents, anyway?"

"We come to help ol' Mack Orcon," Jess informed him.

The drummer came out of the coach. "That old maid—she's still out. I got away from her—" He stared. "I thought this was a holdup, fella."

Carter's beefy jowls were red with anger. "Coupla damn' fool punchers havin' fun at my expense, drummer! Well, they can't make a fool of Hank Carter, believe you me!" He swung a heavy fist without warning.

But Jess Roberts was expecting just such an action. He went down and the fist curled wildly in the air over his head. Hank Carter hit so hard that he lurched ahead into Jess' uppercut.

The blow rocked the cowman to his bootheels. Jess heard him go, "Ugh," and hit him again so hard that he thought he'd break his knuckles. The whole setup was blurred from then on. He remembered the drummer scrambling back inside the Concord and remembered the high screams of the old maid.

He figured Carter had a jaw made out of flint. He'd dropped other men cold with two such blows. But Carter just said, "Ugh," again and went back against the coach, slamming the door shut behind the drummer.

"He tough guy," hollered War Dog.

The stage horses were rearing and fighting the Indian's hold on the ribbons. Carter fought from a low crouch and he was handing punishment to Jess, who had to step back. Jess wondered if he hadn't bit off more than he could chew. Besides being tough as steel, Hank Carter had a smattering of science in his fighting.

His head pulled down between his shoulders. Carter shuffled forward, boots moving dust. He fought hard and relentlessly. Jess hit him twice and took three in return. He had to go backward. They fought in a circle, with Carter standing still and Jess moving around him.

Jess was getting winded. He was doing the work, making the movements, and Carter stood anchored, turning a little as Jess circled. Jess decided to rush him and get him going backward.

He came in, ducking, blocking, hitting. He got Carter against the coach and turned him with a hard right. He got a glimpse of the old maid sticking her homely face out the window. She had a whiskey bottle in one hand and was holding it by the neck. She made a pass at Jess with the bottle. He ducked and she hit Carter across the forehead.

"I got the wrong man," she screeched. "I hit the wrong man—"

The bottle was a heavy one. When Jess stepped back, Carter was down in the dust, knocked cold. Jess grinned up at the homely woman and wiped the blood from his nose.

"Thanks," he said.

She pulled her head back. The drummer looked out. "She got the bottle outa my pocket, fella. I tried to keep it away from her but— Your friend looks like he's out like a chilled beef."

Jess took Carter's gun. He searched the cowman for a hideout gun but Carter didn't have one. The drummer had a fat .38 automatic on him and Jess took that. Then, with the drummer's help, he rolled Carter into the coach. The man was limp and he snored as he lay on the floor.

"You—you brute!" the old maid said.

Jess felt gingerly of his nose. He bent it back and forth and wondered if it were broken. One eye—his left—was swelling shut fast. He chucked the woman under the chin with, "Be nice, honey."

"You—you—"

The drummer grinned. "I'd like to know what this is about, fella."

Jess smiled with difficulty. His lips wouldn't behave. "Just a coupla boys out havin' a good time." After tying his bronc by his hackamore rope to the back of the stage beside the half-breed's horse, he climbed up on the boot beside War Dog. "Let those ribbons out, friend."

It was all down grade into Wishing Springs. The valley was broad, dotted with sagebrush, and Jess figured the land was good—for sagebrush land is good land. When you have soil with greasewood on it and no sagebrush you have soil with a high alkali content and it is no good for farming or grazing.

"Somethin' green over there." War Dog pointed with his whip.

Way across the valley, smack against the far foothills, Roberts saw some green fields. "Prob'ly irrigated by ol' Mack's wells," he said. He shook his head gingerly. "I got another headache, War Dog."

The half-breed asked, "I wonder about that marshal back

yonder? I wonder if the gambler died that you swung by his boots?"

Jess remarked that back in Muleton, a town they had gone through, a bartender had told him that the gambler had lived and was getting well. Jess knew the bartender from over in Arizona and the man wouldn't reveal he had talked to him, he was confident. They'd sent wires up and down the line and the last one had said that he and War Dog had been sighted going toward New Mexico.

The half-breed sighed. "That is good. Soon that charge will be old an' forgotten. Me, I hate to have such things behind me."

"Oh, yeah. That so, huh?"

War Dog was grinning. "Ol' Mack Orcon, he be su'prised to see us, huh? Come into town like big men, with the stage all to ourselves. Get up there, gray horse."

"A three-gaited bronc," said Jess. "Walk, stumble and fall flat. Yeah, ol' Mack's goin' be glad to lay his lamps on us."

The drummer stuck his head out the window and looked up, his oxlike eyes rolling in the dust. "This fella's come to, men. He wants to get out an' fight some more. You goin' stop an' oblige him?"

Jess felt his nose again. He shook his head.

"He aims to jump out."

"Whip up the teams, War Dog."

The half-breed snapped his lash and got more speed out of the four work-broncs. The stage went at a dead run, the wheels lurching and the cab swaying; Jess had to hang on. War Dog braced his boots and made his whip a living talking thing, hanging it continually over the sweating, laboring broncs.

"Carter jump out now," the half-breed muttered, "an' he break his neck, we go so fast."

Carter was hollering inside the stage. The roar filtered up through the roof and became lost in the jar of the wheels and the pounding of wild hoofs. Now and then War Dog would let out with a war whoop. Now and then, too, the old maid would screech: a high sound, much like the screech of a night owl.

Jess Roberts hung onto the rail and tried to grin. They lurched around a bend, the hind wheels skidding out, and almost ran into a farmer with a lumber wagon loaded with groceries and barb wire. The farmer hauled his broncs to one side suddenly, the closer horse rearing and pawing the air in fear, and then the stage was by, showering him with dust and loose rock.

Jess glanced back. Through the boiling dust he could see the farmer staring back at the stage. His hold hardened on the rail as War Dog growled, "Hang on; big bump ahead."

And it was a bump. The three passengers went back and forth like seeds in a dry gourd. Carter, who'd been silent for a while, let out another bellow, and the spinster's screech sounded again, grating on Jess' nerves. Jess was glad when they rounded a sudden bend and saw the Wishing Springs post office a quarter of a mile away.

Across from the post office was a raw, unpainted building that bore the sign: *General Store*. There was a saloon, too, and Jess suddenly remembered how dry he was.

"Quite a city," hollered War Dog.

"Even got a hotel," grunted Jess. "Might be all of six, seven rooms in it, too; that is, countin' the haymow of the barn."

"We stop now," declared War Dog Smith.

And stop he did. Horses skidded, dragged back on their rumps; wheels skidded, screeching against such treatment. And Jess Roberts leaped to the ground, landing hard on his boots.

He jerked the stage door open, pushed the spinster back so hard she landed on the drummer's lap, and jerked Hank Carter out of the stage, dragging the confused, cursing man into the open. He got a hammerlock on Carter and choked him down.

"Where's the law?" he hollered. "Where's the marshal?"

The town of Wishing Springs—what there was of it—came to wild, hurried activity. All of ten or twelve people came out on the street and gathered around the stage. They came running out of the saloon and the store and the hotel and the post office.

"Where's your marshal?" demanded Jess, still keeping his hammerlock. "We got a crazy man here!"

"You're the one who's crazy!" The spinster started beating him over the head with her umbrella and Jess started ducking. But he was still holding Carter when War Dog got the umbrella away from the angry woman. The drummer got his bag out of the boot and ran for the hotel, moving with remarkable speed although he was decidedly fat.

"What's goin' on, stranger?"

The voice was harsh and came from behind Jess, who

turned Hank Carter around. He had expected to see a big man, judging from the harshness of the voice, and he was surprised to see a little runt standing there, shotgun under his right arm, and a star on his open vest.

"You the marshal?"

"I'm Deputy Sheriff Hammerburg, fella. Out of the Watsonville office. We ain't got no marshal."

"Arrest this man, Hammerburg!" stormed Hank Carter.

Hammerburg got down and squinted into Carter's flushed face. "Why, Hank Carter," he marveled. He glared at Jess Roberts, his long mustaches jumping like a cat's whiskers when the cat sees a mouse. "Turn that man loose. He is a reputable citizen, stranger."

"He's drunk," stated Jess. "Either that, or crazy." He still held Carter strongly.

"He crazy, fella!" War Dog shook his head slowly.

A frown formed on Hammerburg's forehead. "What makes you say that, fella?" he asked Jess.

Jess made up a cock-and-bull story about how he'd seen the stage come along the mountain, the team running away and the passengers hollering in fear. He and War Dog, according to him, had finally caught the stage. Carter had been driving with loose reins and whipping the team, holding a bottle in one hand and taking a drink from it occasionally.

Carter's words were muffled but they sounded like, "That's a damn lie." Hammerburg was openly puzzled. Someone in the crowd snickered and the deputy's thin face showed an angry scowl.

"Turn Carter loose, an' let's hear his side."

Jess shook his head. "He's dangerous."

Hammerburg snarled, "I said turn him loose." He stepped forward to jerk Jess' hold loose but his shotgun was in his way. He handed it to War Dog with, "Hold this for me, huh?"

"Sure."

Hammerburg stepped toward Jess, and War Dog shot both barrels of the ten-gauge shotgun. The roar almost stampeded the tired stage teams, but a man grabbed an off-horse. Hammerburg jumped a foot and turned and snarled, "What in the hell—"

War Dog's broad, dark face held a small grin. "I make to swing it aroun', an' my hand, she is on the trigger. It go boom." He swelled his cheeks in imitation. "I lucky I no hit you, huh?"

"They're lying," stormed the spinster.

War Dog looked at her with hurt in his big eyes. "What hard words, miss," he said. "They are not true and you know it."

"They are true!"

Hammerburg spoke. "Close your traps, all of you." Again, to Jess, "Turn him loose, drifter."

Jess released his hold. Carter straightened up, wiped his red face, and then swung on Jess, who ducked. Hammerburg grabbed the cowman and so did the hotel man. Jess stepped back.

"You better get him inside. Is there a doctor around?"

Hammerburg spoke. "Come on, Carter."

"I'm not comin' with you, you halfwit. These two hellions, these—" But they were pulling him toward the hotel. "Them two devils— When I see them again I'll—" They had him in the hotel.

Jess looked at a local citizen and shook his head. "Bad case," he said. He and War Dog went into the saloon, where they ordered. Some townsmen were leading the stage horses toward the barn behind the hotel. The spinster was entering the hostelry, and War Dog watched her through the open door of the saloon.

"What a homely woman, huh?"

"She must be, if you say so. Your taste for women runs bad; you like them homely or purty. She must be ugly."

War Dog shook his head. "Too bad, too."

They ordered whiskey and drank hurriedly. Jess said, "We better get outa town, War Dog. They might believe Hank Carter after a while an' there'll be hell to pay for us." He grabbed another drink out of the bottle.

"Yeah, we pull stakes."

3

The two rode at a long, mile-devouring lope. War Dog Smith was solid in leather, his gross body settled deep between leather fork and cantle, and a craggy scowl played across his dark forehead. Jess Roberts glanced at him and read the half-breed's thoughts aright.

Although on the surface they appeared devil-be-damned, the two men never underestimated, for one moment, the power of Hank Carter. And Jess knew the half-breed was thinking of the war that hung across that range of sagebrush and wild blue-joint grass.

"Buck up, War Dog."

War Dog turned a little and studied his lanky partner. Then a slow grin spread across his face. "That old maid, she was mad, huh? She broke her umbrella on you, Jess. Maybe she love Hank Carter, huh?"

"What a pair they'd make! Nah, she was just excited, an' she took the bit in her jaws, so's to speak. But why think of her?"

"She was so ugly." Stubby fingers waved in the air. "In a bad dream will I see her."

They pulled to a running walk, for their broncs were tired. And Jess allowed his mind to pull its pocket pin and have free range. They'd come into Wishing Springs in a hurry . . . and left in a hurry. They'd not even found out how badly old Mack Orcon was hurt and how he'd got hurt. Well, they'd find out all about it when they talked to the old rascal.

His mental gymnastics completed, he surveyed his own physical condition. Carter had handed him plenty of punishment and a respect for the man's fists continued to grow in Jess Roberts. He decided that, if it were possible, in the future he would evade a fistic encounter with the cowman.

This survey accomplished, he directed his attention to the range over which they were riding. Born in the cow country and raised in the saddle, he was a cowman to the core—his life and his livelihood had always more or less revolved around and depended upon cattle.

And the cattle that grazed on that grass were not in good shape, whereas, by all odds and tokens, they should have been fat at that time of the year. The sun had cured the grass —what there was of it—and turned it to a golden brown, packed with nourishment. But the cattle were poor.

War Dog summed up the situation as it appeared to him. "Too many head of stock and not enough grass for all of them. See that brindle cow over yonder, Jess? She's chawin' on the lower branches of that buckbrush plant, ain't she?"

They drew rein. Jess slung a leg over his saddlehorn and rolled a cigarette, his eyes on the cow as he licked the quirley into a hard cylinder. "Guess that must be Hank Carter's iron on that critter, huh? Hard to read with that shaggy hide on that cow."

"From what I hear, Carter owns only cows on this range. But his cows are not poor. This country needs water."

Jess had his smoke going. "Maybe ol' Mack's on the right track, diggin' them wells. Well, guess we'll mosey on. That must've been his spread we seen back from the hills, that bunch of green stuff to the north acrost the basin."

"That should be it."

"Maybe we should've asked back at Wishing Springs."

"We find him."

Jess allowed that they had plenty of time. Once they saw a rider off to the east, pushing across the country. He was headed south. Their horses, tired to the bone, plodded on. Now and then they got the beasts to a lope. War Dog said he was hungry and Jess also was hungry.

Jess kept thinking of Hank Carter. Carter would be up in arms now; he'd be boiling mad. He wondered if the cowman would swear out a warrant against him and War Dog. He might do that, though Jess figured Carter had more drastic and more satisfying plans in store for them.

Gradually they came closer to the green plots along the edges of the hills. The smell of irrigation water came to them and a mosquito buzzed and landed on Jess' arm, to be promptly killed. War Dog waved his hand in front of his nose to scare another mosquito away.

"Them mosquitoes, they be bad now, Jess. They come with water an' sit along the ditches in the weeds."

"Always somethin' to plague a man," growled Jess.

The wind started and in a few minutes was blowing hard. That held the mosquitoes down. They rode along a fenced lane with alfalfa fields on each side. Stacks of alfalfa hay dotted the hay meadows and Jess remembered how poor Carter's cattle had been. They could have stood some of this hay.

But why was Carter fighting the well-drilling crews of old Mack Orcon? With his cows so poor, a man'd figure he'd run down some wells of his own and raise feed for his stock, instead of letting them run on dry range.

Jess didn't bother long with those questions. The answer was too apparent. For with irrigation, the farmers came in; with the farmers taking up homesteads, the cowman was done, through. For the days of open range—government range open to grazing—would be gone forever. Better to run poor cows than to run no cattle at all. And besides, even if the grass was sparse and thin, that cow shouldn't have been as poor as she'd been.

Ahead, a dog started barking. He came running down the lane toward them, a mutt in late puppyhood. Jess saw a man come out of the log house, look at them, then run inside the house again. He was scowling as they stopped in front of the closed door. If they hadn't seen the man run inside, they'd've figured the spread was deserted. For apparently nobody was on it.

"Hey, there," hollered War Dog. "We look for Mack Orcon, fella! We want to see ol' Mack."

"So you do, huh?"

The voice grated from behind them. They turned their horses and looked at the man who stood there in the doorway of the toolshed, his shotgun on them. He was a young man —not more than twenty-five, Jess figured—and he had the shotgun barrel up and hard against them.

Jess recognized him as the man who'd come out of the house, seen them, then run back inside. The fellow had gone out the back door and circled around into the tool shed.

Jess asked, "What's the play, fellow?" and nodded at the shotgun.

"Yeah," said War Dog. "What do the cards say, *hombre?*" He shrugged with a great gesture and looked at Jess. "For the second time today, another shotgun is coverin' us. They are strong for shotguns aroun' here, huh?"

Jess said, "We're lookin' for Mack Orcon."

"Oh, you are, huh?" scoffingly. "I reckon you aim to kill ol' Mack, huh? Hank Carter's tried to put him outa the way a coupla times already."

Jess understood now. The fellow thought they were Carter riders coming to get into trouble. But the fellow had forgotten one thing, and Jess reminded him of that point: If Carter riders came to fight Mack, would they ride in openly? They'd sneak in, wouldn't they?

"Cain't tell about them hellions. They'd try any trick. What you want to see ol' Mack about?"

Jess Roberts didn't like to look into the black bore of the shotgun. Nor did he like the way the man's fingers trembled on the breech, the forefinger hooked over the trigger. Evidently War Dog didn't like the setup, either, for Jess noticed that his partner sported a worried look.

Therefore he was quick to reveal their identities to the

youth. The shotgun lowered a little at that, the barrel pointing to the ground, and Jess breathed a silent sigh of relief.

"Heard ol' Mack tell you two," the youth said slowly. "Still, this might be a trick. We'll see ol' Mack about this."

Jess started to dismount, but the man's words stopped him. According to him, Mack Orcon didn't live there; he lived around the hill, about half a mile away. The man told them to turn their broncs and ride down the road. He'd walk behind with his shotgun.

"How far to Mack's?" Jess wanted to know.

"Told you onct, fella. About half a mile or so."

Jess rubbed his jaw thoughtfully. "Why not get a horse an' ride behin' us? Then we can make some time. We're ga'nt an' hungry, fella."

"Get movin'!" The shotgun gestured.

They rode along another lane, their horses plodding ahead of the man with the shotgun. Jess gave in, deciding everybody was crazy but himself, and then he began to doubt this. He and War Dog Smith shouldn't have come there to side old Mack. Anybody who'd raise goats for sled dogs—anybody who'd start a fish hatchery . . . But they were there.

Two milk cows gazed in knee-deep pasture. More mosquitoes came out to assail them and the wind mercifully blew them away. Jess was silent and so was War Dog. Behind them the boots of the farmer grated on rock and sand. Neither Jess nor War Dog glanced back.

They rode around a hill that extended out into the valley and from that point they saw a sod shack placed against a hill. There was a lean-to barn and another building, evidently a blacksmith shop. The gate was open and they followed the wagon road up the slope.

Jess sent a quick glance around the spread. There was a conglomeration of junk: well pipe lying in long lengths, some cable and some rope, and a broken down well-drilling outfit. An old steam engine stood beside the barn, one wheel gone and the whole rigging lopping over against the building. Was the barn holding the rig up or was it holding up the barn?

Another dog came out barking. The man said, "Pull in your critters, men," and Jess and War Dog, both grinning, drew rein in front of the plank door. The man hollered, "Hey, Mack!"

No answer.

"Maybe he is in bed," ventured War Dog.

"Mack, oh, Mack!"

Another silence. The dog sat down suddenly and started raking his neck with his right hind leg to dig out a flea. Jess watched him. He was getting a little tired of the way things were going. He was hungry and saddle-tired and his face didn't feel too small. He wondered if both eyes were black or if just one—

War Dog spoke. "There's Mack!"

The old man had opened the door. He carried a diamond-willow cane. He stared up at the two and Jess saw his mouth open in surprise. The cane sailed out into the yard, hit the mutt. The dog ki-yipped and ran off, howling in pain. And Mack Orcon was pulling them from saddle.

"My ol' friends, my ol' friends! War Dog Smith, bless your spurs, you ol' Sioux. Ol' Sittin' Bull hisself. An' Jess Roberts! Man alive, hobble inside; set an' I'll dig out a drink."

The farmer stared at them.

Jess pulled himself out of the old man's claws and asked, "What's the matter with you? Nothin' ailin' you, is there? We heard tell you was hurt an' in bed."

"Yeah," said War Dog. "What she is the matter?"

Mack's face took on a mournful look. "Yeah, I was in bed a spell. Got up two days ago."

"We'll get Hank Carter for that," promised War Dog.

"But it wasn't Carter."

Jess studied the oldster. "All right, it wasn't Carter. Which one of his gunhands was it, then? We'll tend to him."

The mournful look deepened on old Mack's grooved visage. "Wasn't a gunman, either. Fact is, men, it was Nellie Bly that laid me up."

Jess scowled and looked at War Dog. "Who's Nellie Bly?"

A goat bleated behind them. They turned and saw a long-whiskered billy goat standing by the corner of the barn. He had his head down and was shaking his whiskers, pawing the ground. He was ready to attack.

Mack Orcon spoke to the farmer. "Chouse Nellie away, Virgil?"

The farmer got a piece of rope, doubled it, and advanced toward the goat, who stood his ground, pawing and snorting. The farmer beat him around the head until the goat finally turned and ran off to stop a hundred yards away, still belligerent.

"That's Nellie Bly," Mack stated. "O'neriest critter this side of the hot spot. I was bendin' over, savvy, lookin' down a well casin'. . . . Well, Nellie sees me an' comes on the dead run, bent double like a comet. She hit me, too."

"She?" Jess was puzzled. "But that's a billy, not a nanny."

"Yeah," affirmed War Dog Smith. "He should be a he, not a she."

But old Mack Orcon had an answer. "My error, men. When he was a kid, I figured it was a nanny, so I named him Nellie Bly. But I turned out wrong an' I left the name on him. Well, I was bent over, see—"

"An' where did Nellie hit you?" War Dog asked.

Old Mack's look was mournful. "Look, you dumb Injun. I'm bent over, see, an' Nellie comes like the wind— He's behin' me. Where could he hit me, 'cept on one place?"

"Go on," continued Jess.

"Well, my haid smacks into that casin'. Lays me out limper'n a catch-rope on a hot July day. Danged goat hit me so hard he bent my spine. But how come you two scissor-bills hear about me bein' sick?"

They were inside and Mack was pouring drinks. The farmer turned out to be Virgil Barnard. He didn't take a drink. He had to get back to his wife, he said; one of the kids wasn't feeling so well—had a touch of summer cold. Barnard apologized to Jess and War Dog and left.

"Me, I see no wife an' children aroun' there," War Dog said.

"Prob'ly hidin' in the root cellar." Mack Orcon downed his whiskey and poured another drink. "Mighty glad you two dropped in. One farmer's shack has got burned—started fire one night a week or so back—an' the rest of the sodbusters play it close to home now."

Jess studied old Mack. "Why the necktie, fellow? An' you got some clean clothes on, too."

Mack assured them he was waiting for company to come that evening. A woman? asked Jess, grinning. To his surprise, the old man assured him rather solemnly that his company would be a woman. He let the matter drop there and they had more to drink. Jess wanted to know where he had obtained Nellie Bly. Mack said he had raised him; he was one of the goats he'd raised up in Canada for sled goats. That led Jess to ask what had happened to old Mack's fish hatchery.

"Danged thing burned down."

War Dog Smith studied him. "You loco, friend? How could a fish place burn down? Water doesn't burn."

Mack pounded the table with his cane. Jess grabbed the bottle and saved it. "You dumb Injun! I had the fish in a big barn. Of course, they was in steel tanks. Well, the barn burned down an' the fish was in the open. I couldn't leave them without a roof!"

"Why not? Other fishes—the wild ones—they don't have roofs over their streams, do they?"

Again the table shook under the cane. "You ever been in a fish hatchery, Injun? Well, the fish are thick in the ponds, danged thick! A man could almost catch one with his paw if he was fast enough. Well, the Injuns aroun' there—not to mention the whites—they stole my fish. I used to lock the barn, but with it gone—burned—"

"What did you do with them?"

"Sold the whole caboodle to a guy who ground them up for fertilizer!" The whiskers quivered on the pointed chin and reminded Jess of Nellie Bly's whiskers. "Now what happened to your face, Jess?"

Jess told him about fighting Hank Carter. Old Mack stared, his mouth open; then he clicked his teeth shut. "Drawed blood already with the big mogul, huh?"

Jess grinned. "He drawed some from me, too."

War Dog spoke. "A buggy outside, men."

"My company!" Mack got to his feet and ran to the door, forgetting his cane. He was in the yard helping the woman from the buckboard when Jess and War Dog reached the porch.

"Oh, Lord," groaned War Dog.

Jess breathed, "The old maid on the stage! Now what the—"

Old Mack helped the spinster down and hugged her and kissed her. "Now, honey, I want you to meet my two friends — Hey, what's the matter with you?"

For the spinster stood and pointed at Jess and War Dog, her forefinger trembling. "Those two men— They held up the stage—one of them whipped that nice Mr. Carter— Are they your friends?"

"*Nice* Mr. Carter!" Mack Orcon's chin whiskers leaped angrily. "That dirty— This is Jess Roberts, Matilda, an' this is War Dog Smith. Oh, I see. . . . You met on the stage out from Watsonville, huh? Boys, this is my sister, Matilda Orcon."

Jess and War Dog bowed.

"She never got married," said Mack.

Jess murmured, "Some man missed getting a great treasure," and for once the spinster smiled.

4

Hank Carter was washing his face in the kitchen of the hotel. He wiped himself carefully with the rough towel, for his face was skinned and sore. He squinted into the mirror and regarded one eye with a slow deliberateness. Jess Roberts had handed him plenty of punishment.

Carter turned and glared at Deputy Hammerburg, who sat on a stool chewing tobacco. "You little— Dang you, Deputy. How come you didn't arrest them two hellions 'stead of lettin' 'em ride out untouched! Look what that tall gink did to my face!"

Hammerburg stopped chewing long enough to say, "You didn't ask me to arrest them, Hank. If'n you'da asked me I'd've clamped handcuffs on 'em."

Carter hung up the towel. He rubbed his jaw slowly. "You wanta remember I swing a lot of influence in this country, Deputy. I could get you outa your job, fella."

"Why don't you do it?"

"You want me to?"

The runty lawman was standing up, anger scrawled tightly across his face. Carter found himself grinning. Hammerburg looked like a banty rooster right to fight a big Plymouth Rock.

"Hang onto your levis, friend," the cowman soothed him. "I was jus' rubbin' your fur the wrong turn, I expect. Nah, you stay here at this job. I'll see to that."

"I do my duty fair an' square," stated Deputy Hammerburg. "I play no favorites. Look at this nester—this one that had his house burn down. Some folks, these farmers especially, claim you or one of your men started that fire." He held up a scrawny hand to silence Carter. "But me, I dug aroun'—I found out that nester's shack had a bad chimney."

Carter nodded.

"You want to swear out a warrant for them two hellions, Carter?"

Carter pondered that. "Might, later on." He went outside and headed for the saloon. Hammerburg wasn't so dumb. The cook had been listening to them, kneading dough on the bread-board, and Hammerburg had put on a good show for the cook's benefit. Hammerburg was smart enough.

Each month, through the mails, he got a hundred dollars in bills, and in ten-dollar notes. There was nothing else in the letter but the hundred dollars. Neither Carter nor the deputy had ever mentioned this matter, but Carter knew that the deputy realized this money came from him. And a hundred bucks was a lot of money to a man who got only fifty per from the county as a deputy.

Yeah, he and Hammerburg knew each other, and respected each other. Carter got a drink. The whiskey bit into his lips where Jess Roberts' knuckles had broken them. Carter didn't look into the mirror back of the bar. He didn't like to look at his face.

"There goes the ol' gal," the bartender said.

Carter turned, holding his whiskey glass, and watched the spinster climb into a buggy driven by a farmer.

"That's ol' Mack Orcon's sister," the barkeeper explained. "She's comin' out to keep house for the ol' hellion. From New York or Philly, I understand. She's the one that was helpin' you. She was hittin' this Jess Roberts over the head with her bumbershoot."

Carter grinned ironically.

"Ol' Mack'd've brained her if he'da seen her helpin' you, Hank."

Carter nodded.

The bartender restocked his shelves with fresh bottles. He spoke from the top of the ladder. "Reckon they hit plenty of water out on that Jensen homestead, Hank. Sodbuster was in here today an' he claimed they had twenty feet already in the casin'. Good water, too, he said; soft water an' good for irrigation."

Again Carter nodded.

The bartender gave up trying to make conversation and went about his work. They were alone in the saloon. Carter took another snort, and his anger against Jess Roberts and War Dog Smith increased in direct ratio to the power of the whiskey. His thoughts were pretty black when a man entered and put his boot on the rail beside him and reached back of the counter for a glass. He took a water glass, not a whiskey glass, and filled it two inches high.

"Hoss kick you, Hank?"

Carter said, "Don't act funny, Pinto; it don't fit your homely mug." He told Pinto Aggler what had happened and his foreman scowled into his glass before emptying it.

"They brought in that Jensen well today, Hank."

Carter said, "So the bartender told me."

"Lots of water, too, they tell me."

Carter snarled, "Forget that damn' well, Pinto!"

Pinto Aggler winked at the bartender and took another drink. He and Carter had moved into the Wishing Springs country some ten years or so before, driving a herd up from the south. Most of that herd had been steers but, strangely, the bovines had had a good calf crop that next spring; a strange fact, indeed. There had been a few small cowmen in that section and gradually they had gone deeper and deeper into debt with small calf crops. Maybe their calf crops deficiencies were due to the strange phenomenon of Carter's steers having calves.

Once an indiscreet cowman had questioned a steer's ability to produce a calf. Carter pointed out that he had some cows, too; the calves belonged to his cows. The cowman patiently counted Carter's cows and found out, to his surprise, that each cow had about three calves, and pointed out that it was a very rare occurrence for a cow to have twin calves and he'd never heard of a cow having triplets.

Carter had killed the cowman in gunplay and been freed by a coroner's jury. After that, he had the rep of a tough man, and other cowmen sold out to him instead of bucking him. He'd been undisputed boss of the Wishing Springs region until old Mack Orcon and his farmers had moved in, almost two years before.

Hank Carter had not paid much attention to the intruders at first, figuring it was only another wildgoose scheme. He was doing all right. He and Pinto Aggler always managed to get a few head of cattle cheap. These cattle invariably bore an out-of-state brand and were usually moving north, heading toward the Canadian line. Pinto Aggler knew almost every brand in the West and he invariably took cattle that came from great distances. These cattle were always poor, tired from the trail, and they bought them cheap. Sometimes they hijacked a herd from the rustlers who had in turn stolen them.

His men would work the brands over to satisfy any errant stock inspector. But stock inspectors seldom, if ever, got that far from the state office; they liked to loaf in the shade come summer, and in the winter time it was too cold to ride. No use bucking snow, was there?

Carter had remarked that the farmers wouldn't stay long. Come the first hot wind and it would cut their crops down and leave only a dried brown stubble. No use fighting them, he'd said; they'd leave when they found it was impossible to farm that dry-land section.

But the farmers—there had been only six of them besides Mack Orcon—had set up headquarters on Virgil Barnard's quarter section. They'd run down a deep well and put in a windmill and pumped it night and day, running the water into a big concrete tank. When the spring moisture had gone and the sun had got real hot, they'd let the water run out of the reservoir.

Barnard's wheat had begun to turn a little brown. When water hit it, it turned green again, despite the hot, torrid sun. It formed heads—huge heads—and that fall for the first time a threshing machine puffed and chugged in Wishing Springs, threshing the wheat.

The farmers made enough off that first crop to stake themselves, and the next spring found barb wire being strung across sagebrush and buckbrush. And Hank Carter had found himself frowning deeply. He'd called on old Mack Orcon.

He'd stepped down, big and arrogant, and started toward the house. From somewhere came the *pat-pat* of running hoofs. He wondered what made such a sound—not a cow, for the sound was too sharp. He went to turn, and something hit him.

Nellie Bly knocked the cowman down. He went over Hank and stopped, belligerent and pawing, and blatted in challenge. Carter, flushed with anger, didn't get up, for he knew the goat would knock him down again if he did. Lying there, he reached for his gun, grabbed it from holster.

"I'll fix you, goat!"

But before he could fire, another goat—this time a human one with long chin whiskers—had jumped on his wrist. The high heels of Justins had ground the cowman's forearm into the gravel and made the gun slide from his fingers. Scrawny fingers had scooped up the Colt.

"Be careful with your firin' arms aroun' here, Carter!"

Carter had gotten slowly to his feet. Anger had flared in him but he'd held it back by a superhuman effort. The situation required logic, not hot-headed temper. He brushed the dirt and gravel from his legs and chest.

"Go 'way, Nellie Bly!" Old Mack spoke roughly.

Nellie Bly blatted and shook his head, whiskers bobbing.

Old Mack shot once, the gravel spouting at Nellie Bly's front feet. Nellie Bly promptly disappeared around the corner and ran up on the hill, where he started to graze unconcernedly. Old Mack turned to Hank Carter. "Cain't you read signs, cowman? I got one down on my gate that says, *Beware of the Goat*."

"Never saw it," lied Carter. He glared up at Nellie Bly. He'd get that goat, later. A rifle bullet—a .30-.30 shell—could knock the critter kicking. The whole thing had gone wrong and a goat had wrecked his plans. Here he'd intended to ride down on this damned well-driller and order him out of the country. But a goat—a stinking ole goat—had butted him to the earth.

"I come to buy you out," Carter said.

But old Mack shook his head. "Not buyin' me out, mister. I've bummed all over this country an' a few others an' this is where I light until my eyes go out. No money can buy me."

"Ten thousand."

"Nope."

Anger had its way with Carter. "You ol' goat," he stormed. "Here I offer you ten thousan' for this spread—ain't more'n five, six thousan' dollars' worth of hay wire to the whole thing."

Old Mack had shaken his head again. "You can offer me a million, cowman, but I won't leave. Me an' my goat—ol' Nellie Bly—"

"Where'd you get that critter?"

The old man had pulled on his chin whiskers. "She was one of my lead goats, up there in the Yukon. She knew the trail, too, an' she was better'n a dog in the harness. Surefooted on the mountain passes an' she sure could pull a sled loaded down with furs."

Hank Carter had stepped back a pace. He was sure now the old recluse was crazy. Humph, hooking a goat to a sled, in the Yukon! Hell, the old war dog probably didn't even know where the Yukon was! He hurriedly brought the talk back to the question at hand.

But old Mack Orcon would not sell out at any price. Carter was angry and a little puzzled; he couldn't understand a man who hadn't a price. Everybody he'd met in his forty-five years had had a price. But this man didn't have. That didn't make sense; you couldn't scare this old goat nor could you buy him.

The cowman decided old Mack was crazy and rode off. But he made the same mistake others had made—if old Mack Orcon was crazy, he was loco in an intelligent manner. For the steam engine chugged and puffed, either drilling a well or digging for water, and the green plots sprang up on Wishing Springs valley's brown surface, showing the miracle of good water and good soil and a good sun.

"A bullet'll drop that ol' man," Carter had told Pinto Aggler. "A bullet can drop that goat, too."

"Forget the goat," advised Aggler. "The ol' fellow is the one we gotta get outa our way."

But old Mack Orcon was wise. He'd had men after him before. They'd tried ambush and never got close enough for a shot. Fact was, once old Mack had smoked Pinto Aggler out of the brush, just as Pinto was sure he had the old welldriller. Pinto had been lucky to get out of that with a whole skin.

Thereupon Hank Carter had pulled in his horns and tried a new angle. He had hired attorneys—smart lawyers—to go through the homestead entries of the farmers, both in the state capital and in Washington, D. C. He wanted to break the homestead patents.

But the entires were all legal. And besides, both the state and federal governments wanted settlers in the West. Carter's money had been wasted. Lawyers had drawn big fees, pulled the case out to cover as much time as possible, and Carter had obtained nothing—absolutely nothing.

He'd growled, "All right, we'll show them some power, Pinto!"

That night he and Pinto Aggler had lit fire to a farmer's cabin and holdings. The farmer and his family had been out on a visit. Their home burned down and so did their barn and toolshed.

"That'll show them we mean business, Pinto."

Carter had settled back and waited for the farmers to come to him with guns. But none came. They pitched in and rebuilt the burned down farm buildings and restaked the farmer's family with clothes and food. None of them had complained to Deputy Sheriff Hammerburg. Were they wise to him? Were they wise to the fact that Hammerburg was in his, Carter's, pay?

Later Carter had heard that a number of farmers had wanted to go against him and his men but that old Mack Orcon had talked them out of it. Now, more than ever before, Carter realized how cagey old Mack was—he was a human fox, sharp and speedy. And he knew that old Mack had something up his sleeve.

What was it?

Now Pinto Aggler downed another drink. "We better eat, Hank, an' pull stakes for the spread."

They ate at the cafe. Aggler grinned and winked at the waitress, who regarded him with a stony face. Carter said, "She didn't like that, Pinto," and stuffed his mouth full of egg.

Aggler shrugged.

They got into their saddles and rode toward the ranch. The late afternoon was quiet with a silence broken only by the sound of the wind in cottonwoods along the coulees and draws and the bawl of an occasional cow.

Pinto Aggler spat tobacco juice. "We got to act soon, Hank. We can't tetch them through the law; that's out. But we gotta hit an' hit hard an' hit soon!"

Hank Carter rode in silence, heavy in his kak. Finally he said, "That's it, Pinto, that's it. He stroked his bottom lip slowly. "There are plenty of ways we can hit. We can burn down more outfits; more houses an' barns. We can burn down haystacks an' break ditches an' tear up fences."

"Yeah, an' blow up a well or two. I know somethin' about powder, Hank. When I was a button, I worked in the coal mines a spell, 'fore I got wise an' pulled out where the air never had no coal-damp in it."

Carter's eyes were speculative as he studied his foreman. "We got some dynamite at the house, too," he said.

"A man could drop a charge down that well—that new one that come in on Jensen's farm—an' cave it in. That'd make them go to all the work of diggin' a new one, Hank."

Carter stroked his lip again.

Pinto Aggler turned in the saddle. He looked toward old Mack Orcon's spread, some miles away. "They got a big storage tank up on that hill, Hank. Concrete it is; dynamite would lift it danged high."

Carter looked across the distance. His eyes were scheming and slow. Finally he spoke again. "We'll hit that Jensen well first. Then, if that don't make them see the light . . ." His voice trailed off.

They loped across Wishing Springs range.

5

They were going into old Mack's house when Nellie Bly, his head down low, charged around the corner of the barn, chasing the dog. The cur gave a frightened yip and scampered under the porch, and Nellie Bly skidded to a stop and regarded them, his goatee wiggling as he solemnly shook his head.

"Where did you get that terrible animal?" Matilda Orcon sounded shocked.

"Terrible animal!" Jess Roberts read all the signs of anger on old Mack's face. "That's Nellie Bly, my lead sled goat, woman. He come outa the frozen wastes with me—a livin' memento of my sojourn in the frozen Ar'tic wastes."

"I heard about that wild scheme!" snorted Matilda.

Jess Roberts winked at War Dog Smith, but that worthy had no wink in return. "This heifer, she cause trouble, Jess," the half-breed whispered.

Jess nodded.

Matilda stood in the middle of the front room, her skinny hands resting belligerently on her flat hips, and she slowly looked around the room. The men stood silent and old Mack had a pained look on his face.

"What a dirty room! Mack Orcon, I haven't seen you for almost thirty years—and you're just as filthy as you were then, if not more so! You can't even see out of those windows, they're so full of cobwebs and covered with dirt."

"I put 'em that-a-way a purpose, Matilda. With a light in here, nobody can see me from the outside—then that gol' durned Hank Carter or his range boss, Pinto Aggler, can't shoot me down outa the night."

"Shoot you down? Why, Mr. Carter—why would that good Mr. Carter want to kill you? Are you—you drunk—or crazy?"

Old Mack looked at Jess and the cowpuncher saw the de-

38

spair on the old man's face. "Maybe I'm wrong," he said. "Maybe Carter is a nice man." He turned to his old pals. "You boys et yet?"

"We et in town," lied Jess.

"You boys can either bunk in the house or out in the granary. I got a couple cots out there."

Jess glanced at Matilda, who was still studying the mess on the floor. "We'll take the granary, Mack."

The three men went outside, leaving Matilda mumbling to herself. Old Mack was cursing under his breath. "The ol' gal's been threatenin' to come out here," he grumbled. "But I sure didn't expect her to get this far from Boston."

"Maybe she'll go back soon," ventured Jess.

"Don't reckon so, Jess. She ain't got no kin but me an' she's said in her letters she'd come to stay. No, don't figure I'll be that fortunate." He snorted, and the sound reminded Jess of Nellie Bly. "That *nice* Mr. Carter, she says. You notice her umbrella? All busted up, wasn't it?"

War Dog told about Matilda lambasting Jess with the umbrella. "She make things worse," the half-breed said. "With both her an Carter—" He shook his jowls doggedly. "Life will be miserable."

Old Mack cursed again. He showed the pair the cots and they unsaddled their horses and lugged their gear inside. War Dog had some pemmican he'd gotten off a Cheyenne buck and he cut off a piece of this, throwing the dried burro meat over to Jess. Old Mack looked closely at them. "Thought you'd et, fellows?"

"We had to get outa the house," Jess said. "We just couldn't stand it any longer." He chewed on the pemmican. It had a good, dry taste.

Old Mack grunted, "Well, you got this place to hide, fellas, but I gotta stay in the house. Hope one of Carter's stray bullets parts her hair for her some time; then maybe it won't be *that nice Mr. Carter.*" He looked at the house again. Matilda was out on the porch, sweeping hard. "Well, here goes Mack Orcon out of chute number two." He bowlegged up the path.

War Dog hit a harder spot in his pemmican. He dug into a tooth and came out with a beebee. "That Cheyenne musta shot that burro with a shotgun, huh?"

"I'd like some coffee," Jess said.

"There is a coffee pot, Jess. Some groceries are on that shelf, too. Maybe somebody has bached here before, huh?"

While Jess lit some fire in the stove his half-breed companion got some water in the coffee pot from the pump. War Dog was grinning when he came back. "That Matilda, she is bawlin' out ol' Mack. I heard her voice when I pumped water."

"That won't last long," Jess grunted. "He's got a temper, that ol' hellion, an' he'll read the act to her pronto."

The half-breed shook his head. "Sometimes a man takes a lot from a woman, Jess."

They had coffee and Jess made some biscuits. They had a fair but far from a first-class meal. Jess Roberts decided he wanted to get out of the Wishing Springs region. With the old maid there, there'd be more trouble— But he couldn't go, not with old Mack stacking a tough outfit like Carter's.

"I'd like to pull out, too, Jess."

Jess rolled over on his bunk. It was good to stretch his bones out and rest. "We'll push things along, War Dog. We'll carry the fight to Hank Carter, if need be. What say we look around a little bit, huh?"

"Saddle up fresh horses, huh? I see old Mack has four in his barn. Me, I like that black one."

Jess shook his head. "A walk would do us good."

Outside, it was rather dark. Nellie Bly was sleeping on the seat of the buckboard, and he lifted his head and looked at them inquisitively. The cur stuck his head out from under the porch and then went back under it again.

"We tell old Mack we go, Jess?"

Jess grinned. "He's got enough on his hands."

They climbed the hill north of old Mack's cabin. The climb was steep, with boulders and loose shale blocking their progress. Buckbrush and wild rosebushes grew on the steep sides. Once War Dog slipped and slid a few feet in the shale. He got up and took his Colt out of leather. He checked the gun, picked some shale from it, then handed it to Jess.

"Got some in my holster."

He took off his gun harness and shook shale out of the holster. Jess said, "There's a trail over there," and they came to a well traveled trail. Evidently men had packed materials over the trail when the farmers had built the concrete water tank on the hill, the tank that held the storage water for irrigation purposes.

They reached the tank and rested. The moon was coming up and below them Wishing Springs range lay in silence, its dark surface marred by darker clumps of sagebrush. Jess noticed that very few lights shone from the homes down there on the basin floor.

Why? Then he understood. The settlers were expecting trouble from Carter's spread; they kept lights doused or behind heavy blinds. And Carter, too, was expecting trouble; the big ranch, far distant and barely discernible despite the bright moonlight, had no lamps, either.

Jess wondered if the farmers—and Carter also—had guards out guarding their property. He supposed they did have. Was there a guard on that reservoir, too? So far he hadn't met one.

They walked around the big tank once. Lots of work had been accomplished to build the tank. It held plenty of water, Jess saw—many thousand gallons of water. It was built of concrete and some of the outer forms were still in place. They climbed up on the ledge and looked into the water. There was plenty of water there. But it would take more than that to irrigate the big basin below successfully.

"They must figure on building other tanks," declared War Dog.

Jess agreed with his partner. It would take many tanks to irrigate the valley. The farmers would have to build more storage places or find a spot back in the hills where they could build a natural reservoir in the ground.

War Dog scowled. "There are no guards around' this, huh? Now what if Hank Carter—or that foreman of his, what's his name—"

"Old Mack said the foreman was named Pinto Aggler."

"Oh, yeah. What if they came to blow this lake up—"

A voice came from behind them. "Stan' where you are, men. Don't reach for them cutters of your'n! Jest stan' there an' stan' still!"

They had both turned. The buckbrush stirred as if a bear were going through it and a man as big as a bear came out. He had a shotgun on them and he had both hammers eared back.

"Who are you?" War Dog asked.

"Don't cut no ice who I am!" The tone was surly. "The farmers posted me here to guard this reservoir. I seen you comin' an' ducked in the bresh. Figured there might be more of you, so I let you mosey aroun' while I scouted the lay of the lan'. What's your deal up here?"

War Dog played dumb. "Deal? What do you mean, huh?"

"You know what I mean. You two gents is Carter men.

You both pack boots an' guns an' I can see you're cowdogs. Why for you nosin' aroun' our water supply? Speak quick!"

Jess Roberts didn't like that shotgun. It wouldn't have been so bad if the hammers hadn't been back—but they were back, and the gent was rather nervous and (maybe) quick on the trigger.

"We come to side our ol' friend Mack Orcon," Jess was quick to state.

Small eyes studied them with a piggish slowness. The man reminded Jess of that jailer down in the jail out of which he and War Dog had broken. He was slow like that man—ox-like in movements, rolling the way a bear rolls when he walks. Now the man laughed softly.

"You cowmen must think us farmers is dumb, men. My eyes ain't that bad that I cain't tell a cowman from a farmer. Hell, you boys is cowdogs—you think I'm blind completely!"

Jess detected an angry note in the man's voice. The shotgun was shifting a little, and the cowpuncher realized that it took mighty little effort to let a hammer drop, for the weapon might have a hair-trigger. A rim of fine sweat formed under the sweatband on his Stetson.

"Hol' onto your temper, sodbuster. We'll mosey down an' see ol' Mack. He'll tell you who we are."

The man debated with himself. "All right; walk ahead of me. Walk down the trail an' don't start nothin' funny, savvy?"

"Old Mack, he be mad at you," warned War Dog Smith.

"I'll chance that, fella."

Jess and War Dog swung around and started down the trail. War Dog was grinning a little. But there was little mirth in Jess Roberts' skinny frame. This sodbuster might get trigger-happy and start shooting. . . .

War Dog slid and fell down. He landed in a sitting position, his feet sliding out from under him as he stepped on loose gravel. The move was unexpected and the guard, following close behind, almost fell over him. War Dog grabbed the shotgun and turned it to one side, so that both barrels blasted holes in the earth.

Jess was on the man. He jumped his broad back and they went down. War Dog had the shotgun and he got to his feet. The farmer, hollering for help, rolled over on Jess, almost crushing him. He got on Jess, sitting on him, and he pounded at Jess' face. Jess brought his knee up and hit the man in the groin. At the same time, the shotgun came down on the farmer's head. He slid off Jess and lay still on the side hill. War Dog squinted along the shotgun's sights.

"Me, I think I bent the barrel, huh?"

"Don't worry about that shotgun!" Jess snapped his words. One of the farmer's blows had landed on his right eye, the one that had turned black from Hank Carter's mauling blow "Did you fall on purpose, you idiot?"

"What you mean?"

"Listen, don't feed me anythin'! Did you sit down there on purpose or did you really accidentally fall?"

War Dog rubbed his nose solemnly. "I confess, Jess. I sit down on purpose. I see the guard close behin' me—I know he fall over me—"

Jess Roberts groaned. "You could've got us both killed, you loco Injun. Why didn't you let him take us to old Mack? Old Mack'd've got us out of the scrape."

War Dog shook his head. "But that would look bad for us, huh? We come here to help ol' Mack an' a dumb farmer, he jump us. Fine help we would make, huh?"

The anger left Jess and he had to grin. The half-breed's words had logic. This way, even though the farmer'd had a shotgun on them, they'd turned the tables on him. The word would get around through the farmers and they'd respect their powers now. Otherwise, had the guard taken them in—

"Old Mack, he come," War Dog said.

The oldster had a rifle in his hand. He panted to a stop and said, "I heerd a shot up this-a-way. Run over to get you boys outa the granary an' you wasn't there, so I hit this way alone— What happened, gents?"

Jess told him. The oldster rocked back on his heels and grabbed his sides, dropping his rifle. He cackled like a hen that had just laid a double-yolked egg. "That big moose is Tiny Williams. He's been braggin' about how tough he is, men! Now wait till the rest of the sodbusters hear how you tricked him! An' he had his shotgun on you all the time, huh?"

" 'Tain't funny to me," said Tiny Williams.

The man was sitting up, feeling gingerly of his scalp. His hands came away with a little blood on them.

"I'm bleedin'."

"Nothin' that a little liniment an' whiskey won't cure." Mack Orcon was helping the rancher to his feet. "These boys come to help us, Tiny. Tall jigger is Jess Roberts an' the short one is War Dog Smith, one of the Smith boys. Reckon you've heered of the Smiths, ain't you?"

"You're not funny, Mack. My head aches."

"Whiskey'll clear that."

They went down the trail, with Tiny Williams stumbling now and then and with short Mack Orcon holding him when he threatened to buckle. The big farmer was mumbling apologies for having jumped Jess and War Dog. Mingled with these words were curse words directed toward the moonlit world at large. Jess accepted the apologies, saying that Tiny had acted correctly, and he let the curses slide off into space. Thus they came into the yard, with short War Dog carrying both the shotgun and old Mack's rifle.

Nellie Bly bleated from her seat on the buggy. The cur scampered off the porch with a bark and sat down, one eye on them and one on Nellie Bly. The door opened and Matilda Orcon was framed there, a butcher knife in her hands.

"Well, what was it, Mack?" she demanded.

"Had a run-in with some Carter hands," lied the old man. "There was some gunplay, but Jess here an' War Dog run the hellions off. Carter an' his men come sneakin' through the brush. They downed Tiny Williams, our guard."

"Oh, heavens, is he dead?"

"You ever see a dead man walk, woman?"

They all went inside the house. Matilda turned the lamp up higher and Tiny Williams sat on a chair. Old Mack Orcon got some hot water and washed the farmer's scalp. He studied the wound.

"Shaved the hair off'n your scalp, Tiny. Bullet musta jus' creased you, huh?"

Matilda looked at the farmer's hat. "Funny, there's no bullet hole in it," she said.

Old Mack acted fighting mad. "Woman, he fell down, an' his hat come off. Then the bullet hit him. His hat was off when that hellion's lead slapped him to sleep. Now maybe you figure that Hank Carter ain't such a *nice* man, huh? Mebbeso you'll catch the stage back to Watsonville an' the railroad an' head back East?"

"No, I won't, and leave you alone with trouble—I'm staying, Mack."

Outside, Nellie Bly bleated.

6

Hank Carter pushed back his plate and said, "All through, woman; clean up," and looked at Pinto Aggler, who was still eating. "Goin' down to the bunkhouse, Pinto." He stopped in the doorway, hat in hand. "Be moonlight tonight, won't it?"

"Later on there'll be a moon."

Carter looked at the heavy Cheyenne squaw who was clearing the table. He frowned heavily. "Be ready to ride, Pinto."

Pinto Aggler nodded.

Carter went outside. The night was dark yet, but he knew the moon would be up in an hour or two. The wind stirred the sagebrush and brought him the quick odor of fresh sage. The boxelder trees moved in the wind, rustling a little, and an owl hooted from the cottonwoods down the gully a piece.

But these peaceful sounds did not register on the big cowman. He realized clearly that action would break loose, and break loose pronto, on that Wishing Springs range. For with Jess Roberts and War Dog Smith on the range . . .

He bowlegged to the bunkhouse. It was the slack season and he had only five hands on the payroll. They were chosen men, and tested men—chosen for their ability to sling a sudden gun, tested by the acrid smell of gunpowder and the high whine of bullets.

They drew top wages and a bonus. He knew they were not loyal to his friendship; they were loyal as long as he paid them top money. When those wages ceased their purchased loyalty would cease, too. He didn't fool himself on this point. This was a dangerous game and soon it would be a wide open game.

One man sat on a bunk, mending some gear with a sewing awl. He looked up and nodded and returned to his chore. Another lay on the bed, reading from an old magazine, the kerosene lamp on the chair beside his pillow. He did not look up, either. Neither did any of the other three who were playing rummy at the table.

Hank Carter growled, "Howdy, men." He got a series of

grunts and nothing more. The place was close, for the wind outside was cold and the windows were all down. Carter stood there a moment, watching them and evaluating them.

Finally he said, "Smokey, we got a little chore an' we need you."

One of the players shoved back his chair. "Dang it, Hank, why couldn't you pick a warm night to ride in?" He was grinning.

"Night might get warm, later on."

The man looked up from his magazine. "Need any help, Hank?"

Carter scowled a little. Then, "Reckon not, Smutty. Not much of a job. You've handled powder, ain't you, Smokey?"

"You mean in bullets or in sticks?"

"Sticks."

"Yeah, I was a powder monkey for a year, up in the Butte copper mines. But me, I didn't like that hole in the ground we worked in. No use gettin' buried before a man's time is up." Smokey tightened his spur leathers and got to his feet. He took his .45 and gun harness from the peg and checked the weapon. This done, he looped the leather around his lanky waist and followed Hank Carter outside.

"Where to, Hank?"

"That new well they just spudded in. The one over at Jensen's."

"Anybody keep an eye on that place today?"

"Jim was up on the rimrock above the Springs. He watched the rigs leave; most of the sodbusters are goin' home over Sunday, I guess. The way he figured, Jensen is at home alone—he's a single man, I reckon."

Smokey nodded. Pinto Aggler, squat and dark, was in the shadows; he moved out now, quick and sure. "Jensen's spread, Hank?"

"That's the turn, Pinto. Get some powder."

Aggler and Smokey went into the night, spur rowels jingling. Hank Carter went into the barn, where he put his Navajo saddle blanket on a big black stud. He smoothed the wrinkles out of the heavy woolen blanket and tossed his saddle up. He rode a Miles City kak with a low cantle and not much swell in the fork.

The stud pawed and wanted to nip him, but Carter batted him on the nose with his palm. He threaded the latigo through the cinch ring and pulled the double rig tight, tying the latigo. Then he hung his back cinch loose and got a spade bit in the stud's mouth, prying apart the grass-stained teeth. He led the animal outside and he was mounted when Pinto Aggler and Smokey returned, carrying something in a sack.

"Get your broncs," ordered Carter.

He sat his saddle and the stud pawed a little. After a few minutes, the other two rode out—Pinto Aggler astraddle a dark blue roan gelding, and Smokey riding a blood bay. None of the three broncs would show up in the dark. They had selected dark horses on purpose.

"One of you boys got spur rowels that rattle like hell," said Carter. His tone showed his irritable nature. "Better stop that rattle."

"Smokey's hooks," explained Pinto Aggler.

Smokey said, "I'll take them off an' tie them to my saddle when we get there. We ain't carryin' much firin' power, Hank, with just the three of us. We shoulda took them other four riders of ours along, huh?"

"We won't need them."

But they swung to the west instead of going east.

Pinto Aggler said, "We're headin' the wrong direction, Hank. Jensen's place is east, fella."

Carter had no answer.

Aggler did not question the ranch owner again. Carter took the lead, loping into darkness, driving his stud with hard rowels. Aggler and Smokey rode behind him a pace, flanking the man on either side. The sound of their horses' hoofs varied according to the texture of the earth over which they rode. On the hard-pan alkali flats their hoofs were loud, and on sand there was only a muffled whisper to bespeak their passing.

Carter rode hard, for he rode against time. Soon the moon would be up, and the deed would have to be finished by that time. They came down a long hill, braced against the pull of their saddles, and then they were on the level bottom land of Wishing Springs basin. They rode for ten minutes more and then Carter pulled in, the darkness of a clump of wild chokecherry trees shielding them.

"Haystacks ahead," the range man murmured. "They belong to a rancher, don't they? Name of Higgins?"

Pinto Aggler understood now. "That's right," he said. "So that's what the can is on your saddle in the sack, huh? Kerosene?" He was down on the ground and untying the sack from Carter's saddle. He got the gallon can out and uncorked it. "Think there will be a guard out, boss?"

Carter said, "There might be—and there might not. Take that big stack there, the one in the center. It should be dry enough to burn good. Them other two might catch fire from that big one—a haystack gets mighty hot when it burns."

Want me to go with him?" asked Smokey.

Carter shrugged. "No need, fella. Lots of haystacks along this strip an' they can't watch them all. They've probably got a guard back on the hill somewhere, but by the time he gets here—"

Pinto Aggler went into the night and disappeared. Hank Carter and Smokey sat their saddles, silent and glum, and waited. From there to Jensen's it was all of five miles. Carter glanced at the eastern rim and hoped the moon would not arrive for some time.

"He's lightin' it," said Smokey.

Carter jerked his gaze back to the biggest haystack. Flame was licking around its base, running around it to encircle it with a girdle of fire. His stud wanted to rear, and Carter slapped him over the heavy neck with his quirt and brought the animal's front feet back to the sod.

The flames spread fast.

Pinto Aggler came running, the sack swinging behind him. "Took the can back," he panted, reaching for his stirrup. His bronc was revealed as spooky against the glare of the fire and Hank Carter reached down to grab the bit close to the horse's mouth. Carter held the beast in a tight grip while Pinto Aggler mounted. "Didn't want to leave the can behin', Carter. Somebody might prove some way that it belonged to you."

"Good, Pinto."

"Ride out!" gritted Smokey.

Rocks and loose soil spouted behind them as they gave their mounts the rowels. They swung south and rode at a hard, determined lope that put the miles behind them. They reached the rim of the hills and rode along this, following a trail carved out by the hoofs of broncs and cattle and wild game. Down below them, a mile or so away, they saw riders, moving through the darkness on swift hoofs. They passed. Hank Carter grinned.

These were hoemen, hurrying to the burning haystacks. They'd start a bucket brigade and get water from the spring and try to save the rest of their stacks from the fire. His decoy had been put out . . . and it was working.

"There they go," growled Pinto Aggler. He turned in the

saddle as they loped ahead, and a grin pulled at his homely face.

Smokey was silent. Hank Carter was silent. The hills came in and held them; they rode through them. Bullberry bushes snapped back at them and a thorn hit Hank Carter in the cheek, hurting him. Jess Roberts' fists had already beaten that cheek enough without a thorn— Carter thought, "I'll get Roberts. I'll get him an' make him pay."

They pulled in suddenly, hidden by buckbrush. A quarter of a mile away, silhouetted by the rising moon, came a handful of riders, heading for the burning haystacks that lighted the sky.

"More sodmen," growled Pinto Aggler.

Smokey murmured, "Wonder if Jensen rode with that bunch? Too dark to identify any of them, wasn't it?"

Aggler spoke. "Me, I couldn't recognize any of them. Could you, boss?" He turned, one hand on his cantle, and looked back at the red winking fire, a slow smile on his lips.

"Too far away," said Hank Carter.

Ten minutes later they were on the ground, their broncs rein-tied. The trio gathered on the edge of a hill and looked at Jensen's farm in front of them. Smokey had tied his noisy spurs to his saddle and silence held them.

The farm buildings lay in a small clearing at the edge of the hills. Cottonwood trees and boxelders surrounded it and protected it from the winter's strong winds and the summer's hot sun. There was a barn—a small affair—and a log house and some necessary outbuildings. No light showed in the house.

"Jensen's out fightin' fire," Pinto Aggler said.

Carter shrugged. "Maybe. . . ."

The well-drilling rig stood between them and the house. The derrick showed spider-like in the now brilliant moonlight; they could even see the steel cables and the clear outlines of the steam engine that furnished the power.

Smokey shifted. "He should have a dog on the grounds, boss. All them sodmen got dogs. Use 'em for hazin' their milk stock around."

"Jim got the dog this afternoon. He was in the brush and the cur came up and he used his piggin' string aroun' the mutt's neck. Choked him to death."

Carter outlined his plan. Smokey, he figured, knew the most about dynamite; he'd plant the powder in the well. Already Smokey was fitting his fuse and fixing the charge.

"Jus' drop it down the casin', Hank. It'll blow the casin' all to hell an' flatten the hole out an' cover it up. What do you boys aim to do while I'm doin' that?"

Carter explained that, too. He'd circle to the right, moving through the brush and trees, and Pinto Aggler would take the left. They'd meet back of the house. That way, if there was a guard, they'd find him and take him out of the way. "But Jensen's prob'ly rid over to the fire, men."

"I'll wait until you signal me," Smokey said.

The brush seemed to reach out and swallow them, concealing them from Smokey's gaze. Carter had his rifle out and Pinto Aggler carried his shortgun. Carter followed a dim trail, crouched a little, stopping now and then to listen. No sounds but the sounds of the wind and the low croak of a frog somewhere; no alien sounds. He went ahead, a big man with a rifle; a man with a stealthy, deadly tread.

He had a tight spot on his spine, a spot about the size of a man's hand. He couldn't help it. If a man was out there in the dark—if there was a guard out— He should have sent his men to rub out this well. He should have stayed at home or at a safe distance. He had hired hands—men hired to do such nefarious work. Why did he ride with his men?

He knew the answer. He had fought for everything he'd gotten; He'd keep on fighting and he'd never ask a man to do something he wouldn't do himself. That was part of his stern code. He'd never ask a man to top off a bronc because he was afraid he couldn't sit him.

He moved ahead with tense grimness. He was alert, every muscle tuned to possible danger. Once he thought he heard a movement ahead. He stood, rifle raised, and waited, but the sound—if it were one—was not repeated. Were his nerves playing him false?

He saw the cabin ahead and he swung around it. He hunkered at the base of a big cottonwood and waited for Pinto Aggler to arrive. What was holding up the fellow? Somewhere a hen clucked. That was in the henhouse, about twenty feet ahead.

Suddenly the roar of a gun broke the stillness. The report did not bring Hank Carter to his feet, but it stiffened the muscles in his thighs as he crouched there at the roots of the cottonwood. Again a gun roared.

"He got me," screamed Pinto Aggler.

The scream came from the brush. Somewhere Hank Carter heard a man moving. He pulled up his rifle and levered three times, building a square of lead against yonder buckbrush. A man came running, carrying his rifle. He came into the clearing and Carter let his hammer fall.

The bullet hit the man as he ran and he poised suddenly, dead on his feet. He stood like that, stiff against the moonlight, and a second ticked by. Then Carter shot again and his second lead knocked the man down.

Carter jammed fresh shells into the rifle's magazine. He heard Pinto Aggler yell, "Did you get him?" and he waited. He heard a noise behind him and his foreman came into the clearing. He held his .45.

"Me, Carter. You get Jensen?"

"I got somebody, Pinto. I don't know whether it's Jensen. Where'd he get you at?"

"He never winged me. I jus' hollered that to keep him from shooting. Evidently he figured I was alone. He moved and your bullets drove him into the open." He cupped his hands to his mouth. "Shoot the powder, fella; shoot it!"

"Okay, fella."

Carter found himself smiling a little. The tension had left him. "You're a wise one, Pinto," he stated. "I figured sure you was done for when you hollered."

"Old trick, boss."

They went to the man who lay with his nose buried in the sand. Pinto Aggler rolled him over and the limp arm flung itself out as it changed position. Aggler said, "Jensen, an' he's plenty dead."

From the well came a dull, muffled boom. Down in the bowels of the dark earth red flame was smashing through heavy pipe-casing. Flame vomited from the open pipe and the earth rose and settled a little, sucking the pipe down into its belly. The well was done with.

Smokey came running. "We gotta get out. This fella dead?"

"Get our broncs!" snapped Hank Carter.

Smokey ran to where their horses were ground-tied. Carter looked at Pinto Aggler. "Throw him acrost your bronc, Pinto."

"What'll we do with him, boss?"

"We gotta get rid of him! That's the first thing—move his carcass outa here. They might think he got killed, then, but without a body—what can they prove? Nothing."

Pinto got the dead man across his shoulder. While he held the farmer's body, Carter got a bucket of water from the henhouse—the water set out for the chickens—and doused the earth. The blood was thinned out by the water and spread out and soaked into the hungry soil without a trace of redness. Nobody could even tell that a man had died there on that spot, a bullet ripping him in two.

They got mounted, and Pinto's bronc reared, because the dead man's smell was in his nostrils. They headed out on a fast lope to the south. Now and then Hank Carter glanced back across the basin. Had they heard the explosion out at the burning haystacks?

He doubted if they had. The sound had been muffled, its real power stifled by its depth in the earth. Also, the men at the haystacks would be working hard—handing buckets down the line, sweating hard and swearing hard. And the distance between the burning stacks and the homestead had been quite a few miles. . . .

Hank Carter looked down at the burning haystacks. Other stacks had caught fire, it looked like; those sodbusters would have a night's job. He was tired and sleepy and he thought of the dead man. He wished that circumstance had not compelled him to kill Jensen.

He didn't want to create any surplus trouble. He only wanted to create trouble enough to scare the farmers out. If he could have done this without killing one of them—or wounding one—well, that would have been better. But now a dead man—a dead nester—bounced over the fork of Pinto Aggler's kak.

One thing was certain. He had hit and hit hard. Tomorrow many a nester wife would harp on her husband to move herself and her family out of Wishing Springs range. They wouldn't know where Jensen had gone, of course; but many would suspect he'd been killed.

Others might think the farmer, scared by the night's doings, had run out of the country, his feet cold. There would be a series of reactions and statements about Jensen's disappearance. Of course he would be suspected of having got rid of Jensen, but what could they prove?

Nothing. . . .

He was sure of that. They came to the deep hills, and the hills reached out and hid them. Carter led the way; his men were silent, riding the rough hills. The wind came in, cold and harsh. Carter silently cursed it.

They buried Jensen back in the badlands. They made his grave under a cut-coulee, using a spade Carter had thoughtfully tied to his saddle, and late night found them back at the ranch.

They had washed Jenson's blood from Pinto Aggler's saddle. They turned their broncs loose after stripping them, and Smokey went to the bunkhouse and Carter and Aggler went to the ranch house.

"I'm sleepy," murmured Aggler.

Carter shook his heavy head. "There won't be much sleep for any of us from here out, Pinto. Not much sleep for any of us."

Pinto Aggler nodded and went into the house.

7

Jess Roberts and War Dog Smith and old Mack Orcon were the first to reach the burning haystacks. By that time the fire had reached a good start. They'd left Tiny Williams to guard the reservoir and hit for their saddles.

Common sense told them four of the stacks were doomed. They could only try to keep the fire from spreading to the other haystacks. They'd carried buckets over and soon, with the other farmers arriving one after another, they had a bucket brigade going.

"No use dousin' water on them haystacks; they're gone." Old Mack was puffing, his whiskers bobbing as he spoke. "Pour the water on the stubble an' keep the fire from turnin' into a prairie fire. 'Caus if'n it does—"

"Wind is rising," hollered a farmer.

Buckets were going up the line full, coming back empty. The wind whipped against the flaming stacks and scattered brands of fire that drove the workers back. Somebody cursed the wind in a low monotone. And still the haystacks crackled. They were red and hot.

Men stomped out the brands that had landed outside the ring of water-soaked soil. The wind settled down a little and everybody breathed easier. But a sullen anger seemed to grip the farmers. That hay was worth money, and the men had depended on it to pull their stock through the hard winter ahead when snow would be banked deep and cover the grass.

The bucket line was working as fast as possible. And Jess Roberts saw that the ground was so wet the fire could not spread unless an exceptionally strong blast of wind whirled brands out beyond the ring of wet soil. And the ring was so big that this would be impossible, or at least so he hoped.

Most of the farmers were newcomers who'd left the big industrial cities of the East to escape the slavery of factory work. They were a little stunned and uncertain; Jess read this in their open, honest faces. He'd gone through a war or two before and he was mentally looking forward to this one. It didn't seem logical to him that Hank Carter would stop at burning a few haystacks.

"Carter's got somethin' else up his sleeve," he told War Dog.

The half-breed wiped sweat from his bronzed forehead. "Me, I think the same, Jess. But what is it?"

Jess scanned the horizon. "No other fires any place," he said. "Maybe we're wrong."

"The spring is goin' dry," a farmer stated.

Jess nodded and allowed they had a good firebreak built, anyway. He went down the line asking one question, "Have you got somebody on guard at home?" and every farmer, it seemed, had either one of his older sons or his wife on guard with a rifle at home. Jess nodded and remarked that had been a wise move. He stopped beside old Mack. "Anybody missin', Mack? Any farmer who ain't here?"

Old Mack studied the line. "All here, I reckon."

Now another farmer spoke. "Young Jensen ain't here, Mack. He's single, you know; he prob'ly stayed home to guard his homestead, seein' he ain't got no kin to tend to that chore. How about another bucketful, fella?"

"Spring's almost dry," the man next in line stated.

Suddenly old Mack stiffened and listened. "What was that?" he said, his voice awed. "The whul earth shaked, didn't it?"

"Maybe Nellie Bly, he bumped into Matilda," War Dog said.

Jess growled, "I felt it too, old Mack. Hell, that was powder somewhere—I've worked in enough minin' camps to know powder when I— You just finished a well over at Jensen's, didn't you?"

Old Mack spat tobacco juice. "Best danged well I ever dug, too. Water seeped right up in the pipe— Hey, that explosion coulda been over to Jensen's, Jess! Hey—"

Already Jess Roberts was running into the brush after his bronc, with War Dog puffing at his heels. They found stirrups and were up; old Mack Orcon was already on his long-legged mule.

"This way," hollered old Mack.

They pulled their broncs around, moonlight flashing from rising spurs. With old Mack whipping the mule for more speed, they hit along the edges of the hills.

"Quite a ways, boys. By the time we get there—"

War Dog rode close to Jess. "Maybe she was the earthquake, Jess. Once in Texas an earthquake shook like that—"

"Might be," Jess admitted. "But I doubt it."

A few of the farmers had hit saddles also and were strung out behind them, pushing their horses across the moonlight. But they were not horsemen, and they were gradually being outdistanced by the hard-riding trio headed by old Mack Orcon, who whipped his dun mule soundly for greater speed.

They came across a flat, their hoofs pounding the hard soil, and old Mack slanted his mule around a bend. Jess saw that the oldster's hat was back, the brim bent by his speed and the wind. He put his hooks to his mount for more speed and pulled in close to the hard-riding oldster.

"How many more miles, Mack?"

The wind whipped the answer away, dissipating the words into nothingness. And the mule pulled ahead again. Jess had ridden mules down South in the rough country of Arizona and New Mexico, but he'd never seen a mule as fast as that of the old man.

Usually a mule, although sure-footed as a goat, was slow on the run compared with a bronc. But this mule sure had plenty of speed. They came to another flat, roared across it, and reached a hill. Jess glanced back and saw that the farmers had been badly outdistanced. Then the rise of the hill hid them from his eyes.

"No fire ahead," hollered War Dog.

Jess said, "That's good." Maybe they were wrong. Had Hank Carter blown up the well surely he'd have set fire to the buildings, wouldn't he? Jess saw now that Carter had plenty of gray matter. Starting those haystacks on fire had been a decoy to pull the farmers to that end of Wishing Springs valley.

"Hit the bresh!" snapped old Mack.

They dropped their reins, and the broncs skidded to a halt. They hit the ground, rifles in hand; they gathered, a tight knot. And in the distance behind them came the roar of hoofs, for the farmers were still riding.

They studied the house in the clearing. "House looks empty," growled Jess.

Suddenly old Mack stuck out a trembling forefinger. "Look see, men!" His voice was harsh.

The well-digging derrick lay on its side. The steam engine had broken loose from its moorings and lay a distance from the derrick.

"They've blasted the well!" Old Mack's voice was harsh. "That was a decoy to get us out at that end of the range—that's why they burned that hay—" He cupped his hands. "Hey, Jensen! We're comin' in! Friends of your'n—"

They waited. The echoes died, and still no answer came. Jess said, "We scout the brush, men; they might have an ambush. We meet back of the house."

They found nothing or nobody in the brush. Farmers were leaving their broncs as Jess and War Dog went in the back door of Jensen's house. The place was empty. "Where's Jensen?" asked old Mack.

Jess shrugged. He had his suspicions. But War Dog Smith was more to the point. "Maybe he fight with them and they kill him, huh?"

Old Mack kicked a chair across the room, where it slid to a halt against the wall. "If they did—Hades, this basin'll rip open, men! Guns will talk an'—" The oldster's face lightened with a new thought. "Mebbeso he got tender feet an' pulled stakes an' left! Hades, he mighta done that. He was mentionin' somethin' about goin' back East."

A farmer called out of the brush, "Okay to come in, Roberts?"

Jess assured him there was no danger. They came into the clearing and to the overturned derrick. They spread out and inspected the derrick. Old Mack, toting his rifle, came out to join them, leaving Jess and War Dog in the house.

War Dog looked at Jess. "What do you think, fella? He leave or he get killed? Hard to tell which, huh?"

They went outside into the brilliant moonlight. "We'll look for tracks, War Dog. You take that side of the brush; I'll take this. We might find something."

The half-breed squinted at the moon. "Hard to find anythin' in this light. Back in the brush, too, it is dark."

Jess had no reply. He was already going into the scattered buckbrush that was marked by the darker branches of wild rose bushes and diamond willows. No use going over there and looking at the derrick. He didn't know anything about derricks; that was old Mack's job.

But he did know something about tracking. All his life had been spent more or less in the open and he knew how to read sign. And War Dog had taught him much about picking out a cold trail and reading what had happened along it. He found the mark of a boot heel in a soft space. The man had been big and heavy, for the imprint was very deep. A man as heavy as Hank Carter would have made an imprint that deep in soil of that hardness, he figured.

But that was no evidence against Carter. A number of men who were as brawny as the big cowman probably rode that range. The track told Jess that one man—and one alone—had recently traversed that dim trail through the brush. He back-tracked and came upon War Dog, also back-tracking.

"One man, I find his tracks. He go aroun' that way." The forearm made a sweep to indicate the man's path through the brush. "He not very heavy; he walk light. I back-track him to here."

They found where three broncs had been in the thick brush. The ground was trampled and pawed as the horses had turned and ground their shoes into the dampness. Jess, on one knee, studied the sign.

"Don't seem to me that them broncs shoulda made so many tracks, War Dog. What do you say?"

The Indian squatted beside him. "One bronc, he been afraid. He circle aroun' an' aroun' before rider get on him. That mean two things, huh? Either he was still wild—not broke well—and he was afraid of his rider; the other, maybe they load something on him—he no like that, an' he tried to get away, huh?"

Jess nodded.

"Maybe they kill Jensen an' tote his body off. The horse, he hate the smell of blood—all horses hate that—and he make a little trouble."

"That might be it." Jess got to his feet. "All right, they've killed Jensen, we'll say. But where at—where is the blood?"

War Dog kept kneeling. "Here something." He poked his forefinger down and brought it up for inspection. "Look, Jess."

Jess looked. "Blood, huh?"

"We track some more," said War Dog.

A few minutes later, they came to a spot where somebody

had recently saturated the earth with water. They knelt and studied that and Jess said, "They've got water from the spring an' poured it here. Maybe they washed away some blood, huh?"

War Dog shrugged. "Might be."

They got up and walked to the house again. The farmers were still at the derrick. They squatted against the house to get out of the wind.

"He dead," War Dog said. "Jensen dead."

Jess nodded. "Sign reads that way. They've toted him back in the hills to bury him, I'd say." He glanced to the badlands. A man could never find a grave back there. "No use lookin', either."

War Dog nodded solemnly.

"We might cut sign on them and then we might not. And if we did find sign, they'd lose us in the rocks—that man Hank Carter's smart an' Pinto Aggler has prob'ly rid a few crooked twists, too. But we could look come mornin'."

"We do that."

Jess took up a leaf and chewed on its stem. "Look, War Dog, look. What if we tell those sodbusters that we figure Jensen got cold feet an' pulled outa the country? Wouldn't that be better than tellin' them we figure somebody notched off the sodman?"

War Dog frowned. "Me, I figure so. If they find out we think him dead—bingo, they go up to fight. Some of them get killed bad, too. They no fighters; they do not know guns."

"We tell them we think Jensen left, huh?"

They went to the men around the derrick. Old Mack was cursing, as usual; another farmer was also giving expression to his anger through loud curses. The rest were wondering if the derrick could be raised and set up again.

Jess spoke. "Can it, Mack?"

The oldster stopped swearing. He ran an appraising eye over the timbers and cables. "Yeah, we kin raise it, son, but it'll be a hard job. What'd you boys find out back there in the bresh?"

A big farmer spoke. "Yea, what did you find out, men?" Jess didn't like the authoritative note in his voice.

"From the way we read sign, Jensen has drifted stakes."

The big farmer boomed, "Figured Jensen had a yeller streak, neighbors. Well, we're better off without him, then. But this well—" He shook his head slowly. "We suffered a great loss when it was dynamited."

"What we goin' do, Mack?" A farmer scowled.

But old Mack didn't get to answer, for the big farmer answered instead. "We oughta unlimber our shootin' pieces an' go over to that ranch an' wipe out Carter an' his den of thieves. That's what we oughta do!"

"You said it, Parr!"

"I'm for it!"

Old Mack held up a scrawny hand. "Not that, men, not that. We get a wire out of Watsonville to the governor for help. We contact the sheriff in Watsonville, an' if he don't act—"

Parr interrupted. "The sheriff won't do nothin'. He's an ol' gent—why the taxpeyers ever elected him again is beyond me; He'll us' say that Hammerburg is deputy here an' Hammerburg will ride out an' look over this place an' that'll be the end of it!"

"We gotta hit Carter," another man repeated doggedly.

Old Mack looked at Jess. "What do you say, fella?"

Jess summed it up neatly. "Carter's got gunmen; you fellows aren't pistol throwers. Fact is, I figure he's hankerin' for you to come to him so he kin wipe you out."

Silence.

"That's true," a man said quietly.

Jess stressed his point. "How do we know Carter blowed up this well? We guess he did, but can we prove it?"

"We don't need proof," growled Parr.

"Go home an' get some shuteye,' said old Mack. "Tonight we'll meet at Red Hen School to talk it over. Set the meetin' for seven o'clock, huh?"

"Make it eight, Mack. We gotta milk an' tend to our chores."

The meeting time was set for eight. Jess saw some of the tension and hair-trigger readiness leave the grim gathering. Old Mack warned them to have their women folks and older kids guarding their spreads. The farmers got their horses and rode out, splitting up and going into the moonlight.

"Who's this Parr gent?" Jess asked.

"Parr Palm, Jess. Got a half-section back of my place. Why ask?"

"He wants trouble, looks like."

"Hot-headed man," old Mack murmured. "What you boys goin' do?"

"You go home," Jess said. "We aim to scout aroun' a little. Meet you at home in an hour or two."

Old Mack studied them, then climbed on his mule and rode off. Jess and War Dog got their broncs. "You notice that Parr man, he got on horse easy," said the half-breed. "He find stirrup an' go up like cowboy. He bowlegged, too. Farmers, they not bowlegged, huh?"

Jess nodded. "I noticed them things, too."

They scouted the rough country, following the signs of the three broncs as they left Jensen's homestead. The found nothing substantial. A freak rainstorm had hit the badlands in the last hour and wiped out all tracks. That was a common occurrence back here, Jess figured; the rain belt would run a mile or so wide, then suddenly stop.

Dawn found them riding into the Orcon farm. When they rode into the yard, Nellie Bly stood in front of the barn door, his head down and swinging. Jess kicked him to one side and then hit him with his quirt. The goat trotted off to one side and looked at the tall cowboy with a new light in his eyes.

"Him no want to fight now," grunted War Dog Smith.

8

Hank Carter had little sleep. He kept remembering a fresh grave back there in the rough country. Sleep came slowly, and two hours later, when the dawn was fresh in the sky, he was up and stirring.

His housekeeper heard him in the kitchen and got up, a massive woman slovenly dressed in a loose nightgown. She stuck her head in the kitchen door. "I get breakfast, Mr. Hank."

Carter was irritable. He said, "Go back to bed. Get outa my sight. I'll make my breakfast."

The squaw looked at him steadily. She knew his mood and his sudden angers. She shrugged and waddled back to her room. Out in the kitchen, she could hear the rattle of pots as Carter worked.

She knew that he and Pinto Aggler had come in late. She wondered where they had been. She knew they had been out causing trouble. But she'd never tell. She didn't care, in fact. Just so her job went on and she got her wages.

Carter was a good cook. He fried the bacon to a turn and

the hot cakes were a golden brown as he flipped them from the skillet. He set the table and then went down the aisle and opened Pinto Aggler's door. "Chuck's on, fella. Make them blankets break open."

"Damn it, Hank, I just got to—"

"Get out—"

Carter went back to the kitchen. He was eating when Pinto Aggler came in, yawning. Pinto sat down and speared a hot cake.

"Wash first," growled Carter.

Aggler looked at him.

"Get out to the pump and get some cold water and wash."

Aggler finally grinned. "You talk to me like my ol' ma used to, Hank. All right, if you say so."

Aggler went outside.

Carter listened to the pump handle squeak as his gunman got his wash water. He was smiling a little, and the smile, strangely, was rather soft and wistful. He and Pinto Aggler had been raised together down in the Strip. Between them was a deep, undying friendship.

Pinto came in, combing his wiry hair. "All right now?" He grinned and took his seat and tied into the hot cakes. Hank Carter nursed his coffee and watched him eat. He pushed back his chair.

Aggler looked at him. "What today, Hank?"

Carter looked down at the floor. "Well, let's sit tight today, fella. We'll see what effect last night has on the sodbusters. Some of them oughta get cold feet and load up and leave Wishing Springs."

Aggler nodded and cut another piece from his hot cake. "We'll see," he repeated. "We'll see."

Carter turned a cigarette and licked it. He blew smoke idly and leaned back. He felt good with the hot coffee inside him and the good breakfast. "We'll scout aroun' a little, Pinto. Later, of course."

He pushed back his chair and got to his feet. He went outside into the raw early sunshine. The sun had no heat and the slow wind was cold with a threat of snow on the high peaks. He glanced up at the mountains and saw traces of white on the highest boulders. Snow made him think of winter and winter made him think of hay and he remembered the haystacks they'd burned.

With them gone, some farmer wouldn't have hay enough to winter his few head of stock. And Carter doubted if that particular farmer would have any money to buy any hay. Not that there would be hay for sale in Wishing Springs valley. The rain had been short that summer and, as a result, grass had been stunted. All of the farmers would need their hay and wouldn't be able to afford to sell any.

Well, he'd burn more stacks, just to make danged sure no farmers woud have too much hay. He'd starve them out through starving their cattle. After they'd gone, he'd have the run of their homesteads; the wells they dug would be his. Already he had men settling on strategic homesteads. When their homestead patents were granted, they'd deed them over to him; in a matter of a year or two, he'd own it legally with deeds filed for each parcel. He figured the nesters were, in reality, working for him.

He'd let them develop wells and irrigation systems and then run them off. Then he'd have the profits of their hard hours of labor. He stood in the doorway of the mess shack and looked at his riders at breakfast.

Smokey was the straw boss, and he slid into the chair beside him. The riders would take the high country and see what they could see. "Ride in pairs of threes and watch your back-trails. These sodmen might be kinda hot under the collar from last night, Smokey."

Smokey grinned. "Us boys can take care of ourselves, boss."

Carter went back to the house. He got hot water from the tea kettle and shaved, using a hand mirror and sitting at the table. The housekeeper was washing the dishes. Carter honed his straight-edge and scraped his whiskers off. He washed his face in cold water.

"Get two horses, Pinto."

Aggler downed his coffee and went outside. Carter went to his room, got his gun belt and gun, and strapped the belt around him, letting the tie-down strings dangle loosely below his holster. He went down to the barn, where Aggler had tossed kaks on two broncs, a buckskin and a sorrel.

The buckskin was a tough beast with a line down his back. Carter went up and the bronc reared, fighting the spade-bit, and Carter took him down with his quirt across the animal's neck. The fight left the buckskin.

Aggler reined the sorrel and asked, "Where to, boss?"

"Town, and a few stops on the way."

They loped out of the ranch, guinea hens running ahead of their broncs. They did not keep watchdogs; the guinea hens were better than watchdogs. They roosted in the high trees surrounding the spread and any movement of a man below in the brush would cause them to begin their terrible racket.

The sun was higher and had some warmth now. But it still hung pretty low to the southern badlands. The buckskin was fresh and the sorrel pounded at his flank, Aggler deep in saddle.

Carter led the way to the flat where the haystacks had been burned. Aggler was frowning a little in wonder. But Carter had no words for him; they just rode down off the hills and came across the hay meadow. The hay was a pile of charred black ashes.

Carter hollered, "Carter and Pinto Aggler, comin' in, guard!" They rode up and stopped their broncs and looked down at the devastation. Carter's heavy face was without emotion and Aggler was wooden-faced and stiff in saddle.

A farmer came out of the brush, rifle in hand. "What do you want, men?" He squatted twenty feet away and covered them with the rifle, holding it low across his right hip.

Carter said, "We didn't come for trouble, Myers. We saw a fire down this way last night from the ranch—"

"From your place, huh? Sure you didn't see it from yonder bresh after you'd set these stacks on fire?"

Carter looked at him and smiled. "My friend, are you implying that I was the one who set these fires?"

"Either you set them, or else some of your hired hellions."

The cowman laughed a little, but there was no mirth in the sound. Pinto Aggler was quiet and deadly as he looked at the rifle. "That damn' fool's got the hammer back, Hank."

Carter was serious. "You talk like a wild man, Myers. What proof have you got that we fired yonder haystacks? Name your proof."

Myers was silent, then, "Well, none, I guess. Only we figure—"

Carter clipped his words. "Don't accuse us, then. We was goin' ride down an' help you, but we got to thinkin' maybe you'd blame this on us, so we stayed at home. We don't want trouble, fellow—"

Myers cut in. "You're lyin', an' you know it. Now get t'hell off'n my grass, or I'll let this hammer fall."

Anger was deep in Carter, but his voice was level. "As you say, friend, as you say. Come on, Pinto." He spoke to the angry farmer. "You've heard of haystacks catchin' afire by themselves, ain't you? You pack hay too green into a stack an' it gets to smolderin' an' hot an' catches fire by itself. Maybe this happened right here."

"Get out!" repeated Myers.

Carter turned his horse and rode off at a walk. He did not glance back. But Pinto Aggler, plainly nervous, glanced back twice. Myers still hunkered them with his rifle on them.

They reached the hills and rode into a coulee. There they could not be seen by Myers. Pinto Aggler said, "Whew, Hank, that was a bad one! Why in the name of hell did you ride down there?"

"Just to see how much damage was done." Carter was smiling a little. "That farmer wouldn't shoot us, Pinto, as long as neither of us reached for a gun. You oughta know that."

"I figgered that but— Well, a man can't be sure."

Carter swung his bronc to the south. They were in the badlands and they met the strip where it had rained. He remarked about this to his foreman. Pinto Aggler scowled and said, "Well, the rain washed out our tracks, all right. It washed them out, it did."

Carter nodded.

"Where we headin' for, Hank?"

"The line camp."

An hour or so later they rode into a clearing. Here was a line camp made of logs with a small log barn. In the winter time Carter had two riders there who turned back cattle that wanted to wander into the badlands. Sometimes a blizzard drove cattle south, and if they got in the badlands they were as good as dead. For there was no grass there and they would freeze to death.

The place seemed deserted. No smoke came from the stovepipe chimney and the door was closed. They rode up to the cabin and dismounted and let their broncs stand with dragging reins. Carter looked into the cabin and said, "Empty," and Pinto Aggler, who had gone into the barn, came back and hunkered beside the wall with, "He ain't here yet."

"He'll come," Carter said.

They settled into silence. A woodpecker started to work on a cottonwood tree, his bill pounding sharply into the hard wood. He made a monotonous rattle. They smoked and Carter felt the sunshine creep into him and warm him. Pinto Aggler dozed a little, sitting flatly on the ground, his back to the rough logs. Carter let him sleep.

The sun rose higher and had more heat. Carter felt drowsy

and the woodpecker worked on, his sounds echoing though the timber. Aggler was breathing heavily, whistling a little through his flat nostrils. Carter felt sleepy himself.

Now he tensed as a man came out of the brush. He was a big man and he carried a Winchester .30-.30 under his arm. He settled beside Carter and said, "Well, how goes things, Hank?"

Carter said, "I knew you were coming."

The man's brows rose. "How?"

"The woodpecker," explained Carter. "He quit workin' when you scared him. He flew over my head. That meant you'd be coming from the north."

The man toyed with the hammer of the rifle. He said, "The nesters are meetin' tonight at the schoolhouse. I'll be there and I'll report to you tomorrow about what is said."

"How did that strike them when they got them haystacks burned?"

The man scowled. "Some of them wanted to fight right now—they wanted to ride over to your spread an' get the fireworks started. I tried to encourage them to do just that, 'cause I know you'd like to get this over with an' I'd lead them farmers into an ambush at your spread."

Carter grinned.

"This newcomer—this Jess Roberts—he talked sense into them, though. Him an' that new fella, War Dog Smith, an' old Mack Orcon." The big farmer scowled. "Me, I don't know what to think about his Roberts fella—"

"What about Jensen? Somebody claimed he left the country."

Heavy eyebrows rose. "Jensen? Hell, I figured you'd let him have some lead, an' he was dead."

But Carter shook his head. "No, when we hit that well, Jensen wasn't there. He must've skipped out of the country."

The rangeman asked about the damage done to the well and if the derrick could be repaired. According to old Mack, it would be impossible to repair the well, but the derrick would be working again in a few days. Carter made arrangements to meet the farmer on the morrow for a report of the activities at the schoolhouse, and the farmer went back into the brush for his horse. Again the woodpecker stopped working and Carter and his range boss were silent for some time. Finally the woodpecker started again.

"Let's ride," Carter said.

They got their broncs and rode down into the basin until

they came to the wagon road running to the post office. They loped along this and caught up with a lumber wagon laden with family belongings.

A skinny man of about fifty sat on the high seat, guiding the team. Beside him was a heavy woman and back on the tarp-covered load rode two boys of about ten and twelve. When the man saw Carter and Aggler he reached back and got his rifle, but the woman grabbed it from his hands.

"Now, Pa—"

Carter said, "We never rode in for trouble, Webber. You leavin' the country, is that it?"

"It's not my doin's," growled Webber. "I'd stay, but the ol' lady—"

The woman cut in with, "Yeah, were leavin', Mr. Carter. I ain't goin' get my man killed by your hands when he's got a wife an' two young uns to take care of! You can have our damn' homestead—"

Carter smiled and leaned back in leather. He winked openly at Pinto Aggler. "Now those are words we like to hear, Missus Webber. I'm glad to hear you took the same avenue of escape also taken by your neighbor, Mr. Jensen. I understand he left the country, too."

Webber's eyes were sharp points. "Yeah, reckon he did leave, huh? Maybe with a lug of hot lead in his brisket, too!"

Carter overlooked that theory. He leaned low from the saddle. "When you get to Watsonville, folks, go to the bank there. You'll find a hundred dollars waitin' for you if you sign a receipt givin' me your homestead rights. A hundred dollars is better than going out of the country empty-handed, ain't it?"

Webber growled something.

The woman said, "We'll take it."

Carter lifted his hat and Pinto Aggler smiled. They loped on, heading into town ahead of the wagon. Carter said, "The sun is good today," and Aggler nodded.

He spoke slowly. "Maybe tomorrow one of us won't see it, huh?"

"Maybe not," affirmed Carter.

9

There was little sleep for Jess Roberts and War Dog Smith and old Mack Orcon. They were up early, with War Dog grumbling, "A man, he no need blankets here—all he needs is a lantern."

"Where's Matilda?" old Mack asked. "She must still be in bed." He was washing and he blew into the water like a whale. "Hell of a sister she is. Here she comes to cook for me—"

"I'm coming, brother."

Jess said under his breath, "Now breakfast is spoiled for us, War Dog. Bad enough to eat old Mack's cookin' without lookin' at his homely sister—"

"What that?" Old Mack peered over his towel. "Repeat that."

"Goin' to be a nice day," said Jess.

The oldtimer peered at him suspiciously. "That ain't what you said, fella. You don't like my cookin' huh?"

"You got me wrong," Jess assured him. He started a fire in the cookstove, breaking willow twigs. When it got going good he put a stick or two of dried cottonwood on the red willows. Soon the water kettle was steaming and soon Matilda was cooking. What she lacked in looks she made up for in culinary skill, Jess soon realized.

The coffee was really good and the hot cakes and eggs superb. War Dog ate without a word, and once old Mack said, "You sure can cook, sis." Jess watched the homely woman smile and guessed that underneath she had a heart as big as the range, although, so it seemed to him, at times she let her sympathy sway her judgment. He remembered her whamming him over the head with her umbrella down in Wishing Springs.

The meal finished Jess went up and got Tiny Williams. The big man was cold and he hurried down the hill for breakfast, leaving Jess on guard. From that point Jess could see the long stretch of the basin. Smoke was lifting from the chimneys as the farmers were getting their morning chow.

A rider was heading out from town, pushing toward old Mack's homestead. Dust boiled behind his loping bronc. Only once did he slow down, and that was to a running walk that only lasted a scant mile or two. Then his spurs were lifting his pony again for greater speed.

Jess finally recognized Deputy Hammerburg. He went down the hill and was standing in the yard when the runty deputy came in, his bronc lathered. The rattle of hoofs brought War Dog Smith and old Mack out of the barn, where they had been saddling some horses.

"You got nits in your pants, Hammerburg?" growled old Mack. "Or are you jus' tryin' to kill off that bit of hossflesh you're astraddle?"

"Neither, old man. But this mornin' I jus' heard that Jensen's well got dynamited last night. That true, old man?"

Jess grinned as he saw old Mack's hackles rise. *Old man*, huh? "Yeah, that's true, *Runt* Hammerburg. The well was blowed in with powder an' my derrick overturned. The well is ruined beyond repair but I can fix up my derrick again. But what's most important, Jensen has disappeared."

"You mean he's gone?"

"Yeah, he's gone."

Hammerburg looked across space, frowning. "Well, he might've pulled out, men. Last week he was tellin' me his gal was writin' to him from Cincinnati an' she wanted him to come back home. He said he had half a mind to pull out an' hitch up with her an' live on her ol' man's farm in Ohio. He's done that, I'd say."

"He tol' you that, huh?" Old Mack was thoughtfully silent for a moment. "Well, seein' he said that, he prob'ly left. Fact is, I hain't seen him for a day or two, at that. Yeah, he's left, then."

"I'm ridin' over there an' look around." Hammerburg turned his bronc. "Just thought I'd get your ideas first, Mack. Hear tell the sodbusters are goin' meet at the Red Hen School tonight. That true?"

Old Mack assured him it was true. He also mentioned that some haystacks had mysteriously caught fire the night before, too. Hammerburg listened with quiet politeness. Jess kept watching the deputy, trying to catalog him. He got the impression that the runt, although apparently mild on the surface, was plenty tough underneath. Where did Hammerburg stand in this trouble?

"Now that was too bad. But I mind now when that hay

was put up, Mack. Powerful green, it were; I'd say it caught fire in the stack—spontaneous something, they call it. Of course, it might have been fired, as you've said."

"That hay never caught fire by itself. You know that as well as I do, *Hammerhead*." Jess knew that old Mack was deliberately getting a rise out of the deputy by calling him *Hammerhead*. A hammerhead was a knot-headed bronc, ornery and runty. He saw the deputy's lips harden but Hammerburg only nodded.

"Maybe you're right, Old Mack. I'll talk with Hank Carter." He shrugged his thin shoulders. "But, hades, I'm powerless unless I have some direct evidence. Mack. When you farmers get some actual evidence—"

"We've heard that before," clipped old Mack.

Matilda came out just then, carrying some dishwater that she dumped on the ground behind the cabin. She was smiling, and she said. "Howdy, Mr. Hammerburg. Certainly a nice day, isn't it?"

"Certainly is, madam."

Matilda entered the house. Her presence had broken the tension. The deputy turned his horse with, "So long, men," and loped off, heading for Jensen's farm. Old Mack spat and glowered after him.

"I'd sure like to read that fella's mind, men. One minute I swear he's for us; next, I'd accuse him of totin' Carter money in his pocket. Well, we'll see for sure sooner or later, huh?"

"We should," acknowledged War Dog.

"Jensen weren't from Ohiey, men. He was from Pennsylvania. Hammerburg's either got him twisted up with some sodbuster or he's ridin' a windy. Well, we gotta get some tools an' head over to that derrick."

The night's rest had slightly refreshed the horses of Jess and War Dog. But still they were not fresh broncs. Old Mack rode a flea-bitten old gray gelding and he had a suitcase full of tools tied to the back of his saddle. They couldn't make any time because the old gray couldn't travel above a trot and, if he could lope, the tools would bounce around, compelling old Mack to slow him down. Jess and War Dog had to hold in their mounts to let the old man keep even with them.

War Dog rode silently. Old Mack tried to pick up a conversation but got no encouragement, so he dropped it. They came to the wagon road and along it came a farmer and his family, their wagon loaded. Old Mack scowled at the load and the two kids sitting on it. "Where you headin' for, Webber?"

The woman answered. "We're leavin', Mack Orcon. An' don't try to talk my man into stayin'! I'd rather have a live husband, such as he is, than have a grave to weep over."

"Goin' back home, huh?"

Old Mack spat tobacco juice.

"Yeah, we're goin' home," the woman assured him.

Old Mack spat again. "Good riddance, Webber. We needs men with backbones here; not men who tremble when their wife rustles their skirt."

"Now, Mack, don't talk that way. You know I'd stay if'n it weren't for the missus. Her health is poor—"

"Healthiest climate in the world is right here, Webber. Well, drift along the trail, man. Good luck."

Webber clucked to the team and the horses continued their plodding. Jess heard the woman scolding her husband as the wagon creaked over the hill. Old Mack's whiskers were jumping up and down as he chewed. That morning Jess had seen Nellie Bly stand in the barn chewing a hamestrap on a harness. Nellie's whiskers had gone that way, too.

"A good woman can make a man an' a poor one break him. Mind I ever tell you about that time in Panama, Jess? Well, it was like this—"

Jess let the old man continue with his story. He'd heard it a dozen times before, but why tell old Mack that? It made the old man feel good to have an audience. Jess looked over the range and wondered just what was what.

For one thing, he held no brief for the farmers. He was a saddleman himself, and he didn't like barb wire. When the farmers came the cattle went. Here he was, siding a bunch of hoemen.

Well, he was doing it for old Mack's sake, not the farmers. True, he'd met most of the sodbusters—they seemed to be nice folks, good folks. Here and there was a weak stalk among them, but weak men could be found any place.

Of course, he had tangled with Hank Carter, and had almost come out second best. There was his personal antipathy toward the big cowman. Jess felt of his black eye and found himself grinning. He'd like to settle with Carter for that. Of course, he'd handed the cowman plenty of punishment, too.

But that didn't influence him much. He was never one to carry a grudge. He'd had his ups and downs; he could take the bumps along with the smooth places. But if Hank Carter pressed him too hard—

There was a way to end the trouble, he was convinced. Now, riding down the lane with War Dog and old Mack, he sought for this method. The law was clearly out of the picture, he knew. Hammerburg was like the wind—he blew in every direction and did not concentrate his forces at any given point. Maybe he did this because of his nature or maybe he did it because of opportunity. He figured that time would tell.

So the law was out—definitely. A few of the farmers would leave, as Webber was leaving; but most of them—ninety per cent of them, anyway—were there to stay. They had no place to move if they'd wanted to move. They'd left nothing in the East to go back to for the simple reason that they hadn't had anything but bad luck during their sojourn there.

And Carter wouldn't leave. He'd been there before the farmers had come and he'd want to stay—he would stay. Jess figured that Hank Carter had a lot to gain if he could run the sodbusters out of the basin. He'd have plenty of wells to provide water for irrigation for hay. And a cowman needed lots of hay that far north when blizzards swept down from the mountains.

Jess reduced the problem to its simplest form. There were two forces—the farmers and Carter—and neither intended to give an inch. At that point, death entered the picture, grim and ghastly. It didn't stand to reason that Carter could kill off all the farmers, but it did stand to reason that the farmers could kill off Carter and his hands, for the pumpkin-rollers had the cowhands outnumbered.

But some sodbusters would get killed, too.

Jess wanted to get done with this chore and head out. He didn't like fences and he didn't like too many people around and to him the basin was over-populated. He didn't cotton to having Matilda around, either. But he would have to bide his time and wait for the break to come.

Four farmers were already at Jensen's farm when they arrived. Old Mack got down, untied his tools, and slipped the bridle from his ancient crowbait, picketing the horse in the grass. The old bronc fell to grazing and the old man opened the suitcase, selecting a large monkey wrench which he handed to Jess, who still sat his horse.

"What'd you want me to do with this, Mack?"

"Get off'n that cayuse, adjust that thar wrench, an' get to work takin' off them bolts, son."

Jess looked at the wrench. He grinned over at War Dog. "You know how to work one of these, fella?"

War Dog reined his horse out of reach. "Me, I know nothin' about him," he stated. "An' I want to know nothin', too. I like to be iggnerant, huh?"

A farmer laughed.

Jess looked down at the wrench. "Don't know the first thing about it. Somebody tol' me you turned this screw here an'—Wup, I dropped it."

Old Mack picked up the wrench and handed it to Jess, who pulled his horse back out of reach. Old Mack stepped ahead and still the horse moved back. Old Mack stopped and glared, his goatee bobbing.

"That bronc ain't ascared of this wrench, Jess! I seen you curry him a little with your off spur rowel! He ain't ascared of it!"

"No, but I am. Once I heard about a man gettin' killed by a wrench."

Old Mack growled, "You're lazy!"

"An' proud of it. Here comes Parr Palm; he'll be glad to use it."

The big farmer dismounted with, "Mornin', men. All set to go, huh? Give me that wrench, Mack, an' I'll start takin' down these bolts with it."

"Jess wants to use it."

"Give it to him," said Jess. "I'll get another . . . maybe."

Old Mack spat and handed the wrench to Parr Palm, who set to work with it. The other farmers also fell to their jobs. Jess and War Dog turned their broncs.

"Where you two goin'?" demanded old Mack.

Jess grunted, "To town, ol' man."

They loped out of the clearing, heading for Wishing Springs. Arms on his hips, old Mack Orcon glared at them in disgust.

War Dog chuckled. "That big farmer—that Parr Palm—he has strength to turn them rusty bolts. Me, I'm too weak for such hard work. My strength could not stand up long." He sighed.

"Neither would mine," added Jess.

10

Hank Carter and Pinto Aggler met Deputy Hammerburg leaving Wishing Springs. The small man was riding as if the devil were on his bronc's tail. But he pulled in when he saw the two cattlemen.

"Where you goin', Hammerburg?" asked Carter.

"Word came into town that Jensen's well got blowed up an' Jensen is missin'. Me, I figure Jensen left the country." Carter noticed the deputy did not venture to guess who had dynamited the well.

"He mentioned he might leave," said Pinto Aggler.

"I'm ridin' out to his spread," Hammerburg stated. "I'm goin' over to where them haystacks got burned, too." He was grinning slowly, the smile spreading across his thin face.

Carter put his hands on his saddle-horn and looked at the deputy. "Them farmers'll try to lay the blame on us cowmen," he said squarely. "We were all at home last night. We watched the fire from our place. We'd've rid down to help put it out, but we figured them sodbusters would be mad an' they might mistake our act an' start some gunplay. Neither me nor my men want any gunplay, Hammerburg. But if the nesters force us—"

"I know, I know!"

Carter spread his hands out, palms up. "That's the way it is with us, fellow. That's it."

Hammerburg brought his shifty gaze on the cowman. "Look, Carter, look. It's this way. My wages is small. That hundred bucks extra each month—"

"What hundred bucks?"

"Why, that hundred you mail me, of course."

Carter looked at Pinto Aggler with bland eyes. His foreman was smiling a little. "What's he talkin' about, Aggler?"

"You got me, Hank."

Hammerburg was mystified; then he caught the joke. He laughed and said, "All right, Hank, all right."

"So long," said Carter.

Hammerburg lifted his hand and put in his hooks and

loped away, dust stirring behind him. Carter and Aggler continued on toward town, riding at a running walk. Carter said, "He's not so iggnerant, Pinto."

Pinto Aggler nodded. "He knows who owns the bread an' butter that he eats. He knows that."

Carter was scowling. Aggler read his boss' face. Carter was wondering where, and when, and how this thing would end. Aggler was wondering about the same things. Then he decided to let Carter do the worrying.

"What if I gave them each a bonus?" asked the cowman. "What would you say to that, Aggler?"

"How big a payment?"

"A hundred bucks to each farmer."

Aggler considered that. "No, they wouldn't leave. Hell, no, not for a hundred. A thousand, yes. I'd say they'd leave for a thousand apiece. They'd deed their land over for that price."

"How many are there?"

Aggler counted on his fingers. "It would cost about thirty thousand, I guess. Maybe less."

Carter's scowl pulled deeper. "Lots of money," he murmured. "Lots of jack, Pinto. Almost break me, it would."

"But think of the investment. Houses an' wells an' fields. That concrete reservoir back of the Orcon place—"

"Lots of money. I'll think it over."

Aggler was silent for some distance. "Maybe they'll sell for less. Start at five hundred; that'll give you room for bargainin'. Yeah, they might take less. Anyway, money ain't worth a damn when a man has a lead slug through his brisket. Nope, money ain't worth nothin' then. No pockets in a shroud in an undertaker's front room."

"It ain't your money," said Carter.

"It's my blood, though."

Carter looked at his range boss. "Don't try to sneak out, fella. 'Cause if you do, an' I catch you, I'll give you some lead wages."

Pinto Aggler hid a lot under his grin. Under it was anger against Hank Carter's domineering tone. But he said, "I won't, Hank; don't worry. When the last shot is fired, I'll be around." His grin widened. "Even if I ain't standin' up, I'll be there."

"Let's mosey along."

The stage was just leaving when they reached Wishing Springs. Carter called to the driver and instructed him to tell the bank in Watsonville to give the hundred dollars to the

Webbers when they went through that town. They watched the stage leave. Carter was smiling a little.

"I'll try to buy them off," he said. "If only some of them sell out, the odds will be that much smaller against us. Fact is, we got about six new men comin' in; oughta be here any day now. Fellow in Cheyenne hired them for me."

"I'm dry," said Aggler.

They went into the town's only saloon. Carter ordered whiskey and Pinto Aggler ordered rum. Carter said, "Why not take a man's drink?" and Aggler said, "This is strong enough for me."

A farmer started into the saloon, saw them, and then went out again without a word. The bartender was frowning.

"You lose trade when we're in here, huh?" Carter snapped the words.

"Well, them farmers—"

"They ain't got no money for liquor!"

The bartender wiped the counter. "A man always has money for whiskey," he opined, "if he's got a taste for it."

"You've made more money off me an' my men than you've made off them farmers. Just remember the years when my spread kept your doors open, before them farmers come into the basin."

The rag stopped moving. The fingers gripping it were tight. "Don't try to run my business, Carter. I'll jam one of these bottles down your gullet, fellow! You maybe can run this range but you can't run my saloon!"

Carter's eyes were bleak.

Pinto Aggler cut in with, "Holy smoke, he's snuffy this mornin'! You sleep on a hard bed last night, friend?"

The bartender laughed. The heaviness disappeared and the air settled down. Carter said, "Have a drink, friend?"

"Don't mind if I do."

The three of them drank. The bartender lowered his glass, looking out the open door. "Coupla waddies ridin' in, men. Them two that had the fight with you yesterday, Hank—that Injun an' that tall gink."

Carter put down his empty glass and turned to look out the doorway, too. Pinto Aggler balanced both elbows back against the bar. "So them's the jiggers, huh? That tall gent, I take it, is Jess Roberts an' the short one is War Dog Smith. They're stoppin' out in front, too, an' tyin' their broncs. They're comin' in here, ain't they? Sure, they're comin' in here!"

Carter's voice was quiet. "Watch them, Pinto."

The bartender said, "No rough stuff in here, Carter. You break anythin' in here an' by hades you're payin' for it!"

"I'll pay," said Carter.

Carter turned back to his drink. Aggler resumed nursing his rum. Jess Roberts and War Dog Smith came across the floor, boot heels pounding, and stood along the bar at Pinto Aggler's left elbow.

"Whiskey," said Jess. "Two of them. One for my partner."

Pinto Aggler felt mean. The rum was hot in his gullet. "What's the matter, Roberts?" he asked. "Your partner too iggnerant to order for hisself?"

Jess Roberts acted as if he'd seen the pair for the first time. "Well, look who's here, War Dog. My ol' friend, Hank Carter, an' probably one of his watchdogs. What's this button's handle, Carter?"

"You lookin' for trouble, Roberts?" asked Carter.

Pinto Aggler put his shoulder toward Jess, who stepped back a little and let the man bump into War Dog, who hadn't seen Jess. Aggler's shoulder hit War Dog in the mouth and the half-breed smashed a fist into Aggler's face.

Aggler went back against Carter, who was reaching for his gun. The foreman knocked Carter back a little, and before Carter could pull his cutter he was looking into the black bore of Jess Roberts' .45.

"Don't pull," warned Jess.

Carter moved back and stood silent. Aggler caught himself, steadied himself, and spat on the floor. He was stunned a little but not hurt much, and Jess saw his eyes clear. The foreman looked at Jess' gun.

"No gunplay," said Jess.

"You're afraid that I'll notch off this Injun, huh?"

Jess said, "He'd kill you, fellow." He stepped ahead. With his free hand he jerked Aggler's gun from leather. He flipped it across the room, the barrel twinkling as the sunlight found it through the window. The gun hit the floor and skidded against the wall.

Jess said, "Work him over, War Dog."

"The pleasure, she is mine, Jess."

Jess stood back and watched. Maybe War Dog got some pleasure out of it but it looked as if Pinto Aggler got some, too. For the foreman looped in a right that sent War Dog staggering away from the bar.

"Don't break that table!" roared the bartender. "Don't bust that—"

"Shut up!" Jess snapped.

The man stood silent, watching. Carter was watching, too. Outside, somebody hollered, "Fight, men, fight! In the saloon—"

Aggler had followed up his advantage. War Dog steadied on his thick legs, then shuffled ahead. He met Aggler and they clinched. War Dog was solid. Jess had wrestled him, and Jess knew the half-breed's great strength. But Aggler met it and matched it and broke free.

They struggled, locked in each other's grip; they went down, rolling over and over. Jess found himself admiring Pinto Aggler's grit and fight. Aggler was whipping War Dog, he saw.

That brought a frown to Jess' forehead. He boiled at Carter's smooth grin. Carter said, "He's beatin' your dog, Jess Roberts! He's got the cur on the run! Break him, Pinto, break him!"

Townsmen were crowding in the doorway to watch. Somebody was hollering for Deputy Hammerburg and somebody hollered back that the lawman was out of town. "He's always gone when we need him!" a woman screeched.

Now the two fighting men rolled against the wall, kicking and hitting. Pinto Aggler was on the bottom. He got his knees up and put them against War Dog. The range boss kicked and tore loose the half-breed's grip. The mighty blow took War Dog to his feet and Aggler rolled over, reaching for his gun that lay ten feet away.

War Dog kicked Aggler on the wrist. He ground a boot heel across the man's hand and pinned his fingers while, with his other leg, he kicked the gun across the room. It clanged against a spittoon and stopped.

"Now fight!" the half-breed panted.

Jess knew that neither man could stand that pace long. Both were visibly tiring, he saw. There was some hard fighting, brief and savage, and Pinto Aggler suddenly went down. He lay on his side.

"No more," the range boss panted. "I got enough, Injun!"

War Dog Smith was not too steady on his boots. Jess got him into a chair beside a poker table. Hank Carter and the bartender were pouring water over Pinto Aggler, who sat with the liquid running down his face and back.

"That's enough water, damn it!"

The bartender looked over a broken chair.

Carter snapped, "I said I'll pay you! My word's good, ain't it?"

The bartender grinned. "Keep your shirt on, Hank."

War Dog and Jess had their drinks on the table. The half-breed rubbed an eye slowly. "Now I have a black eye like yours, huh, Jess?"

Carter heard the man's banter. He looked up with a harsh scowl and War Dog saw his black eye, too. "He got one, too," he said smiling.

Somebody in the crowd laughed. Carter got Pinto Aggler up and they went out without another word, with Pinto Aggler stumbling a little. They went toward the post office.

War Dog grinned. "I whipped him, huh?"

Jess Roberts' long face was serious. "Some people might claim otherwise," he admitted dryly.

11

Jess and War Dog did not return to old Mack's cabin; they went to the derrick at the Jensen farm. The farmers and the old-timer had worked hard and they had done quite a bit toward rebuilding the derrick.

Old Mack dropped a pipe wrench in surprise. "What happened to you, War Dog?" The other farmers crowded around.

"Me, I walk into the butcher shop, down in town. The butcher he think I'm a beef; he start workin' on me with his cleaver."

"That's a danged lie," stated old Mack. "For one thing, they ain't no butcher shop in town."

Jess told them about the fight. A ripple of merriment went through the farmers and one man slapped another on the back in glee.

"So War Dog whipped Fancy Pants, huh?" Old Mack spat a stream of brown liquid. "Like to have seen that, men." He peered at War Dog's swollen face. "But it looks like Pinto did a little dirty work with his knuckles, too."

War Dog grinned. "He get in plenty; he was tough." He

changed the subject to the drill derrick. Old Mack figured they'd have it up in a day or two. They'd put the boiler back on the next day and rig the cables and be set to go. They walked to the length of pipe-casing sticking a foot out of the ground. What had been a drilled well was now shattered pipe and earth.

Jess spoke. "Remember that meetin' tonight at the Red Hen School, farmers. We better get home an' do our chores an' get over there or we'll be late."

They left a farmer to guard the rig, and got in buckboards and in saddles and rode out toward their farms. Old Mack whipped his gray to a long, bouncing trot. He'd left his tools at the derrick and the gray traveled faster, almost keeping up with the tired broncs of Jess and War Dog.

Jess told the old man that it was rumored around town that Hank Carter was offering a thousand dollar bonus to any sodbuster who would sell his deed to him and get out of Wishing Springs. At that news the old man scowled and spat again. When he spoke his goatee bobbed up and down.

"They won't sell, I reckon. 'Course, one or two might shell out, but the rest of them——"

"A thousand bucks," War Dog repeated. "That is much monies, Old Mack."

"This basin'd cost him a small fortune at that rate." They were riding into the yard. "Now if'n this visitor of mine'd been a male instead of a female, all the chores'd been done, 'stead of me havin' to do them."

They got down and unsaddled and turned their broncs into pasture. Old Mack had some extra saddle horses, and instead of being in the pasture, they were tied to the manger eating hay.

"A team to drive over to the schoolhouse, an' a hoss apiece for you two hellions." The old man scratched his head thoughtfully. "One of the farmer kids must've come over an' got them broncs into the barn."

"Oh, Mack. Oh, Mack, please——"

There was a note of urgency in the voice. They went outside the barn and looked around but saw only Nellie Bly, standing in front of the hen-house door. Nellie was looking at the closed door.

"What is it, Matilda?"

"I'm in the hen-house, brother! This goat of yours—he won't let me out! When I start out he lowers his head and charges——"

"Well, I'll be durned," grunted old Mack.

Nellie Bly saw him coming and jumped to one side, but he jumped too slowly. Old Mack's boot thumped against the goat's high ribs and almost knocked him down. "Teach you to take matters into your own hands, you long-whiskered hellion!" He opened the door and Matilda came out, eggs lying in the recess of her apron. "What you doin' in the hen-house, anyway?"

"Gathering eggs, if you must know! You'll have to get rid of that goat, Mack! All day long he's pestered me. When I went out to get the horses in the barn he followed me, and the minute my back was turned, he was butting me! He goes or I go! Now make up your choice quick!"

"You're mad," said old Mack.

"Who wouldn't be! Having a goat—"

Old Mack looked at Nellie Bly, who was watching him closely. He sighed, and Jess pushed an elbow against War Dog's ribs. The half-breed grinned.

"I've had Nellie a long time, Matilda."

"You've had me longer."

"Yeah, but you bin back East. Nellie's been my pal on the trail an' in camp. You an' me has bin separated—"

"Do you choose the goat? Is that it? You like a goat better than you like your own flesh and blood?"

Old Mack held up his hand. "Please, woman, let me finish, please! No, the goat goes. Come mornin' he goes out to the well derrick with me. I'll picket him nights . . . but I'll miss the old cuss."

"Well, I won't. If it hadn't been for him, I'd've had supper on the table, instead of having to stand in that messy hen-house."

"We sure thank you for gettin' the broncs in," said Jess.

Matilda's homely face showed a happy smile. "Well, I knew you boys would be tired. Mr. War Dog, what happened to you?"

"What you mean?"

"You know what I mean! Your face."

"Oh, him. Well, my horse fall, back on a hill. I slide in the gravel; almost break my neck. Skin up my face."

Jess saw that Matilda doubted the story. Old Mack came in with, "He sure took a tail-winder, too, sister. Me, I figured it might kill him; his neck doubled under him. But a half-breed's hard to kill."

"The Sioux in me," grinned War Dog. "My uncle, he Sittin' Bull."

They went to the house. Jess knew that War Dog was no relation to Sitting Bull. Every Sioux he'd met had been related to Sitting Bull . . . according to that particular Indian. War Dog had made that statement just to impress Matilda but Jess figured she was a hard woman to impress.

Gleaming silverware, definitely out of place in the farm cabin, reposed on a gay tablecloth. The tantalizing aromas of cooking food met their nostrils. The floor was so clean a man could eat off it, and for once you could see through the windows that now had heavy curtains that could be pulled together to make a blind at night. Even the chimney of the lamp, which had been black the night before, was dazzling from its perch on the shelf.

Old Mack stared. "What—what happened, woman? Where did all this junk come from?"

"*Junk!*" Matilda snorted angrily. "Don't call my silverware *junk*, Mack Orcon! That silverware is the finest—"

Old Mack swallowed hard and interrupted. "My buttons, but this place is clean." His face fell. "That means I cain't let Nellie Bly in come a cold evenin'?"

"That goat isn't getting into *my* house."

Old Mack looked at Jess. "Her house now," he said slowly. "An' yesterday it was mine. Oh, well, what the hell? Let's eat."

Jess and War Dog enjoyed the meal and were prompt to tell Matilda so. Jess decided that the best way to handle the spinster was to use flattery. As far as that was concerned, wasn't that the best way to handle any woman? War Dog voiced that opinion when he and Jess were putting on clean shirts and levis in their quarters in the granary.

The granary, too, had undergone sudden transformation during the day. Rag rugs covered the floor and a mirror hung from the wall. Two bunks had been moved in; clean bedding covered them. Their shaving equipment was on a shelf along with a wash basin and some clean towels.

"She must've had all this stuff in her big trunk," said War Dog. "She hard worker, Jess. She make some man a good squaw."

"Not me," hurriedly said Jess Roberts.

War Dog and Jess were riding over to the schoolhouse and old Mack and his sister were going in the buckboard. The partners saddled their fresh horses and harnessed the team and hooked the team to the buckboard, tying the animals to the hitch post in front of the house.

Nellie Bly promptly jumped into the buckboard, got behind the seat, and started polishing his horns against the back of the seat, pawing and snorting.

"That goat, he split up ol' Mack an' his sister," stated War Dog philosophically. He and Jess rode out on a trot. The last thing they heard was old Mack cursing Nellie Bly.

Jess looked back. Old Mack, dressed in his best blue suit, had just kicked Nellie Bly out of the seat, and was helping up Matilda. Nellie Bly was standing on the ground eyeing the woman speculatively.

Jess and War Dog rode slowly. They had time to get to the schoolhouse. At the fork, a big man came out of the brush, following a trail that led to the south. He said, "Howdy, men. I'll ride with you."

He was the big farmer, Parr Palm. He was on a big sorrel and he had a bronc-fighter's rig on the animal—a swell-forked kak with bucking rolls. Jess made a mental note that it seemed odd to see a farmer riding a bronc-kicker's saddle and then dismissed the matter.

Palm had heard about the offer Hank Carter had made to buy out the farmers. They talked about this and Palm said he'd sell out for a thousand bucks, any day. Of course, he had more than that invested in his homestead, but water hadn't reached him yet, and he didn't know when it would get there—he might never get a well if the rig got blown up now and then.

"Maybe Hank Carter give up," volunteered War Dog.

The farmer shook his head slowly. No, he figured it was a fight to the finish, unless, of course, the farmers elected to sell out. He was rather gloomy about the whole affair. From what he'd heard, six new hands had signed on at Carter's ranch.

"An' he ain't hired them to punch cows, men. He's hired 'em to sling sudden guns against us plowhandlers."

Jess admitted that the situation was dark. He wondered if Carter would come to the meeting. Palm said he doubted if Carter would attend.

"Feelin's runnin' high against Carter, Roberts. Many a man thinks that Jensen got killed an' they've planted him somewhere in a secret grave. Webber pulled out, you know. That su'prised me, too. I figured he'd stay sure, but his ol' woman got puttin' the pressure on him—"

"You married?" Jess asked.

"Hell, no. Think I'm plumb loco!"

The Red Hen School was situated in the cottonwoods along Red Hen Creek, a stream that bore a little water in the spring and then remained dry the rest of the year. Horses were tied to the hitchrack and to the wing and the chute-the-chute. Jess saw that quite a few farmers had already arrived. Some had saddle horses, but most of them must have brought their families, for the buckboards were more numerous than the saddle broncs.

They tied their horses to a stout clump of diamond willows and went inside, where the squeaky tones of a violin and mouth-harp rode the night air. Kerosene lamps, sputtering each time the door was opened, hung in brackets from the walls. There was audible only the shuffle of feet and the squeaking of the violin and the mouth-harp—the people were dancing until the meeting started.

Parr Palm moved across the room to talk to some farmers and Jess and War Dog stood beside the door, watching the dance. Jess saw a pretty girl on a bench and said, "Here goes, friend. I'll see you."

"Always chasin' the womens huh?"

The girl, who turned out to be a farmer's daughter, smiled and said, "Why not?" and she and Jess slid out on the floor. She introduced Jess to another girl, and while dancing with her, Jess saw War Dog dancing with Matilda.

"My God," he said.

"You talking to me, Mr. Roberts?"

"Oh, no, no! But look at that. Look at my partner!" Jess swung the girl around so she could see War Dog and Matilda.

"She's taller than he is."

"Yeah, about a foot. Look at his face."

"He's in pain, isn't he?"

"He looks it."

The dance ended and Jess escorted his partner to her bench and bowed in thanks. Old Mack Orcon had gone to the front of the room. Now he beat on the desk with a pointer-stick evidently used by the teacher.

"Order, ladies and gentlemen, order. No more music, please. We must consider the business of the evening, ladies and gentlemen."

War Dog wiped his forehead. He allowed it was awful hot

in there. Jess said it was too cold. "You got het up dancin'," he said.

"I could not help it. She said, 'You dance with me, Mr. War Dog?' an' there we was, goin' 'roun' an' 'roun'."

Desks were being moved back into the center of the room. Farmers sat on top of them and the smaller women sat on the seats, for the men were too big to get behind the desk in these seats, made for kids. Chairs were brought out and again old Mack called for order. Finally the room settled down and the old man started talking.

He resumed the past events, including the dynamiting of the well and the disappearance of Jensen. This latter story caused a grumble to run through the assembly. The old man beat again with the hardwood pointer and silenced the crowd. Various farmers got up and spoke, some urging further negotiations with Carter, others urging that they ride over and clean out Carter's spread at once.

Parr Palm held the floor for the longest time. He stressed his friendship for each and every one of them. He was a good talker, Jess realized. Palm begged them to go slowly, to consider the offer made by Hank Carter to buy out their homestead patents.

A farmer got to his feet. "Maybe Carter won't pay us a thousan' bucks, men. Me, I've never heard of Carter offerin' anybody that. Maybe all that talk is jus' a rumor?"

Old Mack hammered with the pointer. "Now don't jump up an' talk outa turn, Jackson! Mind you that Parr Palm's got the floor! This meetin' is goin' be held regular or not at all!"

"I apologize, old Mack."

"Apologies accepted. Go on, Parr Palm."

"Me, I've had my say, men. But they's a man over by the door that might have a few words to say. How about it, Deputy Hammerburg?"

Jess had seen the deputy come in during Palm's plea for peace. Now Hammerburg went up the aisle, moving with a small man's assumed importance. He liked the center of the stage, evidently.

Old Hank acknowledged the deputy and asked him to proceed. Hammerburg cleared his throat and reminded them that, after all, he was their servant—their public servant. He wanted them to always remember that. He wanted no violence except in defense of property and life itself. His tone was slow and laden with friendship.

"We know all that," a man hollered. "Now tell us somethin' we don't know, fella? Don't rehash that ol' stuff."

"Silence!" hollered old Mack. "Who said that?" He peered over his specs, his goatee bristling.

No answer.

Hammerburg said, "It makes no difference who said it, friend. Perhaps the man was correct, sir. My duties took me to call on Hank Carter. In fact, I just came from his ranch. When I came in the door, Parr Palm was mentioning that Carter had offered a thousand dollars apiece for each of your homestead entries if you held a deed to your property. One man remarked that this was prob'ly a rumor. I can assure you it is no idle rumor."

The deputy stopped and wet his lips. Jess saw that the small man knew how to build up to a climax.

"Proceed," ordered old Mack.

"Hank Carter asked me to ride over here and attend this meeting. He would have come himself but—well, he was afraid you'd mob him. He would have sent his foreman, Pinto Aggler, but Mr. Aggler does not feel well tonight."

Everybody turned and looked at War Dog Smith. "Hurray for War Dog," a man said.

War Dog flushed a little.

Again Hammerburg spoke. "So I am repeating what Hank Carter tol' me to tell you men an' women: for each homestead entry he will pay a thousand dollars cash. These entries must show a deed to the property in question. He will not buy any land that the homesteader has not proved up on. He buys only property with a deed."

There was silence. Finally a man stood up. Old Mack let him have the floor. The man said they all had their deeds. He wanted the farmers to discuss the question among themselves.

Parr Palm said he was in favor of selling. The water was slow to reach his land and his soil was no good without irrigation. This got old Mack's dander up and he said that water would get to each place as soon as they could build ditches and dig wells. Parr Palm again took the floor and stated he would sell. He forced the issue to a vote and less than one half the farmers were in favor of selling out. Jess watched Palm's heavy face as he counted hands.

Palm sat down.

Now another farmer took the floor. He wanted them to think it over for a week and then, inside of seven days, to meet again at the schoolhouse and call for a vote. This proposition drew a lot of support and old Mack adjourned the meeting then and there after a vote had insured another gathering inside of a week. Farmers and their families went out, talking and discussing the issue.

"I still maintain we should sell," argued Parr Palm.

War Dog nudged Jess. "Him, he sure wants to peddle his stuff, huh? He wants to get out, huh?"

Jess scowled. " 'Pears that way, War Dog."

12

Jess watched Parr Palm and Deputy Hammerburg leave the hall. Matilda and old Hank talked with him and War Dog for a while. The spinster's face showed excitement. "Such nice people, these farmers. If only Mr. Carter could really get to know them, he'd stop fightin' them!"

Jess nodded.

Matilda went over to talk to Mrs. Jackson. "She got lot to learn," opined War Dog. "Hank Carter doesn't care about how nice the farmers are. He wants their land, that's all."

Jess and his saddle pal went outside. Rigs were leaving in the moonlight. Jess looked over the horizon and saw no fires. He had figured that, with most of the farmers at the meeting, Carter might have taken up burning again. But maybe Carter was laying off for a spell, waiting to hear the verdict of the farmers on his proposal to buy out their properties.

"There goes Hammerburg," said War Dog.

Jess saw that the deputy rode a black gelding, a horse with a good bottom and long legs. Hammerburg rode into the brush. He switched his gaze back to Parr Palm, who also rode a black horse. Palm was going to the west.

"Let's do some ridin'," murmured Jess Roberts.

He and War Dog found stirrups and turned their broncs around, riding out of the clearing. Jess led the way. They did not ride toward the homestead of old Mack Orcon. They rode south toward the high hills.

"Where we go?" War Dog asked.

Jess pulled in. They were in a clump of high buckbrush. "Look, War Dog, look. We'll say you are Hank Carter. You're fightin' the farmers. You want to know what they say when they meet, what they intend to do, don't you?"

"Sure."

"Well?"

War Dog leaned against his cantle, smiling suddenly. "I understand, Jess. You think maybe there's a spy in the farmers somewhere—one of them, maybe—?"

"Carter's no fool."

War Dog frowned. He started to rub his jaw and stopped suddenly. His jaw was sore from that roundhouse right of Pinto Aggler's. "Who you think he is?"

Jess shrugged. "I don't know. Might be Hammerburg, huh?"

"Might be. He's like a snake—a little water-snake. But still, he carries a badge, Jess."

Jess allowed that lots of star-toters were crooks at heart. Some of them only packed a law-star because they could then legally go about their dirty work. Maybe Hammerburg was that type.

"But he no go to all the meetin's, huh?"

This observation set Jess back a little. He remembered that old Mack had told him that Hammerburg never attended all the meetings of the farmers. Was there another man—a farmer himself—who worked for Carter?

"This Parr Palm, Jess. Me, I don't like him. He no farmer. He ride a bronc-kicker's saddle an' rides like a cowman."

"I'm watchin' him, War Dog."

War Dog pointed below them. A rider was following a hill trail, and in the moonlight, Jess could see the man was Parr Palm on his big black. "That him now," War Dog stated.

"He sure ain't goin' to his homestead," growled Jess Roberts. "He's headin' back into the badlands. What say we follow him, pard?"

"Play hunch, huh?"

They swung to higher ground and followed the ridges. Below them lay Wishing Springs basin, slumbering under the moonlight. Dark spots moved across it with incredible slowness. Those spots were the rigs of the farmers as they returned to their homesteads.

But no fires lapped hungry red tongues into the sky. The seriousness of the situation drew a fine line across Jess Roberts' forehead. He had the feeling that the whole setup would break apart under some slight pressure and war would really move across that grass.

Who would apply that pressure? Would it be the farmers carrying the fight to Hank Carter and Pinto Aggler? Many of the sodbusters were ready to fight right now, he knew. Only the presence of the more mature and more level-headed plowmen had kept peace so far.

Or would Carter and his men provide the spark that would turn the valley into a battlefield? Carter was shipping in more gunmen. . . . Day by day, then, the man-to-man odds were growing against the farmers. Maybe some of them were right. Maybe it would be best to hit now before more reinforcements should be hired by Hank Carter.

Jess realized he and War Dog really had nothing at stake there in the Wishing Springs basin. They owned no land nor any water; they had no woman or child there. They had only their friendship for old Mack Orcon.

But Jess knew all the time that it went deeper than that. Sure, he and War Dog were old Mack's friends; old Mack had practically raised him, given him a home. Sure, the old fellow had had some crazy schemes, but he was old Mack nonetheless, schemes or no schemes. And Jess knew he was as smart as they came.

He had tangled with Hank Carter, fought with the arrogant, domineering man. He had that to settle with Carter. And Pinto Aggler had tangled with War Dog Smith. War Dog had a score to settle there, too.

"There he go," murmured the half-breed.

They had left their broncs and were hunkering in the dark shadow of a giant sandstone that sat on top of a high hill. Below them stretched the labyrinth that was the badlands—somnolent and somber under the moon. The smell of greasewood and juniper was keen on the cold night air.

"Still goin' south," Jess said.

War Dog lifted his forefinger and pointed. "Another rider he come, Jess. They meet, too."

Parr Palm had drawn his horse off the trail and now he sat in a clump of brush. The other rider also rode a black. Parr Palm came out of the brush and the two riders talked and then rode south together.

"Who that other man?"

"Looked to me like Deputy Hammerburg." Jess said, frowning. "Now what is that sawed off runt doin' back here?"

War Dog shrugged.

Jess knew now they were on a hot trail. Palm and Hammerburg had ridden different trails when they'd left the Red Hen School and now they'd met again. And he figured they hadn't met by accident; the meeting had been prearranged. They got their horses and rode south again, letting the rise of the hill hide them from the two men who rode on the trail in the gully.

"Clouds comin'," said War Dog.

And the half-breed was right. The wind came up and moved clouds across the moon, dark and ominous. The clouds stifled the light and turned the range pitch black.

"Maybe they go soon, huh, Jess?"

Jess looked upward. More clouds had moved off the horizon, and he figured the rest of the night would be dark. A drop of rain hit him on the cheek. He silently cursed the luck.

The trail was dead; the range was pitch black. No man could trail on a night such as this had turned out to be. Again, rain hit him; he took his slicker off the back of his saddle.

Suddenly the storm lashed across the badlands, pounding the earth with small pellets of hail. The saddle pals were forced to find a hiding place under a ledge of sandstone that arched out and made a natural roof. They led their broncs under this and hunkered in silence, rain running off the sandstones.

The hail had stopped and rain thundered down, and the sky was split by cracks of lightning and the rumble of thunder. For over an hour it rained and most of the time it rained hard. Jess wondered if the water would drain into Wishing Springs basin. He decided it wouldn't. They were across the divide and the water would drain south into Wind River.

Had it run north, damns in coulees could have been constructed, holding the water for irrigation. That would have made wells unnecessary. But the water drained south. Now he saw why Wishing Springs was always so dry. The divide turned the wind, making what rain there was drop on the other side; the valley therefore got little moisture. A fickle goddess of the weather, he decided, had played a mean trick on Wishing Springs basin.

"When will she stop?" asked War Dog.

Jess shrugged and said he didn't know. But he did know one thing: there'd be no more trailing that night. The rain fell back a little and the partners rode down the slope, heading back toward the basin. Within a mile the rain had stopped and the ground was bone-dry.

"No rain here," marveled War Dog. "Why not, I wonder?"

"The divide turned it back," Jess explained. He was tying his slicker back to his saddle. War Dog was also shedding his oilskin.

They decided to ride over to Parr Palm's homestead and wait there until the man rode back. Jess hit the lead, with War Dog at his horse's flank. The tall cowpuncher was puzzled.

Had they been nosing out a hot trail? He wondered about that. Maybe they were wrong— Yet Hammerburg and Palm had left Red Hen School by different routes; back there in the badlands they'd met and ridden on—

They came to Palm's homestead. The place was along the edge of the hills. They got off their broncs and hunkered in a draw where their horses were hidden by a cut-coulee. War Dog was grumbling and Jess wished he were home in bed.

Almost two hours later, Parr Palm rode into the yard, now colored by the light of the sinking moon. He unsaddled his bronc, turned the animal loose, and slung his saddle over a rail in the fence before he went into the cabin. He did not light a lamp but evidently undressed and went to bed in the dark.

"He had a slicker on," mumbled War Dog. "That means he was back in the rain, Jess."

Jess Roberts nodded. He said, "Well, we found out exactly nothin', War Dog." They rode up the coulee and crossed the hills and came down on the basin floor. "We'll talk with old Mack come mornin'."

They rode at a lope. Jess was tired of the saddle, tired of the trail; so was his partner. They loped across a neck of land and then they saw a rider coming toward them. The partners pulled in and waited.

The rider was Deputy Hammerburg. He wore a yellow slicker and his Stetson was still wet. "Where t'hell'd you fin' the rain?" asked Jess. "We ain't had none here in the valley."

"Been over in the hills. Thought I'd get up high so I could keep an eye on the basin so's if'n a fire did start— You two are up late, huh?"

Jess realized the deputy's statements could not be challenged. He knew that if he were the lawman there he'd have a high point from which he could watch the valley. Maybe he was wrong about the whole thing. Maybe Hammerburg was honest.

But why had the deputy met up with Parr Palm? And where had the two ridden?

Jess decided to let it all ride. He had a hunch something would break soon. Come daylight, he and War Dog would scout the high country. "We took a coppla farmers' girls home," he said, grinning.

"Up late spoonin', huh?" Hammerburg jabbed a thumb against War Dog's ribs. "You ol' Injun, you! If'n you're as handy with your tongue as you are with your dukes, heaven help them girls!"

"So long," said Jess.

They rode on. Once Jess glanced back. Hammerburg was sitting where they'd left him and he was watching them. The next time Jess looked back the deputy was loping toward town.

War Dog frowned and stayed silent. Dawn was close when they rode into old Mack's homestead, unstripped their broncs, and clomped into the granary. War Dog pulled off his boots and rolled into bed dressed.

"Mornin' come too soon. No use undressin', Jess."

13

When Hank Carter and Pinto Aggler rode away from the badland line-camp the rain had stopped. "Looks like it's over with, Hank," the foreman said.

"Jus' beginnin'," growled the ranch owner.

"I don't mean this trouble, Hank." Aggler was grinning crookedly. "I mean the rain, fella."

Carter loafed in his saddle. "So they want time to talk over whether they'll sell or not, huh? That's their deal, huh? What do you think, Pinto? Think they'll sell to me?"

"Why ask me?"

"You oughta be good for somethin', Pinto. You sure ain't no good for fightin'. The way that half-breed whupped you—"

"Forget that!" Aggler's voice was dangerous.

Hank Carter found himself smiling. He liked to rib his foreman, for Aggler had a thin skin. "Yeah, some of them want to sell, from what Hammerburg an' Palm said tonight. Maybe I oughta talk to each farmer alone, peaceful like."

Aggler's laugh was short. "You'd play hell doin' that, an' you know it. Some of them plow-handlers are loaded for b'ar, Hank. You ride into their yard an' some one of 'em might run hot lead through your gullet!"

Carter was frowning. "Reckon that's the truth, huh. Well, what say we post some notices downtown an' on fences? I'll get some printed tomorrow an' we'll get some of the boys to nail them up."

"Don't ask me. I'm no bill-boy!"

Carter laughed a little at that. His laugh died and they rode at a walk, the footing of their broncs uncertain on the slippery terrain. They left the rainy belt and came down out of the hills, heading for the home ranch. Now Carter laughed again, a slow, harsh sound.

"I'll see to it that they make up their minds to sell, and sell pronto. I'll make them damned glad to sell out to me at any price! Sure, we'll post them notices—that'll make it look like we want peace. But our left hand won't know what our right hand's doin', an' you kin bet on that!"

"What's the play, Hank?"

"We take the fight to 'em again, Pinto. We'll push them a little an, make them think a little faster. Fire has a way of makin' a man do some tall thinkin', 'specially if a man is settin' them fires an' they're not accidents."

"They'll be on guard."

"We got men. We got guns."

Pinto Aggler was silent for a long moment. They came into the ranch and came down and turned their broncs over to the hostler. Dawn would be here soon, coming out of a cloudless sky. They went into the house and hit their sougans.

Next forenoon they rode into Wishing Springs, where they climbed on the stage and went to Watsonville. When they came back Carter had some placards printed that announced in huge type that for each and every deed he would pay one thousand dollars. He hired a town loafer to put up the notices in the post office and the saloon and the store, and soon townsmen and nesters were gathered around and reading the notices. Carter and Aggler went into the saloon.

"How much I owe you?" Carter asked the bartender.

The man had itemized the broken items. One chair

smashed beyond repair, a leg broken from a card table—Carter cut in with, "T'hell with what was broken. How much was the bill?"

The man told him. Carter peeled bills off a roll and grinned. "By rights, ol' Mack Orcon oughta pay half of that bill—his hand helped bust that furniture." He was in a good mood.

Aggler grinned. "You dock that out of my wages, Hank?"

"Hell, if I docked you for everythin' you broke up, you'd never have any wages. You'd owe me money, fella. Whiskey for me. Rye. An' you, Pinto?"

"Rum."

Carter groaned. "How can you drink that hogwash?" He downed his whiskey and poured another. A farmer came into the saloon. He was a small man with a skinny face and a prominent Adam's apple.

"I'd like to talk to you, Carter."

Carter shoved over his bottle. The bartender slid out another glass. "Have a drink, Windon. How goes things across the basin, huh?"

"Not so good, Carter. Fact is, I don't know when, if ever, I'll get water on my land. An' a man can't dry-land farm in this country; not enough moisture."

"You want to sell and get out, Windon?"

Windon cleared his throat, his Adam's apple bobbing. "Well, that was my idea, Carter. I don't cotton to trouble; I'm a peaceful man. I seen your sign down in the post office. Me, I voted last night for sellin' out; they voted us down. I got the deed to my quarter section with me."

"Let's see it?"

The farmer dug into the inside pocket of his ragged coat and brought out the legal document. Carter spread it out and glanced through it. "You got a pen, bartender?" Then to Windon, "You sign there."

"I got a pen," said Windon. "Even got a bottle of ink in my pocket. Jus' bought some down to the store for the kid when school starts."

The farmer fitted a pen point to the wooden pen and uncorked the ink he'd taken from a bundle he carried. Carter knew the man was lying: he'd bought that ink for just that purpose, not for his kid when school started. Windon scrawled his signature on the deed, transferring his rights to Carter, who also signed. Then Carter wrote a check on the Watsonville bank.

The farmer studied the check. "Place cost me lots more than that," he said slowly. "But maybe I wasn't cut out to be a plowman. I'm headin' back to Toledo to the shoe factory. Hope they got my ol' job open for me." He folded the check and put it carefully in his wallet. "You kin take possession anytime tomorrow. We're packed to leave."

"Wish more farmers had your brains," Carter said. " 'Nother drink?"

The farmer drank again and left. Outside, there was a sudden commotion. "Looks like a fight," said the bartender, who stood where he could see out the open door.

Carter and Aggler went outside. A big man, evidently a farmer, had just knocked Windon down. Windon sat in the dust, spitting blood; the big man stood on the edge of the sidewalk.

"You danged turncoat," the big farmer growled. "Me an' you come into this section from that damn' Toledo shoe factory. We got tired of the stink of leather an' sewin' on expensive shoes we never could hope to buy with our slave wages. Now you belly out from under—"

"But, Myers—"

"Don't talk to me, you yeller-belly! I should be glad to see you go; you'd be no 'count in a fight. So you sold out to that pistol-totin', ignorant jackass of a Hank Carter, huh? Why, you—"

Carter's hand had jerked Myers around. Carter's left fist came up—a hard jolting blow—and landed unexpectedly on Myers' jaw. Myers went back, his arms flailing, and Carter followed, dropping the farmer with twin blows.

The cowman stepped back. "You talkin' about me, Myers?"

Myers looked at Carter, then at Pinto Aggler. Both men had their hands close to their guns. Fear came into him and washed color from his tanned face. "You don't give a man a chance!" he accused Carter.

"Keep your mouth closed aroun' me!" snapped Hank.

Windon stood in the street. He pleaded, "Don't pull on him, Carter! He's a good man; he's jus' had a drink too many. We was raised together in Toledo—we played together as kids—"

"Close your mouth!" ordered Carter.

Windon stood silent. Other men were silent, too. For one terrible moment, naked brutality was in the air; Carter lifted his pistol a little from leather, and Myers' face was the color of a dirty sack.

"You'd murder me—in cold blood—"

Carter spoke clearly. "You sodbusters had better get out of this basin. Me an' my guns'll run you out—if we don't kill you first. I should start in with you—use you as an example—"

"Hey, stop! None of that!"

Deputy Sheriff Hammerburg came on the run, rifle jutting. His face was flushed and he stopped beside Myers, the rifle on Carter. "What the hell's goin' on here, Carter?"

"I just bought Windon's land. Myers didn't like him sellin' to me. Myers knocked him down. He cursed me an' I swung on him. His tongue ain't civil."

"I've heard times when you didn't use no choice language! We've had enough trouble here—we don't need no more! Now head down the street an' be out of town as soon as your business will allow you!"

Carter studied him. "That might be some time, lawman."

"It won't be too long," threatened Hammerburg.

Carter said, "Come on, Pinto," and he and his foreman went back into the saloon. From the open door they watched Hammerburg and Myers go to where the farmer had his buckboard and team. Myers got into the seat, turned the team, and drove out of town.

"That little lawman's tough," opined the bartender.

The barkeep did not see Carter wink at Aggler. "Anyway, he talks tough. I'd like to trim his horns back for him."

"You had your chance out there," the white-aprons reminded him.

Carter sneered a little. "Chance, hell! With him holdin' a rifle—a cocked rifle—against me?"

"You had your gun almost out when he hollered. He swung the rifle up, an' in that time you could've pulled your sixer."

Carter saw that the man was right. He laughed it off with, "You got a wild man's eye, fella. You been drinkin' your own panther fizz? Or how else could your sight get so bad?"

"More rum," ordered Aggler. "A full bottle this time, not a little bit in the bottom."

The bartender surlily put out another bottle. The two cowmen drank and then went out the back door. They did not go to the livery barn, though; they went down the alley and came into Hammerburg's office by the back door. The deputy was sitting with his feet on his desk.

"Take chairs, men."

"Ain't got time," Carter replied. "You sure put on a good act, fella. Anybody's sure claim you was for the farmers one hundred percent."

"You fell for your cue good." A smile warped Hammerburg's thin lips. "You did all right, Carter. Me, I figure a few of them farmers—mebbe quite a few—will peddle to you."

"Let's hope so."

"An' if they don't sell?"

Carter felt a little anger. The deputy was too nosy. He wondered just how far he could trust Hammerburg.

"We'll see," murmured the cowman.

Carter and Aggler went outside. Back in the alley, Aggler said quietly, "I don't trust that runt, Carter. He's a little man and a little man likes to act big, but when the showdown comes . . ."

"We'll watch him, Pinto."

They got their broncs and rode out of town. They went west and a little south; they reached the badlands. They went into them, into the painted, ugly buttes, and they followed a dim, uncertain trail that twisted across the hills. They heard the bawl of cattle and came to a small park where a guard came out of the brush with a rifle.

"Hank Carter an' Pinto Aggler," said Carter. "This is Kid Jamison's herd, ain't it?"

"It might be; might not be."

Carter scowled and Pinto Aggler grinned. "You're new with Jamison, I take it," stated Carter. He looked out at the herd that grazed on the meadow, nibbling of the short brown grass. "We're ridin' in."

"Ride in."

Kid Jamison was a short, heavy-set man in his late thirties. Crow's-feet pulled at the corners of eyes that were the color of muddy water. He said, "Howdy, men," and turned his bronc to face the herd. "There they are. Look them over."

Carter and Aggler rode around the herd. On the side opposite the outlaw they stopped and talked. "They're poor." Carter rubbed his hand on his saddlehorn. "But they's good blood in 'em. They'll get weight fast."

"They'd do good in the minin' camps, Carter."

Carter nodded. "We should make some dinero here. Unless that damn robber of a Kid wants too much. How many head?"

Aggler counted.

Their count finished, they rode back to where Kid Jamison sat his sorrel. Jamison had three riders they could see and they knew more were back in the brush watching their trail from the south. Carter dickered with the outlaw and Pinto Aggler listened with a great indifference. Finally they came to terms. Jamison and his crew would vent the brands on these cattle and run Carter's iron on them. "Two days' work, Carter."

"I'll be at the ranch. Your dinero'll be there when you come in." Carter pulled his bronc around. "How are things down in Utah, Kid?"

"Utah? Never been there."

Carter smiled thinly. "I'll have to call you a danged liar, Kid. Them cows tote a Utah iron. I worked on that spread a summer when I was a long-legged kid. Ol' Haskins own it yet?"

"Haskins is dead. Died last summer. A big San Francisco outfit—a syndicate of bankers—owns it now."

"I don't like bankers," said Carter. "Hijack some more of their stuff, huh, Kid?"

The outlaw smiled a little. "I might do that, Hank. That guard is green, so I'll ride with you to the trail."

The afternoon was late when the pair reached the ranch. They loped down the wagon road, their broncs leg-tired, with Carter swinging the free end of his lariat, and with Pint Aggler stiff in leather. Aggler had taken the bottle of rum from the saloon and he was a little drunk.

They came in, while the guinea-hens cackled, and they hit the dirt in front of the barn. Carter hollered, "Mozo, take our broncs," and they left the horses with trailing reins and went toward the house. A horse was tied to the hitchrack there.

"Strange horse," murmured Aggler.

"Belongs to a nester, the farmer on Hangin' Butte Crick. Seen that bronc the other day in his pasture. Know him because of them high white stockin's on his front legs."

The farmer was sitting on the bench on the porch. He got up, a slender bearded man dressed in bib-overalls. "I come to sell out to you, Carter."

"Come inside."

They sat down at the table where the farmer took out his papers. Carter studied them and the farmer signed the deed over to him. Carter scrawled out a check with, "Report to me when you leave the valley, fellow. You'll have to drive right past the house to get to town."

"Two days," said the farmer. "I'll be out in two days, Carter." He stopped at the door and looked at the check, keeping his eyes hidden. "The rest of the homesteaders might not like me for doin' this. In fact, they might start trouble with me."

Carter told about Windon selling to him. "Let me know if you get in any trouble. I'll take care of it for you."

"Thanks."

The farmer left. They heard him lope out of the yard, heard the guinea-hens cackle. Carter walked up and down the big living-room. He pounded a fist against a palm.

"More of them'll sell. They got sense, Pinto. They got to sell!"

Pinto Aggler poured some rum into a glass. "Remember ol' Mack Orcon, Hank. He's got a powerful control over them. He's promised 'em water, an' you know what that means?"

Carter stopped, listened.

"It means farms, nice farms. Plenty of hay an' good stock an' a good livin', with dinero in the bank. It means a good home for your kids an' your missus, fellow."

"I gotta get rid of Mack Orcon."

"Yeah, but how? He's got two good gun-riders, an' I don't need to mention names, do I?"

Carter smiled suddenly. "Well, two are leavin'. They got good homesteads, an' when we take over that reservoir we'll run ditches down there an' water an' raise hay—plenty of hay."

Aggler watched him.

Carter said, "Give me that bottle, Pinto." He poured a drink and raised the amber liquid. "Even if it is rum, I'll chance it. Here's to you, fella."

Aggler's eyes were troubled.

14

Old Mack Orcon was mad. He paced the floor, boots pounding on the flooring, and Matilda was seated at the table, a worried frown on her homely face. Outside, Nellie Bly butted against the closed door.

"Damn' that goat, Matilda! Go out an' hit him with a club or somethin'; He'll cave that door in!"

"I'm not going out, brother! That goat will butt me— You promised me you'd leave him nights out at the derrick. Why isn't he there?"

"Hell, he's chawed off his picket-line! He eats a rope right in two, I reckon. I'll get a piece of chain an' chain him. I'll fix him!"

The old-timer went outside. Nellie Bly was five feet from the door, doubled up and ready to butt, when the door opened. He changed his mind when he saw old Mack and turned and ran, the old man after him. Just then Jess Roberts and War Dog Smith rode into the yard.

They drew rein. "Look, he wants to play with the goat, huh, Jess?" The half-breed was smiling widely.

"Two goats together," said Jess. "Go get him, ol' Mack! Bulldog him!"

Old Mack saw them then. He stopped and cursed. "He's tryin' to bust in the door. Lay a loop on him, Jess!"

Jess shook out his catch-rope. Nellie Bly had stopped and now, some fifty yards away, he stood and looked at them, shaking his horns. Jess built a small loop in his hardtwist and sent his hooks into his bronc. The animal started to run toward the goat.

For a moment Nellie Bly stood his ground, shaking his horns in defiance. Then, when the thundering horse bore down on him, he bleated and whirled, running for the tool house.

Jess' bronc pulled in and the loop went down. Nellie Bly stuck his head in the noose that hung for an instant in front of him. Jess' bronc slid to a stiff-legged halt and Jess took fast dallies. Nellie Bly hit the end of the rope, his head and legs traded places, and the goat landed hard on his back where he lay supine.

Old Mack came on the run. "You knock-kneed ijit, Jess! You've kilt him, sure as— I never meant for you to bust him like that! I thought you'd stop him gentle like—"

Jess winked at War Dog. "I reckon I heered his neck snap," he said slowly. "Sure sorry I kilt him, ol' Mack."

The old man was kneeling beside the limp goat. Matilda had come out of the house. She wrung her hands and asked, "Is he—is he dead, brother?"

Old Mack glared at her. "You soun' hopeful, woman. No, he ain't dead; he's jus' knocked out, I'd say! His head busted against yonder rock— Hey, let some slack in that rope, you ornery cowdog! I wanna take the hemp off'n my ol' pet—"

"Pet!" snorted Matilda.

Jess loosened his dallies and old Mack took the rope from the goat. He wiggled the goat's head back and forth slowly. "No, his neck ain't busted. His eyes are openin' now."

Nellie Bly struggled to his feet. He was bleary-eyed and his gaze fell on Matilda.

"I'm going to the house." Matilda left at a fast walk.

Nellie Bly bleated.

"No, his neck ain't busted." Old Mack sighed with relief. "If it were, he couldn't make a noise like that."

Nellie Bly turned and walked into the tool shed. The fight had left him, and after this he would respect a man on a horse—especially if that man had a rope. Jess recoiled his lariat and grinned down at old Mack.

"You was awful hot under the collar when you come out of the house. An ant bite you where you sit down?"

Memory washed over the old-timer and turned his eyes as hard as stone. "You know what?" he stormed. He didn't wait for an answer to his question. "That danged Windon—a farmer—sold out to Hank Carter. He left today with his wagon load—even reported to Carter's ranch when he took the wagon road out. With him was another farmer who'd sold out, too. Nester from the Hangin' Butte Crick country."

"Who tol' you this?" asked Jess.

"Parr Palm was here a few minutes ago. He was down in town yesterday when Carter knocked down Myers after Myers had started to work over that traitor Windon. Accordin' to Palm, Deputy Hammerburg busted in an' kept Carter from pullin' against Myers."

Jess nodded.

War Dog spoke. "Well, two weak ones gone, huh?"

Old Mack's goatee jumped. "That's one way to look at it, Injun. Fact is, we might be lucky we lost 'em, in a way. We might've got in a tight an' depended on 'em— But there's another angle to it, too."

War Dog asked, "An' what is that, Mack?"

Between curses, the old man told them. He was afraid some of the other sodmen would get cold feet and follow the pattern set by Windon and the farmer from Hanging Butte Creek. According to him, some of the women were putting pressure on their husbands, trying to persuade them to leave the basin.

Matilda hollered, "Chow's on, men."

Jess and War Dog unstripped their broncs and turned them into the pasture. There the native grass was green and knee-high to a running horse. Outside of the fence the grass was brown and stunted. The pasture had been watered, irrigated. Jess watched the horses tie into the grass.

Old Mack was right. Water was the thing; with plenty of water, the land would bloom. Fields of oats and wheat and barley and flax would color the basin, giving it strength and power. Cows would graze on fine alfalfa and haystacks would spring up to break the evenness of the pattern. Yes, old Mack was right.

Standing there, looking at the green pasture, for the first time Jess Roberts really understood the old man and his mission. Old Mack was a prophet, a forerunner of prosperity. With no water, only cattle could run on that grass; they would not be fat, either. Without water, there was only room for one man to make a living in that valley.

The weak-hearted and the weak-kneed farmers were being weeded out by the naked gun-threat of Hank Carter and Pinto Aggler and their gundogs. Maybe that was just as well. But old Mack had a strong point when he voiced the opinion that the exit of these two farmers might start a stampede out of the basin.

"Ol' Mack, he gotta win," declared War Dog. His tongue came out and sealed the brown-papered cigarette. "He is in the right. But how he gonna win, Jess?"

"That's simple."

Shrewd eyes peered over the match's peaked flare. "Simple? How you mean it simple?"

"All the farmers have to do is get rid of Hank Carter. Pinto Aggler's no leader; he'll do to follow and back up, but not to lead. With Carter gone, that cow ranch would fall apart."

War Dog blew smoke from his nostrils. "Carter, he no go. Only way he leave is feet first on a slab with bullets in him."

"Maybe he'll get those bullets."

Jess turned and walked to the house, his partner beside him. "We better finish this soon, Jess," stated the half-breed. "Me, I'm tired of stayin' here. I'd like to go back down south, Arizona mebbe? The nights are gettin' cold here an' my overcoat is in Tucson."

"You ain't got no overcoat."

"No, not yet. But it is in a store down there, ready for me

to buy." The squat man was grinning. "We go down there an' buy it?"

"You get to Arizona an' you don't need an overcoat." Jess was serious and his lips showed it. "Wonder what Carter's next move will be, War Dog? What do you say?"

War Dog frowned and pulled on his smoke. "Me, I'd sit still, see if more farmers sell. If they do, all right; but if they don't—"

After eating, the three went to the well-derrick, old Mack riding his mule. He had a rope around Nellie Bly's horns and the goat didn't want to be led. He'd sit down and slide when they came to shale, displaying his protest in this manner.

"He don't want to leave Matilda," said War Dog. "He like her company."

Old Mack put his spurs to his mule. The mule jumped ahead and snapped Nellie Bly out of a hole in which he had braced himself. "Sometimes I figger I'm a danged fool for hangin' onto this refugee from the Yukon, men. I oughta cut his throat an' grin' him up for sausage. Whoa, mule, whoa!"

"Make chaps out of his hide," said War Dog. "Them angora goats they make good chaps, no?"

Jess carried a long, thin chain over his saddle. This was to picket Nellie Bly with out at the well-derrick. He listened to the banter of War Dog and old Mack with an amused smile. But he made no effort to break into their conversation.

The half-breed was right: winter would be there sooner than they expected. Seasons were awfully short there in that high northern country. They came to a hill and Jess stood on stirrups, looking out over the basin.

He was tall and quiet, a serious man in worn levis and bench-made boots, sitting a tough saddle. War Dog sat deep between horn and rim, his eyes running over the trail below. And beside him was the mule of old Mack Orcon. The old man's wizened, leathery face was scowling as he faced the sun's sharp glare. The sunlight played on the brass buckle that held the hat strings of his floppy old Stetson. Nellie Bly braced and pulled on the rope, shaking his head angrily.

"Cain't see no other nesters pullin' out, men." Old Mack spoke slowly. "Maybe they ain't no more of them that'll drift out, huh?"

War Dog shrugged.

Jess said, "Maybe not." He was looking at Carter's spread. "When a wagon leaves the basin, he has to go past Carter's outfit, huh? That the only wagon trail out, ol' Mack?"

"The only wagon trail, Jess. Yep, that's the only one. An'

that gives him the advantage of seein' all farm equipment that comes in along with all other stuff—supplies an' stuff like that."

"He ever try to block that road?"

The old man spat. "Yep, tried it once. Claimed the road run on his property. County surveyor claimed otherwise an' the surveyor won. Can't block a man from gettin' to a railroad, you know. That's Wyomin' homestead law."

Jess nodded.

"Yep, reckon right now Hank Carter knows almost to the dollar how much us farmers has invested here an' he knows jus' what equipment each farm's got. Hell, he seen everythin' hauled in; pulled into the basin right in front of his front door. Well, we better mosey along, huh?"

They rode down the hill, broncs sliding in shale. Below them working-men were laboring on the derrick. They had it upright and were restringing the cables. While Jess and War Dog watched the farmers work, old Mack picketed Nellie Bly to a cottonwood tree. The goat stood and chewed on the chain.

"Look at that damn' fool!" snorted old Mack. "Tryin' to chaw that chain in two! Me, I figgered I'd learned that critter more brains than to try to eat a chain up! But he sure is a good sled goat."

The oldster went to work, giving orders and waving his hands. Most of the farmers didn't pay him too much attention. Jess noticed that old Mack made no effort to get him and War Dog from their saddles to do manual work. And that brought a smile to his lips.

"We'll see you, Mack."

Jess and his partner trotted off. War Dog asked, "Where to, Jess?" and Jess shrugged. "See how the nesters are takin' this thousan' buck bonus stuff, War Dog."

"If I was a farmer, I'd take the money, Jess."

Jess grinned. "So would I, pard. Who in his right mind would want to be a hoeman, anyway?"

"Me, I'm a saddle man. I don't like a plow. Maybe we're different than they are, huh?"

A cow trotted out of the brush. A skinny cow when, by all rights, she should have had some lard on her ribs. Jess pulled his horse around and circled her. She looked trail-weary and her brand was blotched. Now she wore Carter's iron and her original brand had been run out with a flat branding iron, making it unreadable.

War Dog said, "That cow, she is tired, Jess. She has come

up the trail." He looked inquiringly at his partner. "You remember those other cows with vented irons—those ones we saw when we first hit Wishin' Springs grass?"

Jess' eyes were sober.

"He steal cattle, huh?"

"Yeah, or else buys stolen cattle." Jess moved his bronc with his spurs. "Well, no business of ours, I guess. Lots of big outfits do the same thing—jus' so he don't steal from the farmers."

War Dog's dark eyes twinkled. "Maybe he steal Nellie Bly, huh? Holla, Mattie like that, huh?"

"Mattie?"

"Matilda. Mattie is short for Matilda. She told me that."

Jess studied him. "You two are gettin' kinda chummy."

But War Dog Smith shook his head vigorously. "No, not that, Buck. No, no, no! But she is nice womans. She tell me to call her Mattie. Good name an' short, so maybe I call her that."

"Hope she doesn't call us too late for breakfast," said Jess. "She's a powerful good han' with a skillet and some lard."

They called on a number of farmers. Most of them had heard about the departure of Windon and the other sodbuster and most of them, too, had heard of the thousand dollar bonus that Hank Carter was paying for their homestead deeds.

"Damn, Jess, that's a heap of coin!"

The farmer's wife cut in. "Don't dare talk that way, Mike. Me an' you come out here to make a go outa the soil an' to raise our kids civilized-like. Don't think I'm goin' back to a city with you—I'm stayin' here an' fightin' as long as I got me strength to wrap my finger aroun' the trigger of our .30-.30!"

"By crab, Millie, never did hear you talk that fast before." The farmer rubbed his neck thoughtfully. "But damn it, men, this soil is no good without water. An' so far it ain't been runnin' down the irrigation ditches me an' the boys dug by han'. When's the water gettin' here?"

"Go out an' work with old Mack," said War Dog, "an' you'll get water sooner. Build a ditch over from the main ditch an' tap the reservoir."

"We're diggin' on that now."

His wife said, "He's jus' grumblin', men. He don't aim to pull out. Neither does the others of us. As long as that reservoir has water, all we have to do is get our ditches to join up with the main one. Mike, you hustle out an' help ol' Mack with that derrick. He aims to drill on our place next."

The partners contacted other farmers, too. Old Mack was wrong about one thing, Jess saw: the farmers were more undetermined about staying than were their wives. Except in two cases, the women were adamant about staying, and they expressed this in no uncertain terms.

The partners came home at dusk. Old Mack was already home but Jess noticed Nellie Bly was not around. On the long ride in he had been in a serious mood. For things were too quiet there in the basin.

The next day was quiet too, without trouble, and so was the next. And the derrick worked again, but the men who handled it were openly nervous.

"This ain't like Hank Carter an' Pinto Aggler," grumbled a red-haired, bony farmer. "They ain't settin' back unless they got a purpose. Wonder what it is, men?"

"We'll know when we find out," said another. "Hand me that spud-iron, Jim. Carter's got somethin' up his sleeve."

"Yeah, more than his arm's in that sleeve," stated a short man.

15

There was a whiskey bottle on the table. The lamplight reflected from it, the yellow rays dancing across the white tablecloth. The rays ran out and hit the blued-steel of a .45 that lay there, its gun belt beside it. And the lamplight reflected also from the dull brass of the cartridges crammed into the loops on the belt.

A thick hand came down and took the bottle. The cork came off it and the neck tilted, pouring liquid into two glasses. The hand dropped the bottle and corked it, and took up a glass. Now another hand, likewise chubby and hairy, came down and took the second glass.

Hank Carter drank. He put his glass down and looked at the gun. He said, "They ain't leavin', Pinto; they're stayin'. A thousan' bucks ain't enough, I take it. Hell, an' most of 'em never had a thousan' bucks before in their lives! Now they won't leave a piece of worthless homestead lan' for a thousan' iron men! They crazy?"

Pinto Aggler raised his glass and drank his whiskey. "They figure the land will be worth more, maybe." He shrugged. "Anyway, they aren't leavin'. Four days now, an' nobody's left since Windon an' that other scissor-bill. Maybe this ol' Mack Orcon has 'em hypnotized, huh?" He was grinning.

Carter paced the floor. He pounded a fist into his palm. For four days he'd remained idle, watching and waiting, watching and waiting. Playing his cards close and not tipping his hand. But no nester wagons, loaded with personal goods, had stopped in front of his spread to receive a thousand dollars. No wagon of nesters had left Wishing Springs basin.

"Here comes Parr Palm," murmured Aggler.

Palm came in the back door. He stood in the shadows, noticed that the blinds were pulled low, and then he came inside. He said hello and looked at the bottle. Aggler got another glass from the cupboard and tossed it to him. Palm caught it and uncorked the bottle.

Carter spoke. "Well?"

Parr Palm's dark eyes studied the cowman. "Well, what?"

"What do you know?" Carter was abrupt.

Palm drank and lowered his glass. "Skunk juice," he said. "Don't know when I'll work the taste out of my mouth."

"Anybody leavin'?" Carter was sharp.

Palm's dark eyes showed a little anger. "Don't snap at me, fella! I'm no slave of your'n! No, no more nesters has left. And from what I've seen, an' judgin' on my talks with the farmers, none of the rest is leavin', either."

Carter studied him. "Ain't a thousan' apiece enough dinero?"

"Not enough, I reckon."

Palm poured another drink. Pinto Aggler hooked his leg around the arm of his chair, his spur rowel chiming as his boot swung back and forth. The creak of his leather chaps sounded loud in the room.

Carter said, "Why in the hell don't you get hooks that don't make so much noise? Some night we'll ride out on a raid an' they'll hear you a mile off!"

Aggler smiled slowly. "Your nerves are raw, boss." He pulled his leg down, though.

Palm drank.

Carter looked at the farmer. "How many men on the reservoir, Parr?"

"Just one, I think. Tiny Williams."

Carter said, "Break it, an' we'll win. At the same time, we dynamite that derrick again. Only this time we bust it all to hell. Seems funny only one man at that water storage, though."

"What's odd about it?" Palm asked. "The storage tank is right behin' ol' Mack's homestead. He's got two hands there, Jess Roberts and War Dog Smith. Besides that, there's that big hog-wire fence around the reservoir. Fence was finished yesterday."

"You sure about only Tiny Williams bein' there, Parr?"

"You think I'm lyin' to you?"

Anger touched Hank Carter's eyes. His knuckles were white as he gripped the hardwood back of the chair. Gradually the color came back into his jowls. "All right, friend, don't get huffy. Where's Hammerburg?"

"Saw him this afternoon in town. He's stayin' close to town, he says." Palm went to the back door. "So long, men."

He went out silently and somewhere they heard the creak of saddle-leather as he mounted. They did not hear his bronc leave. Carter listened and said, "He moves silent, Pinto." He spoke quietly. "Get Smokey and Ace and Wishy up here to the house, pronto."

"Need any powder?"

"We'll get that later."

Pinto Aggler went out the front door, spur rowels clanging. He was gone about five minutes, and when he and the three gunmen came in, Carter was uncorking the bottle again. They all drank.

Carter talked to them in a low voice. He noticed that Pinto Aggler had left his spurs in the bunkhouse. The foreman listened, scowled, went out, came back with two sacks, each carrying a few sticks of powder and some fuses. He handed one to Smokey.

"Smokey, you ride with me." Carter spoke quickly. "Pinto, you take the other two boys. You three hit the derrick; me an' Smokey'll take the reservoir. Meet here when it's all over."

Pinto said, "We'd better time ourselves. What time will we bust powder, boss?"

Carter asked, "Eleven o'clock, huh?"

His foreman considered that, his face grave. "Yes, that should give us time, Hank. Who's at the derrick?"

"Two men, I understand. Two guards, left there each night."

Ace spoke. He was a thin, hungry-looking man. "What if the guns talk, boss? We shoot to kill?"

Carter thumbed his bottom lip in deep thought. "Yeah, shoot to kill, Ace. They got to learn sooner or later. We'll make them wish they'd sold out to us, the pum'kin rollers. All set, huh? Each man know what he's goin' to do? Everythin' clear?"

He looked sharply at each man, weighing them. Pinto was sure and tough, and so was Smokey. He had tested them by gunsmoke and circumstance. The other two—well, a man never did know what he'd hired until he'd tried them out under fire. . . .

"All set, Hank."

"Okay, boss."

"Let's hit leather."

They went out, leaving Carter alone. He put the gun belt around his middle and pulled the buckle in, finding the hole. He fitted the heavy harness around his hips and tied down his strings. He went down the hall and glanced into a door and into a darkened room. He listened, silent in the doorway; he heard the heavy breathing of the squaw housekeeper. She had slept through their conversation, he figured. What she didn't know wouldn't hurt her.

He went out the back door and circled the house. The night was dark; toward morning there'd be a moon, he figured. He went toward the barn and the knot of men who were saddling broncs there. Pinto said, "Your hoss is inside, Hank. You're ridin' that midnight black, ain't you?"

"That's my pony."

There was the creaking of saddle leather and the muttering of the men as they worked. A horse snorted and a man buried a boot in one's belly, kicking the air out of him so he could pull his cinch tight. These were the sounds heard in the night: the grunt of a cayuse, the mutter and movement of men, the snap of a breech on a rifle as a man inspected its shells, feeling into the dark chamber with his fingers. Now a man went up, shadowy in the darkness.

Carter saddled the big black through pure rote. The horse turned and nibbled the man's shoulder, pulling at the buckskin jacket with his grass-colored teeth. Carter reached his arm around and pulled the pony's nose against him. He held the horse and stroked his forehead and for a moment the horse was quiet, standing in Carter's embrace. Then hardness came over the man again and he pushed the bronc's head back, and pulled his latigo tight.

His four riders were all up now; a horse pawed, pulling against his reins. Carter found his stirrup and went into leather and said, "All right, men; it's our trail."

They went out on a lope, five shadows moving through shadows. They came through the gate, the beam-pole over them, and the dust of the road met their hoofs. This was crossed and only the hard soil of the prairie felt the imprint of their broncs. Carter rode beside Pinto Aggler.

There was nothing to talk about, so they were all silent. A gun harness creaked as its owner moved in saddle. One horse rolled the cricket on his bit, for he wanted to run; he was gay and fresh and hungry for a long trail. Ace pulled him in and cursed him in a dull tone.

Aggler said, "He's only a horse, Ace."

"What do you mean?"

"I don't mind a man cussin', but why cuss against a hoss? He can't understan' you."

"Lissen at him!" Ace's tone was angry. "He talks like a preacher. Remember, big pants, when I hired out to this spread, I hired out to sling a gun, not slobber while I listened to one of your sermons!"

Carter cut in. "Enough of that, you two fools! Am I an ol' woman keepin' two fightin' brats apart? Lay off him, Pinto!"

Pinto laughed a little. "I jus' aimed to start talk rollin', boss." But Carter knew that the man was lying.

They were silent after that, each nursing his thoughts. They came to the hills, and below them were pinpointed the lights in the homes of the farmers. These twinkled and burned and were small against the night and the distance; Carter knew they burned behind blinds, and the light they saw was that which had managed to seep past the heavy curtains.

These lights mocked him.

He thought, I'll put you out . . . an' I'll do it soon." He knew his time had come; he had to hit and hit fast. They were growing stronger, not in numbers but in will; two of them had left, but their leaving had only steeled the others into a blunt determination to weather out the gun storm. He knew this and it rankled in him. For one thing, they would offer more resistance now; for another, it reflected on him and his logic.

He had offered them a thousand dollars a deed. That offer

was a product of his ingenuity; he had thought the idea good. But only two families had taken it. His idea had proven futile.

He had his pride; the pride of a cowman. He had seen the trails in sunshine, bright and clean; he'd bucked them in winter, aslant in leather, snow whipping around him. These nesters evidently had their pride, too. Now the two groups were going to clash in open warfare. There was no other way.

With the reservoir blasted, a summer of work would face the farmers before they could replace it. In view of the double tragedy of the derrick destruction, they should have folded up their tents and left.

He wondered what time the moon would rise. He wanted to get this over with and have no moonlight on his deeds. They came to a fork in the trail. Pinto pulled in with, "We go this way, boss."

Carter said, "Remember, at eleven we let hell rip loose."

"That time, Carter."

Pinto swung his saddle; the horse reared against the bit. Ace and Wishy rode with the foreman, one on either side of him. Smokey said, "We go ahead, boss," and then added: "Wish I had a cigarette."

"Don't chance one here, fellow. Later on when we ride home . . ." The wind and night whipped his words away.

They had almost crossed the basin now. The hills were ahead, folded and ageless; in them was the reservoir. Houses were dark now, for the night was getting late. They came to a coulee and rode along it. The trail was narrow and covered with sand washed down during storms. Therefore it muffled the hoofs of their trotting horses. Carter was glad of that.

He knew the country well and he reckoned they were about a mile from the reservoir. He felt tension across his back, pulling at his muscles. His mouth was dry and he wet his lips, the wind taking the water from them immediately. Here the wind was almost howling.

He weighed this in his mind, and decided the wind was good. Its sound in the buckbrush and boxelders would screen and hide any sounds made by either himself or Smokey. They came to the end of the gully and rode out on a darkened mesa. The wind was stronger there, much stronger. They dismounted in some kin-i-kinick and tied their broncs there. Smokey carried the sack and Carter untied his fence pliers from his saddle.

"How far?" asked Smokey.

"Quarter mile, I'd say. No, less than that. A hundred yards, or a little over. Our horses'll be handy, fellow."

Smokey chuckled. "I'm no hand on foot, Hank. I was raised on a hoss an' my legs don't track right on sod."

Carter got to his knees. He cupped a match to life and Smokey held down his watch. Carter broke the match. "We got ten minutes, Smokey. How you goin' work this powder? Where you goin' place it?"

Smokey said, "I've looked this dam over a coupla times from a distance with glasses. The south side is the side to hit. The rim of it lops over there an' a man can plant his charge there an' crack it an' have water go all over hell."

"That side, then; the south."

They moved through the brush, Carter in the lead; they came to the big hogwire fence. The night was dark and silent except for the wind. Carter started clipping the wires. They fell under the sharp fence-nippers, one by one, and soon he and Smokey were hunkered against the earthen wall of the dam.

Old Mack had carved out the side of a hill and poured the concrete there. One side had solid earth backing the concrete; the downhill side had less earth. They worked toward this spot.

Suddenly Carter stopped. "Man comin'," he said.

16

Old Mack Orcon was an addict of poker—a violent addict. The bug had bitten him in his teens and nothing, not even heavy losses, had inoculated him against the malady. He broached the subject to Jess and War Dog that evening. His blunt fingers played with the greasy deck of cards.

"Try your luck, men?"

"No money," said War Dog.

Jess shugged. "None here, either."

Old Mack snorted. "You got some spare change an' you know it. Set up here while I deal the cards."

Matilda had been washing dishes. She had heard their conversation. She turned, suds clinging to her forearms. "Do you mean you want those men to gamble with you, brother Mack?"

"Gamble? Well, some call it that; I call it just plain poker."

"That is because he always wins," declared War Dog. "It is no gamble to him—it is a sure thing. He's clipped me before."

The spinster's jaw set and Jess knew she was ready to render a verdict. "There will be no gambling in this house while I am here. Back home I was president of the anti-vice league and there will be no playing for stakes while I am here."

"Ah, Mattie, sister—"

"Please, brother."

Jess felt relieved. "She's right," he was quick to state. "Gamblin' is a terrible evil, ol' Mack. I agree with Miss Matilda."

"So do I." War Dog got on the bandwagon.

Old Mack studied them, his goatee jumping. "Three ag'in one," he growled. "All right, no money, then. But can we play for matches, Mattie?"

"That is still gambling."

Jess was reading the Sears Roebuck catalogue. "I agree with your sister." He was grinning. "It is still gamblin', ol' Mack."

"But nobody's got anythin' to lose. I own the matches. I just let you use 'em. That ain't gamblin'. When you gamble, you either win or lose somethin' of value."

Matilda scowled. "All right," she conceded. "With matches, not money." She returned to her dishes.

Old Mack lifted his hand and thumbed his nose at her back. War Dog played, but Jess kept on reading the catalogue, otherwise known as "The Sheepherder's Almanac," so called because every sheepherder had a catalogue. At the table, the old man and War Dog bickered, and cards fell. Matilda finished her dishes and excused herself, saying as she went to her room, "It sure is nice that goat isn't here tonight."

Old Mack chuckled. "Bet ol' Nellie Bly sure is mad, chained to that derrick. Bet right now he's lickin' the grease off'n them cable-drums an' cussin' in goat language." He slapped down an ace. "Got that pot too, War Dog."

Time went by quickly for both Jess, interested in the "Almanac," and for the two poker players, interested in their cards. Old Mack glanced at Matilda's closed door. "Now for some money playin', huh?"

"Not me," stated War Dog.

"How about you, Jess?"

Jess shook his head. "Not me, either. I'm goin' make a turn aroun' the reservoir an' then go in. Somebody goin' relieve Tiny Williams at midnight?"

Old Mack said he was going to be on guard from midnight to morning. Just then War Dog took a fat pot, rolling in the matches, and the oldster's face fell and he cussed in a dull whisper.

"You'd better get some sleep, Mack."

The old-timer dealt the cards, shaking his head. "Don't need none, Jess. Me, I don't sleep even when I goes to bed. Got insomnia, I guess. Your draw, War Dog. King down, huh?"

Jess said good night. He went out into the dark, grinning to himself. Suffering from insomnia, huh? Now whom did he expect to believe that? Old Mack'd hit the sougans and be asleep in three minutes, snoring like a ripsaw going through a hickory knot.

Jess was plainly worried. Four days had gone by, uneventful days. The tension had grown and now it hung across Wishing Springs range, almost visible in the dry air of noon. Now, out there in the darkness, this menace seemed to move, seemed to be a tangible, living thing.

Jess was keenly aware of this. He started to roll a cigarette, then changed his mind; he poked the loose tobacco into his mouth to chew it. He wasn't sleepy and he should have been.

He climbed the steep path that led to the reservoir. The night was so dark he had to feel his way sometimes. He came to the high fence with the gate. He called, "Tiny, this is Jess Roberts."

Out of the dark pattern of the night came the darker shadow of the big guard. "Heard you comin', Jess. Figured you was ol' Mack comin' to relieve me. I'm sleepy tonight."

"I'll take over until ol' Mack comes."

Tiny shook his heavy head. "No, I'd best stick aroun'; it's my job." He locked the gate behind Jess, levering it shut until it was taut. "This fence is the real McCoy. Should have had it up before. Had it been here, I wouldn't've jumped you an' War Dog that night."

They squatted in a clump of buckbrush. Tiny allowed the night was dark, too dark; there'd be a moon around midnight, he figured. Jess listened and chewed some more tobacco. Tiny settled back, his back to a cottonwood tree; he snored a little, the sound thin on the air.

An hour went by and Jess squatted there, wide awake and alert. Tiny kept on snoring, and once he got too loud. Jess jabbed his elbow against him, and Tiny woke up. "I been asleep?"

"You started to snore."

"What's wrong with that?"

"You snored so loud that even if somebody come, I couldn't've heard them. Must be gettin' close to midnight. Let's make the rounds an' meet back of the reservoir, huh? Ol' Mack'll be along soon."

"Okay, Jess."

Jess went to the right and Tiny to the left. Somewhere Jess figured he heard the sharp twang of a wire breaking. He put his hand on the fence, wondering if somebody were cutting its wires. But the wires did not sag.

His ears, he figured, were playing tricks on him. He circled his half of the reservoir and came to the spot where he should have met Tiny. But Tiny wasn't there. Jess hunkered and listened but he could not hear the man.

Suddenly the night was alive with flame. Then the roar of the explosion tore the flame apart. Debris went sky-high and a log landed by Jess' right elbow. The explosion almost knocked him down.

The light died and the sky was black with the smell of burned powder. His gun out, Jess ran ahead; he stopped, listened. Water was roaring from the reservoir and mingled with this was the slap-slap of running hoofs out there in the dark night. He brought his gun up and thumbed three shots.

They were wild shots. He knew they had but a remote chance of hitting. He drew no return lead. Now another gun, speaking from his right by a hundred yards, broke into the fray. He saw it was a six-gun by its flame.

A man screamed. The roar of hoofs died. Now, down on the basin's floor, came the hard flash of exploding powder. It died and then came the rocking roar of its explosion. Jess halted, his gun smoking.

Water was roaring down the cut-coulee and into the basin. Water coming from the dam. It tore at saplings and pulled out brush. He knew that inside of five minutes or so the dam would be dry. A year's work was gone; a sum of money wasted. A year that had gone slowly and money that could not be replaced.

"Tiny!"

"Here, Jess!"

The big man came running out of the brush. He said hoarsely, "They slugged me! In the dark, they slugged me! But I come to. That was me shootin' at them as they headed out!"

"You got one," Jess said. "I heard him scream."

"I wonder who they was, Jess? I couldn't make out in the dark."

Jess listened to the roar of the water. "Either Hank Carter or his men. They must've dynamited the derrick, too. I saw the flame and it looked like it was down by the derrick."

Tiny had his head in his hands. He was down on his knees, rocking back and forth; he was sobbing. "We're broken, Jess! We're done for! The reservoir gone, the derrick shot to hell. We're lucky ol' Mack had his cabin an' buildings on that high rise. Otherwise this water'd take him to hell an' gone!"

Jess was stony-faced.

Old Mack came running, War Dog behind him. "Jess, they hit, huh? Broke the dam to hell, too, huh? You hurt, Jess?"

"They slugged Tiny. Funny, I heard wires snipped, I figured. But still there wasn't no slack in them."

"They were stapled hard to the posts. Some places we tied the wires onto the posts. The slack prob'ly didn't travel down them. Was that other explosion at the derrick?"

"Looked like it."

"Nellie Bly, he's there!"

"T'hades with a goat!" Tiny got to his feet, his nerves steel again. "What about the men down there?"

War Dog said, "There'll be gunsmoke now, men. Carter's gone too far. I tell you, this will be settled now, Jess. Get your broncs an' ride!"

They were running down the hill. The water had left the reservoir now and the gully lay black and ugly with mud under the rising moon. Tiny rode out of the brush on a big sorrel and Jess and War Dog hurriedly saddled broncs while old Mack slung the rigging on his mule.

Matilda ran out, clutching a rifle, a shawl over her hair. "What happened, brother?"

Old Mack bit off his words. He told her to go and tell the neighbors what had happened. Then he hit his stirrups and pushed the mule out after Jess and War Dog and Tiny, pounding out of the yard.

The old man beat the mule with his quirt, driving more

speed out of the animal. All the time he cursed in an angry monotone. Although Jess and War Dog and Tiny Williams rode fast, the mule had caught up with them when they came to the derrick.

"Riders comin' in!" a man hollered.

Jess said, "Jess Roberts an' his bunch." They went down in the light of the flares, their shadows running out ahead of them. Other farmers had come, attracted by the explosions. Old Mack was biting off words, telling about the dynamiting of the reservoir. "Anybody hurt here?" demanded Jess.

"Oliver Lewis stopped a bullet. They took him into town to the doctor. The lead hit him in the shoulder."

"Where's Nellie Bly?" Old Mack croaked the words.

One man looked at another; then someone said: "He's gone, ol' Mack. He went up with the derrick, I reckon. He was settin' by the wench the last I seen of him."

Old Mack was silent for once. Then he said slowly, "Damn' best sled goat that ever put his rump into a crupper. Well, he went the way he wanted to go, I reckon. But I'll sure miss the ol' bugger."

The words, coming from anybody but old Mack, would have sounded foolish, no doubt. But to the solemn men assembled there they held a great significance—a man had lost a trusted friend.

Jess and War Dog circled the derrick. It was a wreck, a complete wreck. Timbers had been blasted apart and steel angles were bent beyond repair. It would be useless to try to repair it, for it would be easier to replace it with a newly built derrick. Jess was silent.

"This rips off the lid," said War Dog Smith.

Jess nodded.

More farmers were coming in, some in rigs and others on horseback. But Jess knew their timbre—they were still in the fight and in for keeps.

"I'm for ridin' over there an' smokin' Hank Carter an' Pinto Aggler an' their den of rats out of the country," a man said hoarsely. "This thing is come to a head, men. We gotta act!"

"Or get outa the country," another farmer added.

The first man pounded his fist against his palm. "By Gad, I'm not pullin' out! I'm here to stay, even if they bury me here! I couldn't live the rest of my life thinkin' I ran from the likes of Hank Carter!"

"Me, neither, Jack. I feel like you, fellow."

Parr Palm spoke. "Zeke an' Jacks's right, men. What say we ride over there right now an' blast them buggers out with gunsmoke—"

Jess glanced at War Dog. The half-breed sported a troubled frown. "That could be the worst thing they did, huh? Carter an' his men would be ready an' they'd pick the farmers off like the pigeons. But Palm he wants that."

"Not so loud," whispered Jess.

The men had broken into groups and stood talking. They made grotesque shapes in the dancing shadows cast by the campfires around them. In the middle of this was the ghostly skeleton of the blasted derrick.

Old Mack stood and talked with Parr Palm and some other ranchers. Somebody mentioned going for Deputy Hammerburg and another man laughed openly, saying that would be useless. Hammerburg could do nothing and, what was more, he'd do nothing against Carter. In other words, Jess realized this was a range without any law.

Riders came in, kids and grown men and sometimes a farmer's wife, and reports showed that the reservoir had drained itself dry, that the base had an enormous crack in it. One man who knew concrete said it could not be repaired; new concrete would have to be poured for a new reservoir. Their whole irrigation scheme had gone up in flame and roar.

"That thousan' dollar offer of Carter's still hol' good?" asked a man.

Somebody said that Carter would probably lower the ante now. Old Mack held up his hand and gathered them around him as he stood on a broken timber of the derrick.

He explained their set-up clearly, showing they were almost out of funds, estimating the amount of damage done in dollars and cents. The farmers listened stoically and a few of the women were sobbing.

Jess had a plan in his mind. A tough plan, sired by desperation, but one that would end the Wishing Springs war. He nodded when the old man said the nesters would meet that morning at ten o'clock in the Red Hen School.

"Mornin' almost here," a man said.

The group broke up then. Jess and War Dog and old Mack rode toward the old man's homestead and Jess outlined his plan. War Dog's face was glum with heavy thoughts and old Mack's seamed countenance showed a sullen anger.

"The only thing we can do, Jess."

"How about Parr Palm?" asked War Dog. "An' Deputy

Hammerburg? We're sure they're workin' for Carter. They'll learn about our plan an' warn Hank Carter."

Old Mack nodded. "Yeah, what about that, Jess?"

Jess rubbed his jaw. "We'll see each farmer by himself, men. We'll ride to each one before the meetin'. We'll tell him what we plan an' take his vote for it or against it."

"An' at the meetin'?" asked old Mack.

Jess grinned. "We'll trick Palm an' Hammerburg. We'll pretend that we're beat, see—"

He talked further. Old Mack looked at War Dog, who grinned. "That should finish it or finish us," he said.

"That's it," Jess affirmed.

17

Hank Carter's boot heels jarred the floor. He rubbed his whisker-coated jaw and grinned at Parr Palm and Pinto Aggler. "So that's the way it turned out, huh? They want to sell to me an' get out, huh? Their lungs ain't made right to inhale powder-smoke."

Palm was seated at the table. He poured himself another drink. "That's what they agreed at the meetin', boss. I jus' rode in from Red Hen School. They talked it over; it didn't take much time to come to a decision. They're all loadin' their wagons with personal belongin's, makin' a wagon train outa them. Then they aim to drive past here, an' you pay them off, one at a time."

"They're whipped, huh?"

Palm nodded. "Plumb whipped. They want that thousan' you offered for a deed. They'll collect that an' go for good."

Pinto Aggler cradled his whiskey glass in his blunt fingers. "You ain't payin' them a thousan' a deed, are you, boss? You got 'em on the run; no use givin' them any cash. Waste of good money."

"I'll pay them," Carter assured him.

Aggler's brows rose. "You loco?"

Carter hooked his thumbs in his gun belt and grinned down at his wagon boss. "No, I'll pay them, fella. Give each one a check for a thousan' dollars on the bank in Watsonville. Then I'll get word to the bank not to honor them."

Palm smiled.

Aggler grinned. "Nice trick, Hank. They think they got a thousan', go into the bank—and the check is no good, huh? They won't come back, either. They'll be tired an' hungry an' busted an' they'll be about thirty miles from here. No, they'll jus' keep on driftin'."

"Man comin' down the back hall," said Palm.

Pinto Aggler moved cat-like to the door, his hand on his gun. He looked down the hall. "Hammerburg." He put the gun away.

The deputy was all smiles. "Well, Hank, you win. I just come from the Red Hen meetin' an' they're pullin' out. Wishin' Springs is your basin, friend. They aim to pull their wagons by this evenin', I understan', an' get their thousan', one by one."

"You're late!" growled Carter. "Parr Palm has already tol' us all this. You ride a slow horse, Hammerburg. Let's hope you don't pull a slow gun."

"I won't, Carter."

Carter spoke to Parr Palm. "Better go back an' see how them nesters are gettin' along, huh?"

But Palm shook his head slowly. "No siree, Carter; I stay here. I don't know whether them nesters suspect me or not an' I'm not goin' fin' out. I'm stayin' here an' sidin' you until them wagons is out of this basin."

Carter considered that. "All right, Parr. An' you, Hammerburg?"

"I'll ride aroun' an' look things over for you, Carter. Then come this evenin' I'll be here to maintain law an' order when you pay off them sodmen." He grinned crookedly and left.

Palm said, "Me for some shut-eye." He went into a room and closed the door. Carter heard him jack a chair under the knob. Nobody could enter that room. The cowman smiled a little. Palm was taking no chances.

"Better get some sleep, Pinto."

Aggler got to his feet. "Damn it, Hank, but I miss Smokey. He was a good man. You buried him out in the hills, huh?"

Carter nodded.

Aggler had a drink in his hands. "Wonder who got him, this Tiny fellow or Jess Roberts?"

"Night too dark," explained Carter. "Look, Pinto, he's dead, that's all. Dead, gone."

Aggler drank. "To Smokey, a good man," he said. He went down the hall and into a bedroom. He did not jack the door closed; he left it open. Carter took a drink and went to the bunkhouse, where some of his men lay on bunks, some sleeping and others just loafing. He changed the guard and went to the barn, where he had a horse saddled. He got the bronc and rode toward town.

He circled through the hills after he caught sight of Hammerburg. He rode hard, and he caught the man, but Hammerburg did not know that he rode in the hills above him. The deputy rode at a running walk.

Carter pulled his rifle from the saddle boot. He verified the lead in the barrel and ran ahead to where the sandstone rocks were high above the trail. He settled there and let Hammerburg ride under him.

Carter found his sights, put them level, lined them against Hammerburg's chest. He waited a second and let the hammer fall. Hammerburg's horse jumped as the deputy fell. Carter shot the running horse and killed him. Then he swung the gun and put three more bullets in Hammerburg.

He did not go down to see if the deputy were dead. He knew Hammerburg would breathe no more, for he knew where he had placed his bullets. He brought his rifle back to the bronc but it lay still. Had there been any life in the animal he would have been moving or kicking.

The rancher got to his feet. Below him were the tumbling hills and below them the flat basin. No riders moved out there; nobody had heard his reports. He picked up his spent cartridges and put them in his chap pocket. He got his bronc and rode down along the lower foothills.

He thought: Hammerburg is silenced forever. I didn't trust him. Now when they find him they'll think some nester has shot him. But what difference does it make? By morning I'll be boss of Wishing Springs range. By tonight, in fact.

He reached the lower rocks and dismounted there to hunker and watch the grass below. He dozed a little, the sun warm on him, his back against a sandstone. Noon came and he stirred and got his saddle, for already farmers were moving on the range below.

Wagons were gathering at old Mack's farm, the white canvas tops shining in the sun. They came in from all directions and were lining up in the yard. Despite the distance he could see men and women moving around.

And inside Hank Carter was a warm glowing feeling. He'd

won despite Jess Roberts and War Dog Smith; the range was his. He had cold jerky in his saddle bag. He cut the dried meat with his knife and chewed it slowly, savoring its good smoked taste. He sat there another two hours, watching the farm below, watching the rigs line up ready to move.

Women and kids were on the rigs. Carter saw various other implements there: one rig carried a stove, the pipe of which stuck up through the canvas top. He watched them load on tables and chairs and desks and other household equipment. They were leaving their farming implements behind, leaving their discs and plows and harrows and seeders. They couldn't take those with them.

All this pleased big Hank Carter. He'd turn these fields into alfalfa and feed stolen cattle he bought off the border rustlers. He'd keep their wells running and raise barley and grain for his stock. And nobody could move in and take the land from him, for he would have a deed for each parcel.

The afternoon was late when he rode down off the rimrock toward his ranch. Already wagons were moving out of old Mack Orcon's homestead. They were thinning out, building a reptilian line, swaying and bending as it crept across the prairie. Even at that distance he heard the commands of the skinners.

Carter watched them go across the prairie, heading for the wagon road out of Wishings Springs basin. He counted the wagons and found there were thirty-odd families below him. He swung his bronc, put home his spurs and loped toward his ranch. Dusk was gathering when he rode into the yard, his horse plowing to a gravel-scattering stop.

His men came running. Some carried rifles. Parr Palm was there and so was Pinto Aggler. They gathered around him and were silent as he told them the nesters were coming.

"What do we do, boss?"

The big rancher had carefully conceived his plan. Pinto Aggler would ride out to the approaching wagon train and look over it to see if any of the farmers openly toted weapons. He would ride to one side and Ace would take the other.

The two went to the barn and soon rode out on a lope.

Carefully Hank Carter stationed his other men, some in the house, some in the barn, some along the buckbrush that fringed the wagon road. Clearly he was taking no chances.

He watched his men take their positions, his lips a little too tight. His squaw housekeeper waddled out. "I go back of hill, Mister Carter. I no like this."

Carter nodded. She moved off.

He had a bench in the blacksmith shop and he moved this alongside the road. Beside it he placed a table he got from the house. He had his checkbook on it and some ink and some pens.

Impatience was sandpaper-sharp in him. He got his bronc and rode along the hills until he could see the wagon train. The wagons were worming their way forward and were a scant quarter-mile away.

He was afraid of a trap. He was afraid that this was just a ruse to get him and his men together and then start a pitched battle. He had his field glasses and he trained them on the lead wagon.

A big farmer sat on the spring seat, shoe against the wagon box; his wife sat beside him, holding their baby on her lap. Other kids were back of the seat, standing up and watching the ground ahead. Some of the precaution left Hank Carter. Surely the nesters would not take their families into a gunfight with him and his gundogs? Surely they would not endanger their wives and children?

Carter came down off the hills, right hand high, and rode to the lead wagon. He waved his hand and said, "Stop in front of the bench, men. Have your deed handy. You'll get your check there."

"We want cash, Carter."

Carter snapped, "Talk sense, Hendricks. You don't think I got thirty odd thousan' dollars in the house, do you? You'll take a check an' like it."

"You're a dirty dog!"

"Dad," the woman said. "Hush."

Carter's lips were white. He held his anger. He said clearly, "You jus' keep your lip buttoned, Hendricks, an' we'll get along all right." He loped down the line, barely glancing at the nesters in the wagons, and stopped his bronc beside that of Pinto Aggler. "Any weapons, fellow?"

"None that I could see."

Just then old Mack's wagon went by. Carter looked at the old man on the seat and smiled as he doffed his Stetson to Matilda, seated beside Mack. "Havin' some sense, huh, Mack Orcon?" He did not wait for an answer. "Where's them two helliors that come to help you?"

"They pulled out, seein' we didn't aim to fight."

"Good riddance."

Carter turned his bronc and loped back. He'd been

wrong; they were peaceful—this would soon be over. He left his bronc with trailing reins beside the table and took his seat. Pinto Aggler and Ace loped up, left saddles, and got on either side of him, standing thirty feet away and a little back. They hunkered there with six-shooters in their fists.

Carter said, "Here they come."

Hendricks drew up, stopping the line. His wife said, "Here's his deed, Mr. Carter. We have both signed it."

Wagons had creaked to a halt. Somewhere a horse neighed; another stomped. For the most part, the nesters were silent. Harnesses creaked and the line moved forward again, then stopped. Hendricks looked at his check and cursed.

"Drive on into town," said Carter. "You ain't needed here no longer."

"I'm waitin' for the others. When the last man is paid, we all go out of here together. We come in together an' we go together."

Carter shrugged. "Have it your way."

One by one the wagons went by. Carter looked at his checkbook. Check number eleven was next. It went to a farmer with a wagon-load of stoves, and he even had his disc inside.

"Your deed, Jackson?"

"Here."

Carter looked at it; it was signed. The nesters had come prepared; the line was moving rapidly. He gave the man his check.

"Next wagon."

One by one they came, got their checks, rolled by the table. Tired men and tired women, beaten by guns and circumstance. The men were silent on the seats now, the women did not chatter. No more banter went up and down the line. And the teams, used to moving ahead a few feet, then stopping, stood silent for the most part, already used to the routine.

Wagon number sixteen turned out to be that of Mack Orcon. Matilda handed down the old man's deed, her fingers trembling. Carter looked at it and then grinned up at her. "You don't need to be scared of me, miss."

She said, "To hell with you! You damn' killer—"

Old Mack cut in. "That's enough, sis!"

Carter smiled crookedly. "They teach you to swear in Boston? All right, ol' man, move that rig on. Who's next?"

"Martin Swenson," said Pinto Aggler.

For a moment Carter looked down at his checkbook. And in that moment the trouble started. Activity broke out in the wagon train. Men grabbed for hidden rifles, cached under the seats, and the women grabbed for the reins, holding the teams steady. Children settled down under the tarps, protected by stoves and implements placed there just for that purpose.

Word smashed up and down the wagons. "Kill them, the dirty— All right, men, wipe them out!"

Pinto Aggler was shooting. So was Ace, the gunman. Carter grabbed for the rifle beside the table. Horses reared and women screamed and guns talked.

Out of the back of old Mack's wagon leaped Jess Roberts and War Dog Smith. The half-breed was hollering a Sioux war cry. They hit the ground and Pinto Aggler went down, his legs blasted out from under him.

"Get Carter!" roared old Mack.

Rifles were springing into action from the Carter men, located in strategic positions. Rifles were talking in the hands of the farmers. Most of them had left their rigs and run toward the buildings. This way they took the fire away from their kin folks and they got close to their enemies.

Jess stood there, guns jutting. Carter was running, zigzagging his way, with bullets kicking sod around him. Jess fired and missed and Carter made the tool shed and disappeared. Later men were to gather and talk, wondering how the cowman had been able to escape that gauntlet of death on his run.

Jess hollered, "Hit for the brush! Smoke them out!" Then he was running ahead toward the house. War Dog had already made the corner.

"Them women an' kids," the half-breed panted. "They should drive those teams away—an' leave fast."

Jess shook his head. "They won't go. They're reserves for their men—if the battle turns an' we start to lose."

"Where's ol' Mack?"

"He went toward the barn, War Dog."

War Dog hunkered. "We light match to this." He had some kerosene-soaked rags under his shirt. He lit these and stuck them under the porch. They flamed up wildly and soon the whole porch was burning.

Jess settled down and reloaded. Yonder lay Ace and Pinto Aggler and beside them lay a dead farmer. He thought:

Enemy an' friend alike will lie silent when the last gun cools. But there had been no other way.

The farmers were in the buckbrush fighting the gunmen. They had agreed on two identifying signals, the words *Gray Horse* and *Hoeman*. Now these words rang back and forth, punctuated by the snarl of the firearms.

The flame of the house grew too hot. Jess and War Dog sprinted for the brush. Fire lanced out from the tool shed and the first ball scattered dirt in front of Jess. They broke into the brush. War Dog fell hard on his face.

"They get you—? That second bullet of Carter's—"

War Dog sat up. "Naw, I tripped. That root there stuck out!"

Jess breathed a sign of relief.

By this time the house was a flaming inferno. Now two Carter men came running out of it; twin bullets stopped them, dropped them.

Jess cursed. "Parr Palm was one of them, War Dog! The dirty traitor—workin' with the innercent nesters—"

War Dog spat. "He was dirty man, huh? Now when this is over we get that deputy an' work him over. Maybe he aroun' here? You see him?"

"No."

The barn and blacksmith shop were afire. Soon the flames had spread to the tool shed.

"Carter, he come out pronto." War Dog grinned crookedly. "That fire drive him out, Jess!"

A man came in from behind them, crashing through the brush. "Gray Horse," he called. Jess and War Dog answered. The farmer came up to them.

"Saw you two men drop them gents that run outa the house. Parr Palm was one, huh? You was right, Jess, when you got us to declare at the meetin' we was gettin' out. Palm must've fell for it. He's prob'ly rid right over to tell Carter."

Jess swung his gun around. "Carter's makin' a run for it. He's comin' out fightin', too!" He held his fire.

For old Mack Orcon had walked out of the brush. Jess heard him holler, "Carter, here I come!" and Carter stopped. He brought his gun up and shot twice and Jess was sure he saw old Mack falter.

Old Mack crouched and shot. Carter, who moved forward a little, now stopped. He seemed to have run into an invisible wall. His hands went down and he dropped his short-gun. He followed it to the sod.

Jess watched, his throat dry. War Dog crossed himself and the farmer stood silent, his face pale.

Somebody hollered, "Ol' Mack's got Carter! He's killed him, sure as hades! He's got—"

The fight was over soon. With Carter gone, his gunmen—those still able to fight—gave up, hollering surrender. Farmers came out of the brush with them at the points of their rifles. They were a broken bunch—some wounded, some dead, some pale of jowl, fearing death at the hands of the farmers.

"What'll we do with them?" a farmer asked old Mack.

"Let 'em hike outa the basin. Make 'em walk out, men!"

Jess and War Dog and old Mack walked toward the wagon where Matilda sat holding the reins.

"Old Mack?" Her voice trembled. "Your arm?"

"Carter got me along the muscle, I reckon. Anyway, don't feel like the arm is busted. Turn the team, sister, and go home."

Matilda kissed her brother's rough cheek. The simplicity of the gesture made a lump rise in Jess Roberts' throat. He climbed into the wagon and War Dog got on the seat and took the lines.

"It was terrible, Mr. War Dog. Some of the farmers died, too. Their families—"

The swarthy man put his arm around her. "Put your head on my shoulder, Miss Matilda. I know how you feel."

Using his free hand, the half-breed turned the wagon and started back toward the farm. Back on the load, Jess was looking at old Mack's arm. The muscle was torn and he bound it, saying that when they got home he'd wash it out with turpentine. Other wagons were moving across the basin, some carrying the dead.

"Somebody'll notify the sheriff in Watsonville," said old Mack. "There'll be inquests an' trouble for all of us, but when a man has to take the law in his hands—" He fell silent.

Matilda was sobbing. Jess was silent. War Dog clucked to the tired team. Old Mack chewed tobacco.

"Well, it's all over, Jess. There'll be a long pull ahead without much money. We gotta rebuild that reservoir an' get a new derrick an' work like beavers. I guess Old Man Time will dry tears and make us forget to a big degree."

"I think so. He usually does."

Old Mack peered at him, his goatee working as he chewed.

He again reminded Jess of Nellie Bly. "Reckon you an' War Dog got itchy boots, huh? Or are you goin' stay for a spell?"

"Not long," said Jess. He looked at his hands. "Mind them callouses, ol' Mack? They come from a rope an' not a plow-handle."

Old Mack sighed. "A saddleman ain't no good on foot. An' you gotta walk behin' a plow."

Jess grinned a little. "That's it, partner."

DOUBLE-BARREL WESTERNS
Twice the Action—
Twice the Adventure—
Only a Fraction of the Price!

Two Complete and unabridged novels in each book!

The Sure-Fire Kid and **Wildcats of Tonto Basin**
by Nelson Nye.

_____2474-8 $3.95 US/$4.95 CAN

Gunslick Mountain and **Born to Trouble**
by Nelson Nye.

_____2497-7 $3.95 US/$4.95 CAN

The Bushwackers and **Ride the Wild Country**
by Lee Floren.

_____2610-4 $3.95 US/$4.95 CAN

LEISURE BOOKS
ATTN: Customer Service Dept.
276 5th Avenue, New York, NY 10001

Please send me the book(s) checked above. I have enclosed $_____
Add $1.25 for shipping and handling for the first book; $ .30 for each book thereafter. No cash, stamps, or C.O.D.s. All orders shipped within 6 weeks. Canadian orders please add $1.00 extra postage.

Name _____

Address _____

City_____State_____Zip_____

Canadian orders must be paid in U.S. dollars payable through a New York banking facility.   ☐ Please send a free catalogue.